AN EPIC
NOVEL
OF MATCHLESS
ADVENTURE

On March 10, 1939, Britain's prize
flying boat takes off on a
fabulous 10,000-mile journey
from Durban, South Africa, to New York.
In unmatched style and splendor she
carries a dozen passengers—six women,
six men—who will be plunged into
a world of scandal, intrigue and murder.

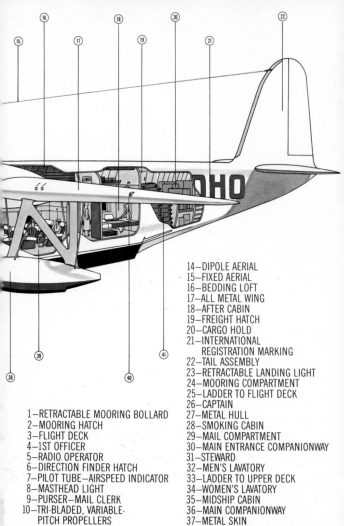

14—DIPOLE AERIAL
15—FIXED AERIAL
16—BEDDING LOFT
17—ALL METAL WING
18—AFTER CABIN
19—FREIGHT HATCH
20—CARGO HOLD
21—INTERNATIONAL
    REGISTRATION MARKING
22—TAIL ASSEMBLY
23—RETRACTABLE LANDING LIGHT
24—MOORING COMPARTMENT
25—LADDER TO FLIGHT DECK
26—CAPTAIN
27—METAL HULL
28—SMOKING CABIN
29—MAIL COMPARTMENT
30—MAIN ENTRANCE COMPANIONWAY
31—STEWARD
32—MEN'S LAVATORY
33—LADDER TO UPPER DECK
34—WOMEN'S LAVATORY
35—MIDSHIP CABIN
36—MAIN COMPANIONWAY
37—METAL SKIN
38—WING TIP FLOAT
39—PROMANADE CABIN
40—PORT NAVIGATION LIGHT
41—MAIL BAGS

1—RETRACTABLE MOORING BOLLARD
2—MOORING HATCH
3—FLIGHT DECK
4—1ST OFFICER
5—RADIO OPERATOR
6—DIRECTION FINDER HATCH
7—PILOT TUBE—AIRSPEED INDICATOR
8—MASTHEAD LIGHT
9—PURSER—MAIL CLERK
10—TRI-BLADED, VARIABLE-
    PITCH PROPELLERS
11—MAIL BAGS
12—GOLD BULLION STORAGE
13—FOUR PEGASUS AIR-COOLED
    ENGINES—RATED 1000 HP

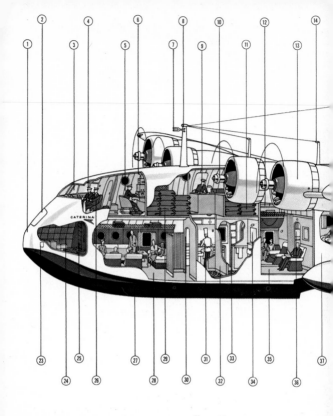

CATERINA —BRITISH IMPERIAL AIRWAYS

REGISTRATION NO: G-ADHO
ROUTE & DESTINATION: SOUTH AFRICA—ENGLAND—NEW YORK
COMMISSIONED: 1937
MAXIMUM CRUISING SPEED: 165 KNOTS
STALLING SPEED: 73 KNOTS
L.O.A.: 88'

CAPTAIN: DESMOND O'NEILL
1ST OFFICER: KENNETH FRAZER
RADIO OPERATOR: RALPH KENDRICK
PURSER: SANDY EVERETT

IMPERIAL
109

IMPERIAL 109

With her gleaming white paint, raked prow and high, sprouting wings, Imperial Flight 109 was Britain's famed S30C Empire-class "boat" and a truly magnificent machine. Propelled by four supercharged Bristol Pegasus XII radial engines, each one capable of 1000 horsepower, lavishly fitted with smoking salons, galleys, private cabins and a promenade deck, the flying palace carried her distinguished passengers up the full length of Africa to the Nile Delta and Cairo, on through Greece, Italy, France and London to the final destination—New York.

Imperial 109

Richard Doyle

IMPERIAL 109
*A Bantam Book / published in accordance with
Arlington Books (Publishers) Ltd.*

PRINTING HISTORY
*Originally published in Great Britain
by Arlington Books, 1977
Bantam Book / July 1978*

2nd printing
3rd printing
4th printing

*Bantam Books are published by Bantam Books, Inc. Its trade-
mark, consisting of the words "Bantam Books" and the por-
trayal of a bantam, is registered in the United States Patent
Office and in other countries. Marca Registrada. Bantam
Books, Inc., 666 Fifth Avenue, New York, New York 10019.*

For my mother

ACKNOWLEDGMENTS

I would like gratefully to acknowledge British Airways and, in particular, Mr. T. E. Scott-Chard, for all the assistance given to me while researching this book. To my sister, who valiantly typed the manuscript, many thanks.

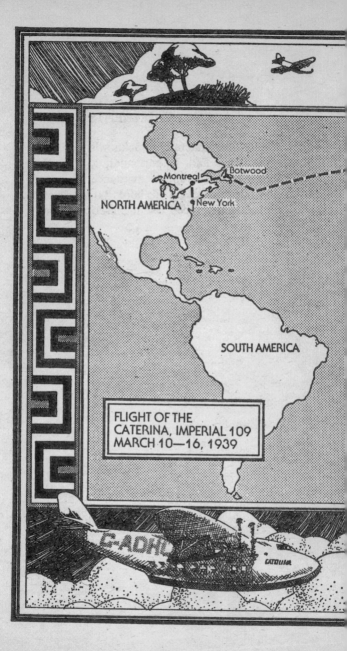

FLIGHT OF THE
CATERINA, IMPERIAL 109
MARCH 10—16, 1939

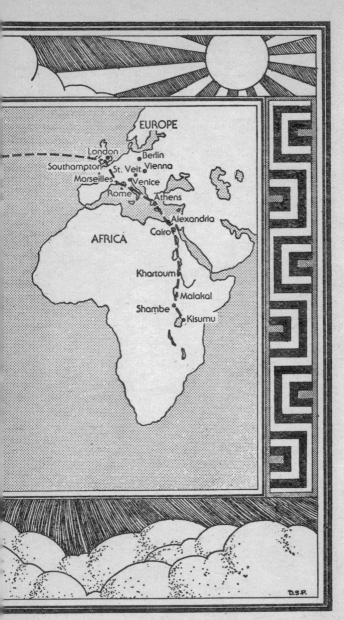

I

Africa

1

By radio: 1310 hrs LOCAL TIME. FRIDAY 10 MARCH 1939. KISUMU UGANDA TO ALL AIRPORTS: SOUTH AFRICA - ENGLAND - NEW YORK MAIL PLANE, IMPERIAL AIRWAYS FLIGHT 109 G-ADHO CATERINA LEFT HERE FOR MALAKAL - KHARTOUM - CAIRO. ETA MALAKAL 1700 hrs. END.

Five thousand feet below the flying boat, the marshes of the Sud stretched out in every direction. From the borders of Uganda, the swamplands run for more than four hundred miles through equatorial Sudan, covering an area greater than England, where the broad Nile all but loses itself in a maze of sluggish channels and creeks. It is a region of neither dry land nor open water but of limitless green papyrus reeds, water hyacinth, stagnant pools, quicksand, and river mud. The fierce equatorial heat, the humidity, and the ever-present risk of disease carried by the millions of swarming insects have combined with the other natural hazards to make the Sud one of the last unexplored areas of Africa.

A heavy storm had lain over much of the region, but now the dense clouds rolled away in the direction of Ethiopia, and the flying boat cruised on in brilliant sunshine. With their gleaming white paint, raked prows, and high wings sprouting from the crests of their hulls, the S30C Empire-class boats of Britain's Imperial Airways were some of the most beautiful aircraft ever to fly, carrying passengers in a style and luxury unmatched since the passing of the great air ships of Germany a decade earlier, and never to be seen again. Spanning the immense distances separating the British Dominions around

3

the earth, the flying boats set standards taken from the
leisured days of the previous century, as if in defiance of
the new order that would soon sweep away the last trace
of the Imperial past.

In the captain's seat on *Caterina*'s flight deck sat Desmond O'Neill. Lean, wiry, an inch under six feet in height,
he had the dark hair, blue eyes, easy charm, and quick
temper common among his Irish ancestors. He glanced out
at the scene below. The Sud never failed to impress him.
Considering, he reflected wryly, that he had probably
flown over the area at least fifty times since taking command of *Caterina* two years ago, he should have grown
used to the sight by now. The section between Mombasa
and Cairo, twenty-five hundred miles of swamp, scrub, and
plain desert, was the worst part of the five-day, Durban-to-
England trip. The long hours in flight were broken only by
refueling stops at dirty, fly-blown river stations in swel-
tering heat. For passengers and crew alike, it was a relief
when they finally reached the delta.

The flying boat lurched slightly in an air pocket,
and there was a momentary surge of power from the
engine as the Sperry autopilot corrected the loss of altitude. Desmond's eyes flicked over the instruments on
the control panels. On the main fuel gauge the fat white
needle pointed to 205 gallons, and Desmond knew at
once it was fractionally too low. He leaned forward and
tapped the dial with his fingernail, a habit left over
from the early days of his flying career, but *Caterina*'s
sophisticated equipment was a far cry from that of its
forebears, and the needle remained obstinately on the
mark.

"You know what that means?" he asked with a sigh.
Beside him in the first officer's seat Kenneth Frazer shifted
uneasily.

"What's that skipper?" Frazer asked in apparent surprise.

"You know damn well," Desmond snapped angrily.
"We've got a fuel leak, and there's only one place it could
be coming from—that port wing tank. Did you check
it out as I told you?"

Frazer's face flushed. He was a tall, well-built young
man with pale features and carefully smoothed fair hair,
more concerned with his appearance and prestige, it

seemed to Desmond, than with attending to the essential details of flying passenger aircraft. "I followed your orders exactly," Frazer answered stiffly. "The engineers stripped off the wing panels, and we examined the tank carefully. As I told you, we found only one small leak, which was sealed. The tank had hardly been touched."

Desmond was silent. There was no point in arguing with Frazer, and in any case the ultimate responsibility was his own. Even so, there was still a strong possibility that the immediate cause was the first officer's negligence. At Mombasa the previous evening, Desmond had let Frazer bring *Caterina* in to land. He had handled the flying boat well, that much had to be admitted, and had made a perfect touchdown, but at the end of her run in, the aircraft had struck a piece of driftwood floating on the surface of the harbor, damaging her port wing float. This had not been serious, and, though annoying, it was pure bad luck on Frazer's part rather than any lack of skill. Accidents of this nature were common.

On shore at Mombasa, Desmond's presence had been required at the Imperial Airways office. After inspecting the damage, he had ordered Frazer to supervise the engineers' repairs. The first officer had subsequently reported that the damage to the fuel tank in the wing above the float would not warrant any significant delay. Desmond had accepted this, and, after assuring himself that the float had been properly repaired, he had taken off again. Now it looked as though his confidence had been misplaced. A glance at Frazer's tight-lipped expression showed that the first officer was evidently of the same opinion.

Desmond's eyes narrowed as he made quick mental calculations. Their present hop was a long one—720 miles from Kisumu, on the shores of Lake Victoria, to Malakal at the northern end of the Sud marshes—and to save weight the flying boat was carrying fuel for only 800 miles.

"Ralph," he called out to the wireless operator at the rear of the flight deck, "can you give me a fix on our exact position? I want to check our fuel reserves."

"Aye, aye, skipper," the reply came back above the background noise in the cockpit. Younger than the two pilots, still in his late twenties, Ralph Kendrick had a lazy good humor that seemingly no amount of frustration could upset. He too had been with the *Caterina* since her commissioning two years ago in 1937.

Ralph unclipped a small hatch in the cabin roof. Wind whistled shrilly through the opening. Beside him, fixed to the bulkhead on a swivel mounting, was a loop aerial for the Marconi direction finder. Ralph locked it in position. By rotating the aerial on different frequencies, it was possible to take accurate bearings on the series of radio beacons located at stations along the route. These could then be plotted on the chart to give an accurate fix on the aircraft's position.

"We're 218 miles due south of Malakal," he reported when he completed his calculations, "and 110 miles south-southeast of the emergency landing station at Shambe."

Desmond figured the answer briefly. There was still enough fuel for them to reach Malakal—provided the rate of leakage remained steady. He looked out the window at the wing on his left. There was no sign of fuel spilling out, but that in itself was no guide. *Caterina*'s thousand-horsepower Bristol Pegasus XII radial engines were gulping fuel at the rate of two gallons a minute.

"We'll monitor the gauges over the next thirty minutes," Desmond decided, glancing at the control panel. "If the situation gets any worse during that time, we'll have to divert to Shambe."

Ralph Kendrick chuckled. "The passengers will love that," he said. "An unscheduled stop with plenty of time for sightseeing in the swamps."

"Damn the passengers!" Ken Frazer snorted angrily. "London will go crazy if they hear their precious cargo is stuck out here."

There was silence. Frazer had touched on a sensitive subject. *Caterina*'s cargo was no ordinary freight load. She carried more than a ton and a half of gold from the South African mines—two million dollars worth at the internationally agreed price of thirty-five dollars an ounce.

All the crews hated these flights. Apart from the strain of being responsible for so much wealth on a journey lasting nearly a week and covering ten thousand miles over some of the loneliest and most hostile country in the world, a high-value cargo meant considerable extra work and inconvenience. A security watch had to be set whenever the aircraft touched down, the holds had to be inspected at frequent intervals, and reports had to be made and permission sought for the slightest variation from the normal flying pattern. If they were forced to make an emergency stop at Shambe, the head office in London would be sending furious signals almost before the aircraft touched the water.

They had seen the gold being loaded at Durban. Forty-four crates brought to the quay at dawn in a convoy of plain trucks, with two armed police in each truck, and, following at a discreet distance, another truck with a squad of soldiers yawning in the early light. The security had been deliberately low-key so as not to attract attention. The soldiers hadn't even gotten out of the truck, and the whole operation had been over in half an hour.

Ian Haggart, Imperial's chief officer in Durban, a stiff, reserved man with a military bearing, had handed Desmond a canvas pouch that was surprisingly heavy. "You had better take these with you," he had said gruffly, with a touch of embarrassment.

Desmond took the pouch without comment. Inside, oiled and wrapped, were a pair of Webly & Scott .38-caliber revolvers and a cardboard box containing twenty-five rounds of ammunition.

For much of the afternoon, the big crocodile had lain in the sun on the edge of a small island of mud and thick grass in one of the creeks on the edge of the White Nile. Basking similarly were a half a dozen others of its species, all in identical attitudes: bellies down, crooked stumpy legs bent up against armored sides, and long mouths slightly agape, exposing orange gums and rows of gleaming teeth. At intervals, the great reptiles would snort and grunt and shift their huge carcasses, sending plovers and water dikkops scattering for safety as the spiny-ridged tails flailed round.

The big croc stood out, not only owing to its age and size—it was starting its second century of life, was fully eighteen feet long, and weighed over a ton—but also because of an extraordinary white scar that ran from just behind its right foreleg almost to the middle of its back, flattening two of the protruding ridge plates. This scar was the legacy of the croc's nearest brush with death, when four decades earlier—already measuring thirteen feet from snout to tail—it had unwisely attempted to seize a small hippo calf when its mother was feeding in the vicinity.

Too large and clumsy to hunt the fish eaten by their smaller fellows, the old reptiles were forced to attack the wildlife that came to the water to drink, and it was two days since the croc had eaten.

There is no more formidable swamp in the world than the Sud, a savage wilderness that spreads for thousands of miles, its endless tracts of reeds split by fetid pools and streams and islands of packed vegetation twenty feet thick drifting in the river channels. All this was perfectly suited to the big croc's needs. Heaving itself up, the croc lurched over the mud and slid quietly into the water. With a few flicks of its tail, it moved out into the midstream of one of the main channels, heading toward Shambe, a mile or two upriver.

The river port scarcely justified the name, consisting as it did of a handful of whitewashed, stone bungalows that housed the few officials who administered the district and managed the landing station. There was a rest house for passengers stopping there, and the huts of a shelluk native village.

There could no longer be any doubt about the leak. Even before the half hour was up, it was clear that they were losing fuel at a rate of more than two hundred gallons per hour. To reach Malakal, still 140 miles away, was out of the question.

"If the loss gets any worse we will have enough problem reaching the emergency landing area, let alone Malakal," Desmond said. "Ralph, give me a course for the station at Shambe. Tell them we're coming in low on fuel, and request emergency services to stand by. Assuming they have any, that is," he added sourly.

"OK, skipper, I have the course for you," the radio operator replied at once. "Steer 310 degrees north. The station is approximately forty-five miles distant. We should reach it in twenty minutes at our current speed."

Desmond peered out of the cockpit windows at the swamp beneath them. "It's going to be hell's own task finding the place in all this muck," he said irritably. "We could circle around for hours looking for it. Every stretch of water looks the same from up here, and we won't be able to see the station till we're right on top of it."

Ken Frazer said nothing, but stared ahead of him, his face set and angry.

The gauges showed eighty gallons of fuel remaining, giving them another forty minutes in the air before they would be forced to ditch, assuming the rate of loss did not increase. Despite Desmond's gloomy prediction, that should give them sufficient time, and they would be able to use the direction finder to help locate the station, even though the instrument would be of limited value at close range.

In theory, of course, they could simply put down on the nearest stretch of open water and wait until boats from Shambe came to get them. In practice, however, this could turn out to be extremely hazardous. The river was so sluggish and muddy that it was impossible to tell if it was clear of obstructions. Just below the surface there could be waterlogged timbers, sand banks, even hippos or crocodiles. During the rainy season, all manner of debris was carried along by the flood, brought down from the forests to the south, and collected in the sievelike marshes. A mud bank or a sizable log could tear *Caterina*'s bottom clean out of her, taking the passengers with it.

Satisfied that he was on the correct bearing, Desmond eased back the throttle levers slightly, allowing *Caterina*'s speed to fall back to 110 knots to conserve the remaining fuel. *Caterina* was capable of cruising at a maximum of 165 knots with a minimum stalling speed of 73 knots.

"Shambe reports landing area clear and all services on standby," Kendrick said.

"Fine," Desmond replied. "I'm taking us down to two thousand feet, so we'll have a better chance of spotting the station." He pushed the control yoke forward as he spoke, putting the aircraft into a shallow descent. "OK, Ken," he said when they had leveled off at the new altitude, "take over and keep her on this bearing, will you? I'm going to have a word with Sandy and let the passengers know about the change in schedule."

Sandy Everett was the flying boat's purser, an enthusiastic, likable nineteen year old who had joined *Caterina*'s

crew six months earlier on leaving school. He had an office in the mailroom immediately behind the flight deck,
and he was responsible for the needs of the passengers.

The purser's true title was that of mail clerk, although
he was always referred to as the purser, the term being
borrowed from the ocean liners whose luxury and elegance the flying boat sought to equal. Mail had been the
real reason behind Imperial Airways' bold decision four
years ago to order twenty-eight of the flying boats
straight off the drawing board as well as fourteen Arm-
strong Whitworth AW27 land planes. Under the Empire
Air Mail Scheme set up that year, it had been agreed that
all first-class mail would be carried by air throughout the
British Empire at current surface rates. Imperial won the
contract and with it a substantial government subsidy. The
aim was to foster the spirit of unity among the Empire's
members, and from the start, it proved enormously successful.

The mailroom was a large compartment, piled high
with canvas sacks—blue, green, or white, according to
destination. At the far end, secure behind a locked wire
grill, were some of the innocuous-looking wooden crates
that contained the gold ingots. There was no sign of
Sandy. Evidently he was down on the lower level. Stepping round the deck, Desmond began to descend the
gangway that linked the flight deck to the passengers' level
below.

Kenneth Frazer's hands gripped the control yoke tightly,
guiding the flight of the eighteen-ton aircraft with angry
concentration. The natural turbulence, often met at low
altitudes, was being increased by warm thermals rising
off the ground and convection currents set up by the sun
evaporating the moisture from the swamps, making constant small adjustments necessary. It was an exercise he
found particularly demanding.

One day in the future, airplanes would be built with
pressurized cabins that would enable them to fly at
heights of thirty thousand feet or more above normal air
turbulence. To Frazer, the prospect was a welcome one.
The new developments being made in aircraft design—
radio beacons, electrically operated flaps, automatic pilot,
and blind flying equipment—were continuing the trend

away from relying on the instinctive abilities of pilots. The captains of the future would be chosen for their technical skills and their understanding of aircraft equipment.

By rights, Frazer considered, he should have made full captain already and been given command of his own craft. He felt that the older captains in the Imperial fleet were contemptuous of the up and coming generation of carefully trained, highly qualified officers. Most of all, Frazer blamed Desmond O'Neill, whose reports on his first officer's fitness to command had, he guessed, been less than complimentary. Desmond firmly believed that pilots should only be given commands of their own after long experience in all conditions.

The memory of Desmond's anger at discovering the fuel leak sent another surge of bitter rage through Frazer's mind. He knew he was wrong. The tank had been damaged quite badly at Mombasa, but a proper repair would have meant a day's delay and a long entry in the log that might well have found its way onto his own report, thus further damaging his chances of promotion. Frazer had persuaded the engineers to do a quick patching job to last until they reached Cairo where a two-day stopover would give plenty of time for more comprehensive repairs. His attempt had misfired. An emergency landing would certainly be held against him.

Kenneth Frazer's father had died when Ken was a child. Raised by his mother, she had indulged and pampered him, and his mother's subsequent marriage to a wealthy London businessman had in no way diminished her adoration for him. Recently she had become friendly with Jack Priestly, Imperial's flying boats operations manager and a long-standing enemy of Desmond. Frazer hoped that with her help he might at last achieve the promotion he sought.

He had been attracted to the world of flying by the glamour and mystery that surrounded the tough, daring pilots and their flimsy machines. The miracle of manned flight was still less than forty years old. Fliers were famous, their names were household words, and in Cairo Desmond O'Neill was a friend of King Farouk's, and Ken Frazer had been determined to be like him.

The reality was far more demanding, more uncomfortable, and at times more dangerous than he had expected. The required degree of professionalism and dedication rapidly bored him. Lacking the natural abilities of many of the young men, he began to fall behind in the struggle for promotion. He was passed from one plane to another as the crews grew sick of his grousing and laziness. His stepfather had offered him a job, the opening was ideal, and he was determined to accept. First, however, he had to prove to himself that he had not wasted his ten years in the air. He had to come out as a captain, someone to be respected and admired. Somehow, he had to gain promotion. It was a desire that was rapidly becoming an obsession.

Bringing his attention abruptly back to the present, he checked the fuel gauges once more and noted the time. The rate of loss had increased slightly; the tanks now held fifty-eight gallons with seventeen minutes to go before they would be over Shambe. The safety margin was down to twelve minutes.

With the exception of the cargo hold in the tail and a small space in the nose used for storing ropes and other mooring gear, the whole of the flying boat's lower deck was given over to the use of the passengers. There were four separate cabins designed to accommodate varying numbers of people according to demand. All could be converted into comfortable sleeping compartments in the event of a night flight, although nights were normally spent at first-class hotels and whenever these were available the aircraft stopped for a while for lunch as well. The immense profitability of the mail loads meant that the passengers traveled in far greater luxury than would otherwise be possible. *Caterina* was eighty-eight feet long, and four double-decker buses could have been fitted into her hull, yet on this trip she carried only eleven passengers.

The double soundproofing on the passenger level reduced the sound of the engines to no more than a hum. The floor was thickly carpeted, and the effect was more like the first-class interior of an ocean liner than an airplane.

Desmond was standing in a passageway directly below the mailroom in the forward part of the boat. In front of him the passage led into the foremost cabin, the smoking saloon, which—as the name implied—was the only place on board where smoking was permitted. The other three cabins—the midship, the promenade, and the after —all lay toward the rear.

The galley door beside him opened with a click, and Sandy Everett emerged into the passage. "Andy and I are just getting the passengers' tea ready," he said, smiling. Andy Draper was the steward. "Shall I bring some upstairs for you?"

Desmond shook his head. "You'd better leave that for now, Sandy," he said. "We're losing a lot of fuel from that tank we holed at Mombasa, and I doubt if we will be able to reach Malakal. I'm going to take us down for an emergency stop at Shambe. We'll be landing in about a quarter of an hour."

"Will we be staying there for the night, sir?"

"No," Desmond told him, "at least I hope not. I've never been there, but I have heard it's the kind of place best forgotten, and God knows Malakal is bad enough. If we can have the repairs done in time, I'll push straight on to Khartoum."

"You'll cut out Malakal then?" Sandy asked. "We've no passengers to pick up there, but there's some mail to deliver."

"We can leave that with the rest at Khartoum, and they can send it up the river on the next steamer."

"Right, sir," Sandy said. "I'll just tell Andy, and then I'll go and inform the passengers that we'll be landing in fifteen minutes."

"I'll do the rear cabins myself," Desmond told him. "Most of the passengers will be there. You can tell the ones in the smoking saloon, and then make sure that they actually get back to their seats before we start to descend."

"OK, skipper, I'll see to it." Sandy nodded earnestly, and Desmond had to restrain an impulse to smile.

"One last thing," Desmond said before turning back to the gangway. "Don't mention that we are low on fuel. Just let them think it's a routine stop to inspect the repairs we had done earlier. I don't want them getting worried."

"Bloody typical!" was Andy's comment when Sandy returned to the galley to tell him the news. "That's your engineers for you. Patch things up just enough to get us right out into the middle of the swamps. I told you we should have stayed longer at Mombasa and made them do a proper job." He was a short, thickset man of about forty who came from East London. He had a quick, natural shrewdness and a particular contempt for the passengers, whom he considered both brainless and a nuisance. However, he ran the lower deck with considerable efficiency.

He had taken Sandy in hand from the moment of his arrival, giving him a great deal of useful advice, all in the same tone of tolerant contempt with which he treated everyone, Desmond included. Andy was expert at anticipating problems and sidestepping them, at smoothing over difficulties and blocking complaints, and Sandy found him invaluable in dealing with the ground staff; there was no trick of the quartermasters or supply clerks he did not know.

"The captain says Shambe is worse than Malakal," Sandy remarked, and the steward snorted derisively.

"Let me tell you, my lad," he said. "I know all about Shambe—and its worse than anywhere. For a start, we don't normally let passengers ashore there if we can help it, in case they catch yellow fever. The mosquitoes bite deep enough to draw blood; it's hot as a Turkish bath, and it stinks of mud."

"So we keep the passengers on board while the engineer looks at the tank?" asked Sandy. "They won't like that."

"Can't—not while they're working on a fuel tank," Andy replied, bending to stow a teapot. "It's the fire risk." Andy was an expert on all airline regulations. "Which means," he continued, "that you and I will have to go ashore and make sure they don't do anything stupid."

"OK," Sandy said. "I'll go tell them the good news."

"One more thing." Andy called him back. "We will have trouble with the female passengers when we land. The natives here don't wear clothes. Not unless you count a string of beads around their waists—and they only wear them if they're married. When I was here before, a general's wife fainted getting into the launch. She fell in the river. Stupid cow said it was the heat."

The promenade cabin, immediately aft of the wings, was the flying boat's greatest attraction and understandably popular among the passengers. The largest of the four cabins, it contained seating for eight as well as a wide area running the full length of the port side that was left free for passengers to stroll about and admire the view through the panoramic windows in the hull at standing height.

Laura Hartman had been gazing out of one of these windows for the past quarter of an hour. She was a pretty girl in her late twenties, small and slightly built. Her face was narrow, with high cheekbones, and tanned. It was an attractive, even beautiful face, with an air of sadness about it.

Laura was bored. She had been bored ever since she had entered the cabin, and she was bitterly regretting that she had been so foolish as to leave the smoking saloon. Standing beside her was a young lieutenant in British Royal Navy uniform. Fresh-faced, popeyed, and, for all his youth, unbearably pompous, Ian Thorne had striven manfully to impress her from the moment they had joined the aircraft at Durban. His opening remark —"I say you're American, aren't you? I can tell, you know, by the accent"—had earned him a look that would have dropped a more sensitive man where he stood. But he had plagued her with constant attention and a never-ending flow of inane conversation. He was either incredibly thick-skinned, she thought wearily, or simply too stupid to notice how offhanded she was being. Unfortunately, there was seldom any way of avoiding him during the flight.

"It's such a pity, Mrs. Hartman," he was saying, "my having to leave the airplane at Alexandria while you go on to New York. It's so nice talking to you." He had a sudden thought. "I say, we stop for a day in Cairo first. Perhaps I could show you the sights. I've been there before, you know."

"Thank you, but so have I," Laura replied dryly. "And in any case I shall have a lot of work to do when we get there."

Thorne looked crestfallen, but before he could reply, they were joined by another passenger. Dr. Van Smit was a

small wiry man of about fifty, dressed in a neatly cut
brown suit. He was very sunburned about the face and
hands and had clever, sharp features. He described
himself as a consultant geologist, although he appeared to
earn his living primarily from card playing and gambling. Both his name and his pronounced accent proclaimed him to be a South African.

"I understand you have been visiting my country, Mrs.
Hartman," he said politely. "Did you enjoy yourself
there?"

"Yes, very much, but I'm afraid I only saw a little of it,"
Laura confessed. "I was there a week, and I had to spend
most of that time in Durban. I'm secretary to Mr. Curtis,"
she explained.

"That would be the Mr. Curtis who is chairman of the
Klerksdorp Mining Company? I have heard a great deal
about him. I gather he is traveling with us, is that not
so?" the doctor inquired.

"He's taken the after cabin," Laura told him. "He likes
to be able to work while he is traveling."

"And you have both flown down to Durban from London for a week, and now you fly back again. That is a
tiring journey for so short a time," the doctor pursued,
his small dark eyes watching her intently.

"Oh, no." Laura shook her head firmly. "Mr. Curtis
had been spending the winter in Cairo with his wife, but
he had some urgent business in Durban, so we flew down.
Mrs. Curtis didn't want to make the trip, so she stayed
behind."

"Do you travel a lot with him?" Ian Thorne broke into
the conversation. He had been standing stiffly by the window. "I mean, it must be quite interesting, I should
think."

"My husband used to work for Mr. Curtis in South
Africa," she said, somewhat irritated. "He was a mining
engineer, and when he was killed in an accident last year,
Mr. Curtis offered me a job as his personal secretary. He
said he needed someone who understood a bit about the
business. It was very generous of him."

The flat tone of her voice was enough to tell the two
men that the subject of her husband was still painful. For
a short while they gazed out the windows in silence. It was
Ian Thorne who spoke first.

"Are you interested in mining, Dr. Van Smit?" he asked and a frown passed over the South African's features.

Before Van Smit could reply, Desmond O'Neill stepped through the cabin doorway and came over to them. "I'm sorry to spoil your viewing," he said, "but I'm afraid you will all have to return to your seats. We are going to make an extra stop, and the aircraft will be landing on the river at Shambe in a quarter of an hour."

"Shambe," the doctor echoed. "Shambe. That is a most unusual place to stop. Is there something wrong?"

Desmond hastily reassured him. "We just want to take the opportunity to check the repairs that were made yesterday," he said. "We won't be delayed very long."

"Well, I'm glad," Laura peered out of the window. "It looks green and cool down there, and Khartoum will be so hot. It will be nice to rest here for a while."

"It may appear pleasant enough from this height, Mrs. Hartman," Dr. Van Smit replied grimly, "but you are looking at one of the most terrible regions in all Africa: the marshes of the Sud. Fifty thousand square miles of fever- and mosquito-ridden swamp. Captain O'Neill must indeed be concerned to be bringing us down in such a place."

Desmond looked at him sharply. Van Smit had a knack of making disconcerting remarks. "I think you exaggerate a little, doctor," he said, keeping his tone deliberately casual. "Certainly Shambe presents no problems to us. The company has maintained a rest house and servicing facilities there for many years." Van Smit gave an enigmatic smile.

Also in the promenade cabin sat an elderly English couple, the Finlays, returning home after a lifetime spent abroad in the colonial service. White-haired and thin, both seemed dried up by the climate in which they had lived for so many years. They sat upright in their seats, books open in front of them, dressed in stiff clothes that were unsuitable for traveling. Desmond suspected that the old couple was dreading the prospect of ending their lives in a country they no longer knew, where their friends were all dead or had long since forgotten them.

The seats in front of the Finlays were occupied by a pleasant-faced, rather plump woman in a floral print dress and her ten-year-old daughter. Their name, Desmond recalled, was Johnson, and the woman's husband, at present in the smoking saloon, was a civil engineer from Kenya, taking his family home on leave. The mother was not in the least disturbed by Van Smit's ominous remarks, and the child appeared to be asleep.

With a quick word, Desmond broke the news of their imminent descent. None showed more than a casual interest, with the exception of Mr. Finlay, who asked several erudite questions about Shambe. Satisfied that all was well here, Desmond went through into the after cabin.

The after cabin was the most luxurious accommodation on board, and since it was the farthest from the engines, it was also the quietest. On this flight, it had been booked as a private stateroom, and its sole occupant was Stewart Curtis.

To Desmond's surprise, the news of the unscheduled landing appeared to irritate Curtis immensely.

"This is a confounded nuisance," Curtis snapped, laying down his papers. "Any delay will be extremely inconvenient for me. I have most important business to attend to. Surely this inspection could be carried out at Malakal?" He was heavily built, with a square, thick-jowled face, somewhere in his fifties, dressed in a Savile Row suit cut from tropical weight cloth. A British multimillionaire with holdings in mining, steel, and armaments who had started as an office boy and made his first big killing by selling off war surplus material in the twenties, he survived the depression to become a leading industrialist and a key figure in the new South African mining market.

"It's damned inefficiency," Curtis snorted. "None of you people would last ten minutes working for me. We were delayed at Mombasa so that damage caused by your crew's carelessness could be put right. I see we shall have this excuse brought out the whole way to New York."

Desmond responded, tight-lipped. "I am sure this will be the last delay."

"It better be, captain," the financier retorted, "because if it isn't, I shall be making complaints to London that will have you back on the ground loading luggage." Indicating that the interview was terminated, he returned to his papers.

"Mr. Curtis," Desmond said quietly, restraining his anger, "I don't know what your understanding of modern aircraft is, but I can only assume it to be extremely limited. Any extra stops or delays will be motivated by consideration for the safety of this craft and its passengers. If I decide that such delays are required, then I will make them, regardless of what you or anyone else may say or do about it." Curtis gazed at him with astonishment. "Furthermore," Desmond continued, "if you are ever again as rude as you just have been, either to me personally or to anyone else on board, I'll put you off at the next stop and leave you there."

It had been a long time since anyone had dared speak to Stewart Curtis in such a manner, and the shock left him speechless. Seeing the rage and surprise evident on Curtis's face, Desmond judged it prudent to withdraw.

Never before had he spoken to one of the company's passengers like that, and it was likely that Curtis might cause trouble. Nevertheless, he felt justified. There was no cause for such rudeness on Curtis's part, and Desmond had derived a certain satisfaction in telling him so.

On his return to the flight deck, Desmond paused at the foot of the gangway. Glancing back down through the doorways of the midship cabin into the promenade deck, he recognized the slight figure of Laura Hartman standing by the window, half hidden by the bulkhead between them. She was talking to the young naval lieutenant, and Desmond felt a momentary regret that he seldom got to know many of his passengers. Collecting himself, he commenced up the stairs. His divorce decree would be final soon, and even after a year, the freedom of bachelorhood still came uneasily to him at times.

Perhaps it was just as well, he reflected. Relationships were hard to hold together in this profession. He was still carrying Pamela's last letter. Even after all this time, his wife's bitterness remained undiminished. Now, it appeared, she had taken a job in London as fashion editor of a women's magazine and wanted to sell the house. She had had a valuation done and, of course, he thought, had taken legal advice. As usual, Pamela had it all worked out. She had decided on a price, hired an estate agent, found a buyer; all he had to do was sign a form of consent, which she enclosed. "I'm sorry to push you," the letter ran, "but I am anxious to move back to London, and you certainly don't require a house that size for yourself."

Desmond had worked hard at his marriage, blaming the difficulties that had arisen on his frequent absence. Looking back, however, he could see that a much more fundamental weakness lay at the heart of their problems. The periods between flights were generous; other pilots were away from home no less often, yet their wives coped. The trouble was, he realized—for all her attractiveness, her intelligence, and the chic so many people envied —Pamela's self-confidence was superficial. Unless she was the constant center of attention, a basic insecurity within her would well up, frightening her into savage attacks on any competing attraction.

Desmond's job had proved to be an opponent she could not match and the result had been inevitable. Their increasingly violent quarrels had driven Desmond to escape more and more into his own world, a reaction that only served to magnify Pamela's frustration. They had been married for exactly three years. He wondered whether Pamela ever felt the regret that he still experienced.

As if the problems with his wife were not enough, another letter had reached him at the same time. This had been a communication from the Admiralty and, although the envelope had read Captain D. M. O'Neill, the letter inside was addressed to Flight Lieutenant O'Neill, Royal Navy Flying Corps Reserve. Arrangements had been made with Imperial Airways, the message ran, for him to spend his summer leave undergoing further training on carrier aircraft with the Fleet Air Arm. Under an Act of Parliament and Orders in Council passed during the previous year, the Admiralty possessed the authority to order him to report to Portsmouth for duty on July 15 for four weeks. As he read the dry official phrases, the threat of war suddenly seemed very near at hand.

Back on the flight deck, Desmond saw at once from Ken Frazer's face that there had been no change for the better. Resuming his seat hurriedly, he ran his eyes over the instruments. Their safety margin was dropping.

"I've cut our speed to 105 knots," Frazer told him, "but it doesn't seem to have made any difference."

Desmond did some rapid figuring. The tanks were draining at an increasing rate, and on the main fuel gauge the needle had swung past the red danger mark. The gauges were notoriously inaccurate at very low readings, and it was possible that the position was not as serious as the gauge indicated; on the other hand, the engines could run dry at any second.

In heading directly for Shambe, their course had taken them away from the main river, which had bent sharply to the east for several miles; the aircraft was now flying over an area where the water was thickly clogged with reeds and mud. A ditching here would almost certainly result in the total wrecking of the aircraft.

"How long before we reach the open river again?" Desmond asked, taking the controls. *Caterina* was still flying sweetly, her four engines in synchronization with each other and no trace of the falterings that would signal the presence of air in the fuel leads. Once that began, they would have only a minute or two in which to select a place to ditch.

"We'll be over the river in approximately twelve minutes," Ken shouted to him, "just before we hit Shambe."

That was little help. There would be no prospect of making a safe landing before they reached the station, and it was too late to turn and head directly for one of the main channels. Twelve minutes. If the fuel gauge was reading correctly, they had barely sufficient reserves to reach the river.

"I'm going down to five hundred feet," said Desmond to the others. "Send a message to Shambe that our fuel situation is now critical."

Down below, ignorant of the danger they were facing, the passengers peered excitedly from the windows at the startled flocks of birds that rose on every side, scattering swiftly as the great plane winged low over the marshes.

○ ○ ○

Siegret Wienzman a pale, pretty seventeen-year-old-girl, lived with her widowed father, David Wienzman, who was head of the department of medicine at the University of Vienna, and one of the most respected men in the city. They lived in a pleasant house on the university grounds, and as she grew older Siegret had assumed more and more of the responsibilities for running their home. She looked after her father's needs and acted as hostess when he entertained members of the faculty or groups of students.

They had been happy years. Vienna had been free from many of the ugly events taking place in neighboring states, and Siegret and her father had many friends. There had been parties, dinners, an active intellectual life, and travel abroad. Then, it had all ceased one terrible day in March 1938.

Anschluss. In a single instant, the borders of the Third Reich had extended one-hundred-fifty miles to encompass the people of Austria. Files of troops—and trucks, motorcycles, and armored cars—slinking in silence through the side streets; endless lines of grim-faced, gray-uniformed men. Neither the soldiers nor the people watching had said a word or made a gesture while the endless columns rolled by.

Later had come the great parade, the buildings hung with the huge red banners bearing crooked swastikas. Siegret had even seen the great man himself drive past at the head of a phalanx of military vehicles. He had been waving and beaming with pleasure, and to Siegret's amazement some of his fierce joy had been communicated to the crowds.

All at once, uniforms and armbands were seen everywhere. Regulations were issued governing people's lives down to the smallest detail. Identity cards had to be obtained from government offices where bullying officials demanded to know every insignificant fact about people's lives. Travel was restricted, newspapers were censored, young men and women were conscripted for state work camps.

The Jewish decrees had started a little later, when the authorities had the country firmly in their grip. In spite of rumors of what was already happening in Germany, it was still a great shock for Siegret to learn of decrees aimed at her and her father, to discover that they were no longer part of the ordinary population, but a separate and suspect minority.

Certain streets were banned to them, for they contained monuments or memorials before which all Germans saluted, and Jews were not allowed to give the Nazi salute. Their passes were now stamped with the word *Juden*, and the letter J imprinted on every page.

It became a common occurrence for Siegret to see uniformed thugs daubing obscenities on the walls and windows of Jewish-owned shops and to see decent men she had known all her life being openly abused and roughly handled. It was common, too, to hear groups of youths jeering at her as she passed. "Little Jewess, Jewish whore, dirty Jew."

Even before the takeover, her father had been worried about their future should the Nazis seize power in Vienna. For the past six years, since the rise of Hitlerism, he had refused to enter Germany on any pretext whatsoever or to allow his daughter to do so.

After the *Anschluss* came, David Wienzman was prepared. Taking advantage of a day when gangs of youths had stormed the university to censor and burn all books and other works declared by the Nazi party to be of a degenerate, non-Aryan nature, he dispatched a letter of resignation to the university governors.

The chanting crowds piled thousands of irreplaceable volumes on the bonfires in an orgy of vandalism, and members of the faculty stood by helplessly. The Wienzmans had packed up their belongings and set off for their old family home in Saint Veit, high in the Austrian Alps, near the Italian border. Siegret could never recall the memory of that journey without a shiver of fear. The two of them slipped away through the mob, dressed as inconspicuously as possible, carrying only a few of their most valued possessions. Her father, a small, upright figure, guided her safely out toward the station, all the time clutching tightly to his chest the parcel containing his precious research records, as though afraid someone would try to snatch it from him.

The journey had been long and wearying. Forbidden to own or drive a car, the old man and his daughter were banned from all but the cheapest of the third-class trains, and for much of the trip they were forced to stand, packed tightly among scores of other passengers. At every stop police had boarded the coaches to check papers, and each time some unfortunate individuals had been dragged off for further questioning. In order to obtain permission to travel to an area so close to a frontier, special passes were necessary, and Siegret had been in terror lest theirs should be in some way defective. Each time one of the strutting guards had examined the precious documents, she had been gripped with numbing fear, her limbs trembling, her mouth dry, scarcely able to whisper the answers to the curt questions.

Not until late at night did they finally reach the small town where Siegret had spent every summer since her early childhood. Siegret nearly cried when they stepped out at the familiar old station and saw the streets and houses she knew so well clustered together at the head of the valley beneath the mountain slopes. The stationmaster himself had greeted them and driven them home in his car, and that night Siegret had slept soundly for the first time in many weeks.

For a little while the spell remained. It appeared that the poisonous atmosphere of the cities had failed to reach the hearts and minds of the independent mountain villagers. The Jewish decrees went ignored and forgotten, and in any case the majority of the regulations were irrelevant here. Local officials were helpful and kindly, the ranks of the police free from the vicious thugs who had terrorized them in Vienna.

The respite, however, was brief. As always, it was among the children and youths that the first signs of trouble appeared. Subjected daily to intrusive propaganda through the schools, educated in the politics of hatred and violence, and encouraged by those in authority to indulge in every kind of outrage against a helpless section of the populace that was already cowed by police action, bands of youths began to carry the campaign against the Jews into the most remote areas of the country.

One afternoon, as Siegret was walking home from school, a gang of boys shouted after her. They were boys she knew, in their early teens for the most part, though there were several older youths among them, and all had run off at the approach of an adult. But the well-remembered pattern had begun again. The older boys took to persecuting her, deriving pleasure in following her about, making lewd and filthy suggestions to her, or leering at her in public.

Life for the young girl became worse than in Vienna. Her natural prettiness, which had increased with the clean air and good food of the mountains, served only as an added incentive to the boys who seemed to appear everywhere. There was one youth in particular who frightened her. Heavily built, fair-haired Heinz Gerdler was the leader of one of the gangs, and his tactic was to pursue and trap her, forcing her to listen to stories of what he had done to other Jewish girls and would soon do to her. Standing around, the other boys would jeer and laugh at her humiliation, until, desperate and in tears, she managed to break through their circle and flee.

Though the youths had so far not dared to extend their attentions to him, Professor Wienzman had observed their behavior toward his daughter with anger, and a bitter frustration at the realization that he was powerless to prevent it. The chief of police for the Saint Veit district was an old friend, Hans Meyer, and Wienzman went to ask his advice. Could something be done to prevent such behavior?

The policeman listened in silence to the professor's complaints. "My friend," he said, shaking his head sadly when Wienzman had finished, "I will do what I can, but I must tell you that there is very little to be done. These young louts," he rolled the word contemptuously in his mouth, "have official backing. It is incredible but true. If I try to arrest them or even hinder them, I will lose my job. I know"—he held up a hand as the old man started to protest—"that should not matter. I should be prepared to do my duty, and I am. But here in Saint Veit I am responsible for many people. If I go, someone much tougher will be put in my place, and then things will be worse. There is nothing I can do. My advice is that you leave this country and go away until these terrible times are over and the streets are safe for decent people again."

"I am too old to leave my home," Wienzman answered, "nor will I be driven away by these ruffians. This persecution cannot last forever. It will pass."

"Professor," Meyer leaned across the desk and spoke urgently, "it is going to get much worse—and very quickly. Already in the cities there are killings and murders every day, and they go unpunished. This evil is spreading. If war comes, who knows what the Nazis may do? For your daughter's sake, if not your own, take my advice and leave while you still have time. At least I can be of some help with travel documents and passes."

"We shall lose everything," Wienzman replied tonelessly. "They let you take nothing with you. Even taxes must be paid in advance for a full year after leaving. What would happen to us both? We would be penniless."

Meyer tried to reassure him. "Professor, a man of your reputation will find a post in any country. If you stay, the Nazis will take everything anyway, sooner or later, and you may lose your freedom as well—perhaps even your life."

The professor admitted that there was sound advice in his friend's words, and after some delay, he began to make preparations for departure. Even with the police chief's help, the difficulties placed in the way of anyone wishing to emigrate were immense. No fewer than thirty-four separate permits and certificates had to be assembled, in addition to the usual passports and visas, all of them involving lengthy visits to the provincial government offices in Klagenfurt. Sometimes the professor went alone, but frequently it was necessary for Siegret to accompany him and take her place in the long lines or in the crowded waiting rooms. The interviews with churlish, overbearing officials were exhausting and dispiriting, and there seemed to be no end to them.

Nothing that might conceivably be of any value could be taken out of the country unless such huge sums were forfeited as to make the exercise worthless. Their house in Saint Viet was sold for a nominal sum to a relative of Siegret's mother, who, since her family was not Jewish, would be safe, with the understanding that the Wienzmans were to continue to live there until their departure and that it was to be resold to them if they ever returned.

With the help of Hans Meyer, a letter was smuggled to an old friend of the professor's now working at the University of Rome, Dr. Augusto Farenzi. Through his aid, Italian visas were obtained, and he also promised to use his influence to persuade the United States embassy in Rome to grant the pair visas for America.

Their preparations occupied the whole of the winter months, but by March 1939 all was virtually complete, and they waited only confirmation of the American visas from Farenzi. Now that the time to leave had drawn near, David Wienzman realized that he found the prospect infinitely more alarming than at first. For all its dark side, Austria had been his home for sixty years. To give up his life there for the uncertainty of a new world seemed to him a tremendous risk, and one he was reluctant to take unless convinced it was truly essential.

At the same time he sensed that time was running out. In both ordinary daily affairs and the official press, the tone of anti-Jewish feeling was becoming more strident. Siegret scarcely dared to leave the house. Even in Saint Veit some shops would no longer serve non-Aryans, and many private homes were barred to them. The decrees issued by the government were increasingly severe.

Without warning, during the second week in March, while the professor was recovering in bed from a chill, there came a devastating and unexpected blow—a peremptory letter from the new chancellor of the university in Vienna. It was brief and to the point. A recent review had shown that the professor's research program on disease immunization was of national importance. He was directed, therefore, to return immediately to continue his work.

The shock of this message, when he had begun to believe that the authorities had forgotten his very existence, struck fear and dismay into the old man. Not so much for himself—he would be safe as long as his work was important—but for his daughter. Now the authorities would never let him send her to safety; she would be a hostage to his cooperation.

"We shall have to go back," he told her helplessly, letting the letter drop.

Siegret regarded him anxiously. The strain of the past year was evident. His hair had become white and was thinning rapidly. The lines on his face had deepened into long creases in the skin, and his cheeks had shrunk and hollowed. Propped up on the pillows she had arranged for him, his hands lying listlessly on the coverlet, he had become, Siegret realized, an old man.

Silently he drafted a telegram message of acceptance and gave it to Siegret to send.

"I will get up and come with you," he said to her bitterly, "since it is not safe for you to be on the streets by
yourself."

Siegret refused him. "It will be all right at this time in
the afternoon," she assured him, "and there won't be any
boys about in this weather. Besides, it's much too cold for
you to go out, papa. She tucked the bedclothes firmly
around him. "I will be perfectly safe," she promised him.
"It's so dark outside I doubt if anybody will ever be able
to see me."

Siegret was more than a little worried. For a fortnight
she had not ventured further than the end of the road,
and twice in recent days she had caught sight of Gerdler
there. She prayed that the bad weather would indeed shield
her from hostile eyes. The back way would be safest.
Tucking her father's message into her pocket, she
slipped out through the back door and set off down the
snow-covered road.

o   o   o

The crocodile is so well adapted to its environment
that it remains one of nature's most successful creations.
Its design has been virtually unchanged for 150 million
years. With its savage jaw, its heavily armored back, its
claws, and its enormously powerful tail, its speed through
the water, coupled with the ability to stay submerged for
an hour or more at a time or to float on the surface in
perfect mimicry of a piece of driftwood, the crocodile is
one of the most dangerous creatures on earth, and each
year claims a greater number of human victims than any
other species except the snake.

Its four-foot jaws slightly agape, throat membranes
closed to prevent the entry of water, and its ton weight
of armor-plated muscle virtually invisible, the big croc
drifted downstream on the current, making scarcely any
movement save for an occasional swing of its tail to correct its course.

While visually scanning the banks on either side of the
channel for any sign of prey, the croc's scent organs were
also alert for traces of food within the water itself. Shambe
was less than a mile downstream.

At five hundred feet, every detail of the swamplands was visible from the flying boat. Flocks of ibis, plovers, and scarlet waders fled from their feeding grounds as the plane's shadow passed overhead. Desmond caught sight of a group of hippos splashing into deep water. He was holding down their speed to ninety knots in a desperate effort to conserve every drop of the remaining fuel. The gauge was flickering about the zero mark, and it was no longer possible to make an accurate guess of how much longer they could remain in the air.

"We should sight the station in the next three or four minutes," Kendrick told him. "We're about nine miles due south of it by my reckoning." Nine miles: six or seven minutes flying time, Desmond thought to himself. If their reckoning was not accurate, if they failed to sight the station when they expected, they would have no choice but to ditch and pray that they and the passengers survived and that, somehow, a rescue party would find them. All three of them were silent, concentrating on the ground ahead, searching among the waving reeds for the first sign of their goal.

"Shall we ask London for permission to start jettisoning the cargo, skipper?" suggested Kendrick, and they laughed, the tension on the flight deck easing momentarily.

They had flown on for another two or three minutes when the inboard port engine coughed several times and commenced to run with an irregular stutter. *Caterina*'s nose dipped sharply. Desmond's hands moved swiftly over the controls, pulling back on the stick to lift her head again and opening up the throttle on the three good engines to boost power and restore stable flight.

Desmond began feathering the port engine, cutting it out completely for a second and allowing the airscrew to spin freely in the slipstream. Turning up the fuel mixture and punching the ignition button, he restarted the engine, hoping to clear out any air locks and set the motor running freely again. The engine gave another series of explosive coughs, and the rackety stutter shook the wing again. Sweating, Desmond switched off and repeated the maneuver; again the engine refused to fire properly. He punched the ignition button a third time, expecting all the while to hear the same ominous sounds from the other engines. The altimeter showed they had sunk to less than 350 feet, and involuntarily Ken Frazer began looking for a place to bring the aircraft down.

Again they heard the familiar stutter as the engine struggled to catch on the weak mixture. Ralph Kendrick's hand strayed to the radio emergency switch ready to get off an SOS signal before they had to crash-land. All three of them were about to give up hope when the engine suddenly burst into a satisfying roar. Desmond knew the danger was not yet over. The fault might have been only an air lock caused by insufficient pressure as the pumps sucked out the very dregs of the tanks, but, unless they sighted the station within the next two or three minutes, he would be forced to ditch in the best available stretch of water, praying that there were no hazards beneath the surface.

He checked the rev. counter and air speed indicators. *Caterina* was flying at only just over stalling speed now. His hand was poised ready to open up the throttle the instant he felt the nose begin to drop, and his ears strained to catch the faintest hint of a check in the rhythm of the engines.

A sharp exclamation from Frazer jerked his attention back to the ground. The sound of the flying boat sweeping low over the reed beds had surprised a herd of elephants browsing knee deep in the mud. The whole windscreen seemed full of heaving gray backs and massive heads tossed up in fear as the great beasts plunged wildly through the swamps, flinging up spray and muck, scattering in all directions.

"Christ! There must be hundreds—I've never seen so many together," Frazer blurted out. "Look at those tusks!" One huge bull, maddened with fear and enraged by the inhibiting mud, had broken into a frenzied gallop and, as the fliers watched in amazement, charged down a young calf, sending it crashing over in the muck. The unfortunate animal struggled to rise, but, even as it did so, others careened into it, and soon several of the herd were brought down, struggling in the mire, their great limbs flailing desperately in their panic.

Then the flying boat was past and the vast herd lost to sight, leaving the men on the flight deck awestruck. All three had heard stories of these herds in the Sud. Sometimes they roamed the swamps a thousand or more strong, secure from attack by hunters in their impenetrable sanctuary.

If the engines had given out back there, Desmond thought grimly, they might well have found themselves crashing into the enraged herd. He could picture the terrorized elephants storming through the wreckage of the flying boat, crushing anyone who remained alive.

"We must see the station soon," Ken Frazer muttered. "It can't be more than a mile or two away at the most. Where the hell is it?"

Desmond glanced at the instrument panel. Speed 81 knots, height 200 feet, fuel zero. Below the gauges, a line of five lights glowed red, indicating that all four main tanks and the reserve were at danger point.

No sign of the landing station. A flock of scarlet ibis rose before them and wheeled away to starboard, climbing rapidly, revealing delicate pink underfeathers on thousands of wings.

"We will have to ditch," Desmond said, "unless we can spot the station within the next sixty seconds. I can't risk being forced down when the engines give out. Keep your eyes open for any stretch of water that looks at all useable."

"Aye, aye, skipper," Frazer replied mechanically. It was evident that he had been expecting such an order.

Below them, the river channels were split by hundreds of small islets and banks to which vegetation clung thickly. Nowhere that Desmond could see was there sufficient space to hazard a touchdown. He reached out to flick on the intercom switch and warn the passengers that a crash landing was imminent and, as he did so, a crackle of static from the radio sounded behind him.

"Skipper," Kendrick called out, "Shambe reports they can hear our engines. They estimate we are approximately two miles southeast of them. The landing area is clear, wind speed seven to eight knots from the northeast." The relief in his voice was plain.

"OK. We should be able to spot them soon enough now." There was no need to tell the others to keep a sharp lookout.

"There it is!" Ken Frazer cried thankfully. "Ahead at two o'clock." He and Desmond sighted the cluster of low white houses almost simultaneously. No more than a couple of miles away, the water opened out, and at the tip of a bend in the river, the station lay half hidden among the reeds. The site allowed them a clear run in at a point where the Nile opened into a broad channel. A narrow wooden jetty had been built out into the water, and a pair of motor launches were tied up alongside. A knot of people had gathered on the shore.

Desmond brought *Caterina* down in a long, slow sweep toward the river. He let her sink gently through the last few feet of air, checking carefully as he did so that he had judged the height correctly.

At landing altitude, the instruments were simply not precise enough to tell the pilot exactly how many feet he was above the water, and the most careful judgment was called for in putting the craft down. When the river surface was very calm and the afternoon light deceptive, an error of only a few feet could result in catastrophe.

If the pilot came in too high at the moment he throttled back and reduced the speed, the flying boat would literally drop into the water, causing herself serious damage, perhaps even breaking up. Equally serious was the risk involved in striking the surface at too high a speed or at the wrong altitude. Then there was a strong chance of a wing dipping and catching in the water, causing the aircraft to capsize.

A fresh bout of coughing vibrated throughout the flight deck as an engine on the starboard wing faltered. Praying, Desmond ignored the sound and closed the throttles still further. Water flashed past the windows; there was a slight jar, a burst of spray, a trembling and hissing as the keel split the surface, and, then trailing a long stream of foam, the aircraft breasted down and settled gently on her planing bottom while one after another the remaining engines spluttered into silence.

2

By radio: 1640 hrs LOCAL TIME. AIR TRAFFIC
CONTROL CAIRO TO IMPERIAL AIRWAYS LON-
DON. RELAYED FROM KHARTOUM. IMPERIAL
AIRWAYS FLIGHT 109 G-ADHO CATERINA
FORCED TO MAKE EMERGENCY LANDING AT
SHAMBE FOR FUEL TANK REPAIRS. PASSENGERS
AND CARGO SAFE. ESTIMATED DELAY THREE
TO FOUR HOURS. WILL ADVISE FURTHER WHEN
REPAIRS COMPLETED. END.

Even before *Caterina* had stopped, the two launches
from the station had started toward her; the channel at
this point was about three hundred yards wide, and the
aircraft came to rest a little over half that distance from
the shore. Directly beneath the flight deck and right in
the prow of the flying boat was a small boxlike space
where ropes and fenders, and other tackle used for mooring, were stored. Reached by a ladder from the flight
deck, it also had a hatch opening out from the prow and a
retractable mooring bollard let into the hull. Ralph Kendrick lifted up the trapdoor in the cockpit floor directly
behind the pilots' seats and dropped through. There was a
bang and a loud click as he undid the hatch. A draft of
warm air filtered up into the cockpit, bringing with it a
smell of mud and the sound of water slopping against
the hull outside.

Sandy Everett came hurrying through from the mailroom clutching his cap and a handful of letters.

"You and Andy better go ashore with the passengers
and see they don't get into any trouble," Desmond told
him. "Make them all go straight up to the rest house and
don't let them start sightseeing or wandering too far."

Since Shambe did not possess the special Braby mooring pontoons that enabled passengers to disembark directly onto dry land, *Caterina* was towed to a fixed mooring buoy thirty yards out from shore and made fast. The two launches, surprisingly smart and well cared for, began ferrying people off, under the supervision of Sandy Everett and Andy Draper. In the cockpit, Desmond and Frazer completed the landing check.

"Do you want to write up the log now?" Frazer asked offhandedly.

"No," Desmond told him, "I'll wait till I hear what the engineer has to say." A scowl passed briefly over the first officer's face. He was anxious to discover exactly what Desmond intended to say about the reasons for the break in the itinerary.

A third boat, loaded with tools and equipment, approached, bringing an engineer to look at the ruptured fuel tank, and Desmond went out onto the wing to talk to him. Frazer's attitude annoyed him, the more so since it was based on bad judgment. However much Desmond might rate him privately for his inefficiency, when it came to writing up the log he would never consider trying to shift the blame onto a junior officer. Frazer's inability to realize this was just another reason why he had a long way to go before the time came to give him his stripes.

The engineer spoke a mixture of English, French, and Portuguese. His usual tasks, Desmond guessed, were confined to repairing the engines of the boats or overhauling the few motor vehicles in the station. He examined the tank for some minutes and shook his head pessimistically.

"Well?" Desmond said. "How long will it take to plug the leak?" The engineer came back along the wing.

"It will not be easy, capitaine," the engineer said apologetically. "In order to make the repairs correctly, I must weld a new patch into position along the seam. The patch there now is too small. Even that will not be a permanent repair, but it will last until you reach Cairo. There the facilities are better."

"How long will it take?" Desmond asked impatiently. The flight to Khartoum, 550 miles away, took three hours. Unless they could get away within the next three hours, they would have to stay at Shambe for the night. Even now he would have to make a night landing at Khartoum.

"Maybe three, four hours." The engineer shrugged. "It is difficult to say. The leak is very bad." That much was certainly true. Even from where they were standing, the smell of fuel was clearly detectable, and when they had opened up the wing to look at the tank, the fumes had nearly choked them. The whole of the inside of the wing must have been swimming with fuel. It was a miracle there hadn't been a fire.

Leaving the engineer to start getting out his tools, Desmond climbed through the mailroom hatch and returned to the flight deck. Frazer was still in his seat, inspecting the river banks through his binoculars.

"See anything interesting?" Desmond asked.

"A couple of native canoes are putting out toward us," Frazer told him, passing over the glasses. "An official from the station was talking to them, but he's just left. You can see him walking back along the bank."

"He was probably making sure the canoes kept out of the way while the launches were busy." Desmond twisted the focus adjuster, and the image became suddenly sharp and clear. Two canoes, more like rafts really, were coming toward them. The natives in them were tall, magnificently built, proud-looking men, apparently completely unclothed. On the leading craft, one of them stood up and waved.

"All secure down below," Ralph Kendrick reported, scrambling back into the flight deck through the trapdoor from the compartment below. "I've wedged a fender up under the nose ring, so the cable shouldn't run out at all."

"I'll have to go ashore and get off a report to London," Desmond told the two men, "before they start calling us. I want you both to stay on board and keep an eye on things." There was no need to say why. "You better each keep one of these with you." Opening the metal locker behind his seat, he took out the canvas pouch that Ian Haggart had given him at Durban. Frazer and Kendrick received the pistols without enthusiasm.

"Must be one hell of a big demand for gold around here," Ralph remarked sardonically, looking out at the tiny group of houses and the vast wilderness. "I'd guess there's a bigger risk of being eaten." He indicated the natives who were circling the flying boat and uttering shrill cries.

Desmond smiled. "I'll be back as soon as I've sent the message," he said. "I want to supervise the work on that fuel tank myself."

The smaller of the two launches was waiting for him. It had space for six or eight passengers beneath the canvas awning and was crewed by a pair of cheerful natives who, in deference to European sensibilities, wore smart white shorts.

Taking off his jacket, Desmond undid his collar and loosened his tie. It was the beginning of the rainy season in Equatoria, the very worst time to be there, but even so he felt glad of the chance to see it. Very probably this part of Africa would never see regular tourists or visitors. With the improvement in range of aircraft, fewer rather than more planes would land.

The shoreline was littered with canoes and rafts and piled balks of timber, evidently flotsam picked up from the river. The small jetty gave access to the rest house; beyond it, tied up to the remains of a rotting wharf, the derelict hulk of an old paddle steamer bore silent witness to the station's past traffic.

A line of duckboards led across the muddy ground to the rest house and airline office. As Desmond stepped out of the launch and dismissed the crew, a gangling man in khaki shorts and shirt came down to meet him.

"Keeling," he greeted Desmond, holding out his hand. "Barry Keeling, I'm the station chief. Welcome to Shambe." He was about forty-five, though his thinning hair made him seem older, deeply tanned, with the agility of someone used to a strenuous existence. He was one of those men, Desmond guessed, who deliberately sought out posts in remote places like Shambe, where he could indulge his passion for hunting and exploration, away from the cares and pressures of the rest of the world.

Desmond explained the trouble with the fuel tank and repeated what the engineer had said. Keeling listened gravely. "I'm sorry to add to your problems," he said when Desmond had finished, "but I'm afraid we've come across an added complication. The fuel in one of our storage tanks has become contaminated by rainwater. We've had heavy downpours for the past week, but the problem was only discovered today. The result is we haven't enough here to get you up to Malakal. I've radioed Malakal, and they are sending down five hundred gallons on board a Calcutta they've got up there, but I'm afraid it won't reach us until seven o'clock at the earliest."

"Everything's going wrong today," Desmond said. "How many gallons have you got still usable?"

"Two hundred. One of the tanks was more than half empty, but the Calcutta will be carrying enough to get her home again, so there should be enough so that you can carry right on through to Khartoum if you want to. You can tranship the mail for Malakal here."

"Yes, that's what I was thinking," Desmond agreed. "If I can have the repairs completed and the fuel on board by half-past seven, I'll make the trip tonight."

Keeling grinned. "Sure we can't persuade you to stay?" he asked. "I mean, look at what we can offer in the way of entertainment."

"Personally, I wouldn't mind at all; neither would the rest of the crew." Desmond grinned back. "But I can't imagine some of our passengers being too happy at the idea."

"No," Keeling admitted as they began to walk back up to the rest house. "That's very true. One of your female passengers has already complained at our allowing the natives to go about naked. Still, it's a pity you can't stay. We might have been able to offer you some shooting, if you enjoy that. Elephant, lion, buck, hippo. It's a hunter's paradise." His eyes glowed as he spoke.

"Any crocs?" Desmond asked with a backward glance at the river. "I should think this must be just the place for them."

"They grow to greater size here than anywhere in the world," Keeling answered. "We lost a woman from the village to one last week," he added quietly. "It took her while she was bathing in the shallows."

Laura Hartman had come ashore in the launch with a middle-aged couple she had met on the plane, Mr. and Mrs. Harold King of Phoenix, Arizona. Mr. King was a short, stout man neatly clad in sporty clothes and a straw hat. His wife was about the same height as her husband, though much lighter in build. Her face, creased and wrinkled by the dry summers of her home, was shrewd but kindly.

A small crowd of officials and residents and curious native onlookers had gathered to meet them at the jetty so that the moment they stepped ashore they were surrounded by a jostling, excited crowd. Laura and the Kings had traveled in the same boat as Mr. and Mrs. Johnson and their daughter. The little girl was fascinated by the strange country, and she danced about the launch, impatient to reach land. Hastening along the jetty after her, Mrs. Johnson suddenly found herself in the center of a chattering throng of stark naked natives. For a moment she stood speechless. Then, letting out a sharp cry, she rounded on poor Sandy Everett.

Her face was bright red with anger and shame, and Sandy felt himself turning crimson as the woman's husband, a serious-faced man in a brown trilby, joined in the outcry and threatened to take his family back to the aircraft.

"I'm terribly sorry," Sandy apologized. "I honestly had no idea about it." Everywhere he looked he seemed to see quivering breasts and genitals displayed by their owners without the least trace of concern. To make matters worse, many of the women in the crowd were young and extremely attractive.

"Well, you should have known," Mr. Johnson told him angrily. Mrs. Johnson broke into loud sobbing.

The situation was saved by Mrs. King. "I know how you feel," she said firmly as she led the weeping woman and her now tearful daughter up the path to the rest house, "but you must remember that these people are quite innocent. They haven't learned our standards of behavior yet, and I think the only thing we can do is ignore them." The remaining passengers followed along the path, and Sandy shot Harold King and Laura a look of heartfelt gratitude.

The largest of the group of whitewashed stone buildings that bordered the river was the airline and river service rest house. The others were houses belonging to the handful of local officials stationed in the town and to the river pilots. There was a mission school and a general store. Behind these lay a sizable village of mud huts and shanty dwellings that had grown up around the station. The air was hot and sticky, heavy with the smell of rotting vegetation and stagnant water, and from everywhere there came the ceaseless whine of insects and the cries of birds.

○   ○   ○

The streets of Saint Veit were all but deserted. The sky was dark with the threat of more snow, and a bitterly cold wind was driving up the valley, keeping people firmly indoors by their fires. She had chosen this particular time because she knew she could count on a clear space of half an hour between the emptying of the schools and the appearance on the streets of the first of the homeward-going workers.

The pavements were covered with frozen snow and slush, interspersed with treacherous patches of black ice. Siegret picked her way carefully, hurrying as best she could, ready to duck down a turning or into a doorway. With luck she might well escape recognition.

Her mind was occupied with thoughts of what she and her father would do in the future. The telegram she was going to send simply informed the university governors that her father had received their letter and would be returning to Vienna at once to take up his work. That much he had to do, even if only to buy time for them to escape. A refusal to undertake work designated "of national importance" would certainly lead to imprisonment in labor camps for both of them.

And the professor's doing such work would not necessarily ensure their safety. The authorities might change their minds about the value of his research. The Nazis might decide to send Siegret to a camp as hostage for her father's good behavior. At the very best, she and her father would have to face all the dangers of Vienna, from which hundreds were still fleeing every day. David Wienzman had never been a particularly devoted Jew; indeed, Siegret's mother had been a Christian, and he had always regarded himself simply as an Austrian. But the persecution had driven him into closer ties with the Jewish community. News of the increasing severity, of the notorious Crystal Night when the synagogues were destroyed and the Jewish shops smashed, of ever-growing numbers of arrests, of the beatings and murders and rapes was passed on to them even in the small mountain town. More

than half the Jews of Vienna, Siegret knew, had already
left the city or been driven away.

The professor had considered leaving his daughter in
the care of some family in Saint Veit, but Siegret had
refused to discuss such an alternative.

As she approached the town square, the streets grew
wider. Cars passed and people hurried about, muffled up
against the cold. Fortunately everyone appeared too anxious to get home to worry about the slight figure that
slipped by, head bowed to hide her face.

Going into the post office itself was the part of the
journey she had dreaded most. There were three or four
people inside, but fortunately they were engrossed in their
own business, and none of them took notice of her. She
filled out the telegraph form, miswriting it in her haste,
and had to begin it again before handing it in across the
counter.

On the way back, all the while she was near the busy
part of town, her heart started violently each time a figure
came toward her. The youths often spotted her in this
area and then followed her home. Usually they waited until the street was clear before beginning the taunts and
jeers, but recently they had become bolder and less
afraid of being rebuked by an adult.

If she could only gain the safety of the less-frequented
back streets, she stood a good chance of remaining un-
observed. If Gerdler or any of the others were near her
house, she could simply rush past them.

She was halfway there when the boys saw her. Six of
them came out of a street so suddenly that they practically walked into her. They were wearing the brown shirts
and shorts of the Hitler Youth movement, and among
them Siegret recognized at least three members of Hans
Gerdler's gang. They must have been attending a meeting
after school.

She turned and ran frantically back in the direction of
the nearest main street. At least there, however much
they might tease and leer at her, they would not dare to
molest her physically. The youths eagerly took chase.
Siegret heard their feet pounding swiftly after her and their
cries of pursuit. The lane she was fleeing down was long
and narrow, and ran for two-thirds of its length, past a

high wall surrounding the local primary school, empty now that the day was over. Panic-stricken, Siegret ran through the gate at the far end of the school and up the steps to the main doorway. The boys caught her as she grasped the handle.

The youths were all in their middle teens, two of them no more than schoolboys, and now that they had caught her they seemed to have no clear plan of what to do next. They held the trembling girl against the door panels while they regained their breath. Had she the strength to tear herself free and run, she might have escaped with no more than a fright, but the months of fear and persecution had sapped her will. So terrified was she that the youths had to literally hold her up.

The noise of the chase had attracted others from the gang, and it was not long before Hans Gerdler arrived with some of the older boys. He pushed his way through and grinned evilly at her.

"So what have we here?" he demanded, seizing the girl by the chin and forcing her head round to look at him. "A little Jewess out on the streets? What were you doing, Jewess? Why did you run away from our patrol?"

Siegret remained silent. Gerdler released her and began slapping her lightly across the face. Her fur hat fell to the ground.

"See how rich these Jews are," Gerdler declaimed, "with money they extort from honest Germans? This Jewess is wearing furs, while the rest of us have hardly got a coat to our backs."

"Get it off her and let her see what cold's really like," called one of them. There was a chorus of agreement, and several of the gang began pulling off her coat.

"Let me alone!" Siegret screamed. "I wasn't doing anything. I was just going home. You haven't the right to do this to me."

"Haven't the right! We'll soon show you what your rights are," Gerdler retorted. "Take her coat off," he ordered. In a few moments she was shivering before them in her thin cotton blouse.

"That's better," Gerdler said, sneering. "Now we can have a better look at you—oh, no you don't!" With a sudden desperate effort, Siegret had twisted away and made a dart for freedom. Grabbing her by the arms, he pushed her back up against the doors, pressing his body against her as she squirmed. The others stood there laughing.

Siegret felt his hands roaming over her body, pinching and squeezing. Her struggles served only to arouse him further.

"Let's get her inside," he called to the others, "and see what little Jewesses are made of."

Siegret let out a scream, but a hand was clamped over her mouth. There was a fumbling at the lock of the door behind her, and she was dragged through into the passage.

"In here—take her in here," Gerdler said as the boys paused. "Put her down on the table," he panted, still holding her tightly. Several more of them grasped her, and she felt herself lifted and flung down on her back on the hard surface of a classroom table. She could see the wooden beams of the ceiling above her and the faces of her attackers leering down at her. Someone tugged off her boots.

"High and mighty Miss Wienzman, who walks about with her nose in the air and thinks she's too good for the rest of us because she comes from Vienna," Gerdler hissed viciously. "Now we're going to show you how to be nice to us." Taking her blouse by the neck and giving it a single jerk, he ripped it open to the waist.

"Hold her down," he snapped at the others as Siegret fought violently. Reaching out again, he tore down her slip and brassiere.

The other boys crowded around, breathing fast with excitement, their faces flushed. Hands pawed at her breasts. "Quick," said another voice she did not recognize, "pull off her skirt." Clumsy fingers fumbled at the fastening at her waist. She tried to kick, but her legs were pinned tightly to the unyielding table. Her skirt and slip came down, stripped eagerly over her ankles. Desperately she bit hard at the hand over her mouth, her teeth meeting in the flesh. There was a shrill cry of pain, and the hand was snatched away. Instantly she let out a scream.

"Bitch!" Gerdler snarled, and he struck her in the face with his fist. "Keep her quiet. We don't want people coming in."

Someone else grabbed her mouth shut tightly, his nails

clawing savagely at her cheek, stifling her cries. Her head was ringing with pain and shock. Fingers pulled urgently at her panties, there was a sound of tearing fabric, and she felt cold air strike her skin. Hands were touching her and feeling all over her body. She heard Gerdler call out harshly, "Spread her legs open!" and her thighs were forced apart.

The other boys were still pawing at her. Gerdler pushed them aside. "I'll go first," he panted. "The rest of you can follow." His weight descended heavily, crushing her against the table. Siegret was aware of his face pressed up against her own, the stench of his breath in her nostrils. The hand over her face was released, and Gerdler's grinning mouth clamped fiercely down on her lips, their teeth grinding together, his fingers probing between her thighs.

There was a sudden confusion, voices raised, shouts and swearing, cries of alarm. The hands that had been holding her down let go. She heard the sound of running feet. The boy on top of her was pulled away. Sick and faint, scarcely realizing that she had been released, she tried to sit up. A face bent over her, a man's. Siegret screamed chokingly and shrank away.

"It's all right," she heard him say. "I'm the caretaker, Stortman. They've gone away. I've got rid of them all. You're safe now."

Through a haze of shock and nausea, Siegret remembered him. They were alone together in the classroom now. The youths must have fled when they heard him coming, ashamed to be caught actually trying to rape someone, even a Jewish girl. The caretaker was a middle-aged, shabby-looking man. He fussed about trying to help, unable to take his eyes off her body. Looking down at herself, Siegret saw that her blouse was in ribbons, the whole of the front entirely torn away together with all her underclothing, and from the waist down she was completely naked, her stockings hanging in shreds about her ankles.

Feebly she tried to cover herself. Her gray skirt lay in a bundle by the door where one of her attackers had dropped it. The caretaker fetched it for her and turned away while she pulled it on and drew the torn fragments of her blouse together to hide her breasts.

"You'd best put my coat round your shoulders," the

man offered kindly, "and come round the back to my room. You can tidy up there, and then I'll take you home to your father. They ought to be punished, those boys," he added as Siegret began sobbing quietly, tears streaming down her scratched and bruised face. He retrieved her boots, and with an effort she put them on and gathered up the scattered remains of her underclothes.

○ ○ ○

Despite Dr. Van Smit's remarks about the unpleasantness and the dangers of the swamps, neither Laura nor the Kings were at all put out by the extra stop. Indeed Laura felt intrigued by the idea of visiting so notorious an area, and the opportunity of looking around the little town attracted her far more than the proposal of iced drinks and easy chairs in the rest house. Mr. King had brought his camera ashore, and Laura decided to ask if she could borrow it before they returned to the aircraft. She had just reached the entrance to the rest house when she met Mrs. King coming out in the company of Lieutenant Thorne.

"Laura, my dear, I shall have to go down to the launch," Mrs. King told her. "Lieutenant Thorne has kindly offered to run me out to the airplane to get my traveling case. I've gone and left it under my seat."

"There's really no need for you to trouble yourself, Mrs. King," Thorne assured her. "If you just describe the case to me, I'll fetch it for you easily."

"No, no, I shall most certainly come," she replied firmly. "I'm afraid I'm not entirely sure where I put it."

"Mrs. King, why don't you let me go across and look for it?" suggested Laura. "I know what your case is like, and it's silly for you to tire yourself in this heat."

"I say, that's a splendid idea," Thorne said eagerly, delighted at the prospect of a few minutes alone in Laura's company. "Mrs. Hartman and I will have your case for you in a jiffy."

The landing stage and jetty were deserted when they reached the shore, and there was no sign of the launch crews or of any of the station staff.

"Don't you think we ought to find someone to take us out?" Laura said.

The young man dismissed the idea at once. "I do know how to handle a boat, Mrs. Hartman," he replied a trifle petulantly, and without waiting to see if anyone would come to stop them, he handed her down into the launch and followed her aboard.

The crowd on the shore had dispersed, and peace had returned to the river. At this time of day, few people were stirring. A pair of gray herons flew silently in, their long legs trailing after them in the air, and only the faint sounds of the engineer and his assistants working on the flying boat in midstream disturbed the afternoon quiet.

The big croc pushed out from the shallows and let itself be carried along with the current, moving very slowly and at a slight angle to the line of the river. Its resemblance to a drifting log was perfect. Its eyes scanned the banks for prey. One or two figures moved about among the huts of the village, and somewhere a pig squealed. The croc was about ten yards away from the end of the jetty when it first spotted Laura and Ian Thorne. Its muscles tensed. Quickening its pace, the croc dove below the surface and thrust forward.

The launch had been made fast at both ends. Thorne went forward to cast off the bow line before going back to release the stern line and start the engine. The stern line was tied to one of the pilings, and he stooped to loosen it. The rope was slimy and tightly tied. Its end slipped out through the young man's fingers and fell back into the water between the stern of the boat and the jetty.

As Thorne bent to retrieve the rope from the water, the unseen crocodile came gliding past the head of the jetty. With a powerful thrust of its tail, it shot forward swiftly, surging through the murky liquid round the pilings, jaws opening wide.

But it was too late. Thorne was already straightening up. His hands and arms were out of reach at the moment the huge jaws came level with him.

Still, there could be no mistaking the danger. The croc's head broke the surface of the water, and the passage of the great reptile driving forward and upward was clearly marked by a long eddy and a trail of bubbles. Thorne had a sudden vision of the huge creature lunging for him out of the depths.

Thorne jumped back with a shudder, and his sudden motion upset the equilibrium of the boat. It swayed violently, throwing him off balance and making him clutch wildly at the gunwale. The crocodile, seeing out of the corner of its wide-angled eyes the white figure once more bending low over the water, lashed upward with its tail.

This terrible weapon, six feet of bone and hard muscle encased in a carapace of armored plate, sharp-ridged along the crest and making up almost one-third of the animal's weight, whipped out, smashing the helpless man clean off the launch.

Instantly the croc arched around, its body banking steeply in a tight turn against the boat. Massive jaws agape, its tail thrashed the water again, and its limbs paddled furiously. The river's surface erupted in an explosion of foam and spray.

Ian Thorne never had a chance. The blow from the tail had broken his left arm and two of his ribs. Choking and sputtering, he struggled weakly to regain the boat; even as he did so, the croc was upon him.

The savage jaws clamped shut on his left thigh in a bone-crunching grip that ripped through the flesh, severing the blood vessels and bursting the femoral artery. A dark trail of blood began to stain the surface as the croc started to drag its victim into mid-river.

Appalling screams broke from the doomed man; his arms flailed in the water with all his remaining strength.

Badly injured and half drowned as he was, Thorne might have stood some hope against a beast of more normal size. Laura's cries, his own screams, the loud smack of the croc's tail on the river's surface, the splashing and struggles in the water had all attracted the attention of people on shore. With a croc of perhaps only eight- or twelve-feet long, he might have been able to fight long enough for help to reach him.

However, he was hopelessly outmatched by the white-scarred monster. Shaking him as a dog might shake a rat, it drew him into the main channel. Then, clamping its jaws even more tightly about the man's thigh, it dived steeply down toward the riverbed thirty feet below.

The water closing over his head spurred Thorne to make one final effort to free himself, wrenching with panic-maddened strength against the teeth that had bitten agonizingly through to the bones.

The croc went into its most fearsome and terrible maneuver. Ceasing its attempts to pull its victim into the mud at the bottom, it allowed itself to float upward for a few feet. Then, even as Thorne, fast losing all consciousness, gained a moment's hope, it tightened its grip again and flung itself into a violent spiral motion, its whole body rotating rapidly.

The terrific force splintered the man's thigh bone from hip to knee, mangling the leg until it was virtually torn from his body. A cloud of blood and fragments of flesh and bone spurted out. The croc twisted again and then backed away, tugging the leg clear of the torso.

It mattered little. Before the crocodile took hold of him a second time, Thorne was dead.

The suddenness of the attack had caught everyone on shore unaware. Barry Keeling kept a heavy hunting rifle in his office, and the instant he realized what had happened, he had seized it and raced down to the water's edge. Desmond had reached the jetty and found Laura in a state of shock in the launch, and his immediate thought had been for her safety. Now, in impotent fury, he stood holding her, watching the struggle.

By this time the trail of swirling blood-streaked water ran a long way out into the river. When Desmond had first gotten there, the struggle had still been taking place near the surface in a furious welter of foam and splashing, and for a brief instant he had caught a glimpse of the young man, his uniform showing very white, slashed with bright lines of red where the great brute had clawed him. Coiled around him had been the enormous green-black body of the reptile, its tail lashing at the water and the man it had seized with impartial frenzy.

Keeling flung the rifle to his shoulder, and the crash of the heavy weapon echoed across the marshes. Clouds of birds shrieked into the air and flapped hastily away as he fired twice more, but the crocodile was too deep now to be frightened off, and the echoes died uselessly. The river surface became calm, the churning ceased, and the bloody tracks in the water diffused and vanished. Before a boat could set off from the shore, the river had returned to its former tranquillity.

○ ○ ○

David Wienzman was hardly able to recognize the battered girl brought home by the caretaker. Siegret had made a brave attempt to clean herself up, but the bruises on her face had already begun to swell and darken. Her eyes were puffy and red from crying, her lips bleeding. Deep scratches covered her body, and she was near hysteria.

Helping her up to her room, he sent the caretaker to summon first the town doctor and then Hans Meyer from the police office. The doctor was a woman and would be better able to see to his daughter.

"But father," Siegret cried, "don't you understand? It's no use going to the police—it's no use asking anyone to help. Those boys are from the Hitler Youth movement, they can do what they like to us; we're Jews, we have no rights. Nobody can protect us." And she burst into renewed sobbing.

The doctor arrived and examined her carefully and dressed her wounds. Ugly marks had developed where the imprints of fingers and nails showed clearly on her skin. The blow she had received on the face had split both lips and bruised the whole of one side of her face. Livid marks and blotches covered her chest, stomach, and thighs, interspersed with deep scratches where the youths had pinched and pawed at her.

"Your daughter has suffered no serious physical injury," the doctor said when she descended to the sitting room. "Fortunately, she was rescued before those young louts could have their way with her. As for her mental condition," she shook her head, "it is too early to be sure. Sometimes a person recovers quickly from such an ordeal; with others it may leave permanent damage. I have given her a sedative, and she is asleep, but—if she is to have a chance of a complete recovery—she needs rest and peace and freedom from fear. I strongly advise that you take her someplace where these may be found."

"What can I do?" the professor asked the police chief helplessly when the doctor had gone and the caretaker, suitably thanked, had returned to the school. "You see what that letter says. I have to return to Vienna—perhaps even go into Germany. What peace of mind will Siegret find there?" Uttering a low moan, he collapsed into a chair.

"Herr Professor," Meyer addressed him with energy, "there is only one course for you to take. You must go; leave Austria at once. Tomorrow morning you must take your daughter and cross the frontier into Italy. From there you must somehow make your way to a country where you will be safe."

"But they will stop us. The Nazis will never give me a visa now. They want me to stay," Wienzman protested.

"You still have time. As yet no word has been sent through to my office ordering that you be refused an exit permit. You are not on the proscribed list. You already have the necessary documents certifying that you have paid your taxes and have no debts. I can issue you a permit and, provided you have no valuables with you, you will almost certainly be allowed through. The Italian frontier is the easiest for crossing."

"No," the professor replied firmly after a moment's pause. "You are very kind, but I could not accept your offer. It would only put you in grave danger, and neither my daughter nor I will buy our freedom at such a price."

"Don't you see? If you go at once, I shall be in no danger. I have received no order to detain you, and we are allowed to permit people, refugees and Jews like yourselves, to leave the country, provided they take nothing of value with them." He leaned forward and spoke earnestly. "Tonight I shall order the arrest of this boy Gerdler and the others. Under the Nazi laws, sexual relations between Aryans and other races are forbidden, even in the case of rape. I doubt very much if the charge will succeed, but at least it will enable me to keep them out of the way while you make your escape. The authorities in Vienna will receive your telegram and will not become suspicious about you for at least two days, by which time you will be in Italy. Of course I will be questioned, but there will be no proof that I have acted improperly. Everything will have been done exactly according to the rules. There may be a reprimand but no more than that."

Siegret's father was silent. When he spoke again, his

face was grave. "There is something else I have not told you about," he said. "There is another reason why I am afraid to return to Vienna, or, worse still, to Germany." Meyer had to lean forward to catch his words. "Many years ago, not long after the war, I was working in a clinic in one of the poorer areas of the city. I was one of three doctors who donated some time there each week. We got all kinds of people, suffering from many different illnesses and complaints. Pneumonia, typhus, diphtheria, and tubercular cases, of course—we had a great many of those." He hesitated again. "I was already specializing in viral infections, and I worked mainly on venereal cases. One day a man came to me to be treated for syphilis. I remember him quite well; it was in the winter of 1924, and he was a strange man, full of wild, irrational talk. At that time I thought he was mentally unbalanced, possibly as a result of his illness."

"And this man?" Meyer was conscious of a dryness in his mouth as he spoke. "Where is he now?"

"Can you not guess? He is so powerful now that to possess such knowledge as I have is certain death, and he must know that I kept records of all my patients. If I am forced to stay on in Germany, if I am taken by the police while trying to escape—" He shrugged. "The secret police, the Gestapo, they have their files. Probably they are searching for me already; maybe that is why I have been ordered back to the university."

Meyer sat up in his chair. "If you return to Vienna, you will probably never get out alive. If you leave tomorrow, you stand a good chance, a very good chance, of escaping altogether," he said earnestly.

"Yes, it is possible, I suppose," the professor's tone was more hopeful. "You are sure we would have no trouble at the frontier? Will we be safe in Italy, do you think?"

His friend gave him an encouraging smile. "It is unlikely that you will have much trouble. Make sure you wear your oldest clothes and appear very poor. The guards only bother with rich people. Above all, take no valuables with you of any kind. If you do, they will certainly be confiscated, and very possibly you yourselves will be arrested. As for Italy"—He shrugged—"I do not know. It is not as bad as Germany and Austria are today, but it

could be possible that the Italian police might arrest you
and send you back if they were asked. For that reason
alone I advise you to travel on as soon as you can. You
have friends there who can help you, do you not?"

"Yes. In Rome. We were students together, and now
he is a doctor. He will help us, I know. It was through
him that I obtained the visa for Italy."

"Good. Then there is nothing to prevent your leaving
tomorrow. I will make out your exit permits myself, and
you can collect them in the morning." Meyer stood up and
reached for his hat.

"Yes, certainly. And yet," Wienzman hesitated, "what if
Siegret is not ready to travel? Perhaps we should wait at
least another day?"

"You heard what Frau Muller said. There is nothing
wrong with Siegret that rest won't cure. The sooner you
get her away from here, the better for both of you." He
spoke sternly and was glad to see that his words had an
effect.

In the hall, Meyer stopped for a moment and placed
a hand on Wienzman's arm. "My friend," he said quietly,
"it is wrong that this should happen—that an innocent
girl can be molested by these young thugs and that decent people are powerless even to punish them. It saddens
me that you should be driven from your home when it is
my duty to protect you, but it would grieve me far more
if you were to remain and suffer worse things. At least
I can be of some use in this way."

There was little in the way of packing to be done.
They would take only what they could be sure of carrying
in suitcases. There was a small sum of Swiss currency he
had managed to keep through the *Anschluss,* enough to
take them as far as America. How they would live when
they got there, he had no idea.

The most vital items were his notebooks. There were a
dozen or more of these, thick volumes crammed with
case histories and records of the past twenty years. He was
strongly tempted to destroy their dangerous contents, but
to do so would not save his life, and they would be
essential to him if he was ever to start work again. Yet
they were too bulky to conceal. He was still wondering
what to do about them when there was a soft sound at

the study door and Siegret entered in her dressing gown.

The bruises on her face had risen in huge purplish and blue patches, her mouth was badly swollen, and her eyes were sunken inside of dark rings. Her father took her by the hand as she moved stiffly toward him. She was very weak and shivering, whether from fear or cold he could not tell.

"I woke and heard you moving about," she said, steadying her voice with an effort. "What are you doing?" She gazed around apprehensively at the books and papers that littered the floor.

Gently the doctor explained the plan Meyer had proposed. Siegret buried her face in his chest and wept, her thin shoulders trembling. The old man stroked her head and talked to her softly, trying to reassure her. But her tears were tears of relief, and when she ceased to cry, she found that she was able to smile at her father again.

"Pack a few of your best and most useful clothes," her father said. "What we take with us may have to last a long time. And no rings or necklaces or any such things."

Siegret laughed. "Father, you talk to me as if I were one of your students," she said, kissing him. "How many rings and necklaces do you think I own? Now give me your notebooks. I will label them as school workbooks. No one will know that I am not still using them, and I shouldn't think a frontier guard will be able to tell the difference between research notes and biology class studies."

At the door of the study she halted and looked back at him. "Father," she said in a hesitant voice, swallowing hard. "Those boys—Gerdler and the others. They didn't succeed, I wasn't—" She colored, searching for a softening word.

"I know," her father answered tenderly. "The doctor told me. We shall be all right, do not fear." Coming back into the room she kissed him once more, and the old man hugged her to him.

○ ○ ○

The crocodile's attack left *Caterina*'s passengers and crew with only one firm desire: to get away from Shambe and the river station as quickly as possible. Where before, Stewart Curtis had been the only traveler to be irritated by the extra stop, now he was joined unanimously by the others.

The chances of their being able to take off again before dusk had never been good. With the delay imposed by a prolonged and unsuccessful search for Thorne's body and the complications of the official report on the incident that had to be composed by Desmond, Keeling, and the local magistrate, a night on the river became inevitable.

After a lengthy argument with Johnson—the civil engineer whose wife had taken the opportunity to resurrect her complaints about the practice of allowing travelers to be greeted at the jetty by naked villagers—Desmond called all the passengers together in the rest house lounge.

"I know all of you are upset," he said, "and that—like me—there's nothing you want more than to get away from here and up to Khartoum and Cairo. If I thought there was any chance of our being able to have the aircraft repaired and tested in reasonable time, I would take it, but the engineers tell me there is no possibility of being ready before nine o'clock, and, frankly, a night flight over the swamps would be foolhardy. I suggest we all settle down and make the best of our night here."

"This is all very well, captain," Stewart Curtis stood up to speak, looking around at the other passengers for support, "but we shall have wasted a whole day here, in that case. Naturally we are all appalled at the tragedy, but I fail to see how our remaining here will help. You were apparently prepared to land at Khartoum in the dark before —why can't you do so now?" His voice had an arrogant rasp that irritated Desmond exceedingly.

"I was prepared to land at Khartoum at night only if we could take off from here and get beyond Malakal and clear of the swamps before dark," he answered. "You've all seen what the terrain is like around here; it would be too easy to get lost and impossible to make a safe touchdown if something did go wrong."

To Desmond's surprise, he had help from Dr. Van Smit. "I for one am only too happy to take Captain O'Neill's advice. I have no wish to find myself struggling in the dark with another crocodile."

An awkward silence greeted this statement, and the passengers began to drift away. Stewart Curtis was still scowling angrily. Van Smit walked over to the bar, and Desmond followed him.

"Thanks for your help," Desmond said, feeling a little self-conscious. He found it difficult to be at ease in the presence of the enigmatic doctor. There was nothing he could put his finger on as being out of place, except perhaps the man's faculty for stating unpleasant truths, yet all the same it was hard to find things to say to him that did not seem trite.

"It was nothing," Van Smit answered. "They were being most foolish. But at times like this such people often are. Even after this afternoon's display, they have not fully appreciated the dangers of the Sud. It is better to arrive at one's destination a few hours late than dead."

The barman came to serve them, and they took their drinks out onto the veranda. It was past seven o'clock, and dusk was falling swiftly as it always did in these latitudes, the cries of birds replaced by the steady sound of croaking frogs and the shrill buzz of cicadas.

The veranda door opened, and Stewart Curtis came through, carrying a drink. Draining his glass in a single gulp, he commenced pacing up and down on the far side of the veranda, his hands thrust deep in his pockets and his head hunched between his shoulders.

"There is a man with a great deal on his mind," Van Smit remarked softly. "I wonder what it is that makes our Mr. Curtis so eager to continue his journey."

There was no chance to ask what he meant, for Keeling stuck his head around the door. "A radio message has come in for you, captain," he said. "It's London again."

The message was the third since Desmond had sent off his report of Ian Thorne's death. It was signed by Perritt, one of Imperial Airways' senior managers, and it consisted of a bald demand for fuller details of the accident. Since these had already been sent off, it seemed likely that a further reply was unnecessary, so after dispatching a brief acknowledgment, Desmond returned to the veranda to finish his drink.

The sky was clear, and a full moon shone brightly on the river, turning the water to silver and gleaming on the reeds. On an impulse Desmond unfastened the screen doors and let himself out. The air was very still and warm, and there was only a faint murmuring and rustling among the rushes. The sound of the frogs seemed extraordinarily loud and close.

Young Thorne's death still weighed on his mind, despite repeated efforts to assure himself that it was in no way his responsibility. As captain of the aircraft, it had been his duty to safeguard the passengers and to anticipate behavior that could endanger them. Perhaps he should have warned them all of the risk of crocodiles before they disembarked; perhaps he should have seen that Keeling posted a guard on the launches.

Aside from the tragedy, there was the knowledge that the remaining passengers and crew would be nervous and irritable for the rest of the flight. When they reached England, there would be further inquests to be faced and questions to be answered.

His relations with Imperial management, never easy at the best of times, had of late been hitting a fresh nadir. In the eyes of Desmond and of most other senior captains and pilots, the company treated its crews shockingly badly. Low pay, long hours, and scarcely any say in the design of aircraft or the routes to be flown had been the rules throughout the airline's history. Three years ago, he and a number of others had founded a pilots' union, and a prolonged struggle had followed. Demands for the installation of de-icing equipment and other safety features had led to several pilots being sacked, ostensibly for disciplinary reasons or inefficiency, and Desmond was well aware that there were men in the company's hierarchy who would welcome an excuse to treat him similarly.

Matters within the company had already reached a position where the government had been forced to step in. A commission of inquiry had recommended nationalization and the recognition of the pilots' union. By the end of the year these would be put into effect, but now there was every indication that the airways board was digging its heels in for a last-ditch battle.

The loss of a passenger, however accidental, would be a heaven-sent opportunity for the board to either dismiss him or to downgrade him to one of the junior routes. If that was the case, he thought ruefully, he would be justified in rejecting Pamela's demand that he sell the house.

A small movement in the shadows caught his eye, and a figure detached itself from one of the tamarisk trees and came toward him. It was Laura Hartman, the moonlight softening her face.

"It's so peaceful," she said. "I can't believe that only a few hours ago—" she shivered, unable to complete the sentence. "I keep feeling that it was somehow my fault, that if only I had asked one of the boatmen to come with me—or you, or anyone who realized what could happen, then Lieutenant Thorne would be alive still."

"If anyone is to blame it's me," Desmond told her gently. "I should have warned you all before you went ashore."

"Oh, no," Laura looked up at his face, "not you. How could you take any blame? You didn't know what we were going to do."

"No more than you could, I agree," he said, "but my superiors certainly don't seem to think so, judging by the cables they've been sending.

"Are you flying through to New York?" he asked as they drew abreast of the landing stage. "Or will you be stopping off in England?" He asked the question in an effort to turn her mind away from its morbid trend, and he experienced a momentary feeling of pleasure at her answer.

"We're going to New York." She sighed. "In a way it's a pity. I'd have liked to stay over in Europe for a while, but Mr. Curtis thinks the political situation is too dangerous, and I guess he's right. Do you think there will be a war soon?" she asked suddenly.

This time it was Laura's turn to be surprised. Desmond stiffened. "Perhaps there will, Mrs. Hartman," he said, "though it seems a pity if, so soon after the last war, we still have not learned enough to avoid another."

"You might try telling that to the refugees and Jews they imprison and torture in Germany," she countered sharply, angered by the rebuke.

"And you might try asking how much misery, how many more deaths would result from another great war," Desmond replied. "And maybe there would be a better chance of settling the problems of Europe if people didn't go around saying that war is inevitable."

Laura glared at him for a moment in the dark. Then turning on her heel and giving an angry sniff, she started back to the rest house.

Stewart Curtis had a great deal on his mind. The enforced delay at Shambe was to him a cause of acute anxiety. Throughout the evening he was seen pacing up and down on the veranda or in the lounge, chain-smoking Egyptian cigarettes, and at dinner, served by Andy Draper and the rest-house staff, he drank heavily and was almost offensively morose.

Returning immediately after the meal to the bedroom that had been prepared for him in the rest house, Curtis flung himself on the bed and lay, staring up at the slow-turning fan that hung from the ceiling. He was tired and half-drunk as well, but he knew that sleep would be a long time coming. He began turning over in his head the problems that faced him.

The first of these, and certainly the most urgent, was the mine at Klerksdorp. Klerksdorp! He cursed the day he had ever heard the name. His experts had sworn that there was gold there. They had been unanimous in their forecasts. The richest mine in the country, they had said. Unlimited reserves of gold waiting to be extracted. And he had believed them. He had sunk millions into Klerksdorp; he had hired the best men and bought the most sophisticated machinery. The crushing and extracting plant was the most efficient anywhere in the world, the envy of every other mine operator.

A massive surface stripping operation, in which huge excavators had sliced away the topsoil, had revealed several veins of ore, and digging had begun in earnest to an impressive fanfare of publicity. There had been a few doubters, but for the most part Curtis had been hailed as one of the new czars of the Rand and spoken of in the same breath as Rhodes and Oppenheimer.

Klerksdorp went ahead with the utmost speed. Of course not all the money was Curtis's, the undertaking was too vast for that, but he had invested a substantial part of his fortune in the company and was its chairman and the person whose name was identified with it. Far more of his money had been put into buying up land around the concession. From studying the history of other great mines, he had come to realize that there was just as much, and possibly more, money to be made from land speculation as the area filled up with people attracted by the gold.

On paper, Stewart Curtis was one of the wealthiest men in Africa. Companies under his control were valued at tens of millions of dollars. His prestige had never been higher, yet there was one fatal flaw that in a few days would ruin the entire structure of his empire.

There was no gold in Klerksdorp. The one crucial factor was missing. His shares in the mine were valueless, no longer security for the loans he had raised against them. His enormous land holdings were worth only a fraction of their current price. The moment the news leaked out, his assets would shrink to nothing as overdrafts and loans were called in, deals suspended, credit refused.

The mineral lodes that at first had seemed so promising had petered out uselessly after a few hundred feet. The ore was too low-grade to be profitable. Trusting the advice of his experts, Curtis had ordered fresh shafts sunk and a further range of galleries opened. He drafted in more men and cutting gear, pushing the work ahead at a furious pace, hoping for some indication of success before news of the fiasco broke. As the situation worsened, he had resorted to more and more desperate means.

Before long he was issuing deliberately misleading statements to the press, going out of his way to show off the mine and its new machinery, and, with the aid of an energetic public relations company, had managed to keep up the fiction that the mine was producing gold in large quantities.

More difficult were his dealings with official bodies—banks, insurance companies, representatives of the world's stock markets. Here he had been driven to juggling assay reports and monthly production figures, actions that might well make him liable to criminal charges if he continued.

The crisis had come a few weeks ago, while he had been on vacation in Cairo with his wife. Summoned by an urgent cable from the Klerksdorp board, he had arrived to find that the company's principal bankers in the Cape, no longer content with the vague reports they had been receiving, had demanded to be allowed to send in their own team of inspectors.

Curtis closed his eyes; he could picture the scene now. The paneled board room in the mine's Durban offices, and old Stuttenheim, the fat, bald bank president, leaning back in his chair and puffing at his cigar, assuring Curtis in his guttural accent that the request was "only a formality in the interest of my shareholders, you understand."

Curtis had understood, all right. The old Boer had guessed what was happening, and now he was sending in his men to make sure. He had readily accepted Curtis's suggestion of a date ten days away for the start of the inspection. That afternoon, when the banker had left, Curtis had telephoned his stockbrokers to confirm what he already suspected. There had been steady but persistent selling of Klerksdorp all day, nothing heavy, nothing the market couldn't absorb, but it was there all the same. The shares had closed a few points down as a result. Stuttenheim was unloading his holdings.

Once the news broke, the panic would be instantaneous, the share price would collapse overnight, and Curtis himself would be ruined. There was no way to prevent that or even to delay it much longer, but there still remained one faint chance of clearing something from the wreck. An American consortium in New York was paying a high price for mineral options on his property interests around Klerksdorp. If he could complete the deal before they heard about the failure of the mine, he would still have something left. Stewart Curtis had come a long, hard road to wealth. The memory of those early, bitter days of poverty was still vivid, and now they loomed terrifyingly near once more. At all costs he had to reach New York and complete the land sales before Stuttenheim pulled the world from under him.

There was a low table beside the bed. Reaching out for his cigarette lighter, his eyes rested for a moment on the silver-framed portrait of his wife, and inwardly he cursed again. Georgina had chosen this moment to start being difficult. That was an added incentive to get back to Cairo as quickly as he could. He looked again at the calm porcelain face and the cloud of dark hair that surrounded it, and he felt a squirm of jealousy.

○ ○ ○

Fifteen hundred miles to the north, amid the formal splendor of a dinner party at the residency of the British ambassador to Egypt, Jacquetta d'Este was watching her husband flirt with Georgina Curtis.

It had been a tiresomely hot day in Cairo, unusual for this time of year, when the generally mild climate drew the wealthy and famous from every country to the city that had become the world's most fashionable winter capital. Even now, toward the end of the season, the hotels and palaces were full. Film stars and millionaires rubbed elbows with Egyptian pashas and the aristocracy of Europe.

Normally, the dinner party would have been enjoyable for Jacquetta. The ambassador and his wife were old friends of hers; she knew enough of the guests to feel at home and not so many as to be bored; she was wearing a new dress from Paris and was conscious that she was looking her best. Added to all of this, there was an atmosphere of excitement and anticipation in the city as the preparations for the wedding of King Farouk's sister to the crown prince of Persia drew to a climax. The pleasure of all this, however, was spoiled by the behavior of Jacquetta d'Este's husband.

A tall, striking woman whose dark hair was set off against the whiteness of her skin, Jacquetta's face was rounded and gentle, at times seemingly sad, as it appeared at the moment, though in fact she was merely pensive. Her husband's antics were annoying rather than hurtful. In the ten years since Luca d'Este had taken her from her father's home in Tuscany, she had learned to live with the knowledge of his constant infidelities. What was less easy to accept was his indifference to the embarrassment he caused her in public.

He caught her look and raised a quizzical eyebrow. At forty-seven, Baron Luca d'Este remained sublimely indifferent to his thickening waistline and thinning hair. The dashing Italian cavalry colonel had been replaced by an aging provincial governor, whose affectations were rapidly becoming ludicrous.

That Georgina Curtis was finding his behavior acceptable rendered her all the more obnoxious in Jacquetta's eyes, although presumably the fact that Georgina's husband, for all his great wealth, was both older and less attractive than Luca, made some difference. There could be no denying, however, that the Englishwoman was beautiful in her hard, superficial way, Jacquetta thought vindictively. A lot of men ran after Georgina, and, to judge by the stories, she let a good many of them catch her.

There was a stir and bustle, and footmen began removing the dishes. The regal pomp of British imperial splendor ran unchecked. Egypt, nominally an independent state united to Britain only by treaty of friendship, was in actual fact a British fief, just as much as was India or Kenya or Hong Kong. Until a short time ago, the ambassador had actually been known as the high commissioner, and it was still common for reference to be made in the world's and Cairo's press to "the real ruler of Egypt."

At her right shoulder, a hand removed her wine glass and replaced it with another. Jacquetta had experienced a hundred such dinners in her life. When Luca had been assistant governor in Tripoli, they had been an almost nightly occurrence, but tonight somehow the dazzling luxury jarred her. The wealth of this city was staggering. Many of the women were literally weighed down with the most astonishing jewelry. Rubies, emeralds, ropes of pearls—there must be several fortunes in gems around this one table.

Her husband and Georgina were talking again, Luca with a ridiculous, gross leer on his face, his eyes fastened greedily on Georgina's bosom. Perhaps it was his title that attracted her; certainly it could not be his conversation or his looks. The Englishwoman rested a gloved hand lightly on his wrist for a moment in a coquettish gesture. Glancing up and catching sight of Jacquetta watching her, she gave an overfriendly, condescending smile.

Trying to hide her anger, Jacquetta realized that the man on her left had been speaking to her.

"I'm sorry," she said.

Courteously, the man, an elderly and important member of a visiting French delegation, repeated his remark. "I understand," he said carefully, "that the government here is concerned by the numbers of Arab tribesmen who have been crossing the border into Egypt. It is said that several sheiks from the great Senussi family have arrived recently."

Jacquetta caught the allusion. The Italian colonies of Tripolitania and Cyrenaica to the west of Egypt were maintained by the presence of a sizable army. Periodically the land erupted in warfare as one hostile tribe or another rebelled against their European masters.

The Arab raiders were ruthless men, accustomed even in days of peace to an existence on the edge of survival. Their fight against the invading enemy was vicious, and the Italian troops had responded in kind. Torture and brutality were commonplace, and occasional bloody reprisals were permitted to demonstrate the futility of revolt. On both sides a degree of hatred had brewed that nothing could extinguish.

Luca d'Este had been assistant military governor in Tripoli, Libya, when they had first been married. To Jacquetta, the post had meant no more than the comfort of colonial life and the satisfaction of knowing that her husband was one of the territory's senior officials. Italian rule had made Tripoli into an attractive town, its surroundings planted with groves of olives and citrus trees and great vineyards. The fighting had been hundreds of miles away, utterly remote from the tranquil life of the capital and its rounds of parties and horse races and receptions.

Only later had Jacquetta learned of the part Luca had played in the suppression of rebellion. Ferocious atrocities against the families of the ruling sheiks had been carried out on his orders. Intended to cow the populace, they had only succeeded in creating a legacy of hatred. Luca had been precipitately recalled two years ago, and successive administrations had succeeded in restoring peace to the area.

The Senussi, the largest and most powerful of the hostile tribes, were the Italian occupation army's most persistent foes. Luca indeed was under sentence of death by them out of revenge for the execution of a Senussi sheik that was carried out on his orders.

"It is two years since my husband resigned from colonial government service," Jacquetta replied to the man beside her. "I'm afraid I am quite out of touch with the news from the colonies, but I thought things were generally supposed to be quiet there now.

"Will you be watching the race on Sunday?" she asked, changing the subject.

"The motor race to Fayum?" the Frenchman took a

sip of wine. "I will watch the start, of course, but I fear I am no longer young enough to follow it through the desert. Since your husband is taking part in the race, I presume you will be expected to see it through to the end. I hope for your sake the weather remains cool."

"So do I," Jacquetta echoed fervently. "Fortunately, we won't be following the exact course of the race. We will cut out a large loop in the official track and be at the finish line in time to see the winner pass the flag."

"I wish the baron good fortune; I am told he is highly favored to win."

"You are most kind." Jacquetta placed her knife and fork neatly on her plate. "It would make Luca very happy to win. On Monday we leave for New York, and it would be nice to end his stay in Cairo with a victory."

On the opposite side of the table, Luca and Georgina Curtis were laughing at some private joke. The irony was that Luca had asked her to invite Georgina to watch the race with her. The two of them would have to spend the whole day together.

In their suite at the Italian legation that night, Jacquetta's feelings about his behavior at the dinner came to a head, causing a bitter row.

"I fail to see what you are complaining about, my dear," Luca answered blandly when she protested. "I was simply being polite. It is true that Georgina Curtis is a beautiful and charming woman, and it is natural that I should be attracted to her. What of it?"

"You were pitiful." Jacquetta was brushing out her hair, watching him in the mirror as she spoke. "Contemptible. She was playing with you—anyone but a fool could have seen that."

Luca's expression hardened. "I will not have you speak to me in that fashion," he snapped. "What do you know about how people think? Until you married me you were nothing but a little country bitch living in a shack."

"And, not content with making a fool of yourself," Jacquetta continued, ignoring his retort, "you make me look stupid by inviting that woman to drive out with me for the race tomorrow. The whole of Cairo will be laughing at us."

"Bitch. When I met you your father was so poor he'd have sold his daughter to anyone who'd have offered to repair his roof."

"Your money, my breeding," Jacquetta answered easily, putting down her brush and going over to the bed. "You had to have someone to show you how to behave after the Duce had given you your title and was sending you off to play dictator with the Arabs." The moment the words were out of her mouth, she knew she had gone too far. Luca d'Este was exceptionally sensitive to any criticism of his birth and background. Swearing savagely between his teeth, Luca stepped toward her and hit her hard, twice, aiming for her face. Ducking, she caught the first blow across the side of the head, and the second slammed into her neck.

Choking for air, her head singing, she fell to her knees, while her husband stood over her venting his fury. "You will never again dare to criticize myself or my family! Do you understand? Or speak disrespectfully of the Duce and the work he is doing for Italy. Or allow your infantile jealousies to make you impolite to my friends and my guests." His voice was high-pitched with rage, his face flushed. He had drunk heavily during the meal.

"Do you think I don't know what you were doing in Tripoli all that time?" She spoke with difficulty, her breath still coming in gasps. "Do you think I didn't hear what they said about you when we were there? 'That butcher d'Este,' that was what they called you when your back was turned. Oh yes, you were so brave fighting a few bands of unarmed tribesmen and showing off your uniform in parades. Well, it may impress women like Georgina Curtis, but to me you're nothing but a posturing bully." She braced herself for another blow, but Luca's anger seemed strangely to have burned itself out.

"I will sleep in my own room tonight," he announced curtly, drawing his dressing gown about him, "and trust that in the morning you will have recovered your manners."

○ ○ ○

On the other side of the world, where the ice and frozen snows of the long winter months had only just begun to give way before the onset of spring, Pat Jarrett stood at the head of a small lake among the pine-covered hills of New Hampshire.

It had taken months of searching before he had found what he was looking for. Warren Lake, a five-mile stretch of clear, deep water on which the ice had already broken up and was now fast melting.

Every feature was perfect. A good north-south lie, among hills that were not high enough to pose difficulties for an aircraft yet provided an effective screen against the outside world; a dirt road sufficiently clear to enable him to bring the truck up yet discouraging to other drivers. By renting one of the houses, he could establish a legitimate cover. Warren Lake was only a few miles off the direct route between Montreal and New York's La Guardia Marine Terminal.

There was still some snow on the shoreline, and Jarrett had to pick his way between the deeper patches. He reveled in the clean, cold air; he felt invigorated and fresh again after the long drive in the pickup. His plans had really taken shape.

The dirt track wound back along the eastern shore of the lake past the big house on the point that he had already picked out as his base. Standing a short way into the water, it had a small natural anchorage as well as a sizable wooden boathouse, large enough to conceal a small float plane, and a good long jetty. Here he would live and work for the next eight days.

He doubted whether anyone had visited the lake during the past five months. Perhaps an occasional hunter in late fall or a workman repairing one of the houses after the summer visitors had left, but certainly no one since then.

The snow had turned the ground to mud that clung to his boots as he walked the few yards back to the shoreline. The sensation brought back a host of memories. France 1917—his first visit to the trenches to see the kind of war they were fighting on the ground. The mud and the stench and the sight of those dirty, shivering, gray-faced men were as fresh in his mind as if it had been only a few hours ago.

At age nineteen Jarrett became a pilot with the newly formed U.S. Army Air Corps. An ace with six kills to his credit, he was a boy hero, the favorite of his squadron. Jarrett's family, especially his mother, had been proud of him.

But Pat Jarrett had returned to the United States from the battlefields of France to find that the world had changed in his absence. People wanted only to forget about the war, they had no use for heroes anymore; every bar held half a dozen veterans willing to tell their stories for the price of a drink. Jobs were scarce and money tight, and Pat Jarrett, former flying ace, was just another unemployed veteran.

Flying was the only thing he knew, and the discipline and demands of the life had suited him, while the hours in the air had given him the chance to excel at individual combat. He had enjoyed the comradeship and toughness of body and spirit that the service instilled. Back at home he found himself despising the soft civilians with their slack habits and easy existence. He resented having to defer to them, to plead for jobs from men whom a year ago he would not have deigned to notice. And it seemed that the girls wanted men with cars and fat wallets. Good looks and military decorations were somehow no longer enough.

Abandoned and rejected, Pat Jarrett had drifted from town to town, hanging around airfields, picking up odd jobs, and begging flights from friendly pilots when he could no longer afford to buy them. He became morose and bitter, living in a world of his own imagination, preparing for the day when the air force would need him again.

Discipline became an obsession with him. Each day he exercised rigorously, building up to a point where he was spending more than two hours a day in weight-lifting sessions and calisthenics. He was scrupulously neat, his clothes always cleaned and pressed even when he could hardly afford to eat. Remembering the ignorance of most pilots about the mechanics of the aircraft they flew, he went to night school and took jobs in airline repair sheds, all the time avidly following every development of aircraft and flying, learning the characteristics of every plane.

Paradoxically, Jarrett's intensity was the very factor that prevented him from obtaining a job with the airlines, when passenger aviation and mail flights blossomed in the twenties and thirties. By this time there were any number of hungry young pilots available, and airline directors were suspicious of the taciturn, stern-faced veteran who was so desperate to get into the air that his hands shook uncontrollably during the interviews.

Then Britain had started to rearm in preparation for another European war. The crisis had died away in September after Munich, but the expansion of the armed forces continued, and in pilots' mess rooms around the United States, the word went out that the Royal Air Force was signing American flyers for combat training. Jarrett had applied at once, traveling to the British embassy in Washington at his own expense.

The British wanted pilots, but they wanted young men, not forty-one-year-old relics from a previous war with limited experience of modern aircraft. The interview panel had been kindly and had taken time to explain their reasons for turning him down. They had even held out a faint chance of a posting on the supply staff. "But I'm afraid what we're really looking for are qualified commercial airline pilots," a young wing commander told him. "We don't even recruit our own people beyond thirty-five."

Jarrett surveyed the lake again. He had better be moving. There was much to be done and not over long to do it in. The date was Saturday, March 11. In eight days, the first of the bullion flights, Imperial 109, flying boat *Caterina,* piloted by Captain Desmond O'Neill, would be in the United States, en route for New York.

3

By radio: 0730 hrs SATURDAY 11 MARCH 1939.
AIR TRAFFIC CONTROL CAIRO TO IMPERIAL
AIRWAYS LONDON. RELAYED FROM KHARTOUM.
IMPERIAL AIRWAYS FLIGHT 109 G-ADHO CAT-
ERINA LEFT SHAMBE. ETA KHARTOUM 1035 hrs
LOCAL TIME. END.

The passengers were still gathering themselves sleepily
together and cursing the night's delay when Desmond
came down to the jetty to take a launch out to *Caterina*.
Dawn was only just breaking over the river, and patches
of mist still hung over much of the swamps, heightening
the sense of remoteness.

The villagers were going about the first of their daily
tasks. Desmond saw a boatload of muscular black fishermen pulling toward the entrance to one of the smaller
channels. They waved their spears in greeting.

"A fine looking people, captain." The sound of the
voice made Desmond turn with a start to find Mr. King
standing behind him, smiling politely. "I beg your pardon
if I startled you," he said.

"Not at all," Desmond told him. "And you're right,
they *are* a fine-looking people. I think I rather envy them
their way of life here."

Harold King faced Desmond squarely. "I should like
you to know, captain, how deeply upset my wife and
I are over Lieutenant Thorne's death. It was a terrible
tragedy, a shocking thing. Mrs. King feels very much responsible for what took place. If only she had not forgotten to bring her case off the airplane or had not asked
Lieutenant Thorne to fetch it for her, he would still be
alive."

The American was genuine in his distress. "Of course, it was in no way any fault of your wife's," Desmond assured him. "As I told Mrs. Hartman, Thorne was quite wrong to have tried to take a boat without a crew on board. I'm afraid he was very largely to blame for his own death—that is, if anyone was." He felt awkward speaking ill of Thorne so soon after the accident.

"That's very kind of you, captain." King's voice was plainly relieved. "I know Mrs. King will feel greatly eased when I repeat your words to her. Mrs. Hartman will be happier, too, I am sure." He stood on the jetty, watching as the launch pulled out from the shore and moved in the direction of *Caterina*.

The fuel tanks had finally been repaired after dark the previous night, and Desmond had gone over every inch of the work with the engineer, then grudgingly pronounced himself satisfied. Even so, now he took care to make the launch take him underneath the wing to allow him to check for signs of any fresh leakage since the tank had been refilled. Satisfied, he boarded the aircraft and went straight up to the flight deck. On his way he met Andy Draper.

"Everything's fine, skipper," the steward reported. "Passengers are being assembled now. Purser's sending them on board at half past seven."

Desmond glanced at his watch. It was ten minutes to seven. That gave him forty minutes to go through the preflight checks and send a radio report off for transmission to London.

"Were there any complaints about the accommodations or the food?"

Andy shook his head, "No, sir—barring Mrs. Johnson's, that is. She was still shook up about seeing all them natives undressed, sir, but in the end we got her quieted down."

"Glad to hear it. Let's hope she stays that way. You'll be serving breakfast as soon as we're airborne, I take it." Desmond suddenly realized that he was very hungry.

"Aye, aye, sir. Should I bring one of my specials upstairs?" Andy's breakfasts—bacon, eggs, kidneys, and all the trimmings—were legendary.

Desmond said, "I'll have it in the smoking saloon." It was time he showed himself among the passengers again.

Ralph Kendrick met him at the top of the stairs. "No problems of any kind, skipper," Ralph answered his captain's look of inquiry. "Andy's got a pair of boys cleaning ship below, and he's keeping an eye on them. Ken Frazer went out and had another good look at the portside wing, but it's still there and no sign of any leakage. We've just started the preflight check. Oh, and I've had a weather forecast from Khartoum—it should be fine all the way up to the delta."

"And how's our cargo?" Desmond asked. "Is it still there?"

"Any mice, you mean?" Ralph laughed. "Not a sound all night. Andy rigged a bed in the mailroom last night. Ken and I tossed to see who should sleep in it, and he lost. He said he never slept better in his life. We counted the boxes as soon as we woke up just to be sure, and I'm glad to report all present and correct.

"Forgot to mention one thing," Ralph continued as they returned to the flight deck. "There was a signal passed through from Khartoum late last night after you had turned in. It seems the Canadian people have been getting worried about our falling behind schedule. Anyway, London has had some query or other from Botwood, Newfoundland, over whether we were canceling or not. London tells us they've answered that we will be making up the time en route and sticking to the original schedule."

"A polite way of telling us to get moving," Desmond replied moodily. There was no reason for Botwood, a tiny airfield on the remote Newfoundland coast, to start worrying. The place was no more than a steppingstone—a refueling stop for the handful of transatlantic flights.

So far he had received no less than fourteen separate signals from London, first on the fuel tank delay, then, and more copiously, over Thorne's death. Aircraft captains were not supposed to lose passengers. The navy was evidently of the same opinion, having chimed in with a curtly worded demand for "fullest details to be forwarded to the Admiralty forthwith." He was in for a hard time as soon as the plane reached England.

Ken Frazer had come to the same conclusion. In other circumstances he would have welcomed any event that might possibly damage his captain's career and thereby open the path for his own promotion. This case, however, was different. That there would be an inquiry into Thorne's death he was sure. He was equally sure that the reason for *Caterina*'s unscheduled touchdown at Shambe would come out, and the board might well delight in having a second scapegoat on which to load the blame. As soon as they reached Cairo, he would have to send off a telegram to his mother in London, telling her to use all her influence to have his part in the business hushed up.

During the later part of the previous evening, Frazer and Ralph Kendrick had discussed the tragedy and its consequences. Like Desmond, the radio engineer held Ian Thorne largely responsible for his own misfortune and was angry at the thought that the blame might be cast elsewhere. Kendrick had been nervous and preoccupied during the evening and subject to fits of irritability. He had drunk quite heavily before turning in for the night, all of which Frazer had put down to reaction to the killing.

The galley was only eight-feet long, less than half the width of *Caterina*'s main cabins, yet the steward was capable of producing at an hour's notice, an elegant, four-course meal for up to twenty people.

Andy had carefully planned the breakfast he would offer the passengers as soon as they were in the air. The juice would have to be tinned, for the remaining supply was no longer fresh enough, and he did not trust the local fruit. The fish was still good, though, a fine king-fish caught at Mombasa. Andy had seen it cleaned and gutted and placed on ice in the refrigerator within a quarter of an hour of its being landed. He had intended to serve it for dinner—it would have made an excellent centerpiece on the serving trolley, surrounded by a nice salad garnish. Now, however, he would make a kedgeree. His eye flicked to a shelf—yes, there was plenty of rice.

There would have to be bacon and eggs as well as kidneys, cooked with all the usual trimmings—fried bread, tomatoes, and sausages. The passengers had a right to expect a choice, and Andy was convinced that any traveler with a good meal inside him was likely to be far less trouble for the remainder of the flight.

Of course, some passengers, particularly the women,

would prefer cereals, and all would finish with toast and marmalade or honey. Mrs. Hartman, he remembered, had told him she enjoyed a continental breakfast, and he had bought some small rolls for her during the wait in Kenya.

It was fortunate that Sandy, the purser, was a friendly, easygoing young man, willing to do a share of the kitchen work. Andy had been working for the airline for twelve years, and before that he had spent nearly as long serving as a cabin steward with Cunard on the transatlantic run. A lifetime spent ministering to the comforts of wealthy travelers had taught him to sum up a passenger's character after only the briefest acquaintance. He could spot at a glance the troublemakers, "the professional moaners," as he referred to them privately, who liked to occupy their hours in the air in making him run. Their cushions were never comfortable, their drinks were never mixed correctly, and they were either too hot or too cold. There was always one such person on every flight, and this time Andy had even less trouble than usual in picking him out. Arrogant and irritable, convinced of his own supreme importance, Stewart Curtis treated those he thought inferior with contempt, and he almost appeared to enjoy humiliating people.

So far, Curtis had complained of the service twice to Sandy Everett and once to the captain. Andy knew his captain well enough to be sure that Curtis would be listened to politely and no more. Nevertheless, Andy resented the financier going behind his back. Had Curtis but known it, he had managed to ensure for himself the maximum discomfort and inconvenience possible during the remainder of the voyage.

Desmond sat at the controls, watching the distant shore through the wide cockpit windows. Judging by the heavy clouds spreading across the sky from the east, another torrential downpour would reach them soon. With luck, they would be away before it struck.

The atmosphere in the cabin was tense. The entire crew was sensitive to the fact that they had lost a passenger, and everyone's nerves were on edge. Ken Frazer went about his tasks with an angry defiance, as if determined to show that he did not consider himself in any way responsible for what had happened. Ralph Kendrick was all too obviously very upset, clearly worrying as to what the reaction of the London office might be.

There were the inevitable delays in starting. The passengers had been slow in getting ready and even slower in coming down to the pier to embark. One of the launches was discovered to have a defective engine, so one boat had to fulfill a dual role of ferrying passengers, as well as baggage, supplies of fresh water, mail, and clean linen out to the aircraft. Then, too, there had been some final and grisly arrangements to be made with Keeling about what to do if Thorne's body should be recovered. His possessions had been gathered and placed in a bag in the mailroom until the airline received instructions on where to send them.

Now the crew waited for final clearance before starting up the engines and taxiing out into midstream. Desmond and Frazer had gone through the preflight procedure, running over the course they would follow to Khartoum and on up to Cairo, and estimating the fuel loads required. An excess of fuel meant increased weight and hence increased consumption. On the transatlantic route, the aircraft burned up so much fuel getting into the air that they had insufficient reserves left to reach the far shore. Consequently they had to be sent up with half-empty tanks and be refueled in midair from another aircraft, an experiment that seemed to work surprisingly well, though the necessity for it would disappear within two or three months when the new and larger G-class flying boats with their increased range came into service.

A slightly bigger wave than usual rocked *Caterina*, and Desmond saw the starboard float dip and touch the water for an instant. She was listing a trifle to port. It was seldom possible to trim an aircraft exactly, and the slightest motion of the water would send her rolling to the swell. He could feel the tension building within him, a growing impatience to be off, to be back at his job.

"She's all yours, skipper, they're ready to go." The words were hardly out of Kendrick's mouth before the two pilots had their hands on the controls.

"Switch on master." Ken Frazer leaned forward and pulled the master ignition switch. "Master on," Frazer confirmed.

"Check fuel levels in all tanks." *Caterina* had taken on

much less than a full load, but they had enough to see them safely to Khartoum.

"Oil pressure normal?"

"Affirmative," Frazer echoed.

"Radios functioning?" There were a series of clicks behind them as Kendrick tested the three separate sets.

"All radios functioning, skipper," he sang out.

"Fuel pressure normal?"

"Affirmative."

"Ready with the pyrene gun, Sandy?" Desmond called over his shoulder, and again it was Ralph who answered. "He's all set up, skipper. I can see him standing by the hatch."

"Starting number two engine." Punching the ignition buttons, Desmond heard the nearside starboard engine spring into life. The aircraft gave a surge forward and began to slew around toward the far bank as the propeller bit the air.

Back in the mailroom, Sandy Everett crouched by the open hatchway and peered out at the spluttering engine. This was always an anxious moment for him. If an engine should overheat and catch fire from the rich fuel mixture fed in for ignition, it was the purser's job to crawl out onto the wing and pump foam from the pyrene fire extinguisher into the cowling. This was no easy task at the best of times, with the aircraft pitching through the water and the slipstream tearing at the purser's fingers as they clutched the slippery wing, while trying to keep hold of the heavy pyrene gun and praying he wouldn't be left standing by a burning engine, having dropped the extinguisher into the water.

For the rest of the crew, the purser's antics on these occasions were always something of a joke, although the airline had actually lost one purser this way. This time, however, there was no trouble, and the engine settled down to run smoothly.

When all four engines were firing, Desmond worked the throttle, making sure that each one ran smoothly, feeling the power surge die away beneath his control.

"Check for carburetor heat."

"Aye, aye, sir." There was a momentary drop in revolutions on each engine as Ken Frazer pulled the switches that pumped warm air from the engines into the carburetors via a small hatch. In freezing conditions or at high altitudes, such a facility was vital to prevent ice from forming round the inlets.

"Carburetor heat functioning correctly. Switching back to normal." Frazer closed the switches as he spoke, and the aircraft's speed increased with the restoration of power.

"Check alternator load. Check oil pressure." This could never be done too often. A fall in the oil pressure gauge was often the first and only warning of imminent engine failure.

"Check fuel pressure. Check oil temperature. Check manifold pressure. Check suction gauge. Check exhaust temperature. Close throttle." The power died away, the noise ebbing from the cockpit as the engine returned to idle and the needles on the rev. counter sank back to the 500 mark.

"Test power flaps." With his right hand he worked the levers controlling the electrically operated wing flaps.

"Flaps operating normally," Frazer confirmed.

"Set gyros." This was the first officer's task, and Desmond waited as Frazer fiddled with the setting of the gyro compass and flicked up the cover of the magnetic compass beside it.

"Open artificial horizon and direction indicator.

"Check turn and bank indicator.

"Set altimeter." The altimeter gave a height reading based on the air pressure outside the aircraft, but it was essential that the instrument be set at the correct ground pressure for the particular area. A wrong setting could bring about a totally false reading.

Under his captain's watchful eye, Frazer took the readings and made the settings correctly and went on to check the airspeed indicator and the rate of climb and descent indicator while Desmond brought *Caterina*'s head into the wind and prepared for the final run.

"Request take-off clearance from shore," he said to Kendrick, and the radio operator bent over his microphone.

"Hotel Oscar to Shambe station. Hotel Oscar to Shambe station," Kendrick repeated. "Imperial 109 requesting clearance to take off." There was a crackle of static. "OK, skipper," he called out, "we're cleared to go."

Trailing a long streak of white foam, *Caterina* raced

along the water, spray flying from her sides. As her speed increased, she rose onto the planing step of her keel, and she seemed to skim along the surface. The vibration, severe at first, became easier as she went faster. The water flashed by outside the windows, and the banks sped past. Then, as though severed suddenly by a knife, the foaming trail was cut off, the vibration ceased, and the great plane rose slowly from the river and climbed away into the sky. Desmond set about the task of synchronization—setting all four engines to run smoothly in time together.

"Autopilot on, sir?" Frazer's hand was on the switch.

Desmond shook his head. "No," he said. "I'll fly her for a while." It was a relief to have his hands on the controls, to feel the aircraft responding, sensitive to the slightest movement of the rudders or steering yoke. They were still climbing slowly toward cruising height. With no high ground between the marshes and the scrub and desert plains through which the Nile ran for the next two thousand miles, 5,000 feet would easily be sufficient altitude. The sun was warming the air, creating powerful thermals that now and then caught the plane, lifting her and with equal suddenness dropping her back down a hundred feet or more. Antcipating such forces and compensating so that the passengers were scarcely aware of any break in level flight was a source of satisfaction to him.

A little over three hours to Khartoum at the junction of the two Niles, then another seven hours up to Cairo, with a stop at Wadi Halfa for more fuel. With luck they should reach Cairo at dusk, but it was going to be a long day.

A sudden lurch as the flying boat struck an air pocket recalled his attention to the present. At least for the next few hours, he could concentrate on his job. Settling himself in his seat, he eased the aircraft back toward cruising height.

By common, though unspoken, consent among the passengers, no mention was made of yesterday's tragedy. Accordingly, once they were in flight and Andy was handing around the breakfast menus, the passengers began to move about and talk, much as they had on the previous day.

Their attitude was noted by Sandy Everett with relief as he helped the steward organize the meal. Sandy was worried about Laura Hartman and the Kings. Unlike the rest of those on board, they felt a degree of personal responsibility that could not simply be ignored. They were sitting in the midship cabin in silence, eating mechanically, staring out of the windows. Several times during the flight, Sandy went in to talk to them. The tragedy seemed to have driven the three Americans closer.

Early on in the journey to Khartoum, Laura was summoned to the after cabin by Stewart Curtis, and, during the conversation with the Kings, Sandy realized that the couple had adopted a protective attitude toward the girl.

"I don't like Laura working for that man," Mrs. King said, with a defiant glance in Sandy's direction. "I don't care how rich he is—he makes her work too hard and take on too much responsibility."

"Now Sarah," her husband said, "we have no reason to speak against Mr. Curtis. He is Laura's employer, and that is between them."

Sarah King sniffed. "A good employer doesn't keep a girl up till all hours or make her travel about alone with him. I think he behaves much too selfishly, and if I see him, I will tell him. He doesn't even let her use his cabin, he just keeps the whole place to himself. I'm surprised the airline allows one man to take up an entire cabin like that." She looked hard at Sandy.

"Mr. Curtis's wife is joining him in Cairo," he explained apologetically, "and she's traveling with her maid. I suppose it is easier for them to have a separate cabin. We only allow it when there are plenty of other seats, but if someone is willing to buy up all the seats in one particular cabin, there's not a lot we can do."

Harold King gave a low whistle. "Six seats in all—and they're flying through to New York. That makes one expensive trip."

"It's even more than you imagine, sir," Sandy said. Like Mrs. King, he disliked Laura's employer and was glad of a chance to criticize him. "I know for a fact that Mr. Curtis has booked luxury suites at every hotel we stop at en route. He must be spending a fortune."

Harold King did not seem pleased at this revelation. "I am not sure you should be telling us this, young man," he answered gruffly. "Mr. Curtis's travel arrangements should be his own private business." Sandy flushed at the rebuke and shortly after, found an excuse to return to the upper deck.

At his seat at the radio desk, Ralph Kendrick was gripped by nerve-breaking panic. Every muscle trembling in an uncontrollable spasm, his two hands gripped the metal edge of the table fiercely, his face contorted as he fought the attack, sweat pouring from his body.

Soundlessly he sat, locked and rigid for nearly half a minute, before the fit passed, leaving him weak and spent. He looked across at the other two, noting their motionless, unseeing backs with relief. That was the third attack since the trip began—how much longer could he conceal them? Desmond had already begun to notice.

He ran his tongue over his gums. His mouth felt parched. Another two-and-a-half hours to go before Khartoum. He needed a drink badly. His eyes strayed to the locker by the radio spares box. A bottle of whiskey was in there, hidden among the repair tools, left over from last night, when the strain of the forced landing and Thorne's death had driven him to seek relief. Almost one-third of the bottle had been needed to steady his nerves. He dared not run the risk of Desmond smelling the alcohol on his breath this early in the morning. He would have to wait.

That damned transatlantic crossing. Just when he thought he had finally laid to rest the ghosts of the past— the ghosts of a flight seven years ago. He shivered at the memory.

They had been in the air ten hours and were more than 1,100 miles out over the North Atlantic. They were flying at about 5,000 feet between banks of violet cloud.

"Carl, be a good fellow and switch on the panel lights." There were three of them on board the Junker monoplane. Bell, the captain; Carl Huessen, the German copilot; and Ralph as radio operator. Their task was to make a survey flight over the route between Ireland and Newfoundland, preparing the way for the airliners of the future.

Carl pushed the switches, but the instrument panel remained unlighted. "I'll check the connections. It's probably

*only a fuse," Carl said, but when he tried the switches
again, it brought the same result. Bell swore irritably.*

*"It's a nuisance that's all; either you or Kendrick will
have to shine a torch on the compass." This far out over
the open sea, even so small a failure as this seemed ominous. Ralph looked down at the rapidly darkening expanse
of the Atlantic below them. There was a heavy swell running, the crests of the waves foaming white. Far off to
the left, a lone iceberg drifted with the current.*

*Huessen checked their speed. "Ninety miles per hour.
We must be hitting head winds. Fuel consumption is
steady, though."*

*Then the Canadian weather bureau came on the air.
"Severe storm moving eastward over Nova Scotia, high
winds and some snow."*

*"We may have to fight these head winds all the way
to the coast. Let's hope they don't get any worse." There
was no need for Bell to elaborate.*

*Ralph did some calculations. "Seven hundred miles to
go. About eight more hours at this speed."*

*"Provided we're on the right course," Bell grunted. He
stabbed at the dial with a stubby forefinger. By the light
of the torch beam, Ralph saw that the needle was flickering and jumping beneath the glass. He felt a knot of fear
tighten in his stomach. If the compass was faulty, they
were indeed in trouble.*

Inwardly, Ralph cursed Desmond O'Neill for accepting the offer of the transatlantic command, though it
should have been obvious that anyone would jump at the
prospect. Only the cream of the airline's pilots were being
picked for the route.

Kendrick had five days left before he had to either come
up with a way of getting out of the flight and letting the
airline send a replacement or face again the nightmare
that had nearly destroyed him and now threatened his very
sanity.

○ ○ ○

The train had been halted at the approaches to the pass
for the past three-quarters of an hour, at the small siding
in the Carnic Alps that held the frontier control post for

Germany's border with Italy. A few passengers descended and were walking about the platform in the cold clear air, gazing up at the mountain peaks glistening in the sunlight. Among them moved the watchful figures of the frontier police.

The majority, however, preferred to stay inside the heated carriages. It was eleven o'clock, and the sun had not yet succeeded in warming the day. Also, a significant number of the passengers were refugees reluctant to abandon the train. They waited nervously while the inspecting police worked their way slowly through the carriages checking the complex documents and permits needed before a citizen of the Third Reich could travel beyond its borders.

Siegret and her father sat in silence. Some people had already been ordered off the train. They could be seen from the window, a miserable, pathetic group standing on the platform surrounded by piles of baggage, watched carefully by two guards.

The police had reached the next carriage, and Siegret felt herself begin to tremble. Her father squeezed her hand. The others in the carriage seemed equally apprehensive. One was a businessman, she thought: he was too well dressed to be a refugee. He was traveling with his wife, a stout, brassy blonde in her forties who smoked incessantly. Nearer to the door, an old couple sat facing each other. Both were frail and worn out, and like the Wienzmans they were shabbily dressed. The old man caught Siegret's eye and gave her a fleeting smile.

The voices in the next car rose and fell interminably. Once or twice Siegret heard snatches of dialogue as some of the occupants were interrogated. There was more slamming of doors, and then there were uniformed men in the corridor. The door was pulled back, and two guards and a plainclothes man entered the carriage.

"*Ausweis, bitte.*" With the peremptory demand for their papers, Siegret was at once acutely conscious that their whole escape depended on this moment. All the elaborate plans, the sacrifices they had made, the risks taken would have been in vain if these men were not satisfied. All the work she and her father had put into collecting passes and permits, in obtaining passports and visas, had been directed to this one instant.

On the journey to the pass, her mind had been occupied in speculating what their fate would be if they were caught at the frontier, either through some error or deficiency in their papers, or because the guards had already been warned to watch for them. In the eyes of the Nazi authorities, their actions would certainly be treasonable. Even if they needed her father's work too badly too harm him, they would have an excellent excuse for sending her to a labor camp for "political reeducation," where she would be held as a hostage to guarantee his cooperation. The thought made her sick with fear. She had heard about the camps. Her chances of ever being released again, once inside, would be nonexistent.

The old couple by the door were the first to be checked. The plainclothes man took their papers and ran his eye over them, frowning. "Jews," he remarked wearily. "More Jews. I see nobody but Jews on the trains these days. Do ordinary Germans never travel?" The old man and his wife made no reply. "Baggage?" he asked curtly.

"One trunk," the man answered in a quavering voice, "in the passage, and my wife has a basket."

"Go and take a look," the policeman nodded to one of the men with him. Apparently satisfied that their papers were in order, he moved on.

The blonde woman and her husband were German nationals employed in Italy and returning there after a holiday in their homeland. Their visas had evidently been countersigned by some important official, for they were subjected to only the most cursory examination, and their baggage was left untouched. The policeman handed them their papers with a small bow of respect. Finally it was the turn of the Wienzmans.

David Wienzman handed over the two bundles of documents to the plainclothes man who started to examine them page by page, checking every detail. Siegret watched out of the corner of her eye, not daring to look at him too closely. His face was sallow and impassive, as he concentrated on his task. He turned the pages of the passports slowly, creasing each one down with his thumb as he went.

At first he was silent, studying the elaborately printed papers. Then, without raising his eyes from the page, he spoke in a quick, flat tone. "Purpose of journey?" he demanded.

Taken by surprise, Siegret's father stumbled over his words. "Emigration—we wish to emigrate," he managed at last, his face pale and sweating.

The policeman ignored him and turned another page. "More stinking Jews," he said contemptuously. "Search their baggage carefully," he told the guard. "They probably have property stolen from the Reich concealed there." The professor lifted their suitcases down from the rack and opened them. The guard began pulling out the contents, shaking the folded clothes loose to see if anything was hidden among them. Siegret and her father watched apprehensively. Their sole contraband, the notebooks, were at the bottom of Siegret's suitcase, which was still to be searched, but the police might easily take exception to something else.

"It says here—" the policeman spoke again, this time his voice slower, as if puzzled by something he had found. Both instantly recognized it as a sign of danger. "It says here," he repeated, tapping the page and glaring at the professor, "that your profession is that of doctor and lecturer at the University of Vienna. But in your passport," he turned back to the reference he was seeking, "you call yourself a professor. Which is the correct description?"

The man's tone was casual, but the inference was only too apparent. It was clear that he suspected that he had here a highly qualified intellectual who was trying to slip out of the country by pretending to hold a much lower-grade post. Siegret's father was prepared for the trap. He had, indeed, realized that as a mere lecturer he would arouse considerably less interest when applying for permits. Only his passport revealed his true status. "Lecturer is my correct title," he answered, forcing himself to speak calmly. "I was provisionally made professor of my department in 1938, and at that time I applied for the passport, but after the Anschluss, my appointment was not confirmed, and I remained a lecturer until I was dismissed later in the year."

"So you had to go back to your old job," the policeman sneered. "You must feel bitter toward Germany," he suggested.

"No," Wienzman said, "I am not bitter, but since I am unable to find work in Germany, I am forced to go abroad." At the quiet way in which he answered, disguising the deep loathing she knew he held for the regime, Siegret felt a surge of respect for her father. The policeman snapped the passport shut and tossed the whole bundle back into the professor's lap.

Meanwhile the guard had finished with the professor's two suitcases. "Put that stuff back," he told Siegret, pointing to the belongings that lay strewn over the seat. "Which are your cases?" Siegret stood up and lifted her two small suitcases down. The injuries she had received the previous afternoon had caused her muscles to stiffen, making her movements painful and awkward. To her alarm, this caught the attention of the plainclothes man.

"What's wrong with you?" he asked sharply, giving her a hard look. Siegret made no reply and turned her head away, pretending to be busy repacking her father's belongings. She was terrified that the guards would become suspicious of the bruise on her face where Gerdler had hit her. She had done her best to disguise the marks with powder and make-up and had wound a scarf around her head, but there was no hiding from close inspection.

The man was not to be put off. Grasping her by the shoulders, he pulled her toward him. "Answer when I speak to you, Jew," he snapped angrily. "What happened to your face?"

Before she could reply, her father intervened. "My daughter was attacked in the street by some youths," he said. "She was beaten about the face and body. I must ask you to speak gently to her, she is still very upset."

"Shut up," the policeman retorted viciously. "What are you, some kind of whore that you fight in the streets?" he demanded of Siegret. "Did one of your clients give you a beating? You filthy Jewish bitch." His tone brought back all the horror of the assault in Saint Veit, and she was seized by a fit of uncontrollable trembling. Tears began to stream down her face. The two police laughed jeeringly at her, and the plainclothes man tugged the scarf from her head.

"Leave her alone!" Siegret heard her father's voice above the jeers and laughter and saw that he had swiftly risen to his feet. "How dare you say such things to an innocent girl? Have you no children of your own that you behave like this? Is this the greatness of the new Germany we are told about?" Anger and disgust at the treatment of his daughter lent a power to the old professor's voice that stopped the two men short. For a moment they stared at him, amazed that anyone should dare rebuke them.

"Listen, old man, your daughter is nothing but a dirty little Jewish whore—and you're her pimp," the senior of the two retorted. "You keep quiet unless you want to be arrested and sent off to a camp." Placing his hand on the professor's chest, he pushed him down back into his seat. The uniformed guard laughed again. "What do you want to do with the girl?" he asked. "Shall I send her back to the post for questioning? Maybe we could find some more bruises on her."

Siegret waited, transfixed with fear, for the policeman's decision. His eyes flicked over her as though she were no more than an article of baggage. Plainly he was undecided. Then, just as he opened his mouth to give his answer, there came a commotion from out in the corridor. "What the hell's going on?" he barked angrily. Another guard put his head around the door, and behind him Siegret recognized the anguished face of the old man who had been sitting in the corner.

"We've found a whole load of silver—this old nut was trying to get away with it," the guard informed the plainclothes man.

"It's not true!" the old man shrieked in protest. "I have certificates of ownership!"

"Take them away and put them under arrest. We'll sort it out when the train's gone." The second guard took the man's wife by the arm and dragged her to her feet. "Put them with the others," the policeman ordered, following them out. "Stinking Jews. How anyone can sit in the same carriage with you I can't think," he spat. Then he was gone, and the protests of the old couple, interspersed with shouts from the guards, receded down the corridor.

Siegret's father hugged her to him, patting her shoulders gently. The train whistle gave a short warning blast, and the train pulled slowly out of the station. The last thing Siegret saw was the old man and his wife standing with the other prisoners. With hopeless expressions they watched the train leaving them behind as it steamed off toward the frontier.

The train's smoke was still hanging in the air above the pass when the telephone rang in Hans Meyer's office in Saint Veit. "There is a call for you from Berlin," the operator informed him. "A Herr Rintlen from Gestapo headquarters." With sudden foreboding, Meyer waited for the connection. It was impossible that the Gestapo should already have heard of the Wienzmans' attempt to escape. They could scarcely have reached the border, and, in any case, had they been arrested, his own office would have been the first to receive the news. All the same, the call was ominous.

"Superintendent Meyer of the Kriminalpolizei, Saint Veit?" a voice demanded curtly. "This is Standartenführer Rintlen of the Sicherheitsdienst. I wish to speak to you on a confidential matter concerning a person known as Professor David Wienzman, at present registered as a resident in your district, formerly a lecturer in medicine at the University of Vienna."

Hans Meyer's mind was racing. The Sicherheitsdienst —the S.D.—was the secret intelligence division of the S.S. itself, controlled by Reinhard Heydrich, the most feared man in the whole of the Third Reich, the evil genius behind the rise of the black-shirted S.S. and, many said, in reality more powerful than Heinrich Himmler, his nominal master. It had been Heydrich who had masterminded the slaughter on the terrible Night of the Long Knives in 1936 when Roehm's brown shirts had been purged of all opposition to Hitler. The S.D., the most secret and most powerful organization within the Nazi state apparatus, was the means whereby Heydrich maintained his hold upon the S.S. and the Gestapo.

"I am instructed to inform you, Superintendent," Rintlen continued, "that the work of this man Wienzman is considered to be of the highest importance. It is essential that he and his family be sent here under guard at once."

Meyer could picture the man on the other end of the line who spoke in the harsh, arrogant tones he had heard so often from the Aryan supermen of the black shirts. Although the police chief had spoken confidently to David Wienzman of the ease with which he would be able to deal with the inquiries of such men, he felt a cold fear in his stomach.

"I very much regret, Herr Standartenführer, that the

man you refer to was permitted to emigrate recently. He obtained the necessary permits from the ministries in Vienna, and I issued him a frontier pass myself several days ago. By now he will certainly have left."

"You idiotic fool!" A torrent of abuse came over the line. "You allowed a man of vital importance to leave the country. My God but you'll pay if this is true."

"Whatever has happened," Meyer responded, "the fault is not mine. Wienzman was in possession of permits from your office in Vienna, as well as from the Foreign Ministry, the Economics Ministry, and the Office of Emigration. I merely issued the frontier pass for which he already had authority. You must look higher if you wish to find someone to blame."

"Tell me this much," Rintlen snapped, "since you have so signally failed in everything else—when and where did the professor cross the frontier, and who was with him?"

Meyer had to delay the pursuit. He glanced at the clock on the wall opposite. It was quarter to eleven; they were probably crossing the border at this very moment. A single telephone call might stop them.

"The professor was to travel with his daughter," he answered carefully. "The pass allowed them to cross into Italy at any point within this police district. As to the time of their departure," he hesitated, "of that I am not sure. Would not the best course be for me to check at once with the border guards? It may even be that they are still on Austrian—on German soil. In which case I can deliver them to you."

"Do that, and telephone me here the moment you learn anything." The line went dead. Meyer turned his gaze thoughtfully toward the window. The mountains stood out clearly against the bright sky. With luck, he thought, he could delay any pursuit for a couple of days at least, and that might give the professor and Siegret a chance to get out of Italy and beyond the reach of the Gestapo.

In Berlin, Paul Rintlen sat for a moment in thought; then, picking up the file of papers in front of him, he went out into the corridor and along to a door at the far end. Unlike Hans Meyer's image of him, he was dark and slim, with the light build of an Austrian. His face was intelligent and would have been good-looking except that his chin was too narrow and pointed, an awareness of which had given him the habit of constantly stroking and kneading his jaw, as though trying to hide the defect.

The door at the end of the corridor opened into a large room containing a leather· sofa and several chairs for visitors. At a small desk sat an officer dressed, like Rintlen, in a black uniform trimmed with silver.

"Is the chief free, Lindeman?" he asked. "There is a problem with the Wienzman case."

Giving a nod, Lindeman rose and knocked softly on a door behind him. "Standartenführer Rintlen," he announced.

Hated and feared more than any other single man in the Third Reich, Reinhard Heydrich epitomized, in the eyes of many, everything the nation's government stood for. Tall, blonde, strikingly handsome, he had an air of irresistible power and vitality and a ruthless, driving ambition that had brought him to the topmost circle within the state. In some quarters it was whispered that Heydrich, by far the cleverest mind among the Nazi hierarchy, was the only man in Germany feared by Hitler. Certainly the chief of the S.D. had amassed detailed and incriminating files on every person of significance including both his current boss Himmler and Prime Minister Hermann Goering. Perhaps among those carefully guarded papers there were records of secrets that the Führer himself would wish to hide.

Rintlen had been a little surprised to have been given so routine a task as the tracing of Wienzman, and even more so when he had been ordered to report directly to Heydrich. There must be something special about the case, and it was with some trepidation that he related the failure of his efforts.

For a moment Heydrich remained impassive; then his face twisted in a scowl and he swore once, with such venom that Rintlen started.

"There is a good reason, Obergruppenführer, to believe that this man and his daughter are now in Italy. If that is so, a special request to the Italian ministry of police should produce results."

Heydrich waved him to silence. "This is not a case of

some little professor fleeing the country," he said thinly. "Professors are two a penny—the Gestapo can take care of them.

"Wienzman is important not because of what he is or does, but because of who he was." He lit a cigarette and tossed one to Rintlen, who smiled inwardly. As far as the general public was concerned, Heydrich was a man without indulgences such as tobacco and liquor. "Wienzman is being sought by Goering's people, ostensibly to continue his work on medical research. That, however, is only a cover. I am certain that Goering has discovered a link between this man and a high state official. Naturally, it is my duty to investigate."

Rintlen felt a shadow of fear fall on him. The risks of entering a struggle between such antagonists were terrifying. Whatever the result, he would be bound to offend one of the country's most powerful men.

"You will go out to this place, Saint Veit," Heydrich went on, "and find this man Wienzman and arrest him and any member of his immediate family. You will go alone, and, if you are forced to use local police support, you will tell them nothing.' No record will be kept of the arrest or of any associated action. You will also bring away, unread, all personal documents you find."

"And if he has already crossed into Italy?"

Heydrich gave him a cold, hard glance. "You will follow him wherever he goes and carry out your task. Our missions abroad will be instructed to give you any assistance you require."

"I understand, Obergruppenführer. You can rely on me." Rintlen rose and saluted. "Heil Hitler."

"Heil Hitler." Heydrich smiled grimly. "Our salutes demonstrate our reverence to our leader. Nevertheless, I trust that in this particular mission you will at all times remember to whom you owe your immediate loyalty, even should this appear to conflict at times with your loyalty to the Party and its officers." Again he paused. "Perhaps even conflict with the supreme authority."

Back in his room Rintlen poured himself a stiff measure of schnapps. His fingers, he noticed, were trembling slightly. There had been brutal jobs in the past years that he had carried out without qualms. The road to power in Germany had been tough and merciless, but this one. . . .

He shivered again and took another swig. Of the implication of Heydrich's final words, there could be no doubt.
Wienzman was to be eliminated, and the incriminating
documents placed in Heydrich's hands, and not even the supreme authority in the state was to be allowed to prevent it.

○ ○ ○

Desmond had already guessed at Ralph Kendrick's
fears. The radio operator's growing nervousness had been
apparent ever since the news of the Atlantic flight had
been broken to them two days ago at Durban. As yet, Desmond was not sure what to make of it. All flyers were
afraid at times. Bad weather, faulty equipment, engine
failure—at any time one might be seconds away from
death. Desmond remembered some of his own experiences,
flights that had gone wrong or nearly so. A crash-landing
in the Pyrenees; engine failure off the coast of France; a
fire in the air at Croydon during one of his first trips for
Imperial.

Every flyer had similar memories. If modern techniques
and equipment were rendering their tasks less dangerous,
this was being more than compensated for by the constant
striving after ever more difficult achievements. Night flying, trans-Saharan flying, flights across the Andes and over
the Pacific. Always longer and more arduous journeys,
and the most difficult and dangerous of all was the North
Atlantic; the route with the worst weather in the world.

Ralph had had a bad crash, and the fear would probably always remain with him. Far more to the point was
whether he possessed the toughness, the determination
of spirit, to push back the fear and carry on. One way or
the other, Desmond thought, this flight would prove the
answer.

Privately, Desmond was sure that his radio operator
possessed those qualities along with the dedication that
made a good flyer. A trip might be good or bad, as easy
as sleeping or so exhausting that when you finally stepped
down from the cockpit it was all you could do to stand
upright. One seldom ever mentioned these things. What
counted was getting through, delivering the cargo and the
passengers, and keeping to the schedule. Private fears and
hopes, private lives, everything came second to this. If a

man could not accept it, there was no point in his flying any longer.

O O O

The rain was sleeting down on the road, blowing in off the Chesapeake. Jarrett paid the cab and squelched across the yard to the small office. The windows were steamed up, and inside he found three men sitting round an oil stove, drinking coffee in a thick, stale atmosphere. They looked up with hostility as he entered.

"I've come to pick up my plane," he told them. "The Supermarine S4." None of the men made a move. Eventually, one of them, a fat, balding man in dirty white overalls, heaved himself to his feet and approached the paper-strewn desk.

"The Supermarine S4, the Supermarine," he repeated to himself, sifting through the mess until he came to some kind of registration book. "Yeah, I remember." He ran an oily finger down a list. "Ain't seen yer for a week or two, Mr. Jarrett. You used to be down most evenings working on her. What you aim to do with her? Only got one seat 'n no space for baggage. Heavy on the gas and been smashed up once."

"Ach, she's a fine bird for all that," one of the other two men threw in unexpectedly. "Sister to the one that won the Schneider trophy in '27."

"She was smashed up on trials, though," the older man answered without raising his head. "That's why they sold her."

"What you planning on doing with her, then?" the second man asked.

"I collect historic aircraft. I buy them and try to restore them. Got a Curtis Navy Racer CR-3 and a Fairey F17 Compania." As he had expected, this explanation established him as a wealthy fool with more money than sense, and the men's interest in him disappeared at once. "Is the plane ready?" he asked. "I'm short on time, and I've got a long way to go."

"She's ready," the fat man admitted reluctantly, squinting through the window at the rain dancing on the tarmac outside. "You want to take her out in this?" Seeing Jarrett nod, he sighed and reached for a black oilskin. "OK then, fellers. Let's get the man his plane."

It took the combined efforts of all four of them to roll back the dilapidated hangar doors. The metal was freezing to touch, with water cascading down the gulleys of the corrugating. Toward the rear of the hangar, Pat saw the silver-white outline of the Supermarine sitting in its launching cradle.

"We'll hook her up to the tractor and back her down the ramp till she floats off." The foreman wiped the rain off his face.

Some twenty-seven feet in length with a slightly greater wingspan, the racer had an impressive, streamlined appearance. The nose, float struts, and upper wing surfaces were all plated with polished duralumin; the remainder of her body glistened a freshly painted white. She was built for speed and power.

Three-quarters of an hour later, the airplane fully fueled and the preflight check complete, Jarrett was sitting in the tiny open cockpit, snug in a heavy leather flying coat, fur-lined helmet, goggles, and leather gloves.

The elegant little aircraft began to skim across the water. Jarrett was conscious of the spray flying up at him, and the engine noise now rose swiftly to a high, keen pitch as they howled across the bay.

For the next few minutes, oblivious of the rain flung back at him over the cowling, Jarrett put the thoroughbred machine through her paces, climbing, diving, banking, loops and rolls, lost in his exhilaration. Not since the end of the war had he known such pure pleasure.

O O O

Khartoum was hot and humid. The air, once the doors were opened, struck the flying boat's occupants like a blast of steam. Set on the point of the triangle where the swift-moving waters of the Blue Nile meet the turgid, discolored White Nile, the city of "Chinese" Gordon, of Speke, of Livingstone, and the Mad Mahdi impressed them as no more than a stifling harbor whose peeling waterfront sheltered only a handful of dhows and a solitary river steamer. The town had been rebuilt since its destruction by the Mahdi's fanatics and its subsequent recapture by Kitchener forty years earlier, but it still remained a remote colonial outpost, the capital of one of the world's most sparsely populated lands, and everyone was relieved when Desmond announced that they would resume the flight as soon as refueling was complete. Lunch would be served aloft.

They flew on in the harsh sunlight, the desert unfolding slowly below, streaked and mottled with the marks of hills and dried watercourses. The bright ribbon of the Nile flowed steadily northward.

The weariness of the long flight and the strain of the previous day was telling on the crew. With the autopilot on and no hills to avoid or course changes to observe, they sat in silence, each occupied with his own thoughts, their minds numbed by the noise and rattle of the engines, their eyes aching from the glare.

They made their final refueling stop of the day on the Egyptian waters of Wadi Halfa. At quarter-past one, they were ready to take off once more. The thousand or more miles they had covered since dawn seemed to have made only a slight difference in the heat and humidity. There was a hot wind blowing out of the Nubian Desert, and the air was heavy with dust.

"The hot weather's returning early this year," the airline's representative at Wadi Halfa told Desmond. "We'll have a long summer of it." He gazed out over the river. "I hear you're taking the flight across the Atlantic this time," he remarked suddenly, giving Desmond a quick look. "Good luck to you in that, you'll need it."

"I've flown the route before," Desmond answered him shortly.

The man looked away again. "It'll be winter out there, and here the summer's starting. Wonder if I'll ever see a real winter again—back home, I mean. Do you think there'll be war this year?"

"Who can say?" Desmond shrugged. He felt a sudden longing to be away.

"Heard about your spot of trouble down in the marshes; bad thing to happen. These crocs—never see 'em coming," the man said slowly. It was hard to decide whether or not he was talking to himself. "Company won't like it—

never do, especially a passenger. The rest of us, you and me, we're not so important."

That much was true, Desmond thought, as he climbed back to the flight deck. It was likely that command of the Atlantic flight would be taken away from him. And he would be left to work his way back and forth along the Cape to Cairo route, passing and repassing the scene of Thorne's death. His mouth tightened as he settled behind the controls. If the board tried to pin the blame for the accident on him, he'd fight them every inch of the way.

The other men on the flight deck noted the signs of their captain's anger and kept silent. Only when they had been flying for several minutes did Ralph Kendrick tap him on the shoulder. "Think you'd better see this, skipper," he said, passing him a slip of paper. "It's a weather report just in from Cairo. It looks bad, I'm afraid."

4

By *radio*: 1330 hrs LOCAL TIME. SATURDAY 11 MARCH 1939. CAIRO TO IMPERIAL AIRWAYS FLIGHT 109 G-ADHO CATERINA. MET. OFFICE REPORTS STRONG DEPRESSION MOVING IN FROM LIBYAN DESERT. PRESSURE 998 mb. FALLING. GROUND TEMPERATURE 70°F WINDS 40 KNOTS FROM S.W. SEVERE STORM IMMINENT. END.

"That's a khamsin," Ken Frazer commented when Desmond passed the message across. "It must be moving right onto our path judging by this." His eyes strayed to the open map on his knees where a moment earlier he had been marking off their progress. "I suppose there's a chance we might outrun it," he said doubtfully.

"That's what we'll try for," Desmond agreed. It had, in fact, been his own immediate reaction on reading the message. With a little under three hours to go until they reached the delta, there was a chance, if they flew at maximum speed, that they might be able to cross the path of the khamsin and get ahead of it. The winds would be operating in their favor; the only questions were how far the storm center was from the city and the speed at which it was moving.

"Give me our exact fuel requirement for maintaining maximum cruising speed to Cairo," he told Frazer, "and check that we have sufficient reserves."

Frazer moistened his lips with his tongue. "You won't worry about the wing tank then?" he asked, the nervousness just evident in his voice.

"I'd rather take a small risk on the repair holding up than try to land through the middle of a khamsin."

Desmond's tone was curt; he felt in no mood to pander to his first officer's anxieties. "The tank has given us no trouble so far today." For flyers, these storms were particularly terrifying. Caught in one, a plane's engines were swiftly choked and stopped by the fine particles blowing in through the filters and inlet ports. Tossed and buffeted by the air pockets, the pilot would strain his eyes in vain to see through the swirling dirt. Planes had disappeared in these clouds never to reappear, even their wreckage swallowed up by the sands.

Their alternative was to land on the river and wait until the khamsin had passed over, but at ground level the effects of the scorching wind and sand were at their worst. Aside from the difficulty of mooring *Caterina* securely in such conditions, there was a very real possibility that the engines would be so clogged with dust that restarting them would be impossible.

"Of course, if we meet it in the open desert, we should be able to fly above it," Frazer continued hopefully.

Desmond made no reply. Although in theory Frazer was right, it was far more likely that the storm would strike them as they were nearing Cairo, when they would be having to lose, not gain, height.

"We'll continue at maximum speed," Desmond announced when they had checked the fuel figures. To Ralph Kendrick he said, "Tell Cairo I want everything they hear about the storm as soon as they get it." The desert surface continued undisturbed, the horizon a flat, clear line, unbroken by any hint of cloud; an hour, perhaps a little more, would see the full weight of the khamsin bearing down toward them on a converging track.

○ ○ ○

"Have we not seen enough? Why do we wait?" The howl of the sandstorm snatched the words from the Egyptian's mouth, rendering them barely audible.

Crouched near the top of the dune, Rashid al Senussi peered down onto the road two hundred feet below. Conditions were rapidly becoming impossible. Great gusts of wind were tearing sand off the crests of the dunes in long, ragged streams and driving the dust furiously across the open plain. The two men were shielded to some extent by the small hollow in which they sheltered, but even so their position was exposed and uncomfortable.

"We have seen everything. Why waste time?" the Egyptian repeated. "Let us go back. We will return tomorrow." He gave a tug at Rashid's robe. "Let us go back."

Rashid struck the man's hand away angrily. "Be still," he said curtly, "and watch the road. It is only a little wind." Damn these Egyptians, he thought. Peasants and farm dwellers—they were useless in the desert. A few hours without water, the threat of a storm, and they were finished. Generations of easy living had softened them to a point where they would be of less account than a woman among the nomadic tribes of the true desert.

Thank God he had a few of his own people with him. Tough raiders out of the Sahara, men who could travel all day on a handful of dates and half a cup of brackish water and still fight hard at the end of it. Men who were not afraid to risk death in battle rather than submit to the rule of an alien master.

For himself, he could no longer conceive of any other life. Almost his earliest memories were of trekking off into the hills with his father's tribesmen, out of the reach of the Italian artillery, clinging flat against the rock faces as the planes swept the narrow valleys with machine-gun fire and shrapnel bombs. He could vividly recall the terrifying roar of aircraft diving down at them; the explosions as the bombs blasted the column, the sound echoing off the sides of the gorge; the sharp smell of cordite; the screams of the women and other children around him; and wounded men and horses struggling together on the ground, their blood mingling in the sand.

The enemy had overwhelming strength, and it had been a long time before the Arabs had come to terms with this new method of fighting. Rashid had ridden in more than one mad horseback charge against Italian forts—charges that had turned into bloody routs when the machine guns and mortars had opened up. He had seen his three closest friends blown into rags a scant ten yards ahead of him.

Unable to compete with such armament, the Arabs had fallen back on the old ways, raiding in small groups, attacking by stealth at night, laying ambushes and melting away in the vast empty regions beyond the coastal strip. A boy warrior at thirteen, by the time he was fifteen Rashid was a battle-hardened guerilla with a price on his head.

That price had been collected one day in 1933 when a military detachment had surprised him at his father's house near Tobruk in Cyrenaica. Seized before he had been aware of what was happening, by decree of the military governor, the young sheik had been dispatched across the sea to Italy as a hostage for the good behavior of his father and his people.

Somewhat to his amazement, he had been well treated. There was a new policy in force at that period under which the sons of Arab chiefs and sheiks from troublesome areas were to be educated and instilled with an understanding of the Italian way of life in the belief that this would make them sympathetic to colonial rule. Rashid was determined to continue his fight for freedom; yet he was filled with a passionate desire to acquire the knowledge that gave his enemies so much power.

His father had written to him:

My son, for us the war is lost, and to fight on would be useless, bringing death, hardship, and misery to our people. We must wait and trust that with our children the times may change, that our enemies may grow weaker, and that you will one day return and show our people how to throw off the yoke that has for so long lain upon our necks. Take what your captors offer, accept what they have to teach, but never forget that you are of the desert—you are a prince of the Senussi, and your home is with us.

From that day, there was no more dedicated student of European culture than Rashid. So pleased were his superiors that they even allowed him to be sent to the Victor Emmanuel Military College in Rome.

"Baron d'Este will come by this road tomorrow, of that I am sure," the Egyptian pleaded, plucking once again at Rashid's sleeve. "It is always the same course." There could no longer be any doubt that they were about to experience a full khamsin; the wind strength had increased markedly in the past few minutes, and furious gusts were cutting across the dunes, driving the sand off them in solid sheets. The road below was entirely obscured.

"He will come, as you say"—Rashid turned angrily on his companion, who cringed against the wall of the hollow—"unless your information is a pack of lies."

The unfortunate Egyptian whined with fear. "No, it is true, I swear it, my sheik, upon my mother and my sister. Luca d'Este will drive in the big race. His car is a red one. It is said he may win."

Luca d'Este—d'Este—the memories evoked by that name grew more bitter each time he heard it, renewing the force of the oath he had sworn. Three years, no more, since an urgent message had transformed him into a hunted rebel once more as he fled to his homeland— a message bearing that name, whose contents were to remain forever burned into his brain.

"He must come," the Egyptian pleaded, his face a mask of anxiety. "He leaves the country for America in two days' time, and his wife goes with him. Tonight he will attend the king's ball at the palace; tomorrow he drives in the race to El Faiyûm. There—I have told Your Highness all that I know. Believe me!"

"Is there any reason why I should not?" Rashid demanded. "Since you know that your life depends on it." He pulled the hood of his robe over his head. "I have seen enough; we will collect the horses and return to the city to fetch my men. When d'Este comes past tomorrow, we will be ready for him."

Jacquetta d'Este had been wrong in supposing that her husband was having an affair with Georgina Curtis. So far they had not progressed beyond the stage of mild flirtation. Which, while most enjoyable, could hardly be considered a great romance, Luca thought as he sat alone drinking brandy after lunch on the terrace at Shepheard's Hotel, and it was a state of affairs he was determined to alter.

Jacquetta had gone riding, a frequent pastime of hers of late; indeed, so frequent that at one point Luca had begun to wonder if she was meeting a lover. For a time he had even felt jealous. His wife was certainly beautiful enough to have attracted any number of admirers, and he doubted whether, in the light of his own past behavior, she would suffer any guilt in deceiving him. Discreet surveillance had, however, revealed that her time was genuinely spent riding among the sand dunes and watercourses on the edge of the desert.

The wide marble terrace of Shepheard's Hotel was the most celebrated rendezvous in all Cairo, and equally famous throughout the whole of the Middle East. A carpeted stairway led up from the street, and the guests lounged, idly watching the pavement below where there milled a crowd of snake charmers, donkey men, souvenir hawkers, touts, dragomen, and itinerant peddlers, all prevented from entering the hotel itself by the gorgeously uniformed *suffragi* standing at the steps.

"Good afternoon, baron. You honor us with your presence. I trust everything is to your satisfaction?" The speaker was a man of medium height in his late thirties.

"Your cooking, my dear Freddy, is far superior to that of the embassy," Luca greeted the newcomer affably. "Will you join me in a brandy?" Luca turned to the waiter who approached soundlessly. "Some brandy for Mr. Müller."

"And so, Freddy," he went on as they sipped their drinks, "another season in Cairo draws to an end. It has been a good one, I think."

The hotel manager reflected for a moment. "Yes," he answered at length, "it has been a good season—one of the best. Indeed, I should think the best for ten years at least if not more, but perhaps—"

"Go on." Luca was watching him carefully.

Freddy collected his thoughts. "I was going to say," he continued, "that this last season has been the brightest and gayest in many years. Cairo has never seen so many distinguished visitors. The women have never been more beautiful, their clothes more elegant. There have been more lavish and glittering parties than I can ever recall. Hardly a night has gone by here at Shepheard's without a ball or a dance or grand dinner party, and now with the marriage of the king's sister to the future emperor of Iran, the celebrations have become more spectacular still. Yet I seem to sense an undercurrent of urgency, almost of desperation, as though people thought in some way it could not last forever."

"Come, come, Freddy," Luca gave him a laugh. "Like

all Swiss, you're a national pessimist. People are happy now because last summer they all thought there would be war in Europe, and now that has been avoided. I agree it's been a marvelous season, but this air of desperation as you call it—no, I don't find it anywhere."

"Well, baron, perhaps as you say I am a pessimist and an oversensitive one at that. You do not believe there will be war, then?" He took another sip of his brandy.

"War, there is always war somewhere," Luca responded carelessly.

"No, I meant—" Freddy began.

"You meant a big war, between Germany and France say, or Britain." Luca dismissed the idea with a wave of his hand. "I think there is small chance of that. Hitler's eyes are to the east. It is Germany and Russia who may fight one day, but there will be no war in the west for a while, I think."

"But the British and the French are rearming," Freddy murmured.

"So are Germany and Japan and Italy; it does not mean they are about to go to war with one another. Enough of this depressing talk. Tell me, how do you rate my chances in tomorrow's motor race?"

"It is said that you have the fastest car," Freddy responded suavely, "with perhaps Captain O'Neill as the next challenger. As to the driving skills"—he spread his hands—"I am no judge, but the betting is lying in your favor."

"Well if I win," Luca told him jovially, "I shall give a great party at Shepheard's to celebrate. With a dinner and dance in the gardens afterward."

"I confess we are already making preparations to accommodate the winner," Freddy told him with a grin, "and I shall pass on your intentions to the chefs. I only hope that the wind will have dropped in time for the race."

"It will have passed by this evening, and tomorrow the day will be clear and cooler." Luca said optimistically. "I must go." He rose to his feet, and the hotel manager at once stood up. "I have promised to escort Mrs. Curtis to the palace of Prince Suleiman."

Prince Suleiman was a Syrian of unequaled wealth who lived in a rococo palace on the western side of the river in a predominantly Arab quarter whose mean and crooked streets and squalid homes served to emphasize the extravagant lines of what was said to be the most beautiful of Cairo's many palaces. Now a widower in his seventies, the prince was once one of the leading figures in Cairo society, and invitations to his palace were still much sought after. Luca, who knew the old man well, was hoping that the grandeur of the buildings and the splendid gardens would assist him in his seduction of Georgina.

The prince sent a boat to fetch them, powered by a dozen oarsmen—an oriental affair with gilded timbers and a silk canopy over the high, carved stern. The wind was now stiffer, but not unpleasantly so, though Luca could see that their return would have to be made by road.

Beneath the white facades of the buildings, the river banks were fringed with tamarisks and palm trees and were bright with bougainvillea and oleander; nearby, opulent houseboats rode at anchor. A string of feluccas moved slowly upstream ahead of them, their huge single sails bellying out in the wind.

Luca eyed Georgina keenly, barely suppressing the desire he felt. His gaze lingered on the firm outline of her body beneath the thin silk of her dress.

Was it simply the desire for physical satisfaction or aesthetic attraction that made him crave her so? he asked himself. Was it because his instincts told him that she would be an exciting lover, or was he merely aroused by the difficulty of the conquest and by the thought of her stripped of her beautiful clothes and robbed of the coolness and poise with which she kept him at bay?

"It's such a pity there should be a khamsin," Georgina remarked, frowning. "I should have loved to have come here on a really perfect afternoon."

Luca did not reply. A woman's complaints on such matters were to be ignored; treated with respect, they tended to assume exaggerated importance. He put his faith in the splendor of the prince's palace to make her lower her guard. This afternoon was his last chance before her husband returned, and Luca intended to make the most of it.

The boat drew in at a point where the gardens ran down to a marble-faced embankment, in the middle of which lay a white marble pier set with silver lamps and sil-

ver handrails—like an enormous piece of jewelry. Music
reached them faintly over the water; concealed musicians,
Luca realized, must be stationed nearby to greet the arriving guests. Liveried servants waited on the pier to receive them.

The scene could not have been more perfect. He heard
Georgina give a small gasp. Taking her arm, he confidently
conducted her off the boat and up to the palace grounds.

Jacquetta d'Este had not found the wind too troublesome. She had driven out beyond the suburbs some
twenty miles to where her horse was kept at stables on the
edge of the desert. The horse was a fine bay gelding named
Balbo whom she had brought with her from Italy for the
season, a present from Luca on her birthday three years
ago, during one of his rare spells of affection.

The majority of riders from the stable invariably made
for the Pyramids and the Sphinx. Today, however, only
a few tourists were defying the blowing dust. Even so,
Jacquetta turned Balbo's head toward the open ground to
the southwest. This afternoon she felt a need to be as far
away from others as possible; she had even made the
groom who normally accompanied her remain behind
with the chauffeur.

As soon as they had left the vicinity of the stables, Jacquetta gave the horse his head, and at full gallop they sped
toward the hills. Exhilaration swept through her as she felt
the wind and heard the swift drum of Balbo's feet on the
sand, and sensing her excitement, the horse quickened his
pace.

When at length she slowed him to a trot and then a
walk, she realized that she was halfway to the hills and
that the dust blowing into her face was considerably more
unpleasant than she had at first thought. The fact annoyed her, just as anything that threatened to interfere
with her daily ride annoyed her, and, urging Balbo back
into a trot, she pressed on toward the shelter of the
broken ground. In a few minutes she came upon the
course of a dried stream that wound torturously back toward the hills. Its wide bed offered an easy path for a horse
to follow, and, though the banks on either side were not
high, they gave a fair amount of shelter.

She rode slowly, partly to give the horse a chance to

pick its way among the stones littering the ground, and partly to allow herself time to think.

Her thoughts ran, as they so often did these days on Luca, and their future together. Her position seemed to have become increasingly intolerable. Her husband's affairs had become more and more blatant, and lately he appeared to care nothing about the impression he gave in society. He humiliated her constantly in public, and in private he abused and ill-treated her. At heart a bully, he seemed to derive an actual physical pleasure from watching her suffer, a pastime that his constant heavy drinking was causing him to indulge in even more frequently. Sexually he ignored her for months at a time, and, judging by the stories being bandied about, Luca was rapidly degenerating to a point where only the stimulus of a new conquest was sufficient to arouse him.

A highly sensuous woman, to whom lovemaking had been one of the chief delights of marriage, Jacquetta hated Luca all the more for making her spend her nights alone and unsatisfied. The obvious answer was to do as several of her friends had done and take a lover herself, but she felt she wanted a more final solution, some form of separation that would allow her to live apart from her husband, though in her heart she knew Luca would never permit it.

Thus preoccupied, she rode steadily on. The shallow channel turned into a small ravine with sides that were steeper and rockier than before. The sky had darkened, and the wind was howling outside the ravine, driving the sand before it in a stinging spray. But sheltered by the rock walls, Jacquetta scarcely noticed the approach of the storm.

"Why must it be d'Este who must die, Highness?" the Egyptian asked when they had covered nearly half the distance back to the city and were taking temporary shelter in the ruins of an abandoned village. Outside the mud walls, the sand was blowing thickly enough to choke anyone unprotected by a head cloth, and they had been forced to rest the horses. The Egyptian was reluctant to move on, and, he kept up a flow of questions in the hope of putting off the moment when Rashid would drive him out into the storm once more.

"Why do you hate this Italian so much, Highness?" he asked again. He crouched in a corner, watching Rashid anxiously.

"He murdered my father and my sister," Rashid told him in a flat tone that was meant to discourage further conversation. The Egyptian, however, broke into voluble comment on the iniquity of such a deed and the understandable need for revenge. Rashid paid him no attention, vividly recalling the moment when the news had reached him in Italy: "Your father is dead, murdered by the soldiers. Your sister, Rathine, they have carried off to the palace of the governor in Tripoli."

Once, as a boy, he had seen a killing done that way. The Italian soldiers had surrounded the village during the night and moved in at dawn. They were looking for rebels and arms.

He had stood and watched while the tents and houses were searched and the people's possessions were strewn over the ground outside. The soldiers had picked them over, taking some things and smashing others with their boots or the butts of their rifles. The men had been separated from their families and made to stand in lines. Rashid remembered them shivering with cold and whispering nervously to each other, striving to appear unafraid. Then an informer wearing a black hood had been brought out, and he had walked along the lines with two of the officers, stopping at intervals to reach out and touch the chests of the men he betrayed.

The beatings and interrogations had gone on for most of the morning. The cries of the tortured men had been audible all over the village, and the rest of the people had waited and listened, and the smell of pain and fear was everywhere. For the most part, the soldiers had lolled about in the shade, drinking wine from flasks and smoking, but near the edge of the village Rashid had seen two of them rape one of the girls, stripping her at knife point and taking turns holding her down. Later that evening the same girl had hanged herself from the branch of a thorn tree.

Not that the soldiers would have cared. The purpose of the expedition had been to teach these tiresome rebels a lesson rather than to capture large numbers of men and guns. After the interrogations were over, one or two of the men were released and the remainder were loaded into a truck. The villagers noted this with a certain degree of relief. According to previous experience, the prisoners would be taken off to one of the forced labor projects near the coast. At least they would be allowed to live.

The sound of the aircraft's engine had come as a surprise. The Arabs had learned to fear the machines that scattered death from the air in the form of shrapnel bombs and tracer bullets and watched the movements of the tribes as they crossed the sands.

The plane landed on a patch of firm ground beside the camp and switched off its motors. With much shouting and blows with their rifles, the soldiers drove everyone into the center of the village, where the officers stood. Beside the officers, between two guards, stood the sheik of the tribe.

One of the Italian officers spoke for a while. Rashid hadn't been able to follow his words, for the man's Arabic was poor. Instead, his eyes had been fixed on the sheik. The old man, until that day the undisputed master of his people, their judge, leader, and prophet, still retained his dignity. His eyes still held their accustomed pride, but now Rashid saw confusion and bewilderment in them, too. Something was about to happen that even the sheik did not comprehend, and this frightened the boy greatly.

The officer stopped speaking, and for a brief moment there was silence. Then he motioned to the guards, and they fell upon the sheik, with ropes, binding him, not in the normal fashion to prevent escape, but trussing him up like a turkey being taken to the market.

Amid the laughter of the rest of the troops and the horrified cries of the women and children, the soldiers dragged the old man across the sand to the airplane, lifted him up, and bundled him in. The door was slammed shut, the engines started up with a clatter, and the plane raced across the ground and lifted off into the air, climbing swiftly.

Their task apparently complete, the soldiers climbed into their lorries and began to move off in the direction they had come from, with their prisoners. Soon only a slowly disappearing cloud of dust marked their progress.

The villagers remained in a group. With their sheik and half of the men taken away, their homes looted and ruined, nobody had a clear idea of what to do.

When they heard the plane again, the first reaction of many had been the thought that their sheik was being returned to them, and they waited eagerly for the buzzing speck in the sky to descend.

But the plane had not descended. Approaching from the north it circled high above the village, while the eyes of those on the ground strained to follow it. Rashid had not seen the tiny black missile drop suddenly toward them, but he heard cries of horror, and there was a scattering for cover. There had been a sound in the air above like that made by a bomb, and he had been expecting a loud bang, but there had been only a heavy thud on the ground behind him, and he had turned his head just quickly enough to catch sight of the tattered bundle leaping high into the air as it bounced on the blood-spattered sand. This man's death, as well as Rashid's father's, had been ordered by Baron d'Este as a warning to the Arabs.

At least his father had died quickly. Rashid still felt an impotent fury when he thought of his sister's fate. The Italian governor had had a great palace in Tripoli, with golden domes and marble fountains set in the gardens. The officers had liked to force pretty Arab girls to dance naked in the fountains for them, and Rathine had been very beautiful. She had died on her second evening in the palace, hurling herself from a balcony in a grim parody of her father's death.

She and Rashid had been very close. Their mother had died when they were still young, and their father had been occupied with the affairs of his tribes, so they had looked to one another for company and comfort throughout their childhood. Later, when Rashid had been fighting with the rebels, he would return to see her as often as he could. Her death had struck him even more deeply than his father's.

○ ○ ○

Desmond O'Neill made his way to the smoking saloon for lunch, his mind preoccupied with his crew. There could be no doubt that Frazer would have to go. Desmond was fairly confident that for all the young man's boasted influence with the airline board he would be hard put to block an official request for his transfer. Perhaps some other captain in the fleet would find him easier to stomach, though Desmond doubted whether anyone would willingly take on the arrogant first officer. But one thing was certain: he was not going to remain on board *Caterina*.

Of Ralph Kendrick, Desmond was much less sure. Ralph was a steady, reliable radio officer whose solid qualities were to be respected, yet he was obviously suffering acutely at the prospect of another flight across an ocean that had once nearly claimed his life. The simplest way out would be to suspend him from duty when they reached England. Any pretext would do; he could be sent off for a medical check or on a new equipment familiarization course. However, what Ralph needed was to beat his fear. If he took, or was given, an easy way out, then for the rest of his life he would be a failure in his own eyes. The question was how far Desmond was justified in risking the safety of the aircraft in order to give the radio operator the chance to prove himself.

In the passageway he met Sandy returning from the smoking saloon. The purser was looking flushed and angry.

"Mr. Curtis is in there having lunch, sir," he said with a nod. "He's been wanting to know if you'll be cutting short our layover in Cairo in order to make up for the time we've lost. I told him that I thought, if anything, we would be staying longer while the engineers did a thorough inspection job on the fuel system, and when he heard that, he really hit the ceiling. You'd have thought we were doing it just to spite him."

"All right, Sandy, I'll see to it," Desmond assured him. "Are the rest of the passengers behaving themselves?"

"All except Mrs. Johnson; she's complaining Draper's been rude to her. He probably has, but that's only because she's been giving him hell all morning. I told her she must have misheard him, and I made Andy apologize, but she's still pretty cross."

"Do we lose her at Alexandria?" Desmond asked. Several of the passengers would leave them at the delta, and others would be boarding.

"No such luck," Sandy answered gloomily. "The Finlays are leaving us there, and an Italian couple are joining us at Cairo as well as Mrs. Curtis. I just hope she's not as bad as her husband."

Desmond smiled. "Cheer up, Sandy, at least then he'll have someone else to complain to besides you. Who are the Italian couple?"

"A baron and baroness. He's some kind of big shot in government circles apparently; he and his wife are going all the way to New York with us, and I've been told to see they get red-carpet treatment. They're friends of the Curtises, I think."

Desmond passed on into the smoking saloon. Curtis was holding forth on the shortcomings of the airline and especially the flight they were now on, but he greeted Desmond without any trace of embarrassment.

"Captain, your purser tells us we can expect further delay when we reach Cairo. Is this true?" he demanded. "I should have thought you would want to push on as quickly as possible to make up for lost time." There was a murmur of assent from Mr. Johnson. Laura Hartman and Dr. Van Smit said nothing.

"You are correct, Mr. Curtis, in thinking that I intend to make all possible speed," Desmond said equably, "just as soon as I am satisfied that the aircraft is safe." He glanced toward Laura as he spoke.

"You were apparently satisfied enough to fly nearly two thousand miles up the Nile," Curtis said rudely. "Why should you change your mind?"

"I had temporary repairs made to allow us to reach the nearest port where there are proper servicing facilities." Desmond said. "When we leave Cairo we shall have to cross open sea as well as fly over the Cévennes Mountains. I would think you would be glad of my taking extra care."

"How long will these repairs take?" Curtis asked.

Desmond shrugged. "That depends on what they find, but I don't expect we shall be delayed for more than about half a day. We will probably leave in the afternoon on Monday instead of first thing in the morning. After that, it depends very much on whether we have a clear run straight through to Rome or have to stop in Athens."

Van Smit gave a low chuckle. "But at least, Captain, there will be plenty of time for you to drive in the motor race in Cairo on Sunday. Your purser was telling me

earlier that you have a Hispano-Suiza. A magnificent car
—you are most fortunate. How did you find such a car
in Egypt?"

"Magnificent but old, I'm afraid," Desmond said. "She
doesn't have a great chance against some of the new
machines. I managed to buy her from King Farouk. His
father left him more than a hundred cars when he died
three years ago.

"Ah, then you know the king?" Van Smit remarked.

"Hardly at all," Desmond said, "but, like a lot of
people, he's interested in airplanes, and I've flown him on
a couple of occasions." He did not add that one of his
most serious quarrels with Pamela had been over his refusal to accept Farouk's offer to become his personal
pilot.

Stewart Curtis's voice cut across the conversation. "You
apparently fail to realize, captain, that I have important
business commitments that make it imperative that I reach
New York without delay. You have seriously inconve-
nienced me. I am due to attend a ball at the king's palace in Cairo tonight with my wife, and thanks to your
tardiness, I may well arrive late. What excuses will you
have me make *then*, I should like to know?"

Desmond's jaw tightened. "I can assure you, Mr. Curtis, that you will be in Cairo in plenty of time for King
Farouk's ball." He paused before adding, "I have been
asked to attend myself."

There were smiles from the others in the cabin at the
financier's visible discomfiture. For a moment he appeared
about to retort; however, he rose abruptly and stalked out
of the saloon.

"I think, captain, that you have just made an enemy,"
Van Smit said in his soft voice.

At this remark, Johnson, who had been sitting quietly
in a corner with his pipe, taking in the conversation,
bridled unexpectedly. "I see every reason to sympathize
with Mr. Curtis's feelings," he said pompously. "It is extremely annoying and inconvenient for some of us
to have our travel arrangements upset in this manner."

Laura Hartman leaped instantly to Desmond's defense.
"I call that a very selfish viewpoint, Mr. Johnson," she
said with spirit. "Why, you're asking Captain O'Neill to
put your personal convenience before the safety of the rest

of the people on board." Johnson looked taken aback at this sudden attack, and Desmond intervened hastily to cool the situation.

"It's annoying for all of us," he said. "For myself and the crew every bit as much as for the passengers. We had been hoping to have time to make an extra stopover at Bastia in Corsica. There's a special landing area there by a little fishing village where they give us fresh lobster tails for dinner."

"But can you do that?" Laura asked with surprise. "Stop and come down anywhere you want like that?"

"Not quite anywhere." Desmond smiled back. "We're supposed to stick to the scheduled ports, but I like to vary the trip a little if I can, so I admit I tend to look for excuses."

"Yes. We were warned of that in Durban." Van Smit showed his teeth in an answering grin. "The Imperial Airways officer told us that there was no alternative landing area you had not used at least once."

Desmond made a wry face. "Unfortunately, they were wrong. I hadn't been to Shambe." An awkward silence descended on the cabin.

"We should be having a news bulletin after lunch," Desmond said to change the subject. "We thought you would all like to have the four o'clock broadcast from Cairo put through on the intercom."

"Ah yes," Johnson agreed, "I shall look forward to that. I regard it as most important to make an effort to keep up with the news at home when one is abroad."

"It's all so gloomy I sometimes think I prefer not to hear it," said Laura, glancing involuntarily at a *Pictorial News* magazine on the table.

Andy Draper entered with the dining trolley and set about serving lunch.

"Nile perch," Van Smit commented. "Your caterers certainly know their job, captain. I shouldn't have expected such excellence from Khartoum."

Desmond thanked him. "We may not always run on time," he said, "but we do our best to give you a good meal."

The doctor filled Laura Hartman's wineglass and Mr. Johnson's before attending to his own. "And tell us, captain," he went on, "what kind of weather can we expect in Cairo?"

"At this moment they are experiencing a khamsin sandstorm," Desmond told him. "But with luck," he added, seeing their faces fall, "the weather will clear soon. These storms don't usually last long, though they can be nasty. By this evening it should be fine again."

"Just right for your ball," Van Smit remarked. "Mrs. Hartman tells me she will be there as well. Mr. and Mrs. Curtis are taking her in their party. You will be able to show her the Abdin Palace, captain."

Desmond and Laura looked at each other with some embarrassment. Laura gave a nervous smile and began to ask about the forthcoming race.

"We drive out to Fayum on the morning after the ball," he explained. "It's an oasis about sixty miles from Cairo, but the course takes a big sweep out into the desert, so the total distance is about one hundred and eighty miles. Part of the way is tarmac and the rest is dirt track across the sand. It should be a good race."

"Will you have much competition? I mean, will there be many other cars in the race?" Laura took a sip of wine.

"I won't know until I get to Cairo," Desmond said.

The flying boat gave a slight lurch, and Desmond glanced at the window. The horizon was clear; still no sign of the storm. They must be passing through a patch of local turbulence. As if in response to his thoughts, he felt *Caterina* lift, as up on the flight deck Ken Frazer increased altitude to take them up into smooth air again.

There was plenty of time before they could expect any marked deterioration in the weather; all the same, he was anxious to return to the controls. He began to hurry through his meal while the three passengers talked.

○ ○ ○

Jacquetta d'Este could see no more than a few yards through the storm. Blindly, she kept going, head bowed to escape the stinging blast of sand and dust. Her sense of direction had vanished. All she could do was to concentrate on keeping the wind at her back and hold the bridle of her horse, forcing the unfortunate beast to stagger along in her footsteps.

She knew that the fields of irrigated land that fringed the desert lay only a few miles away, yet in the choking clouds she no longer knew where to turn. It was very possible that she was heading away from safety and out into the empty wastes to the south.

Terrified as she was, Jacquetta found it hard to accept the idea that in the space of only two hours, conditions had changed to a point where they threatened her life. When she had first climbed up out of the dry wadi, it had been hot, and the sand had blown uncomfortably hard, but not so much as to alarm her. She had ridden on, hoping to find shelter among a line of dunes and from there make her way straight back across the desert to Mina rather than go to all the trouble of retracing her steps along the path she had taken.

The dunes themselves had afforded protection from the blowing dust, and it was only when she got out onto the flat plain beyond, that she became aware of the severity of the coming storm.

The whole of the horizon and sky behind her were blotted out by a dark wall of dust, towering thousands of feet into the air, traveling toward her at immense speed, devouring the ground in front of it, sucking up the surface of the desert in great twisting spirals of dirt that billowed out of sight into the sky.

Urging her horse to a gallop, Jacquetta made a futile attempt to outrun the storm. With frightening speed the wind had built up and with it the fury of the driven sands. Almost before she knew it, she was enveloped in a stifling cloud of dust that swallowed up the landscape about her, burning her face and eyes and leaving her hardly able to breathe.

It became impossible to ride. Slipping down from Balbo's back, she began to lead him by the bridle, trying all the time to head in the direction where she thought the city lay.

She tried to remember the features of the land she ought to be crossing. Although at first sight it had appeared to be quite flat, she knew this was deceptive and that quite soon she should reach an area of hilly ground with outcrops of wind-eroded rock. The land rose there also for a space before falling away again into another long level stretch, beyond which lay Mina and the Pyramids.

The Pyramids. For all it mattered, she might have been hundreds of miles deep in the Sahara instead of a couple of hours' ride from the tourist hotels and monuments of the Nile. Jacquetta had no illusions about her chances of survival should the khamsin continue. It was frighteningly easy to become lost in the desert even in fine weather, no more than a mile or two from safety. Unused to the sands, people wandered off into the dunes and lost their bearings. The sun did the rest. Nineteen hours, the experts always said—a man could last in the desert without water for nineteen hours. If she was headed in the wrong direction now, she could wander in circles all night, and by midday tomorrow she would be dead, her shriveling body buried in the sand drifts.

The heat was taking its toll. In Cairo the temperature in spring rarely climbed above seventy degrees, but here in the heart of the khamsin, it must be at least thirty degrees above that. The effort of walking in the wind was draining her fast. Balbo, too, was tiring, and he had begun to trip and stumble. Very probably, if she let him go now, he would simply lie down and die.

She forced herself on. To stop even for a moment would be fatal. Like the frozen deserts of the Poles, the Sahara would seize the first instant of weakness and turn it into surrender. The urge to give up, to stop and rest, must be resisted at all costs. There was still some small hope of coming through alive—if she could only keep going until the storm blew over or she managed to reach the edge of the desert, Meanwhile it was possible that search parties would be starting out to find her.

Though the khamsin was severe, its center would pass some way to the southwest of Cairo, and only its trailing edge ever reached the city itself. Nevertheless, this was sufficient to bring hot, stifling winds and dry, dust-laden air into the streets and houses. The inhabitants retreated inside if they could, fastening their shutters and windows. These periods of discomfort were brief, and by evening the city would be cool again and the winds still.

Luca and Georgina had found it too hot to wander far

in Prince Suleiman's palace gardens, and they had retired inside to join the other guests. The interior was truly sumptuous. Retainers in tarbooshes and white robes opened magnificent doors of beaten copper to reveal rooms whose marble floors were inlaid with beautiful mosaics, from which slender columns of alabaster rose to painted ceilings with chandeliers of colored crystal. They passed through a seemingly endless succession of rooms whose walls were hung with paintings by every artist from the old Italian masters to Dali, and each room was more magnificent than the last. They crossed floors inlaid with ivory and saw themselves reflected in a hundred mirrors as they followed the silent feet of the palace servants.

The old prince received them in a small salon. He reclined among embroidered cushions on a divan, listening to the talk of his guests and watching them shrewdly, all the time smoking an elaborate silver hookah.

This was the first time Georgina had come in contact with an Egyptian nobleman who still clung to the old oriental style rather than following the western fashions adopted by the courts of King Farouk and his father. Luca was gratified to see that she was pleased and not a little awed. The other guests were part of the smart clique of wealthy cosmopolitans with whom the exotic and unashamed opulence of the prince's living, as well as his disregard for the conventions of society, were much in vogue.

Surprisingly, in view of the prince's age, the palace was a meeting place for the radical anti-British element in Egyptian political life. With increasing popular pressure for the withdrawal of British troops and the rapidly rising power of the Fascist regimes in Italy and Germany, there were those close to Farouk who were urging him to safeguard his throne by adopting closer relations with these new powers, especially Italy, whose army of one hundred thousand men on the Libyan border constituted the most formidable force in North Africa.

Beneath the surface of the capital, a fierce power struggle was taking place between the pro- and anti-British parties, with Farouk's court attempting to hold a middle course. Already a number of leading Egyptian politicians had been assassinated in the streets, and scores of others had been threatened. The stakes were colossal: despite desperate poverty among the majority of the people, the country was prosperous and a small number of men and women staggeringly rich. In Cairo alone there were estimated to be more than five hundred millionaires. The king himself personally owned one-seventh of the land in the country. Nowhere else in the world did such magnificent displays of wealth contrast with such misery, disease, and starvation. The rewards of power in Egypt were very real.

More than that, Egypt was of vital strategic importance. With control of the Suez Canal, the gateway to India and the east, as well as to the oil of Arabia, a nation could place a stranglehold on the British and French colonial empires and perhaps control Africa as well. Small wonder that the spies and agents of half a dozen governments swarmed throughout the city and that the king's secret police watched everyone. Corruption, treachery, and savage torture raged unchecked behind the tranquil facade.

Today the conversation in the prince's salon was more guarded than usual; and a swift glance about the room soon told why. In a corner opposite the prince lounged the plump, pampered, elegantly dressed Yousouri Pasha—light featured and soft haired, more like a woman in appearance than a man, the Albanian blood in his ancestry proclaimed by the pallor of his skin. Behind the indolent mask, Luca knew, was one of King Farouk's most trusted advisors, and for that reason one of the most powerful and most feared men in Egypt.

Presenting Georgina first to the prince, who bowed amiably and waved them to seats among the cushions, Luca found them places next to Yousouri. Half an hour or so of gentle conversation would suffice before he would suggest taking Georgina on a tour of the palace. Behind the principal rooms there were secluded suites designed for just such a purpose as he had in mind.

"You are both leaving shortly, I am told." Yousouri proffered a bowl of sweetmeats to Georgina. "It will be a sad loss to our little community," he added with elaborate courtesy.

"Your Excellency's presence today is an unexpected pleasure," Luca responded with equal politeness. "We had not expected to see you before the ball tonight." What twist and turn of local politics brought so sinister a figure here at this moment? he wondered.

"His Majesty sent me with greetings to His Highness." Yousouri took a sugared pastry from the bowl and examined it idly. "I am no more than a humble messenger who has remained out of curiosity to meet the guests." He popped the pastry into his mouth, flicking his fingers to remove the sugar that had stuck to them. "It is coincidental that I should meet you here though, baron," he continued, "for a little earlier today your name was mentioned in my presence in an unusual context."

He spoke casually, smiling at Georgina. Luca was suddenly conscious of a hollow feeling in his stomach. As a foreign diplomat, he was theoretically beyond Yousouri's reach, but in these times one could never be sure, and there had been unpleasant rumors of unexplained disappearances.

He forced himself to speak naturally. "I trust you heard nothing to my disadvantage."

Yousouri transferred his smile from Georgina to Luca. "It was merely an expression of interest. A man who was here had met another man—quite recently it seemed—who knew you and had asked after you. It is of passing interest, nothing more." He leaned against the cushions, closing his eyes. Around them the quiet conversation continued; in the background a lute was being played with exquisite skill. Luca cursed the necessity for this indirect form of speech. Why couldn't these Egyptians ever say what they meant? he thought angrily.

"I meet so many people," Luca replied. "It is not always possible to remember them."

"It seems that the man of whom we speak was until recently in your country, which must, of course, be where he met you. He himself, however, is a native of Libya, although his family is related to that of the prince here." Yousouri indicated their host with a wave of his hand. "His name is Sheik Rashid al Senussi," he said, looking intently at Luca.

"I have heard of the man, though to my knowledge we have never met," Luca said shortly. "His father was a noted rebel during my appointment in Libya, and he was dealt with severely." He could not quite bring himself to admit that on his orders the man had been put to death.

"Then the man I spoke to must have been recently in Libya, for where else could he have met Sheik Rashid? Certainly, not, I am sure, here in Egypt."

"Your Excellency would be better placed than I to know that," Luca answered.

The Egyptian nodded. "That is true, and in any case you yourself are leaving soon. However, I heard that you are to take part in a motor race," he said. "It is to be hoped that you will exercise great care; these events are dangerous, and accidents can easily happen."

"Thank you. I will heed your advice. And now if you will excuse us," Luca stood up. "I should like to show Mrs. Curtis some of the beauties of the palace."

The pasha made a regal gesture of dismissal. "By all means. And, if I may advise," he said to Georgina, giving her a bland smile, "the galleries on the first floor are particularly worth viewing. But I am sure the baron knows that already."

Luca led the way out of the salon and into the hall beyond.

"This is the most beautiful place I have ever seen," Georgina whispered, slipping her arm through his. "But who was that man you were talking to? He seemed very odd even for an Egyptian. Did you say he was a pasha?"

Like a great many newly wealthy women, Georgina Curtis believed that a title was indicative of personal merit, an attitude that Luca hoped would soon prove to be of use.

"Yousouri Pasha? He's just one of the king's advisors," he told her with deliberate casualness. "Quite a powerful figure, in his way."

"And what was all that about the sheik from Libya?" The hall was lined with huge mirrors in ornate gilt frames, and Georgina was looking at her reflection as she spoke.

At least, thought Luca, he could make some use of the Egyptian's remarks, although he still couldn't decide whether they had been intended as a warning or a threat. "Sheik Rashid al Senussi?" he shrugged. "He is just someone who has sworn to kill me, that is all."

"Darling, how terrible!" Georgina squeezed his arm excitedly. "Why ever should he want to do such a thing?"

This was playing straight into Luca's hands, and, giving what he hoped was a regretful sigh, he said, "Rashid's father was a criminal whom I was obliged to sentence to death several years ago. I did not wish to do it," he went on, striving to convey the impression of a misjudged ruler, "but he was guilty, and it was my duty to enforce the law."

Georgina gazed into his eyes with exaggerated wonder. "But aren't you frightened at all? I know I should be." Looking down into her upturned face, her dark eyes full of admiration, her red lips parted, Luca felt his pulse quicken. They had reached the door to the first of the private suites, and opening it, he drew her into the seclusion of the room beyond.

"One is more sorry for the young man than afraid for oneself," he said, anxious to maintain a role she evidently found attractive. "If he goes about saying he is going to kill people like me, he will be arrested and sent to prison." Georgina was still looking up at him, her eyes shining. Greedily taking her into his arms, Luca kissed her hard on the lips.

Yousouri Pasha heaved his corpulent body up and made his way across the room to the prince's side. The other guests withdrew a little at his approach to allow the two men a degree of privacy, though Yousouri knew that, for all their apparent disinterest, they would strain to hear every word.

"And so?" the prince said to him quietly. "You delivered your warning?"

"I delivered the warning. Whether d'Este will heed it or not is another matter. For the moment I think he is too busy to concern himself with so mundane a business as a threat to his life."

The prince took a long suck on his hookah and passed the coiled pipe across to his guest. "He would be wise to take precautions. Rashid is no simple desert youth."

"I explained the close link to Your Highness." Yousouri put the pipe to his mouth and drew deeply on the smoke. "Yet I doubt if he realizes the danger."

"Then you will take precautions?" the old man queried.

"Yes, such as I can. Rashid must certainly be thwarted, at least while he is on Egyptian soil. As to what happens afterward—"

"You are right," the prince agreed. "I have no love for this Italian. Whatever these fools may think," he gave a contemptuous glance at the rest of the room, "I wish to see the British out of our country forever—but I do not wish simply to replace them with Mussolini's governors."

"Nevertheless, we do not wish to anger them needlessly, and the British themselves would give us no peace if d'Este was killed."

"Then you had best see he is not," the prince answered. "Find Rashid if you can and lock him up until d'Este has left the country, but take care you treat him well. I will not have a kinsman of mine ill-used as though he were a common criminal, and Rashid is fighting for a cause many of us believe in."

"His Majesty's instructions are similar to your own, Highness. It shall be as you ask."

Jacquetta had lost count of the number of times she had stumbled and fallen during the past half hour. For what seemed like an eternity, she had been clawing her way up the slope of a hill, the wind tearing at her. There had been no such hill anywhere within sight when the dust clouds had closed around her, but there could be no doubt now that the ground was rising steeply.

She slipped and fell heavily once more, dragging at Balbo's reins, causing him to toss his head and squeal. If she could keep him with her, she might stand a better chance of making her way back when the storm eased. She heaved herself to her feet. The heat and exertion had given her an appalling thirst, and her eyes, mouth, and nostrils were caked with sand, so that she was forced to drag herself along, half blind, while the dirt caught chokingly in her throat. According to her watch, she had been lost for two hours, and she doubted if she could last much longer. The realization that she must have wandered far off her intended course had all but drained her remaining willpower.

Her repeated falls had torn her hands to shreds on the sharp rocks that littered the surface of the desert and the spines and thorns of the tough scrub plants. She was thankful that she was wearing leather riding boots and breeches. Without them she would have given up long ago.

Abruptly, the terrain flattened out, and Jacquetta pushed forward with relief. She had no idea of how high she had climbed or of how steep the descent might be, she was only thankful to be released from the desperate uphill struggle. She encountered a shallow slope, and she began to follow it, fighting the savage gusts of wind that were strong enough to knock her from her feet.

When she had progressed a few hundred yards, she found that her descent had brought some shelter. Wiping the dirt from her eyes, she saw that in front of her lay a wide valley. Her heart sank as she gazed down at it. The far side was very largely obscured by long fingers of sand blowing off the ground, but from what she could make out, there was more of a gorge than a valley in that direction, with high, nearly sheer walls of rock occasionally split by sharp vertical fissures. There would certainly be no escape there.

To her left the valley flattened into what appeared to be an endless void of dunes and sand drifts, across which the dust was driving. The very emptiness frightened her, making her feel lost and hopeless.

To her right the floor of the valley narrowed and the sides grew steeper. At least there would be some shelter there, and there was a faint chance that she might find water. Scrambling down the hillside, she began to make her way up the valley and into the gorge.

Once on level ground she found it possible to ride again. Provided the wind dropped by morning and she was able to hold out through the night, she decided there was a fair chance that she might be spotted by a search party or an airplane.

As she neared the start of the gorge, she realized that the cliffs were higher than she had thought. Their crumbling sides split and pierced with cavelike openings, they loomed above her in the swirling dust, drawing gradually closer together until at length she was riding down a deep narrow canyon whose walls rose far above her.

Although there was less wind here, there was still a

great deal of dust and sand being blown in from above or wafting up the pass in both directions. Stones and pieces of rock crashed down from the cliff faces from time to time, alarming her and startling the horse. Her spirits fell again. She felt dead with exhaustion and lack of water, and even the effort of guiding Balbo was almost more than she could manage.

Suddenly the ravine opened out, the walls fell back. Some great geological upheaval of the past had opened a vast amphitheater in the desert floor. There was much more dust and sand in the air here, but Jacquetta could distinguish several smaller, narrow passes opening into the one in which she was riding. The cliff faces of these were all heavily pierced with caves, and in the gloom they had a sinister and unwelcoming appearance.

She had halted at the sight; now she rode on slowly, keeping to the center of the pass, hoping to see a way out on the far side. The ground was littered with old rubbish and the crumbled remains of what had once indeed been dwellings of some sort.

Jacquetta was still wondering what kind of people had lived in so lonely a spot when she saw a movement near the dark mouth of one of the nearby caves. Her heart leaped in fear, and she spurred her horse onward. As she did so, a wild, tattered figure sprang out at her from behind a heap of rocks and made a grab at the reins.

She let out a scream, and Balbo shied away from the ragged creature and made a break for one of the nearby ravines. From every cave and hole, more figures appeared, leaping down from the rocks and swarming toward her. More hands reached out, clutching for her. The horse reared and snorted, and for one terrible second Jacquetta thought she was about to fall. Hideous faces leered at her through the dust, their features distorted repulsively it seemed to her blurred vision. Maimed, fingerless hands waved in front of her eyes, agile cripples hopped across the ground waving their stumps from beneath the rags that bound them. Shrill cries resounded dimly above the noise of the wind.

Jerking Balbo around, she made a vain attempt to get back down the gorge the way she had come, but the creatures were too many for her. Blocking her path, they drove her back with flailing arms. Jacquetta struggled to control the horse and force him to charge through the mob, but his strength and rising fear were too great, and in panic he swerved aside and raced blindly around along the valley wall among the refuse and broken hovels.

An opening in the cliff face loomed ahead amid the storm, and seizing her only chance, she steered Balbo for it, urging him on past the figures at the entrance. The way was only a little less wide than the path she had originally come down, and she prayed frantically that it would prove to be a way out. She could hear the sounds of the chase close behind as the inhabitants of the caves hurried in pursuit.

Balbo gave a sudden start as they rounded a bend in the canyon. In the dust they had all but run into a horse and rider coming down the pass toward them. At the sight of the tall hooded and cloaked figure, Jacquetta's nerve broke. Screaming with terror and lashing out with her free arm, she tried to force a way between the rider and the sheer wall of the canyon.

The newcomer was too quick for her. As she drew level with him, he reached across and grasped her reins. Jacquetta cried out and beat furiously at his hand with her fists, but the iron grip did not relax. She collapsed, sobbing, onto her horse's neck.

Georgina Curtis responded to Luca with a readiness that surprised and gratified him. Pressing her open mouth against his, she kissed him long and passionately, her body pressing urgently against his own. His excitement flared as his hands caressed her back and fondled the soft curves of her bottom. He could feel her thighs close against him and the pressure of her breasts on his chest.

Luca was aware of his own body stiffening with desire as her passion aroused him. His heart beating swiftly with anticipation, he drew her over to a wide, silk-spread couch in a window that was shielded by half-closed drapes.

Drawing the curtains, he lay beside her on the couch in the dim light that came through the stained glass. Their hands explored each other's body, touching and stroking, their hunger removing all barriers between them. Unfastening her dress, he let his hands roam over her warm, naked back, feeling the play of the muscles beneath the velvet-soft skin.

At that very moment, to his fury and surprise, there came a loud tap at the door. "Baron d'Este," a voice called. "Baron d'Este—please come quickly. A messenger from the embassy has arrived. You are needed urgently."

"All right, all right, I am coming!" Luca swore viciously under his breath. Georgina was already sitting up, hastily doing up her dress and tidying herself.

"Come quickly, baron!" the voice called again.

"Yes, yes, I will, damn you!" Luca shouted back. He stood up and helped Georgina to her feet. "I am sorry," he said. "Why do these things always happen at exactly the wrong moment? There will be other times, I promise you."

Putting her face up to his, she gave him a hard, quick kiss on the mouth. "Lots of times," she grinned as she checked her makeup with a vanity mirror. "Although," she gave him a sly chuckle, "it would have been fun in a real palace. You must go and leave me here. It will be quicker for you and look better for me. The prince will send me home in a car."

Her self-possession was truly incredible, Luca thought, as he hurried from the room after one final embrace. Most women in similar circumstances would have been angry or upset, very possibly both. Yet Georgina was able to sit down and repair her makeup as though nothing out of the ordinary had happened. Such coolness and imperturbability on the surface, such fire and passion underneath. What more could a man ask for in a mistress?

An anxious major-domo was waiting outside. "The messenger is in the main entrance hall, baron," he said in English with a deferential bow. "It appears that your wife has become lost on her ride. There are fears for her safety in the khamsin."

Once again Luca swore under his breath as he followed the major-domo. It was ironic that his wife should succeed in thwarting his plans at the very moment of success. He found himself vengefully hoping that Jacquetta would not be found. His marriage had long since ceased to bring him pleasure, and nowadays he was conscious only of its inconveniences.

After listening to the courier's message—no more than

the information that Jacquetta has failed to return after her ride and that there was now a severe dust storm blowing in the vicinity—he left immediately by car for the embassy.

○ ○ ○

On board *Caterina*, a long, dark line like a smudge of dirt on the horizon appeared shortly before four o'clock. They were still 180 miles short of Cairo. As they drew nearer, the men on the flight deck saw it grow until it extended directly across their line of sight. The massive storm clouds became more distinct, and the slowly sinking sun tinged their crests with ominous fire. The crew had experienced similar storms and were only too well aware of the battering the aircraft would receive if they were forced to descend.

"What's the last word from the met. people?" Desmond asked after a while. "Tell them I want the exact speed and course of the storm, Ralph, as well as the strength and direction of the winds."

"Looks to me as though it's heading almost due west," Frazer muttered as Kendrick began tapping out morse on his key, "in which case it may be missing Cairo altogether."

"We'll know that when we get the weather reports," Desmond replied shortly. "There's no sense arguing about it beforehand." Even the simplest discussion led to bickering between them nowadays, it seemed. Frazer had an uncanny knack of putting his back up.

"Storm moving west-southwest at approximately thirty-five knots on a front estimated to be one hundred miles wide," Ralph Kendrick informed him. "Wind speeds with the front averaging fifty knots plus, with gusts up to seventy." He bent over the charts on the table beside him. "Assuming it holds this course for the next hour, we should be able to fly over it and land at Cairo without any particular difficulty. The met. office estimates the limit of air turbulence at 12,000 feet."

Frazer's face flushed with triumph.

"Very well then," Desmond said to Frazer. "Go and ask Sandy to warn the passengers that we'll be climbing to high altitude shortly. He'll want to make sure they all have sweets to suck and blankets."

The copilot's face darkened with annoyance. "You could put it out over the intercom loudspeakers."

"And I could send you off to tell Sandy quietly, which is how I'm going to do it," Desmond answered. For a second the first officer appeared about to make a retort, but the look in Desmond's eyes made him bite it back.

When Frazer had left the deck, Ralph Kendrick let out a whistle of amazement. "I don't know how you take it from that man. He's got the biggest chip on his shoulder of anyone I've ever met, and he unloads it all on the rest of us."

"I know, Ralph," Desmond said, "but he's the only copilot I've got, and we'll have to live with him until we can find another."

"And in the meantime he's down below kicking hell out of poor Sandy."

As Ralph had predicted, when Frazer returned he began at once to complain about the purser's behavior. "He's useless, that boy," he said spitefully. "The least upset in the normal routine, and he goes into a flap. He had no idea of what to do down there."

"Maybe it's just you who puts him into a flap, Ken. He seems fine to the rest of us," Ralph said, with an edge to his voice.

"That's because I'm not soft on him like you are," Frazer snapped back.

"Break it up, you two!" Desmond told them. "We're all tired after this last couple of days; let's not take it out on each other. Shouldn't that news bulletin be on soon, Ralph? It's almost four o'clock."

"Coming up in a couple of minutes, skipper," Kendrick replied. "I'm tuned in already."

"What about the storm?" Desmond had his eyes on the dark clouds ahead. "Will that cause interference?"

"Uh, uh, the storm's nonelectrical. Here we go." He flicked the intercom switch, and they heard the familiar hiss as the loudspeaker circuits warmed up.

There was a crackle of static, and then the voice of the announcer came over the air. "This is the Overseas Service of the BBC. Here is the British Empire and for-

eign news: Drastic measures have been taken in Czechoslovakia to suppress Slovak separatism. The autonomous
Slovak government has been dismissed, and Czech troops
are mobilizing."

○ ○ ○

Arm in arm, Siegert Wienzman and her father were
strolling round the Piazza di San Marco. It was chilly,
the Venetian sky was overcast, and puddles from rain
earlier in the afternoon still remained. Most of the tourists had returned to their hotels for dinner and with them
had departed the seed sellers, the pavement artists, and
other itinerant traders. To the two refugees, the scene
could not have been more beautiful.

After their harrowing experience at the frontier, Siegret
had almost refused to believe that the nightmare might be
over. To be able to walk about freely in the streets without listening for the sounds of pursuing feet or hearing
the jibes and insults of the Nazi bullies was an incredible
joy. She was intoxicated with her new freedom and her
release from fear. Grasping her father's hand, she
danced round the square, bubbling like a child.

For David Wienzman, there could be no surer proof
that he had acted rightly than the change their escape
had brought about in his daughter. In the space of a few
hours, a fair measure of her former spirit had returned,
and the color was returning to her bruised face.

"Remember, we are still not completely safe," he cau-
tioned her. "We still have to reach America."

"Yes, I know. But papa, Dr. Farenzi said he was sure
it was going to be all right about the visa."

Immediately on their arrival, the professor had telephoned his old friend in Rome. Farenzi was delighted to
hear of their escape and assured him that he had already contacted the American embassy authorities and
they had expressed their willingness to grant a visa. "Of
course, there are formalities to go through; it may take a
little time—but you will both stay with me in my house."

"All the same," the professor repeated his warning to
Siegret, "we must still be on our guard. If the Nazis
knew we were here, they might persuade the Italians to
send us back to Germany."

"Oh, they could not do that." Siegert's face went pale. "Oh, say they could not do it, papa!"

Her father felt instantly contrite at the effect of his words. "There, there," he squeezed her shoulders. "We are too small fish for them to bother about, and even if they did, they could never find us now."

His daughter relaxed. "Don't ever talk about going back again, papa," she said in a hushed voice. "I couldn't bear it. It would be the end of us both." They stared at one another for a moment, and then with a laugh Siegret shed the seriousness that had fallen on her, and they walked on. "Papa," she said when they had reached the other side of the piazza and were preparing to return to their hotel, "if we really are safe, can't we stay here for a few days? There's so much to see and do, and if we go to America, we may never have a chance again."

"Stay here, in Venice, you mean, and not go to Rome?" her father asked.

"Only for two or three days. It would be like a holiday. Oh, do say we can, papa."

The professor smiled at her. "Two days will be enough? You're sure?"

"Yes, yes! Oh, papa, thank you! I'm so happy!" Flinging her arms about him she burst into tears.

Two days will make no difference, her father thought as he held her close and patted her hair. He would telephone Farenzi and warn him of the delay. It would be good for the child to rest; and tomorrow was Sunday, anyway. They were safe enough here in Venice; there was no need to worry.

○ ○ ○

The horseman made no move to touch Jacquetta, but neither did he relax his hold upon her reins. Instead, he shouted in Arabic at the pursuing mob. Gusts of wind were shrieking over the canyon walls, but his voice sounded clearly above the noise. A chorus of cries and shouts rose in reply, but the man shook his head decisively and repeated his words, letting go of the reins of his own horse as he did so and unslinging the rifle he carried on his shoulder.

"You are safe now; they will not come near you."

Hearing him speak English, she looked up with a start. The man bending over her horse wore a loose white, dust-stained cloak and a Bedouin headdress bound with black braided tassels. To protect himself against the sand, he had covered his face with a fold of black cloth, but he had pulled this aside to speak, revealing a young, handsome face with finely drawn aquiline features. He looked so proud and fierce that she felt afraid to speak.

"You are safe," he repeated. "Who are you, and what are you doing out here in this wind?" His voice was authoritative, with surprisingly little accent.

"I was riding and lost my way," she answered in English when she found her voice. To allow him to believe she was a British subject might be more sensible. "I am staying at the embassy in Cairo," she added, in the hope of impressing on him that friends would be searching for her.

There was another man behind the rider who now pressed forward, saying something urgently, glancing at Jacquetta. He was a smaller, less attractive man, with quick, shifty eyes. Dismissing him with a few words, the rider turned back to her.

"Come with me," he said. "I am going back to the city, and I will show you the way. If you remain out here, you will certainly die." Releasing her reins, he handed her a leather water flask, and Jacquetta drank greedily. "Ride between us," he ordered. "I will keep these creatures away."

The mob gave way before them as they emerged into the circle of cliffs. There were more than two hundred of these people, she guessed, of all ages, crowded into the caves and passages. Now that she dared look at them properly, she realized that everyone of them was deformed or crippled.

"Who are they?" she asked her rescuer. Even with his protection, they still inspired her with fear and loathing. The servant evidently felt the same way, for he rode close behind them. "Who are they, and why do they live out here?"

The man looked at her with scorn. "Can you not guess?" he said. "They are lepers, and they live here because they have been driven from the city and from their villages.

There is nowhere else for them to go except for these holes, so they live here like rats."

Jacquetta shuddered. "You will keep them away, won't you?" she cried, for the lepers were showing signs of coming closer. "You won't let them touch me. Can't you frighten them off with your gun?"

Her companion did not answer. Putting a hand inside his robes, he produced a small leather pouch, and taking out a handful of coins, he flung them in a wide arc behind the crowd. At once they scattered, scrabbling in the sand and scuffling with one another over their finds. Pausing only to toss another handful, the rider continued across the center of the clearing and into a cleft in the far wall.

"That is easier than using a gun," he said, "and they can give money to their relatives to buy food for them."

Jacquetta tried to thank him, but he brushed her words aside.

"We must ride quickly," he said. "Put this over your face; it will keep out the sand." He handed her his black head cloth. "It is two hours or more to the city by the route I must travel. There are men hunting me on the desert road."

Jacquetta accepted the cloth gratefully. It was wonderfully fine and light, woven with gold thread and perfumed with some scent she did not recognize. At his words, however, some of her alarm returned.

"Who are you?" she asked, "and why are people hunting you? Are you a bandit?"

"I am called Rashid al Senussi," the man answered. "I am not a bandit, but men hunt me all the same."

Jacquetta gave an audible whimper, but thanks to the wind and the clothes they were wearing, it went unnoticed by Rashid and the Egyptian.

For the whole of the past year, since she and Luca had left Libya, they had known of the young sheik's threat to revenge the deaths of his father and sister. For a while, in Rome, they had lived under armed guard, in case Rashid should be capable of seeking them out and killing them, even in Italy.

Luca had never shown the slightest fear. So great was his contempt for the Arabs, whom he had never fought except when the odds were overwhelmingly on his side,

that he refused to take the assassination threat seriously.
On the contrary, she suspected, he rather enjoyed describing himself as a marked man—as though this brought him additional glamour in the eyes of the world.

Even the news that Rashid's men had systematically hunted down and killed a large percentage of the soldiers and airmen who had taken part in the raid of his father's village had not worried Luca unduly. When the security police had suggested that it might be unwise to spend a month in Cairo before taking up his new appointment in Washington, he had dismissed their advice.

Jacquetta's feeling toward this desert prince who so desperately wanted Luca dead had been mixed from the start. Although Luca himself had been reticent about the reasons that had sparked off Rashid's desire for revenge, she had learned the details from other members of the governor's staff, and what she was told had horrified her. When she had faced Luca with the truth, he had brushed her accusations aside, claiming that he had acted for reasons of state, which a woman could not be expected to grasp.

Now, here she was, her very life in the hands of Rashid al Senussi. Yet, if he was to learn who she was, she might be in greater danger.

Wild plans flashed through her head of making a break for freedom when they reached the edge of the desert or of trying to seize the rifle he carried negligently on one shoulder. There was a faint hope that he might run into the men who were looking for him, whom she presumed were the Egyptian or British authorities, although the young sheik appeared too competent and assured to be captured easily.

They rode in silence, heads bowed against the wind. How Rashid could find the way in such trackless sands, where the dust blotted out all features in the landscape and had shuffled the dunes over the face of the desert, she did not know. Occasionally he paused to confer with the Egyptian, and once he made a sudden, unexpected detour back on their tracks after he had climbed alone to the crest of a low rise and scanned the ground ahead. Jacquetta guessed that his unexplained maneuver was connected with the need to avoid interception.

She was at first surprised and finally a little annoyed

to discover how little interest her rescuers displayed in her. Apart from turning his head a few times to check on her riding ability, Rashid scarcely looked at her. His eyes restlessly searched the desert, the hawklike leanness of his young face emphasized by the barrenness of the land.

She felt ashamed to recall how feeble and weak she must have seemed; her fear and loathing of the lepers must have made her ridiculous in his eyes, justifying the contempt he displayed for her presence. Jacquetta had never before met a true Arab from the deep sands. Her previous acquaintance had been only with the degenerated tribes of the town, and she was unprepared for the concentrated self-discipline, the sheer physical and mental toughness that singled out these men. She felt overpowered in Rashid's utterly self-reliant, ruthlessly masculine world.

Toward five o'clock she realized that the wind, which had been dropping steadily for the past hour, had virtually ceased. They were riding more easily now, the horses' hoofs thudding monotonously on the packed sand, on what appeared to be a path of some sort. The sun was sinking, the coolness a marked contrast to the suffocating heat of the afternoon. Shadows crept out from the sides of the dunes, carving the scenery into strange geometric shapes that had been sculpted by wind.

At length, she began to distinguish the squat outlines of the Pyramids. like regimental toys against the horizon, and then, quite suddenly, she saw, about a mile distant, the beginnings of the cultivated land.

Rashid reined in his horse. "Do you see that building ahead?" Shading her eyes against the dying rays of the sun, Jacquetta saw a square white blockhouse standing beside a road. "That is a police guard post on the road between Fayum and Cairo," he said. "The men there will take you back to the city."

Jacquetta's heart stood still at the thought of what was going to happen when her identity was revealed to him, but Rashid's next words removed her fears. "It is not possible for me to go with you," he said, "since the men in the post probably have orders to arrest me, but you cannot lose yourself now."

Her relief was so great that she was profuse in her gratitude. Rashid cut her short. "I have been honored to have been able to help you," he said dryly. "Farewell, and take care you do not ride alone in the desert again. I may not always be on hand to rescue you."

○ ○ ○

Frazer, Kendrick, and Sandy Everett were discussing the implications of the news from Czechoslovakia. The purser had returned to the flight deck and was sitting on the radio spares box behind the copilot's seat. All three were drinking coffee brought by Andy Draper at Frazer's request.

Desmond listened to their conversation with half an ear. With *Caterina* only a few miles from the edge of the storm zone, the ground beneath them had become hazed with dust. At times the line of the river and the green strip of cultivation that clung to it were completely obscured. He was flying on manual, concentrating on the feel of the controls, alert for the first signs of turbulence that would mean the time had come to climb above 12,000 feet.

"What do you think, skipper, will Hitler go in?" Sandy appealed to him.

"It'll be war if he does," Frazer put in before Desmond could reply. The copilot was making a visual check of the instrument panel as he spoke. "Starboard fuel tank is nearly dry. Shall I trim the other tanks?

Desmond nodded.

"I don't see Chamberlain taking the country to war over Czechoslovakia," Kendrick replied to Frazer's remark. "He didn't at Munich, and anyway there's nothing we could do to help them."

"We're preparing for war some day soon," Frazer continued. "You heard what it said on the news. 'Expansion of the Fleet; air raid precautions; plans to evacuate children from London; 250,000 pounds a day being spent on aircraft for the R.A.F. conscription.' What's all that for if it's not for war with Germany? Don't you agree, skipper?"

"You're probably right. I don't know," Desmond said, though as he spoke he knew this was untrue. He thought of what he had heard and seen during the past six months and of the letter from the Air Ministry. However unwillingly, Britain was moving toward war. Even so, he could not bring himself to admit it.

The aircraft trembled and dropped sickeningly through a hundred feet or more as they struck an air pocket. Loose equipment rattled across the cabin floor, and Sandy cursed as hot coffee spilled down his uniform trousers.

"You'd better go back to the passengers," Desmond called to Sandy over his shoulder. "I'm going to take us up above this, but it may be rough for a while."

Opening the throttle to counter the fall in speed as the plane's nose lifted, he set her into a steady climb. All sight of the desert below had vanished, covered by a thick barrier of black clouds shot with streaks of lighter brown.

"Must be one hell of a storm down there," Ralph shouted above the engine noise, watching the cloud base receding beneath them. "They say a wind like that can strip the paint clean off a car in a couple of hours."

"Or choke an engine within a few minutes," Desmond suggested, watching the needle swing round on the altimeter. He swallowed to clear his ears. Twelve thousand feet. This would do.

The weather report had said the storm front was one hundred miles deep. If they were flying at 165 miles per hour, they would be clear to descend in forty minutes, by which time they would be only another fifteen minutes' flying time from Cairo. For all Frazer's casual dismissal of the khamsin as weather one could fly above, that left them little room for maneuvering. At low altitude, the winds could play some nasty tricks.

Desmond realized suddenly how tired he was. He had had little sleep the previous night. The shock of Ian Thorne's death and its subsequent complications, Kendrick's nerves, and Ken Frazer's ill temper, to say nothing of the behavior of passengers like Stewart Curtis, had all taken their toll. He half wished that he did not have to attend the ball in the evening, but remembering that Laura Hartman would be there, he changed his mind.

Fortunately, *Caterina* encountered little more turbulence as she skimmed over the storm front. Once or twice she was buffeted by small air pockets, but Desmond caught her smartly and lifted her back. Almost to the minute of his prediction, they reached the limit of the clouds and began a slow descent preparatory to making a final approach when Cairo came in sight. The Nile, wider than at any previous point, as it neared the end of its four-thousand-mile journey, flowed between green and fertile farms that were sliced by tiny irrigation channels, a sharp contrast to the desert that began where the irrigated land left off and ran on as far as the eye could see.

"ETA Cairo, twelve minutes," Frazer reported. "We should be able to see it by now."

"Coming down to 2,000 feet," Desmond said as the altimeter wound slowly back.

"Speed down to 140 knots," he ordered, and Frazer eased the throttle levers back.

A descending airplane with a nose-down attitude would automatically pick up speed as she came down and, unless corrected, this would bring them in too fast for a safe touchdown.

"Cairo acknowledges our ETA," Kendrick reported from the radio desk. "Winds twenty knots from the southwest. Visibility clear."

"Then why can't we see them?" Frazer asked. "Christ! What's that?" Ahead of *Caterina,* at the same altitude but a little to starboard, a small dense cloud had appeared out of nowhere. With incredible speed it mushroomed outward, sucking up dust from the desert surface far below and spewing it into the sky.

At once they were upon it, and the aircraft was enveloped in an opaque yellow cloud of swirling sand. "Hold tight!" Desmond shouted as they felt the giant hand of the pressure bulge lift the flying boat dizzily upward as though it was no more than a chip of wood. "Give me full revs!" he called urgently, struggling to hold *Caterina* against the fierce crosscurrents. Frazer slammed the throttle levers open again, holding them hard against the stops to ensure that every ounce of power came through.

Engines screaming, Desmond banked the aircraft steeply to port, seeking the safety of calm air once more. In a dust bubble of this intensity, it would be only a matter of minutes before choked valves and air intakes left them with multiple power failure. Within seconds, however, a monstrous air pocket opened beneath them, and the plane fell four hundred feet with stomach-wrenching speed.

A red light glowed on the instrument panel in front of him. "Number three engine overheating," Frazer called out. "Shall I reduce power?"

"No!" Desmond shouted. "Keep it on full!" Their best

hope lay in breaking free from the grip of the pressure spiral before they suffered serious damage. The flying boat was taking a terrific hammering. Again he made a tight banking turn to try to bring them clear. Another air pocket struck them and then a third, and this time the fall was truly frightening. Before their horrified eyes, the needle of the altimeter wound back to less than a thousand feet.

Another warning light signaled a second engine overheating to danger point. Props clawing at the air, *Caterina* fought to shake herself clear of the tenacious squall. Again they fell, as the pressure vacuum snatched the support from around the plane.

The nose dipped violently, threatening to throw them into a spin. Hauling back on the controls, Desmond's eye was on the altimeter: 700 feet, 650, 600—there were seconds in which to pull the flying boat out of the dive— 550 feet, 500—the jerking needle was slowing—480— *Caterina* was responding to his weight on the stick—450 feet—the needle was hovering, the nose was coming up. She was leveling off.

So thick was the dust that it was only by watching the instruments, the artificial horizon, and the altimeter that it was possible to tell if the plane was flying on a straight course. The sky was the color of pea soup. Both remaining engine temperature warning lights came on simultaneously. The next two or three minutes would decide whether *Caterina* was to be brought down by engine failure due to dust choking or fire. Unless, Desmond thought grimly, another air pocket like the last one dashed them to the desert floor. He was climbing steeply, but, with less than five hundred feet beneath them, there was little chance of pulling *Caterina* out of a spin, and he dared not reduce his engine speed and lessen the fire risk until he had gained some height.

Frazer was white with strain, his eyes glued to the altimeter dial and the temperature gauges. Every few seconds he made a quick glance out of the windows to check the engines for smoke, although in the murk it was impossible to see beyond the inboard motors.

Then, as if a curtain had been pulled away, the men on the flight deck found themselves blinking in the sunlight.

"Jesus!" Frazer wiped a hand over his face, "What on

earth was that?" He had relaxed his grip on the throttles and was easing them back.

"Don't shut them off more than a quarter way, Ken," Desmond said. "All four engines are probably so choked with muck after flying in that dust they're probably just waiting for an excuse to die. I'd rather risk a fire at the moment."

"Understood." Frazer adjusted the settings. "There's Cairo coming up," he said, pointing ahead. Fortunately, their wild gyrations had thrown them only a few degrees off course. "What caused that squall back there?" he repeated.

Desmond shook his head. "I don't know," he said. "It's some kind of rare pressure phenomenon. For no reason at all, the sky just seems to bubble like that, carrying the sand to immense heights. You find them in the Sudan and in Jordan in the desert beyond Lake Tiberius, but I've never met one as strong as that.

"Ralph," he called out, "will you go see if Sandy needs any help? The passengers must be pretty shaken up after that little experience." There was no reply from the radio desk, and he strained around to look over his shoulder. Ralph Kendrick was ashen-faced, staring rigidly out of the porthole next to him. His mouth was working convulsively, his eyes distended.

"Ralph!" Desmond called sharply again, the radio operator took hold of himself and turned to face the captain. "Did you hear what I said? Go down and help Sandy."

"Aye, aye, skipper," Ralph whispered hoarsely; he rose wearily to his feet. "I'm sorry. I felt a bit sick back there for a second."

"Did you see his face?" Frazer demanded unnecessarily as soon as he was gone. "He's cracked up—his nerves are gone."

"Maybe," Desmond answered coldly. "We shall see."

"But you can't let him go on like that," Frazer persisted. "He isn't fit to fly."

"I'll decide that, not you," Desmond replied. "Keep your mind on your own job and let me deal with the crew."

Biting his lip with rage, Frazer turned away, his knuckles clenched white on the bars of the control yoke.

A short while later Ralph was back, the traces of the spasm gone. "Luckily Sandy and Draper had them all strapped in and the breakables stowed, on the off chance that we might hit trouble. I think everyone was more surprised than anything else. The Johnsons' child was crying, and Mrs. Johnson was upset. There were a few glasses smashed in the galley. Mr. Curtis's papers were scattered all over his cabin, and he's cross about that."

"Somehow I can live with that," Desmond said. "OK. Thanks, Ralph. Call Cairo air traffic control and tell them we are coming in."

II

Cairo

5

By *radio*: 2030 hrs GMT. SATURDAY 11 MARCH 1939.
IMPERIAL AIRWAYS LONDON TO BRANCH OF-
FICE LA GUARDIA MARINE TERMINAL NEW
YORK. IMPERIAL AIRWAYS FLIGHT 109 G-ADHO
CATERINA DELAYED 24 HOURS AT CAIRO FOR
SERVICE AND FAULT CHECK. WILL CUT OUT
ATHENS STOPOVER TO MAKE UP TIME. TRANS-
ATLANTIC FLIGHT WILL DEPART AS SCHED-
ULED AND ETA NEW YORK REMAINS UN-
CHANGED AT 1600 hrs EST FRIDAY 17 MARCH.
END.

In Cairo, it was the custom of Imperial Airways to
book their passengers into Shepheard's Hotel. This was by
no means always easy. During high season the hotel was
overcrowded, yet so great was the attraction of the famous hotel that people were often prepared to pay simply
to be allowed to spend the night on the couches in the
lounges.

Luxury hotel, fashionable rendezvous, gentlemen's club,
Shepheard's was the unquestioned center of Cairo's
social world. To many people, it was the first place they
wanted to see, the only place they wanted to stay.

"You wouldn't believe the trouble we had getting you
in this time," Keith Payne, the company's local manager,
said when Desmond came ashore after their landing at
Kasr el Nil, just north of the city. "It's this blasted wedding.
The world and his wife have come to Cairo this week;
they've actually got two kings staying at Shepheard's—
two! Can you imagine? There's so much bowing and
scraping and 'Yes, Your Majesty' and 'No, Your Majesty'
that no ordinary person can get a look in."

"What about the bullion?" Desmond asked. "What happens to that while we're here?"

The manager frowned. "We were going to leave it on board under guard, but when you said the plane would need servicing, we decided that was too risky, so it's being transferred to the army barracks under cover of dark.

"We heard about your trouble down at Shambe," he added. "I'm sorry that had to happen."

"Have you any idea what the company wants to do next about it?" Desmond asked. Keith Payne could be a bit of a pedantic old woman at times, but he possessed a shrewd insight into the minds of Imperial's management back in Britain.

"There's to be an inquiry held by the airline when you reach Southampton," he told Desmond. "I've been instructed to let you know that officially. Unofficially—"

"Go on, tell me the worst," Desmond said.

"Unofficially then," Payne went on, "some of the top men see this as a chance to crucify you. On the other hand, they are short of pilots to fly the transatlantic run, so the general feeling is that you may come out of it relatively intact. For the present, that is, and so long as your passengers and crew are prepared to support you."

The formalities at the pier head complete, Desmond left *Caterina* to be unloaded and then towed off to the service wharf. The rest of the crew had already gone their separate ways, and now Ralph Kendrick took his leave shamefacedly.

"We should have a talk," Desmond said to him, "and see if we can get things sorted out. Why don't you drop by my room before I go off to this party tonight? And don't forget I'm depending on you for the race tomorrow, okay?"

"OK," Ralph agreed unhappily. "I'll come by at about seven." And he left without another word.

In the taxi on his way up to the center of Cairo, Desmond thought over what he had learned from Keith Payne. From the sound of it, the inquiry in England on Thorne's death could be the breaking point of his career. Desmond was under no illusions about the lengths to which his enemies among the Imperial management would be prepared to go to get rid of him. They would never have a chance like this again—and they would make the most of it.

His job was threatened, perhaps his flying career—and none of it need have happened, he thought savagely, if Frazer had bothered to do his work properly. If he managed to come out of the inquiry still in command of a plane, that young man was going to go.

The familiar sights and sounds of his favorite city drained away some of his anger and tension. The city's night life was just beginning. In an hour's time, he would have to set off for the palace. At least, Desmond reflected, he could put aside all the worries and decisions for the next forty-eight hours and enjoy himself in Cairo.

○ ○ ○

Rintlen's interview with Superintendent Hans Meyer of the Saint Veit police had not gone well. In fact, he thought as he sat over a glass of schnapps at the town's sole hotel, it had not gone at all. The big policeman had been apologetic for the unfortunate error that had resulted in the Wienzman father and daughter being granted permits to cross the frontier, but he had been careful to point out that his own part in the business had been entirely covered by the orders of his superiors in the various ministries.

No one, Meyer had assured him, could be more anxious than he to secure the arrest and conviction of the enemies of the Reich. Had he known that Wienzman was needed for questioning, he would not have had the smallest hesitation in detaining him. As it was—Meyer shrugged. It was not his fault that Rintlen's call had come too late to enable the train to be interrupted. Of course, it would have helped if they had known which route the fleeing couple were intent on using, thus avoiding the delay that had ensued when the more westerly passes had been contacted first. But this had been a legitimate assumption, based on the knowledge that the majority of escapers crossed as near to the Swiss frontier as possible.

Rintlen had never visited the Austrian mountain province before; his experience had been confined to the major towns of Germany, with a brief spell in Vienna immediately after the Anschluss, and he was finding the sturdy independence of the people a shock after the easily cowed Berliners. Meyer, he had no doubt, was concealing something. Whether the police chief had actively assisted the Wienzmans or was simply covering his own inefficiency was impossible to say, but so long as he stuck to his facts and put the blame on the officials in the government ministries, he could not be touched.

Rintlen swallowed another mouthful of schnapps and signaled the hovering waiter to refill the empty glass. The worst feature of the affair was that he had nothing worthwhile to report to Heydrich, and the chief of the S.D. was not a man who took failure lightly. Rintlen had an instinct that this case was not one in which any failure or half measures would be acceptable. If the stakes were really as high as he suspected, Wienzman had to be tracked down—or he, Paul Rintlen, might suffer in his place.

He tried to decide what to do. The long flight up in the plane and the interview with Meyer had left him tired, and the cold air had sapped his strength. He ought to go on into Italy and search for Wienzman. He took out a map of the border area and the northern Italian cities and opened it on the table.

The railway line the professor and his daughter had taken crossed over the border at Tarvisio hard by the Yugoslavian border and then wound through the Venetian countryside as far as Treviso. Here the two tracks divided; one line ran eastward to Trieste, another west to Rome, a third line continued south for twenty miles or so until it came to Venice.

The more Rintlen gazed at the map the more certain he was that Venice must be his starting point. Not only was it a convenient day's journey from the border, making it an ideal place for the escapees to rest after their recent ordeals, but it was a seaport, with excellent connections by rail and road to other parts of the country. It was highly likely that the Wienzmans would remain in the city until they could board a ship to take them on to another country. Or they would make for Rome. Rintlen was inclined to dismiss the possibility of their taking the westerly route toward Switzerland. If that had been their intention, he reasoned, they would have attempted to cross over straight from Austria.

There were other problems to be faced. The first and most important was the difficulty of finding and identifying the Wienzmans. The only available photographs were either of the passport type or scaled-up extractions from group portraits, and none were of good enough quality to be of any real use. There was a strong chance that the two Jews would have registered in a hotel under an assumed name or even taken rooms in a private house as paying guests.

What was really needed was a full-scale police hunt using all resources. Street identity checks, hotel and boarding house searches, and checks at every port, railway station, and highway exit. Heydrich, however, had specifically forbidden calling on the Italian authorities for help.

An idea struck him. He replaced the map in his briefcase and drained the remainder of his schnapps. "Here you," he growled at the waiter. "Take the drinks out of this." The money was insufficient to pay his bill, but no innkeeper would dare to bring a complaint against an officer of the S.D. over so small a matter.

He found Meyer in his office. The police chief welcomed him cordially and insisted on Rintlen seating himself so as to catch the warmth of the fire. "How can I be of assistance, Standartenführer?" he asked. "My staff and I await your orders."

Keeping his temper with difficulty, Rintlen answered, "The youth Gerdler who led the attack on the Wienzman girl. You say you have him under arrest."

"Yes, indeed," Meyer responded. "Under the new laws governing racial purity, relations between Aryan and non-Aryan are strictly forbidden—but then I expect you know that, Standartenführer," he said with a trace of irony. "I have Gerdler here in the cells."

"Good. Bring him out. I want to talk to him."

"To Gerdler?" Meyer looked surprised. "I doubt if he will be able to help you. He was certainly no friend of the Wienzmans."

"Nevertheless, I want to speak to him, and quickly," Rintlen snapped. "Have him brought to me at once."

Hans Gerdler, on first sight, proved to be an unprepossessing young man, strongly built, with loutish features. However, Rintlen noticed a gleam of sly cunning in his coarse face.

"Very well, you may leave us," Rintlen said, dismissing Meyer. His deliberately casual tone toward the police chief made a visible impression on Gerdler, who stood watching the newcomer with a mixture of apprehension and admiration.

"Do you know what authority I represent?" Rintlen asked him.

The youth ran his eye swiftly over the black and silver uniform, taking in the unit badges and the stripes. "Yes, Standartenführer," he replied nervously. "Sicherheitsdienst!" He pronounced the name dry-lipped.

Rintlen nodded his approval. "Yes, the S.D. That is correct. And do you know why I am here?"

Gerdler shook his head violently.

"I am here to find out what has become of a man called David Wienzman and his daughter. You know of them at least, I take it."

"Yes, Standartenführer." Gerdler's voice was hardly more than a whisper.

"Very well. It seems that Wienzman left the country in great haste this morning. This may have been because he discovered that he was wanted by the authorities in Berlin, or"—he paused to give weight to his words—"it may have been because a gang of half-wits tried to rape his daughter." He let the last part of the sentence ring out harshly, and the youth wilted in the face of his anger.

"I swear, Standartenführer," he stumbled, "we were only playing with her a little. We didn't know, nobody knew she was wanted. It was just a bit of fun," he ended lamely.

"Possibly," Rintlen said dryly. "The question is, are you prepared to make up for the trouble you have caused us?" He cut short Gerdler's expostulations. "Good. Would you be able to recognize Wienzman and his daughter, even if they were attempting to disguise themselves by wearing different clothes or by cutting their hair, for instance?"

"Certainly, Standartenführer," the boy agreed. "The girl more easily than the old man." And he flushed.

"Excellent." Gerdler was exactly what Rintlen needed. Having experienced the humiliation of his quarry being snatched from him, he would be tireless in his efforts to find her again. "You will return home therefore and meet me here again at nine o'clock tonight, bringing with you ordinary civilian clothes, enough to last you a week, do you understand?"

"Yes, Standartenführer, I mean, no, Standartenführer. What is it you want me to do?" the boy asked desperately.

"I want you to come with me to Italy to search for the couple whom your actions frightened away. You are being offered a chance to perform a special service to the Reich. Do you refuse?" Rintlen demanded.

"No sir, of course not. At nine o'clock I will be here." Drawing himself up hastily, Gerdler saluted, "Heil Hitler."

"Heil Hitler," Rintlen acknowledged with a half-wave of the arm. Now, at least, he reflected as Gerdler hurried out, he had a means of identifying the Wienzmans. It only remained to find them.

○ ○ ○

Laura Hartman and the Kings arrived at Shepheard's while the light of evening still lingered. The sun was slipping below the hills in a brief but spectacular performance, the temperature had eased, and a slight breeze from the north had cleared the dust and lifted the stale atmosphere that had clung to the streets.

The bars and cafés had begun to fill, and the heavy traffic of the day—lorries and carts and jostling, noisy crowds—had given way in the smart districts of El Gezira and the Garden City on the Nile's eastern bank to limousines, taxis, and innumerable horse-drawn garries conveying the wealthy to their evening's enjoyments. From the minarets of the mosques, the wailing cries of the muezzins echoed above the streets, calling the faithful to prayer.

Imperious doormen drove off the peddlers and beggars who surged around the taxi as it drew to a halt at the red-carpeted steps. Efficient clerks entered their names in the register. "What a place," whispered Mr. King to Laura as they went up in the elevator. "Did you see the flags on the roof as we came in? Royal standards! They say there are two monarchs staying here."

"Bulgaria and Albania," his wife snorted derisively. "Hardly among the world's great kingdoms—and one of them has lost his throne, anyway. The staff needn't think they can ignore the rest of us because we have not got titles to our names. I don't hold with them in any case." And she glared severely at the nearest bellboy.

"Now, Sarah," her husband said mildly, "I'm sure we shall be very well taken care of."

"Maybe," Mrs. King responded, "but they might as well understand right away that I won't stand for being treated second best." The elevator came to a halt, and the doors were pulled back. "I guess we separate here," she said to Laura. "You be sure to come and show us your gown before you go; it's not often we see a girl going to a royal ball."

"I thought you didn't approve of monarchs," Harold King reproved her, winking at Laura.

"I don't approve of them, but that doesn't mean the girl shouldn't enjoy herself," his wife replied with conviction.

On her previous stay, Laura had been given a bedroom and bathroom across the passage from the Curtis suite on the third floor, but on this occasion, in order to make room for the royal contingents, the whole of that floor had been cleared and the Curtises were now staying on the second floor, and Laura's rooms opened off the private hall of their suite. Georgina Curtis had not been at the pier to greet her husband when the plane landed, but Laura heard her voice, raised in argument coming from the sitting room.

"Every time I turn my back you're off playing around with a new man," Curtis was shouting angrily. "I'm away for two weeks, and you're so busy with d'Este you haven't even time to come and meet me when I return."

"I was having tea at Prince Suleiman's, if you must know," Georgina snapped back, "and your flight was delayed, so how did I know when it would reach here?"

"You could have found out easily enough," Curtis said furiously. "And I know damn well that Prince Suleiman

is a crony of d'Este's. You were there with him, and the
whole of Cairo knows the kind of tea parties they have at
that palace. First it's a German ski instructor, now it's
this slimy bastard. Well, I've had enough—do you hear?"

Laura slipped into her room. The cause of their quarrel
was familiar to her. It was always a surprise to those who
did not know him well, to learn that Stewart Curtis loved
his wife and was passionately jealous of her frequent
affairs.

Laura had never been able to decide quite what to
make of Georgina Curtis. She invariably treated Laura
with kindness, and at times with generosity. It had been
Georgina who had asked her to go to the ball with them
and had even provided a dress for her to wear. Yet she
was also hard to the point of ruthlessness—a greedy, un-
scrupulous woman who frequently admitted that she had
married Stewart for his money and who made a point of
refusing to accompany him on business trips so that she
could enjoy herself unhindered. In a way, Laura supposed, Stewart Curtis and his wife were well matched.

Leaving his room to go downstairs for a drink in the
Long Bar before the ball, Desmond came face to face with
Laura Hartman coming out of a suite on the same corridor. She wore an evening dress of heavy cream-colored silk
embroidered with flowers and so great was the transforma-
tion in her appearance that he almost failed to recognize
her.

"Why, Captain O'Neill," her face shone with pleasure,
"how smart you look."

Desmond gave a deprecating glance at his evening
tails. "Beside you, I am very ordinary. You look magnificent," he said with sincerity. "That is a most beautiful
dress."

Laura laughed self-consciously. "Yes, isn't it just," she
admitted. "The Curtises gave it to me. It's my Main-
bocher. Do you know," she said with a trace of awe in
her voice, "it cost more than my whole salary for a year?
I feel a bit strange wearing it."

"Well, it was worth every penny," Desmond assured
her. He held out an arm. "I'll take you down the stairs.
You can't possibly go in the lift in such a dress."

The Curtises were sitting in the main lounge, a large,

dimly lighted room with a vaulted ceiling, thick Persian carpets, and alcoves arranged with couches and low tables. Several groups of people in evening dress were sitting there, talking in low voices. Desmond led Laura across to the Curtises' table and was introduced to Georgina.

Beautiful, proud, willful, cunning, and sensual, she sat very upright in a white satin dress trimmed with black velvet. Unlike most of the other women in the room, her black hair—instead of being pinned up—had been brushed off her face to hang in Egyptian style on either side. The effect was striking and dramatic, and she knew it. She was the center of a small circle of admirers.

"So you are the aviator who will fly me across the Atlantic," she said after Desmond had been introduced to the rest of the party and Laura complimented on her appearance by everyone present. Georgina appraised him thoughtfully. "Tell me, is it safe?"

"No," Desmond returned her gaze steadily, "it is not safe." There were disconcerted murmurs, but Georgina remained unmoved.

"Not safe?" her eyes widened in feigned astonishment. "How is that, captain? Surely you would not take us on a journey that was not safe."

"Professional pessimism," commented the man next to her in accented English. "People always want to make us believe their jobs are dangerous." He gave Desmond a contemptuous glance and began screwing a cigarette into an enameled holder. "The crossing is safe, or the airline would not be making it."

"Hush, Luca." She tapped him on the knee with a crimson-nailed hand. "I am sure Captain O'Neill has excellent reasons for saying what he does. Is that not so, captain?"

"No flight over thirty-five hundred miles of ocean where the worst weather conditions in the world exist can be called safe," Desmond said flatly. "We try to keep the risks to a minimum; nevertheless, they remain."

"You make it sound exciting. Don't you agree, Stewart?" Georgina questioned her husband.

"I think Captain O'Neill's superiors," Stewart Curtis emphasized the last word, "would be displeased to hear him talking in this manner. And I confess I am surprised," he continued, frowning heavily, "to find him going to a ball so soon after the tragedy in which he was involved."

"Then you feel that any regret on your part is unnecessary?" Desmond suggested, and Curtis's frown deepened to a scowl.

"I fail to see—"

His wife cut him off. "I see you are no mean opponent, captain," she laughed. "Certainly not a man to be trifled with. Perhaps Baron d'Este here ought to be worried. You and he are competing in the race tomorrow."

"I'm afraid I haven't had time to examine the lists," Desmond said politely to d'Este. "What car will you be entering?"

"A Delahaye." Luca inhaled his cigarette. "The same car as the one that won the Le Mans twenty-four-hour race last year. She has the fastest acceleration of any car on the road today," he told the party proudly, "from zero to sixty in eleven seconds."

"The captain is driving a Hispano-Suiza." Laura Hartman entered the conversation. "He'll give you a run for your money, baron."

"Ah yes, an excellent car," Luca answered complacently, "but no longer modern, of course."

"It's top speed is equal to a Delahaye's, and it's a race-proven design," Laura responded warmly. "I'd back a Hispano any day."

"Do you see the interest your presence arouses?" Georgina said to Desmond with a smile. "You must join us for the evening. I do so want to hear more of the dangers of flying the Atlantic. Shall we wait for your wife?" she said to Luca d'Este, who was still disputing the merits of the two cars. "Baroness d'Este was caught in the khamsin while out riding, and she was almost lost in the desert," she confided to the others.

"No, thank you. She is still resting at the embassy and may join us later. Fortunately, some Arabs found her and brought her back to the city before she suffered any harm," Luca said, amid general expressions of concern. "She was foolish to go riding without her groom."

"Then let us be setting off for the palace," Georgina said. "Captain O'Neill shall escort me in the car because I want to talk to him about flying. Stewart, give Mrs. Hartman your arm."

Desmond obeyed reluctantly, feeling that he was being asked to desert Laura. To judge by the expression on Stewart Curtis's face, he too disapproved strongly of his wife's behavior. Whatever happened, Desmond seemed fated to arouse the financier's hostility.

What worried him most, though, was the fact that Ralph Kendrick had failed to come to his room as they had agreed.

At the hotel's famous Long Bar, the haunt of generations of travelers and explorers, Ralph Kendrick was getting drunk. He had left the flying boat with the firm intention of drinking himself into oblivion by the end of the evening in an attempt to silence the fears that wracked him.

Staring glassily into the bottom of his whiskey, he told himself for the twentieth time that he was finished. His utter collapse during the squall had removed any hope he might have had of maintaining the fiction that he was going to be fit to fly the Atlantic. The violent lurches of the air pockets, the shaking of the airplane caught in the fierce eddies, the sightless windows of the cockpit had brought back to him, more acutely than ever before, the memory of his seven-year-old horror.

He shuddered; whiskey spilled from his glass, and he watched the trickle drip to the floor. The barmen were hastening to and fro with cocktail shakers, and no one cast more than a casual glance at the morose, lone figure.

He felt badly about letting Desmond down, but Ralph had found he couldn't nerve himself to face his captain—though there would be no real escape, he thought, for sooner or later Desmond would come looking for him. Quite apart from his responsibilities as flight captain, Desmond was relying on him to act as engineer and navigator in the race tomorrow.

The bar was becoming too noisy for comfort. It was time to move on. Shepheard's was no place to get drunk alone, and Ken Frazer might show up at any minute.

Weaving his way through the throng, he went past the great pillared gallery and onto the terrace steps. The night was warm and unclouded. A tout approached him offering his services, but Ralph brushed him aside. Three or four streets away there was a quiet bar where a man could drink in peace.

Ken Frazer was not, in fact, contemplating coming down to the bar. He had ordered the room service waiter to bring him a pink gin. He was not seeking to avoid the company of his fellow crew members, but he had important business to attend to.

Weighing on his mind was the thought that he might be held in part responsible for the emergency landing at Shambe and thus by extension for Ian Thorne's death. An unemotional man by nature, he had had no difficulty in absolving himself of any possible moral blame, but there was still the nagging doubt that the committee of inquiry might think otherwise.

The solution, as he saw it, was to make sure that Desmond took all the blame. Not only would this relieve Frazer of criticism, but it would open the way to have Desmond transferred, perhaps demoted, and possibly even dismissed. In which case, Frazer considered, he himself would stand a strong chance of being given command of *Caterina.*

The essential thing was to see that the board and senior management of the airline were made aware of Desmond's general failings as a captain. If Desmond could be made to appear incompetent and irresponsible, then the findings of the inquiry would be a foregone conclusion.

To this end, Frazer was composing a letter to his mother in London, to be sent by tomorrow's mail plane. In it he presented her with a catalog of his captain's faults and errors in judgment during the flight up the Nile, and he urged her to do her best to bring them to the attention of Jack Priestly. He wrote:

I am utterly convinced that Captain O'Neill means to make me the scapegoat of this whole dreadful affair and thus duck his responsibility. More than that, his behavior throughout the trip has been disgraceful. As well as being rude to several of the passengers and causing delays by demanding extra servicing to the aircraft in order to give himself time to take part in motor races here in Cairo, he is also allowing a crew member, our radio officer, to continue his duties even though the man's nerve has gone

completely and he is drinking heavily. You can imagine
the danger into which this puts us all, both passengers
and crew, and I only hope that this state of affairs is
brought before the management prior to our setting out
across the Atlantic.

Altogether, he decided, as he sealed the letter and took
it by hand to the purser of tomorrow's aircraft with a
request to have it delivered by special messenger on arrival in London, he had provided his mother with ample
ammunition to bring Desmond O'Neill's career to a halt
forever.

○ ○ ○

Darkness had fallen by the time Pat Jarrett had the
Supermarine safely landed and berthed within the enormous interior of the boathouse. He used the launch to tow
her in for the last part of the way, being very careful
not to scrape the wing tips. With the doors shut and the
overhead lighting on, there was ample room to work,
undeterred by conditions outside or the risk of being observed.

He began bringing his tools and other equipment down
from the house and stowing them in one of the rooms in
the back of the boathouse, mentally listing the tasks that
lay before him. The engine had not been running as
smoothly as he would have liked on the way up—such a
race-bred machine needed careful tuning before each flight.
That would be a day's work, but it was a job that could
be left until last.

Far more important was the radio. The Telephony
transmitter-receiver had to be installed in the cramped
cockpit, and that was going to mean cutting away part
of the instrument panel, possibly repositioning some of
the gauges—a couple of days work, even if there were
no snags.

Finally, from under a pile of rubbish in the cellar, he
pulled out a long, narrow wooden box. He grunted with
the effort as he lifted it. Inside the boathouse he laid it
on a bench top beneath the lights. The wood had been
tightly fastened down with nails, and it took much lever-
ing with a chisel before the lid came clear. Inside, a num-

ber of cloth-wrapped bundles lay packed in shavings, held in place by battens fastened to the sides. Impatiently, Jarrett levered these aside and lifted out the contents.

A moment later, he was gazing rapturously at the gleaming, oiled metal lengths of two air-cooled, electrically fired .50-inch Colt machine guns, complete with ammunition trays, mountings, remote firing control gear, and optical sights suitable for use in a single-seat fighter aircraft. The racer was about to be given some teeth.

○ ○ ○

The festivities at the Abdin Palace were at their height when Dr. Van Smit, using a locksmith's key prepared on his arrival in Cairo, opened the door of the Curtis suite, paused momentarily, and, entering, shot the bolt firmly home behind him.

Two bedrooms and a bathroom, used by Laura Hartman and Georgina Curtis's maid opened off a small hallway; the doors opposite led to the suite's sitting room and master bedroom—spacious rooms, each of which had a luxurious balcony and was furnished in the style of the third Empire. The sitting room especially might have graced one of the city's finer residences, occupying as it did a corner of the hotel overlooking the rear gardens.

It was to the sitting room that Van Smit turned his attention first, setting to work to pick the lock of the massive desk situated to the right of the door. He had little fear of being interrupted, for Laura was at the ball with the others, and earlier in the evening he had seen Georgina Curtis's maid slipping out of a side entrance of Shepheard's in the company of another guest's valet.

The lock proved stiff and troublesome, and to the doctor's annoyance the desk yielded only a handful of unimportant papers—passports, travel documents, and the like. Glancing at the bundle of airline tickets, he noted that the entire group was booked right through to New York.

Evidently Curtis kept his more valuable possessions elsewhere. A walnut sideboard yielded only a selection of liquor bottles and glasses; a cupboard beneath a bookcase was empty and unlocked. Van Smit was about to move through into the bedroom when the sound of the hall door being tried froze him where he stood.

The door rattled as the person on the other side kept turning the key in an effort to get in, and the doctor held his breath, thankful that he had remembered to fasten the bolt. A chambermaid would have a master key, capable of overriding the bolt, but he had waited until the rooms had been prepared for the night. With luck, whoever was outside would go off to find help. Most probably it was Georgina Curtis's maid returning unexpectedly early.

The noise ceased, and instantly the doctor moved swiftly into the hall and put his ear to the door to catch the sound in the corridor outside. The thick carpeting would absorb all footsteps, but voices nearby or other doors being opened would be audible. Satisfied that all was clear, he took a deep breath and, striving to appear as normal as possible, he unlocked the door and stepped out into the passage.

He closed the door behind him and made off down the corridor in the direction of the stairway. Turning the corner he saw he had not been a moment too soon. Coming toward him was the Curtises' maid in the company of the second-floor room waiter, brandishing a pass key.

Inside the Byzantine Hall of the Abdin Palace, Laura Hartman and Desmond O'Neill stood together among more than a thousand guests awaiting the entrance of King Farouk and his royal household. They had both been reluctantly released by Georgina Curtis when her husband had insisted on exercising his right to escort her up the marble steps of the main entrance, and now they talked quietly.

"I've never seen such a fantastic place in my life," Laura whispered. "It's as though Hollywood and Versailles got together to throw a party."

In the great hall, gilded columns soared toward a many-domed ceiling studded with intricate stained-glass panels and hung with huge alabaster lamps. Along the walls stood chests of bronze and sandalwood, holding the jeweled costumes of the palace dancing girls. Sculptured marble fountains surrounded by flowers played among the richly dressed throng gathered to await the king.

"They say the royal apartments are even more unbelievable," Desmond told her. "Staircases with crystal banisters and floors inlaid with ivory and mother-of-pearl. And this is only one of Farouk's five palaces."

"It's like a fancy dress ball." She repressed a laugh. "And the men are worse than the ladies."

Desmond followed her gaze. Representing the cream of Cairo society, the guest list encompassed more than twenty nationalities, providing a glittering array of military and diplomatic uniforms as well as Egyptian court dress.

Tarbooshed pashas moved among Indian rajahs in jeweled turbans and Arabian sheiks in gold-spun robes, the light sparkling on diamonds, pearls, and rubies. There must be several fortunes in precious stones here tonight, Desmond thought. To Laura he said, "I feel very ordinary in such a dazzling collection. You, on the other hand, are outshining all competition."

Laura flushed with pleasure. She had noticed a number of the women looking at her dress. "When do you think the king will enter?" she asked.

"I'm afraid that's anyone's guess," Desmond said. "Farouk is notoriously unpunctual, and in any case he hates functions like this. Sometimes he keeps audiences waiting for hours."

"You know him quite well, don't you?" she asked. "I mean as a friend, not as a king."

"Not really. I'm not sure anyone can know him like that. I've only taken him flying a few times and gone shooting on the marshes at Dashur with him when he's asked me. I think he likes to get away occasionally from all the grand people surrounding him."

"You sound as though you feel sorry for him," Laura said. They were speaking in undertones to avoid being overheard.

"A nineteen-year-old boy who has inherited one of the world's greatest fortunes along with one of its poorest lands? Everything in the country depends on him, yet he isn't really master of Egypt. He's surrounded by fawning, corrupt courtiers and condescending foreign diplomats who laugh at his attempts to impress them," Desmond said. "Yes, I am sorry for Farouk."

"A very convenient attitude for one whose nation virtually rules Egypt." Luca d'Este's sneering voice caught both Laura and Desmond by surprise. Looking around they saw the baron in company with the Curtises. The others looked embarrassed by his remarks, and Georgina interrupted before Desmond could reply.

"My husband does not dance, captain," she said, smiling at him winningly, "so I turn to you for an escort when the music starts."

"I should be delighted, Mrs. Curtis," Desmond answered sincerely, "though I am afraid I have already engaged the first dance of the evening with Mrs. Hartman."

Georgina's smile remained unchanged, but a momentary glint of annoyance came into her eyes. "That will be nice for you, Laura," she said patronizingly. "I see I shall have to take second place."

"My dear Georgina, I should be honored—" d'Este pressed forward.

Georgina's expression hardened. "Yes, yes, of course, Luca, of course," she said shortly and turned to say something to her husband. Luca fixed Desmond with an angry stare and seemed about to speak when from the far end of the room there came a sudden buzz of excitement. Looking up, they saw the massive, carved, bronze doors opening at the head of the stairs.

Down the steps there came a pair of trumpeters who took their stations on either side of the door. Behind these followed a double line of courtiers dressed in red tarbooshes and dark blue, tight-fitting jackets stiff with gold frogging. They filed gravely into the hall, pressing back the crowd of eager guests, creating a clear avenue into the center of the room. Suddenly, expectant silence fell.

At an invisible signal, the trumpeters raised their instruments. The king and the crown prince appeared at the head of the steps. The ball was about to begin.

For all her husband's promises, Jacquetta d'Este had no intention of joining the celebrations at the palace. Arriving at the Italian embassy residence in the police car, she had given Luca and her hosts only the barest outline of her adventure before pleading utter exhaustion and retiring to bed. She had deliberately not mentioned Rashid al Senussi, except to say that she had been found and brought in by a party of wandering Arabs.

Lying against the silk pillows in the dimly lighted bedroom, she tried to analyze her motives for shielding the sheik. Gratitude alone was not enough to explain her reluctance to expose a youth who, after all, had sworn to kill her husband.

She found it difficult to dismiss Rashid's lean figure and proud features from her mind. For the space of a few hours, she had glimpsed a harsh, uncompromising world where the smallest weakness of body or spirit meant death, where men still followed a code of honor and chivalry in the midst of a ruthless struggle for survival.

The shallowness and dishonesty of men like Luca—with their endless pursuit of wealth and power, their trivial amusements, their vulgar intrigues, and their pathetic displays of arrogance and temper—paled beside Rashid's fierce thirst for revenge, his savage pride, and the single-mindedness and self-discipline with which he pursued his aims. Rashid, she realized, attracted her more than any man she had ever met.

King Farouk had spared no expense for the climax of his sister's wedding week. Four separate orchestras, specially imported from Europe and America, played in different rooms throughout the night. There were cabaret dancers, troupes of acrobats, jugglers, fire-eaters, magicians, and singers. A sumptuous buffet was served, followed by an hour of brilliant fireworks set off in the garden behind the palace. Bursting stars, silver rain, and brightly colored rockets exploded over the domes and minarets of Cairo in a display of extravagant beauty, while the guests watched awestruck from torch-lighted terraces.

Desmond and Laura spent the evening together, dancing and talking with the many friends the Irishman had made during his frequent visits to the city. "This city seems almost like home to you," Laura said as they strolled out onto one of the balconies.

"I suppose you're right," he agreed. "Cairo's full of people like me—men who come and go all the time, without any fixed place to live."

"Do you have a home anywhere?" Laura asked, and almost before he realized it, he found himself telling her about Pamela and the house in England and the bitterness of the divorce.

"She sounds as though she feels very angry and hurt," Laura said. "I guess I would, too, if I hadn't been able to make my marriage work."

"We were mad to try in the first place," Desmond answered. "You can't expect a marriage to succeed when the man is away flying half the year."

"That's not true, and you know it. There are thousands of people with jobs that take them away from home, and they don't all get divorced." She spoke with a firmness that surprised him.

"I'm sorry," he said. "I shouldn't be boring you with my problems."

"You weren't boring me," Laura answered. "Anyway, I owe you an apology—for being angry when you said you didn't believe in war," she explained. "Sandy Everett told us about your brother being killed flying in the last one. It must have been terrible for you."

"Yes, a terrible tragedy and a terrible waste." For a moment his brother's laughing face flashed into his mind as he had seen him for the last time, waving jauntily from the car on his way back to the front. "Mark was nine years older than I, and I worshipped him. When he died, it was the worst day of my life."

He stopped abruptly, remembering too late that Laura had lost her husband little more than a year ago. Their eyes met, and they smiled at each other in understanding. Instinctively and without noticing, they had stopped walking. In the flickering light of the torches, Laura's upturned face was very beautiful. He felt an enormous desire to take her in his arms and kiss her.

"I would like to go back to the hotel soon," Laura confessed. Having stepped apart a little self-consciously, they began wandering back into the ballroom. "It's nearly one o'clock, and I'm afraid I didn't sleep very well on the river last night."

"I'll see you back there," Desmond said. "I want to make sure of a good night's rest myself before the race tomorrow."

When they announced their intentions, Luca d'Este and Stewart Curtis appeared pleased. Georgina, however, was less happy at the news. "I simply must have another dance before you go," she insisted, brushing aside the protests of the Italian who had been promised the next turn.

She was an excellent dancer, and, as in their first dance of the evening, she held herself close against him, flirting with an intimacy that embarrassed him. In more normal circumstances, Desmond might have been susceptible to her overtures, for Georgina was an undeniably attractive woman, and there was a certain honor in being singled out for her attention in this way. As it was, however, with Laura Hartman looking on, as well as the lady's husband and friends, Desmond felt only annoyance.

"You're very formal tonight," she whispered. "Has something offended you?"

"Not at all," Desmond said hastily. "I'm afraid I am very tired. We had a long flight up and not a lot of sleep the night before."

"I know, you poor man." Georgina's eyelids fluttered as she gazed at him in feigned sympathy. "And tomorrow you are driving in a race. Poor Luca is furious," she laughed. "Everyone is saying you will win, even the king himself." Desmond had seen her dancing with Farouk in the main ball room. Evidently the king's praise of him had raised his desirability in her eyes.

The music changed to a slower rhythm, and Georgina settled herself more firmly into his arms. "Tell me— how are you getting on with little Laura Hartman?" she asked with too obvious casualness.

"I like her very much. She is a sweet girl," Desmond answered shortly.

Georgina gave him a sudden, intent glance. "I see I shall have to put you in the picture there," she remarked obscurely. He was still trying to puzzle her meaning when the music ended.

At Georgina's insistence, Desmond and Laura agreed to ride with the Curtises in their limousine back to Shepheard's. The main courtyard of the palace was packed with an array of cars, and they had a lengthy wait. By the time they arrived back at the hotel, most of the guests had gone to bed or left for home, but the pavement near the steps was still crowded with beggars hoping for generosity from late returners. Laura shivered as a blind cripple and his child keeper were turned away by one of the doormen.

"Egypt still horrifies me sometimes," she said. "I don't know how people can accept the contrasts so easily."

"It's the same everywhere in Cairo," Desmond said. "There have always been a handful of immensely rich and millions of poor. The villas of the Garden City right next to the hovels and slums of the City of the Dead." He was about to add that Shepheard's itself backed onto a huddle of shanties and vermin-infested tenements when he heard his name called loudly from across the street. Turning, he saw Ralph Kendrick lurching toward him.

"Skipper," he cried again as he stumbled up the stairs to where Desmond and Laura stood beneath the canopy. "Skipper, I'm sorry I didn't make it this evening," he slurred, clutching at the awning pillars for support. "I couldn't come, just couldn't come," he repeated. "Wanted to—but just couldn't."

Shepheard's was used to high-spirited revelers returning late at night, but Desmond could see that the doorman was looking doubtfully at Kendrick, who had torn off his jacket and tie and was carrying them in his hand with a half-empty whiskey bottle. His face was flushed and sweaty.

"Hell, Ralph. Why do you have to get yourself into this state?" Desmond took him by the arm and began to steer him through the hall. "You had better let me deal with him," he said to Laura, but the girl was calmly relieving Kendrick of the jacket and the whiskey bottle.

"Take him through," she said. "I'll get the key and follow."

Not without difficulty, for he was a heavy man, they managed to get Ralph upstairs to his room and onto his bed, where he collapsed into a stupor. Desmond removed his shoes and left him covered with a blanket. "Thanks," he said to Laura as they returned to their own floor. "You were a great help."

"Oh, it was nothing. I'm used to all that, I've had to do it hundreds of times." Her tone made Desmond glance at her sharply.

"My husband." She answered his unspoken question in a flat, tired voice. "He was an alcoholic. I did this for him again and again and again."

"I'm sorry," Desmond said gently, "I didn't realize that. It must have made dealing with Ralph a lot worse for you."

"I'm used to it." She shook her head sadly. "At first I used to cry every time. That was how he was killed in the end. He started going down into the mine when he was drunk, he got careless, and there was an accident. Snap!

No husband." She made an empty gesture with her hands. "All over in a second—just like that.

"What will you do about Ralph?" she asked as they reached the door of Stewart Curtis's suite.

Desmond shrugged his shoulders. "I'm not sure yet. I'll have to think about it and decide tomorrow. Right now all I want to do is get some sleep." Gently kissing her goodnight, he returned to his room.

6

From:

THE EGYPTIAN GAZETTE
Sunday 12 March 1939

His Majesty King Farouk will today honor the Cairo Motoring Club by starting the club's annual race to Fayum at 3:30 P.M. in the Abdin Palace Square. His Majesty will be accompanied by His Royal Highness the Crown Prince of Iran. Members of their suites will also be present, together with the British ambassador and members of the diplomatic corps.

○ ○ ○

In the big house on the point at Warren Lake, Pat Jarrett woke to the sound of his alarm just as the sun was climbing above the rim of the surrounding hills. He leaped out of bed, as he had done every morning since he went away to the war. Rising at dawn—never lying in for a moment once he was awake—was an important part of his rigorous code of self-discipline.

Scanning the lake from the window, he checked to see that all was as it had been the previous evening. The sky was clear, and the surface of the water was calm. If the weather would stay like this for another five days, everything would be perfect.

Grabbing a towel and a pair of shorts, he hurried out of the house and down to the pier. Usually he began the day with a cold shower or splash-down, but since his arrival at the lake, he had taken advantage of the opportunity to have a proper swim.

After his swim in the icy water, he set off for his daily run—five miles regardless of weather conditions. Except when snow was on the ground, he ran barefooted to keep his soles hardened.

His body felt renewed and invigorated. Not only did he feel in peak condition, but the knowledge that his years of denial and self-discipline were at last being put to use had brought a sense of excitement back into his life.

Returning to the house, he showered and rubbed himself down once more before putting on a clean shirt and starched white overalls from the supply he washed and ironed daily. Pride in appearance was the hallmark of the good soldier, he reminded himself as he shaved and trimmed his hair. Today he would begin to fit the radio transmitter. Everything was going according to plan.

○ ○ ○

The race was due to begin at three-thirty to suit the convenience of the king, who had announced his intention of starting the cars off and presenting the winner with his prize. Most of the drivers were in favor of an afternoon contest since this meant they would miss the hottest part of the day. The first cars were expected to cross the finish line in the Palace Square at about six o'clock, just as dusk was falling, with the last of the drivers home by six-thirty. The final leg would be the most spectacular, the cars roaring through the spectator-packed streets, headlights blazing in the failing light.

Desmond had been working on the Hispano-Suiza since early morning, following a brief visit to Kasr el Nil to check on the work being done on *Caterina*. He was inclined to rate his chances in the race as low. Unlike the other contestants, he had been unable to practice over the course during the past three weeks, and now he would have to do without a mechanic as well. Against him would be men like Baron d'Este with a brand-new, expensive car and any number of chauffeurs and mechanics to help him in his preparations.

The Hispano was kept in a small garage not far from Shepheard's, in a narrow cul-de-sac that housed several small businesses as well as the homes of a number of taxi drivers who were among his staunch supporters and whose children's greatest joy was to be allowed to help polish the fabulous racer.

In 1924, the Hispano-Suiza Boulogne had been the ultimate in luxury and performance. The breathtaking twelve-foot body was hand-built from tulipwood and powered by an eight-liter version of the famous wartime aero engines, representing a pinnacle of engineering and coach-building craftsmanship that would never be attained again. Every leaf of the beautifully grained, red-brown tulipwood body had been shaped and fitted by hand into the car's sweeping elegant lines, studded every few inches by brass screws, so that the overall effect was a rich combination of deep red and gold, which gleamed and sparkled in the light.

Nine months ago, on a tour of Farouk's palace garages, Desmond had seen the car lying abandoned and decaying behind the ranks of more recent models, and he had persuaded the king to let him buy her. Since then, most of his spare time had been spent in hunting down parts and restoring the car.

All things considered, the Hispano was in extraordinarily good condition. Desmond lay on his back tightening the sump guard bolts. True, she was fifteen years old and lacked the acceleration of the new Delahayes and Jaguars, but given a straight road and room to maneuver, the huge engine was capable of equaling the speed of most cars and holding the pace without straining.

On this afternoon's course, reliability and strength would be as important as all-out speed. The desert road was marred by deep ruts, potholes, and loose stones. Split tires and broken wheels and axles could easily result, especially among drivers unused to such hazards. There was at least a chance that he might be well placed at the finish.

Sliding back a short distance to begin a scrutiny of the steering assembly, he heard the door to the street being tugged open. As he squinted around past one of the front tires, he saw a pair of small feet in neat white tennis shoes topped by white overalls with the bottoms turned up. A moment later, Laura Hartman's face was peering at him.

"I figured you'd need a helper, so here I am," she said when Desmond had hauled himself out from under the car. "Your Mr. Kendrick is still out cold." She had caught her hair neatly back in a scarf. "I know," she continued as he protested, "but my husband, I told you, was an engineer, and almost the only thing he managed to teach me about was motor cars." She cast an appraising eye over the Hispano.

"She's beautiful," she said, running her fingers lightly over the gleaming woodwork of the bonnet. She gave him a stern look. "Hispano-Suiza Boulogne, 1924 model. Six cylinder, eight-liter engine with overhead valves. Nicknamed the Tulipwood Boulogne, it is the only one of its kind in existence and was built for André Dubonnet of the French wine family, who raced it in the Targa Floreo in 1924."

Desmond stared at her and then burst into laughter. "Did he teach you all that?"

The girl shook her head. "No, Freddy Muller, the hotel manager, told me. He told me where to find you as well; but I do know what I'm talking about, so do I get to go with you?"

He looked at her doubtfully. "The race may be dangerous. It will certainly be tiring and dusty," he answered. "A lot of the track runs through the desert, and the roads are pretty bad there."

Laura's jaw tightened. "I can handle a little dirt," she said. "I can also change a wheel and grease an axle. And anyone else you find will only weigh more," she added defiantly, and Desmond laughed again.

"That much I have to admit," he agreed. "It seems as though I have no choice—and you certainly look the part. Where did you find those clothes?"

It was Laura's turn to grin. "Your purser Sandy Everett found them for me at the airline store. He's given me this pair to work in and another clean set to wear for the race."

"You'll need a helmet and goggles as well," he told her. "I'll see about getting hold of them for you when we knock off for lunch. I just want to finish checking her over, then we'll take her out for a run." He glanced at his watch—it was already eleven o'clock. They had less than four hours.

The entire square in front of the Abdin Palace was taken up by the rows of cars, drawn up in order according to ballot. Forty-two drivers had joined the race, though less than a quarter of these were serious contenders for the prize, the rest being older cars whose owners were entering more for the fun of the drive than for an attempt at victory.

About each of the polished and gleaming machines were clustered a throng of admiring onlookers, watching the final adjustments being made to the engines and discussing their merits critically and volubly. On the king's instructions, a police cordon held back the ordinary spectators, but this had not prevented practically the whole of Cairo society from entering to watch their friends and see the king start the race.

At the edge of the square, Jacquetta d'Este stood beneath an awning erected by the Cairo Motoring Club for its guests. The hottest part of the day was still not quite over, and out on the unprotected tarmac the noise and dust and smell of exhaust fumes had been too much for her. Several of her friends chattered excitedly about the prospects of the various contestants. Her husband had seated Georgina Curtis behind the wheel of his maroon Delahye and was explaining the controls to her. Through the milling crowd of supporters, Jacquetta could see the Englishwoman's wide-brimmed hat nodding from time to time.

Since their debut at the Paris Motor Show in 1938, and subsequent victory in the Le Mans twenty-four-hour race in the same year, the big streamlined Delahayes had attracted great attention. To Luca's satisfaction, the crowd had gathered thickly, admiring the glossy maroon paint, the whitewall tires, and the rich luxury of the leather and walnut interior.

From Luca's temper that morning, Jacquetta realized that all had not gone well for him at the ball. Later she heard that Georgina had spent the evening running after the good-looking pilot, who would be flying them to the United States. It also appeared that Georgina had had to face competition from her own husband's secretary. Jacquetta wondered how she had enjoyed the experience.

Luca had been allotted a favorable position in the

front rank of the start, between an enormous bright yellow Isotta-Fraschini and a square-nosed Bugatti belonging to a Syrian. Desmond O'Neill's Hispano-Suiza was on the far side of the second rank.

A stir of excitement ran through the square, and from the crowds in the road beyond the cordon, there went up a loud chorus of greeting. Looking around, Jacquetta saw that the palace doors had been thrown open and a phalanx of soldiers, uniformed courtiers, and distinguished personages was descending the steps. The king and his brother-in-law, the crown prince, had arrived. The crowd continued to roar. Unlike his miserly father who had despised his people and refused even to learn their language, Farouk was a popular king. The glittering cortege began to move slowly along the rows of cars, pausing now and then to exchange a few words with the occupants.

Georgina joined Jacquetta under the awning. "It's so hot out there," she complained. "I pity those poor drivers. Luca let me sit in his car," she went on proudly. "It really is the most marvelous machine. I do hope he wins."

"I should have thought you would be supporting Mrs. Hartman and Captain O'Neill," Jacquetta replied innocently and she was gratified to see her words bring a faint flush to Georgina's cheeks. For all her sophistication and grandeur, Georgina Curtis was little more than a spoiled child who enjoyed leading men on—especially married ones whose wives she could taunt.

The king stood on the podium, and the noise of the spectators died away expectantly. For the space of a few seconds, the cars quivered on the starting grid, a glittering array of brightly colored metallic creatures. The king raised his arm, there was a sudden bright flash and a loud report, and the cars leaped forward with a tremendous blast of sound. The colors flashed away, blurred by the speed and dust—green, blue, red, gold, silver, yellow, it was hard to separate them. Jacquetta caught a glimpse of Luca's Delahaye turning out of the square in front of the Hispano, and then they were gone, the crowds racing down the road in pursuit.

The first few miles of the course, through the streets of Cairo and along the Pyramid road leading out of the city to the south, were too narrow and restricted to allow the race to develop properly. The leaders were held together in a tight bunch.

Crowds cheered wildly as the cars swept round the tight bends along the riverside avenues, fighting grimly for position. The khamsin had left a considerable amount of fine dust on the roadside and in the gutters, and the sudden, violent passage of the cars stirred this up, adding to the hazards facing the drivers.

Desmond and Laura were well up among the front dozen cars and only a length or so behind Luca d'Este's Delahaye. Although the Italian had been more favorably placed at the start, he had failed to make use of his advantage. His shortcomings as a driver were beginning to be apparent in his nervous, jerky handling and poor positioning on the corners. Despite the fact that the Delahaye was the newest and most expensive car in the race, Desmond felt confident that his own driving skills would give him an edge.

For the present, however, Desmond was content to hold his place, striving to avoid a collision with cars whose drivers were recklessly trying to force their way through from behind. When the open road was reached, most of these cars would inevitably fall back, unable to compete with the faster machines, but at the moment they were turning the road into a dangerous melee, swerving to avoid one another in the confusion.

A red Daimler Double-six cut in ahead of him, forcing him to brake hard and pull out to the right. As he did so, he saw the nose of another car accelerating past him on the outside. There was a momentary glimpse of the driver's goggled face screaming at him. Then the speeding machine had flashed by, its tail barely visible in the dust. If this kept up, there was going to be a serious crash, probably involving several vehicles, and he began to regret bringing Laura with him.

Luca was driving with increasing wildness in his anxiety to fight off pressure from the rear. Desmond could see him swinging the big Delahaye viciously across the track. Obviously the Italian would not surrender his lead willingly, and anyone trying to overtake him could probably expect to be crowded off the road or even risk deliberate ramming.

Yet overtaken he must be, if not here in the city, then on the tight bends of the road through Fayum itself. For on the flat straights through the desert, the Delahaye's superior speed would render the task impossible, and Luca knew it.

Past the tree-lined suburbs, the road opened out, and the squat, yellow shape of the Giza Pyramids became visible. The race grew more frantic as the faster cars pulled out onto the packed sand on the edge of the road to overtake those in front, raising great clouds of dust in their wake. Pressing his foot down hard on the Hispano's accelerator, Desmond felt an immediate response, and with a deep crackle from the exhaust, the Hispano thrust forward. The Delahaye was already pulling away ahead as Luca d'Este made full use of the tremendous power that had carried the marque to victory at Le Mans.

Laura felt the excitement mounting within her as one after another the leading machines were overtaken and left behind. The speedometer was touching almost one-hundred miles per hour when they turned off onto the secondary road into the desert. The whole car was shaking with the strain, the thunderous howl of the engine filling her ears. Desmond sat hunched over the wheel, using all his strength to hold them on the road. Both of them were caked in a layer of fine gray dust.

Only a handful of contestants remained ahead of them, four or five at most, she guessed, and judging by the way Desmond was handling the Hispano, there was a good chance that they might be out in front with only the Delahaye to beat by the time they reached Fayum, ninety miles across the sands.

There, in the oasis, all drivers had to make a compulsory stop to take on fuel and give a hurried check to their vehicles before setting off for the high-speed dash down the main road back into Cairo. At all costs, she and Desmond must wrest the lead from Luca before then.

The oasis of Fayum, set in the desert sixty miles out from Cairo, is the vast garden and fruit orchard of Lower Egypt. Its heart is Lake Karoum, fed by water draining in from the Nile. Lush groves of almond, apricot, orange, fig, and lemon trees intermingle with graceful acacias and eucalyptus, tamarisks, and tall date palms. From the shores edged with silver sands, irrigation chan-

nels and water wheels feed fields where water buffaloes
wade through green rice paddies and gangs of fellahin
slash at high purple sugar cane. On all sides rich acres of
wheat, cotton, maize, clover, and every kind of vegetable
stretch to the horizon.

On the glassed-in veranda of the Hôtel de Chasse,
Yousouri Pasha sat looking out over the shining surface of
the lake. Sighing, he transferred his attention back to the
police colonel who stood anxiously by his chair. "So you
have failed in your task," he said disdainfully.

The officer cleared his throat uneasily. "We have not
failed exactly, Excellency," he pleaded, "but events did
not quite go as we planned. There is still time."

Yousouri selected a sweetmeat from a plate on a nearby table. "Your orders were to apprehend Sheik Rashid
in order to prevent him from trying to assassinate Baron
d'Este. All you have succeeded in doing is driving him into the oasis—where he will be impossible to find—and
at the same time warn him that he is being hunted."

"The sheik must have known it, Excellency. His Bedouin were waiting in the ruined city to the west. They had
pickets out, and as soon as they spotted us, they retreated back to Fayum," the colonel said.

"Fool," Yousouri's voice rose angrily. "Did you expect
a man like Rashid to walk into your arms? Of course he
had pickets out, and of course he retreated. You should
have been prepared and had men at his rear."

"What shall we do now, Excellency?" the man asked
plaintively.

"Do! Why, find him, of course! Call out your men,
comb the orchards and cane fields, send patrols through
the woods," Yousouri snarled. "You have less than an hour
before the cars come through. And I promise you,
colonel," he added savagely, "if you bungle this, if
Rashid slips through the net and succeeds in killing the
baron here in Egypt, you would have done better not to
have been born. Do you understand?"

From a mimosa thicket on the eastern end of the lake,
Rashid al Senussi scanned the ground about him and
cursed. The spot was ideal for an ambush. Less than fifty
yards across a field, the road down which the racing cars

must come skirted the lake shore and bent sharply to the right around a clump of trees before continuing on through a series of bends to join the main road to Cairo. Any approaching vehicle would be forced to slow down.

One thing marred the plan, however. Parked under the trees by the edge of the road was a military truck with a dozen well-armed Egyptian police inside. Rashid had four of his own followers with him, and, in ordinary circumstances, he would have regarded the odds as acceptable. Today, however, was different. The oasis was crawling with police and troops, and the sound of firing would draw scores of reinforcements. Outnumbered and cut off, the Bedouin would be trapped with the lake at their backs and picked off one by one.

Since early morning, nothing had gone right. Details of his intended attack on d'Este had evidently reached the authorities, and Rashid and his men had all but walked into the arms of an ambush themselves. Rashid had been forced to withdraw, and only by sending some of his men off to lure the pursuers into the desert had he been able to slip through and reach Fayum.

Now they were bottled up again. It was unlikely that they would have another chance to get so close to the road. At the other end of the lake was the refueling stage, but that had virtually been sealed off by the police, and patrols were working steadily through the fields on both sides of the road. Rashid would have to create a diversion.

The mimosa pollen fell about his head and shoulders like dust as he crawled back to his companions. Lean, desert-hardened men like himself, they were waiting with the horses in a small thicket while he reconnoitered. Calling them round him, he told them his plan.

A short while later—from his earlier position—he watched the four Arabs lead their horses quietly out from behind the thicket and ride off in the direction of the river. Before they had gone far, a cry went up from the waiting Egyptians, and the truck set off rapidly in pursuit.

With a smile at the ease with which the trick had worked a second time, Rashid slipped across the field and into the concealment of the trees on the other side. From here he could see a long way down in the direction from which the cars would approach.

The ground was thickly overgrown with weeds and

mimosa, and it sloped up to a low ridge. Once there had been an orange grove here, but now the irrigation ditches were choked, and the water wheel stood disused and broken.

To his left, beyond the field, lay the reed-fringed marshes bordering Lake Karoum. Before him, the road skirted the orchard and bent to run beside the lake, receding into the distance a mile or two away. Down that road would come the cars.

Unslinging his Manlicher rifle, he settled in a small hollow behind a fallen tamarisk branch halfway up the slope. From here he would be able to directly fire upon d'Este as the baron approached down the straight section of road, then slowed to take the corner twenty yards away and a little below.

Now that the troops had gone, all was quiet save for the chatter of birds and the faint music of hundreds of water wheels. The sun was sinking; he would not have long to wait.

After the hour-long drive through the desert, the sight of the trees and lush fields of green was a welcome change, even though Laura knew it heralded the start of the most urgent phase of the race. Three cars remained ahead of them: a Bugatti; the red Daimler that had passed them earlier, driven by an English army officer stationed in Cairo; and Luca d'Este's maroon Delahaye.

The Delahaye led by a quarter of a mile. On the straight roads over the sand, there had been little scope for skill, and each driver had pushed his car to the limit.

The fifteen or so miles through the twisting lanes around Lake Karoum would be crucial. A driver who could succeed in putting a substantial distance between himself and his nearest rivals was virtually assured of victory. The tarmac road back from Fayum was broad and straight— one of the best in Egypt.

The flat landscape with its neat fields and luxurious vegetation was a novelty to Laura, and it was pleasant to feel a smooth road again after the bruising ride over the desert and to see spectators waving as they flashed past.

They struck trouble immediately. Taking a corner too

quickly, Luca skidded hard and slithered off the road into
the grass. It took him only seconds to regain control, but
in that time the others had closed the gap and were on his
heels. With only a few feet between them, the four cars
raced along the narrow track, squeezing every split second
of advantage out of the bends.

The pressure was telling on Luca, and soon the driver
of the Bugatti seized an opportunity to draw level with
the Delahaye on the inside. Nose to nose, the two hurtled
along, the greater power of the maroon car balanced by
the superior skill of the Bugatti's driver.

Then Desmond saw d'Este put his wheel hard over in
an apparent effort to force his rival off the road, repeating the tactics he had been using earlier to prevent others
from passing him.

On these fast bends the maneuver was so insanely dangerous that Desmond instinctively eased his foot off the
accelerator, opening the gap separating the Hispano from
the three leaders. As he did so, the Delahaye's front
bumper struck the Bugatti's offside wheel.

The thin cycle wing mudguard crumpled, and with a
sharp-pitched bang, the Bugatti's wheel sheared off and
went bowling crazily along the road as though possessed
of some extraordinary power of its own. The two cars
bounced apart, and for a moment the Bugatti rode upright while its driver stared, transfixed, at the runaway
wheel. Then, with a sickening screech of metal, the right-
hand wing dropped to the ground and slid jarringly along
for fifty yards, gouging a furious track in the roadway.
Desmond and Laura could see the driver trying futilely to
steer as his car slid and twisted across the path of the
vehicles behind him.

Then without warning, the Bugatti pitched end over end,
leaping high in the air, clear of the road; the car bounced
shatteringly and crashed to rest against the bank of an irrigation ditch, scattering debris in a wide area around
it.

Almost before Desmond had realized what was happening, they were speeding past. Laura was left with a con-
fused impression of images superimposed one upon the
other—the wheelless car still driving upright, the horrify-
ing somersault over the road. Looking back she saw the

Bugatti lying on its back like a broken toy, the first rescuers hurrying toward it through the trees.

Desmond made no comment but drove with a fierce
concentration on Luca's tail until they halted at the fuel
stage, less than a mile away, in the parking lot of the
Hôtel de Chasse. Scores of spectators and race mechanics
mingled with officials in a scene not unlike the confusion
that had prevailed at the start of the race. A large crowd
had driven out to the oasis to see the finish of the first leg,
and a field next to the parking lot was packed with
vehicles of every description. Six large petrol wagons
were waiting on the tarmac, and the mechanics had begun to refill the Delahaye's tank and were checking the
wheel casing for damage when Desmond drew up and,
vaulting out of the Hispano's driving seat, ran over to
where d'Este was talking to a group of race officials.

"You criminal idiot!" Desmond accused him hotly, ignoring the eagerly clustering spectators. "You caused that
accident deliberately."

The Italian was in a highly nervous state, and he
flared up at Desmond's charge. "The Bugatti was responsible!" he shouted. "He cut in on the inside of the corner
—I could not help what happened."

"Damn you." Desmond was white with anger. "I saw
you put your wheel across with my own eyes. It was deliberate ramming."

One of the officials interrupted. "I am sure you must
be mistaken, captain," he said. "Nobody would do such a
thing."

"Ask any of the other drivers—ask Mrs. Hartman," Desmond told him. "This fool's been driving like a madman
all the way out here."

"O'Neill is right." The owner of the Daimler joined the
group, a big florid-faced man with a mustache, "The man
ought to be banned—as clear a case of ramming as I've
ever seen."

More cars were arriving to take fuel, their drivers and
mechanics hurrying to get started again. Luca d'Este's
face took on a hunted expression; he could see the race
slipping from his grasp. "It was an accident, an accident,"
he repeated. "The Bugatti's fault—not mine."

In another moment the track officials might well have

decided to call off the race, or at least forbid Luca to continue, but just then another man came running over.

"They're all right!" he cried. "The Frenchmen in the Bugatti. They were shaken up, but the ditch saved them from being crushed by the car. There's hardly a scratch on them."

Sighs of relief went round the group, and a look of triumph flashed onto Luca's face. "Now perhaps we can continue with the race," he snarled, climbing back into the Delahaye, which stood refueled and waiting nearby. His action was the signal for an immediate scattering of the other drivers back to their cars.

Desmond leaped back into the Hispano, which Laura had had refueled and ready for him. Slamming it into gear, he roared off through the hotel gates in pursuit of the Italian.

To Rashid's annoyance the immediate area was still crawling with armed police. From where he lay, twenty yards from the bend, he had so far observed three trucks similar to the one he had seen earlier grind past, the men inside sitting upright against the sides, clutching their rifles between their knees.

A section of a dozen men was combing the ground along the shores of the lake, working steadily toward him through the marshes. Whether they were aware of his presence or simply taking extreme precautions, the young sheik had no means of telling. For the moment he was safe enough from detection, but the sound of a shot would reveal his position at once.

All he could do was lie still and pray that by the time the cars appeared along the road, the patrol would have moved far enough past to enable him to scramble through the trees and get clear. With luck, he thought, the echoes of the shot on the lake would confuse the searchers.

The sun sank steadily as he crouched in the hollow, watching every movement in the fields. The soldiers drew level with him and continued past, the nearest less than a hundred yards away. Their search was painstaking and methodical, coordinated by an NCO from the center of the line. Rashid cursed their slowness. The first cars were already overdue, and, although the failing light would give him some slight assistance, the soldiers were still within easy sighting distance. His hands were sweating where they gripped the rifle, and he wiped them nervously.

So intent was he on watching the patrol that he did not at first hear the low hum in the distance that signaled the approached of the cars. Suddenly, however, he recognized the sound and switched his attention back to the road. The sun was very near the horizon now, making it difficult to distinguish shapes far away, but he could just make out the rapidly nearing trail of dust thrown up by the cars.

Cuddling the Manlicher tightly, he made a minute adjustment to the rear sight. He would put the first shot into d'Este exactly as the Italian reached the bend. The car would be moving at its slowest then. The soldiers in the field were still too near, but Rashid no longer cared. His father would be avenged.

Laura had gathered that the driver of the Bugatti was uninjured, but more than that Desmond had been unable to tell her, for it required all his attention to follow the twists and turns of the road. Certainly the conversation at the fuel stop had aroused his anger, she could see, for he was driving with a furious determination, sticking relentlessly to the Delahaye round every corner and bend, trying every device he knew to overtake the maroon racer.

For the first time since the start of the race, Laura felt frightened. The cars rocketing along the narrow roads between sharp corners at up to one-hundred miles an hour was nerve-racking enough, but what really terrified her were the crazy tactics Luca was resorting to in order to fight off the Hispano, as well as Desmond's disregard for the risks he was taking.

Coming out at last onto an open stretch along the eastern end of the lake, Luca pressed his accelerator into the floor in a furious effort to draw clear of the pursuing car. The engine note lifted to a high-pitched whine as the revolutions mounted and the speedometer needle climbed past 110. Luca's mechanic paled at the sight of the bend rushing closer.

Behind them in the Hispano, Laura was gripping the side of the car. Unless he slowed up, there was no way Luca could take the bend, and the two cars were now so close that a misjudgment by the Delahaye would involve them both in an appalling crash.

Five hundred yards away, Rashid snapped the Manlicher bolt shut and sighted in on the speeding car. He heard the squeal of tires and the sudden bellow of protest from the engine as d'Este braked desperately and changed down through the gears. Even from the ridge, it was possible to see that the Italian had begun to slow too late.

Less than a hundred yards from the corner, the Delahaye's brakes locked, and the big car went into a skid, swinging broadside across the road, tires shrieking. Luca spun the steering wheel in a vain effort to regain control before the Hispano-Suiza smashed into him.

Desmond reacted with lightning decision. A deep ditch ran along the right-hand edge of the road; the opposite side was a narrow but unobstructed strip of grass. Braking hard he swung out along the grass off the tarmac, praying that the Hispano's weight would hold her steady at this speed. There was a violent bumping, and clouds of dirt and sand shot up as with inches to spare they flashed past the Delahaye's nose into the corner.

Putting the wheel hard over, Desmond felt the car's tail break free and start to slide round as they regained the road. Releasing the brakes and dropping another gear, he spun the wheel again, correcting savagely.

There was a split second of stomach-churning fear while he thought the heavy car would refuse to obey, and then, miraculously, they were around, and he was accelerating out of the corner and away.

Just as the Hispano roared clear and the Delahaye's still-squealing rear wheels slid backward into the ditch, Rashid squeezed the trigger of his rifle.

The crack of the shot echoed sharply out over the flat landscape, alerting everyone except those in the cars. Rashid saw the Delahaye slide headlong over the partly filled ditch and lurch over the ground beyond, to land on its side among the trees, spilling its occupants out behind it.

There was no way of telling if he had hit d'Este, and, with his quarry hidden by the car whose still-spinning wheels faced him, and the soldiers in the nearby field running in his direction, there was no chance of a second shot. Shouldering the rifle, Rashid scrambled to his feet and made off through the orchard.

The noise of the Hispano's engine accelerating away from the corner had completely drowned out the crack of the rifle shot. Twisting around in her seat, Laura witnessed the crash and overturning of the maroon car, but she knew nothing of the bullet—or of the fate of Luca and his partner.

"They must be unhurt," Desmond yelled back when she reported what she had seen. "The Delahaye's a big, solid car, and she must have lost a lot of her speed by the time she hit."

"Can we win now?" she cried against the wind. "Can any of the others catch us?"

"We've a good chance, if we can just hold the lead till we reach the main road," he shouted.

Fortunately they had only a little further to go before striking the Cairo highway, and though even in that space the red Daimler crept ominously close, once they were out on the open road Desmond gave the Hispano her head, and the awesome power of the engine drew them clear again.

Hurtling along the empty road in the dusk at more than 115 miles an hour, the wind stinging her cheeks, and her ears filled with the deep howl of the exhaust was an experience Laura would never forget. Their lead built up increasingly and, by the time they reached the Pyramids, they knew they were uncatchable.

Moonlight was glittering on the Nile as they sped on into the city, palm trees giving way to jacarandas and flame trees flashing past in the incandescent blaze of the headlights. Then they were racing through the streets, the pavements jammed by crowds wild with excitement. Suddenly they were past the flag and into the Palace Square, and it was all over.

○ ○ ○

"He is uninjured? He doesn't even realize he was shot at?" Prince Suleiman's tone was incredulous.

Yousouri Pasha made an expressive gesture. "I know it is unbelievable but, nevertheless, true. The bullet broke the steering wheel, it must have missed his head only fractionally. Luca d'Este was too worried trying to save the car to notice, but my men found it embedded in the wing, and there was a hole in the dashboard to match." Reaching into his pocket, he drew out a flattened lump of metal and placed it on the table.

The two men were sitting in a summer house in the gardens of the prince's palace. Deaf-mute servants, slaves in all but name, were ministering to their wants. The prince ignored the spent bullet. "It was fortunate for us all that Rashid missed," Yousouri continued.

"Fortunate, perhaps," the prince agreed, "but I cannot share in any rejoicing at d'Este's continued escape. He has, after all, murdered my kinspeople."

Yousouri recalled the stories he had heard of the beautiful Senussi girl the prince had brought out of the desert and married more than forty years ago. She had died in her first childbirth, but, for all his want of an heir, the prince had never married again.

"We are united in condemning d'Este's crime," he assured his host, "but we must agree on the disastrous consequences that might result if he were to be slain in Egypt. I can see to it that this attempt does not come to light and that the man leaves the country tomorrow morning." He paused and regarded the table thoughtfully. "I have been instructed—" he put a slight emphasis on the words and hesitated for an instant to let their full weight sink in—"to ask for Your Highness's word that Rashid al Senussi will not be permitted to carry out any further attacks on Baron d'Este while he is still here in Egypt."

"You assume that I have greater control over the boy than may be the case." The prince's tone did not change.

"That may be so; nevertheless, in so far as you are able, I must ask. Baron d'Este is to dine at Shepheard's and then return to the embassy, and the whole area is now under heavy guard. Tomorrow he will be escorted to the airplane by the police. An attempt could not possibly succeed. However, there must not be any such attempt."

Prince Suleiman leaned forward and picked up the crushed bullet. "The boy has not yet returned," he said, turning the metal over between his long fingers. "When he does, you have my word that he shall not harm d'Este." There was a pause. "So long as the baron is in Egypt."

Yousouri rose and bowed low. "Your Highness has been most understanding," he murmured. "I am sure His Majesty will be pleased to hear of the assistance you have given us."

O O O

Heinz Gerdler was walking the streets of Venice with an increasing sense of frustration. Although he and Rintlen had not arrived in the town until the early hours of the morning, the S.D. man had permitted only a brief interval of rest before beginning their search. While Rintlen remained in the room, working down the list of hotels and boarding houses in the telephone directory, Gerdler had been sent out to wander around the stations and tourist places in the hope of catching sight of the refugee couple.

That had been ten hours ago. Gerdler had walked unceasingly through the crowded streets until his legs ached and his mind grew dizzy with fatigue. Privately, he was inclined to believe they were on a hopeless mission.

Venice was already starting to fill with tourists for the spring, and hordes of people streamed past him everywhere he went. At least a dozen times he must have caught sight of a figure in the distance who looked like the Jewish girl, but when he had struggled through the crowd, he had discovered that it was someone quite different.

A task that at first had promised adventure and excitement was proving to hold nothing but boredom and hard work. Worse still, when he had returned to their hotel at lunch time to report, he had found Rintlen in a sour temper after a fruitless morning on the telephone. Gerdler was afraid that if their venture was to fail, his own part in the Wienzman's flight might be dragged up, and this anxiety increased as the afternoon wore on into the evening.

The failing light was making it difficult to pick out the features of people on the other side of the street, yet he shrank from the thought of returning empty-handed to confront Rintlen. Turning abruptly on his heels, he resolved to try once more in the Piazza di San Marco.

The evening was clearer and warmer than that of the previous day, and consequently there were still many tourists about, watching the sunset over the Campanile and the pigeons wheeling away to their perches. Courting couples strolled hand in hand or sat in the cafés, and children ran to and fro among the chairs. In the center of the square a handful of amateur artists were putting the finishing touches to drawings and watercolors. Among them was Siegret Wienzman.

The Weinzmans were staying only a few minutes walk from the square in a small hotel which, since it was un-licensed, was not listed in the telephone directory. Father and daughter had spent most of the day in Venice muse-ums and art galleries until the professor had pronounced himself exhausted. He returned to the hotel, giving Siegret his permission to take her sketch pad to the square.

She had just packed her belongings and was about to return to the hotel when she caught sight of the figure of Heinz Gerdler. There could be no mistaking him.

With a gasp, Siegret ducked her head as the coarse-featured face peered in her direction. She was hardly able to believe that she and her father could have been detected and followed in so short a time, yet there could be no other explanation. The youth was obviously searching the square for her. Her feelings of helpless ter-ror returned with undiminished intensity.

Not daring to look at him fully, she watched Gerdler make a circuit of the square and take a seat in one of the cafés. For a while she sat half mesmerized, trying to de-cide what to do. Then, clutching her basket, she rose slow-ly and began to walk away from him, trying as best she could to mingle with other passers-by, although in the past few minutes, these had thinned out greatly.

Every few steps she glanced back to see if she had been spotted. It was this that was her undoing. Hard by the steps down to the Canale di San Marco, where the gondolas were bobbing and swaying in the water, Gerdler's search-ing eyes met hers. With instant recognition he leaped to his feet and began running toward her. Siegret looked frantically for a way of escape, the memory of the last, terrible chase paralyzing her limbs. In blind panic she ran down the steps and jumped into the nearest gondola.

She was in mid-channel before she saw a second craft

putting out in pursuit of her. At first she thought the lead
they had was too great, but straightaway the other
boatman gave a series of loud hails, to which her own
gondolier responded, pausing in his strokes on the oar.

"Please," she cried in agitation, "you must hurry. I am
frightened." In broken Italian she tried to explain, but
the two boatmen were evidently under the impression
that they were taking part in a romantic chase between
two lovers, and to her dismay she saw that they were
gradually allowing the distance between them to close as
they crept along the canal.

Growing more and more frantic, Siegret appealed to the
boatman to go faster, but the man only grinned good-
humoredly and gave her an incomprehensible answer.
Gerdler was clearly visible now across the intervening
thirty yards of water, an expression of fierce triumph on
his face as he bore inexorably down on her. Numerous
other craft were moving up and down the canal in the
warm evening, but their occupants remained seemingly
unaware of her cries, too intent on enjoying the beauty of
the churches and palazzi that lined the waterfront.

The address she had given was a small church only a
street or two from where she was staying. To get there
the gondolier was forced to turn off into one of the
smaller waterways criss-crossing the city. A short way
past the turn, a small flight of mildewed steps ran down
the canal wall to the water. A boat approaching from the
other direction made them pass close beside this and, at
that instant, Siegret screwed up her courage, stood up,
and made a grab for the rusty iron railings lining the
steps.

Before anyone in either gondola realized what had happened, she had pulled herself onto the steps and was running up them into the streets.

"You idiotic fool! Stupid, careless oaf! Above all things
you were told not to let them know we were here."
Rintlen's rage vented itself upon the unfortunate Austrian. "What good did you think it would do to chase
after the girl like that?"

"I'm sorry, Standartenführer," Gerdler stammered,
sweating with fear. "I was trying to follow her to find

out where she was staying. I thought that was what you wanted."

"Yes, but not by running and yelling after her like a bull," Rintlen snapped. "This isn't the Reich anymore." The anger that he had built up during the long day wasted on the telephone was boiling over, and he cursed the youth savagely. To have been right in his guess at the Wienzmans' plans, to have had them so nearly in his grasp only to be frustrated by this last minute clumsiness, was infuriating. Less than an hour ago, he had received an urgent message from Heydrich, via the German consulate, demanding that the mission be accomplished with the utmost speed. The crisis over Czechoslovakia was worsening hourly, and war was looming.

"We must hurry. There is no time to waste," he told the boy, putting aside his anger for the moment. "We must get to the station at once."

"To the station?" Gerdler's face wrinkled in perplexity. "But why? Where are we going?"

"Half-wit! What do you imagine Wienzman will do as soon as his daughter tells him she's seen you? He'll take the first train out of the city. We must be there to follow them."

Venice's central station was surprisingly busy for a Sunday. Loudspeakers were blaring a series of unintelligible instructions while the staff attempted to deal with the hordes of travelers clamoring for attention and help. Several trains were standing at the platforms. Two big expresses were scheduled. One to Milan and Turin, and the other to Rome.

"They might take either of these," Rintlen said, examining the destination boards. "At a guess, Rome is the more likely, but we have no way of telling. They may not even be intending to take a main line service at all, or for that matter they could have gotten away already. We took long enough getting here, and I doubt if Wienzman would delay any longer than he had to."

Sending Gerdler off to check the queues at the ticket booths and watch the people boarding the Milan train, Rintlen bought himself a paper and sat on a bench from where he could see anyone approaching the barrier to the platform at which the express to Rome was standing. In his pocket he had tickets for himself and Gerdler to both destinations.

The minutes crept by, and he began to suspect that he might have guessed wrongly as to Wienzman's reactions when, just as the ticket collector was about to close the gate, a pair of figures detached from a party of tourists standing not far away and made a dash for the barrier.

Despite the fact that he had seen only poor reproductions of photographs of Wienzman, Rintlen had no hesitation in identifying him or his daughter. Their pale, worried faces left him in no doubt. He cursed the old man's cunning in timing their exit so well. There was no chance for anyone to follow them. The train was pulling out as the two clambered aboard, smoke from the engine billowing up to the roof.

Hurrying over to the other platform, he located Gerdler. "Here—go and get the money back on these"—he thrust the Milan tickets at him—"and find out when the next train leaves for Rome."

"They took the express to Rome?" Gerdler asked unnecessarily. "What are you going to do now?"

"Idiot! You and I will go after them at once, but first I must call our office in Rome and see that they are followed when they leave the train. They may think they've escaped, but they're not clear yet."

○ ○ ○

With the passing of the weekend, Stewart Curtis's anxieties over Klerksdorp began to trouble him again. Monday would see the investigating team starting their work on the mine, sifting through the assay reports and production figures and checking these against actual output. How long would it be before they found what they were looking for?

According to his own estimate, he had no more than a week at the outside before the banking syndicate headed by old Stuttenheim broke the news to the world. He based this reasoning not so much on the time it would take the investigators to uncover the fraud—in all probability they knew all they needed already, or at least guessed it—but on the ease with which the financiers would be able to unload their large holdings of Klerksdorp stock on the market.

This coming week would decide whether he was going to be able to salvage anything from the wreck for himself. The Southampton-New York flight was due to touch down at 4:00 P.M. on Friday, and on the same day Curtis had a 5:00 P.M. meeting scheduled with the American group who was purchasing his land options. Desmond O'Neill's decision to cut out the normal overnight stopover at Athens meant he could still just make it, but the margin was slim indeed.

Sitting in the Long Bar, Curtis read through the reports in the *Financial Times*. The steady selling of Klerksdorp shares that had been recorded for the last fortnight in both London and Johannesburg had eased on Friday, and there had actually been a slight gain on that day. Probably Stuttenheim was being careful not to frighten off potential buyers. Until he had managed to put the American deal through, Curtis didn't dare try and sell his own stock, for the same reason.

"Good evening, Mr. Curtis, I see you did not go to witness the finish of the race." Curtis recognized the figure of Frazer, *Caterina*'s first officer, standing beside him at the bar.

"I'm due at a dinner the Motoring Club's giving your captain, though at the moment I have rather more important matters to worry about," Curtis answered sourly, "such as wondering how long it will be before we make New York."

"Then I have good news for you, sir." Frazer said. "I was down at the moorings while the captain was out winning races," Frazer said virtuously. "*Caterina* has been given a clean bill of health. We shall be leaving first thing tomorrow."

"Do you mean there was nothing wrong with the plane at all?"

"Practically nothing. The chap in Shambe had done a pretty good job, it seems. Our people here replaced a couple of fuel leads and cleaned the air filters, and that was it."

"This is excellent news," Curtis nodded approvingly. "I

am glad to note that at least one crew member re-
tains some concern for the passengers' convenience."

Signaling the barman to bring Frazer a drink, Curtis put
his newspaper aside. "What continues to annoy me," he
went on, "is the fact that we have another delay in England
before we can fly on to New York."

"I suppose they could run the flight a day earlier,"
Frazer said thoughtfully. "Particularly since, as far as I
know, no extra passengers are joining us for the Atlantic
crossing. With your party, as well as Baron d'Este and his
wife, Dr. Van Smit, the Kings and some Turk or other
who's booked to join us at Alexandria, we shall be almost
up to our limit. We can't carry more than twelve or
thirteen passengers over such a long distance."

"In that case, we could fly straight on the next morning."

"Yes, indeed," Frazer agreed as a new thought entered
his head. "You could be in New York by Thursday afternoon. There's just one problem, though."

"And what's that?" Curtis demanded.

"You'd need to persuade Imperial Airways to put on a
new crew. You see Captain O'Neill is due to fly this
crossing, and he will certainly refuse to take off until he's
had thirty-six hours' rest. Exactly as he has done here,"
Frazer said pointedly.

It was Curtis's turn to look thoughtful. "So it's O'Neill
who's holding us up again. Well—I might just be able
to do something about it this time." He gave Frazer a
shrewd, speculative look. "I'm grateful to you for your
help—very grateful," he said as he drained his glass.
"Keep me informed if you have any more ideas."

Ken Frazer watched him with a smile of satisfaction.
The net around Desmond was closing in.

○ ○ ○

It was late before Rashid finally returned to Prince
Suleiman's palace. After his shot at Luca d'Este, Yousouri's police and soldiers had hunted him for three hours
among the rice paddies and sugar cane fields. They had set
up roadblocks at strategic points, and in the end he had
been forced to escape by hiding in a truckload of vege-
tables. He felt intensely weary and despondent.

The prince had left word that Rashid was to be brought to him on his return. As soon as he had washed and changed his clothes, the young sheik joined the prince in his study.

"So," the prince raised a quizzical eyebrow, "you have decided to favor me with your presence at last?"

"I have been at Fayum," Rashid told him. "Luca d'Este was there, and I wished to avenge the deaths of my father and sister."

"Yousouri Pasha has been here to tell me what you have been doing—or perhaps trying to do would be more correct," the prince replied. "I presume you are aware that you missed?"

"I know." Rashid flung up his hands. "The devil protects that man. The car overturned as I pressed the trigger. But he cannot escape forever. Next time I will kill him, even if I must pay with my own life."

"That I do not doubt," the prince said quietly. "However, you will not do so in Egypt. I have given Yousouri my word on it."

Rashid stared at him. "You gave your word?" he cried. "You promised to stop me bringing justice to the murderer of my own father and your cousin? I cannot believe it. No man would do such a thing, no man of honor or courage would so demean himself."

"You forget yourself." The prince's tone was icy. "I do not need a young boy to remind me of what is honorable. Nor do I forget your father. Since your own attempts have proved such signal failures, I suggest you follow my advice for a change. It is only thanks to me that you are not even now in one of Yousouri's prisons."

"I am sorry," Rashid apologized humbly, "truly sorry. I spoke without thinking." He gave a sigh.

"I have made arrangements for you to join d'Este's aircraft at Alexandria. If necessary you can journey all the way to New York with him. Neither he nor anyone else on board has ever seen you before, so you will be safe from recognition. I have your tickets, money, and passport and papers in the name of Ahmed Yalchin Bey, a Turkish nobleman who has been visiting Egypt for the wedding ceremonies."

Rashid took the old man's hands in his own and kissed them. "How can I thank you?" he said with emotion.

The prince came out from behind his desk and embraced the young man. "You must leave at once, a car waits to drive you to Alexandria. May God grant you success and a safe return."

○ ○ ○

As soon as the prize ceremony at the palace was over, and he and Laura had received the huge silver-gilt cup from a beaming Farouk, Desmond slipped away to *Caterina*'s moorings at Kasr el Nil to talk to Keith Payne and the engineers.

"I've kept the boys working round the clock," the manager told him. "We found nothing major wrong, but you were right to insist on a thorough hundred-hour overhaul, and I'll back you up in my report."

"Thanks. I suspect I need all the support I can get right now," Desmond said.

Payne shook his head. "Things may go all right for you," he said. "It's hard to tell. I wish you luck, though. At least you'll be back on schedule again.

"We'll launch her at first light tomorrow," Payne added, "and put the gold on board straightaway, before the passengers—or anyone else—are around." He gave a thin smile. "For God's sake don't have an accident with any of that, or you really will be in trouble."

The Cairo Motoring Club was giving a dinner to honor the race winner at Shepheard's that evening, but first Desmond wanted to find Ralph Kendrick. Returning to the hotel, he ran into Sandy on the terrace.

"I've contacted all the passengers and warned them we shall be leaving at 7:30 tomorrow," the young purser said, after congratulating his captain on his victory. "Ken Frazer has spoken to some of them already. Mr. Curtis was very pleased."

"How's the passenger list? Any last-minute changes?"

"There's a Turkish chap joining at Alex," Sandy answered. "Oh—and Dr. Van Smit has decided to fly on all the way to New York with us."

"I can't make him out at all," Desmond remarked. "Have you any idea what he does?"

The boy shook his head. "I think he's involved in mining in some way," he hazarded. "Certainly he always seems very interested in what Mr. Curtis is doing."

Ralph Kendrick was not in his bedroom when Desmond called there. Searching the bars and sitting rooms on the ground floor, Desmond finally found him alone in the garden by the open-air dance floor of the night club.

The radio operator greeted him sheepishly. "I'm sorry about last night," he apologized, "and for ducking out of the race. I've let you down pretty badly all round." He was pale and careworn, Desmond noticed, but at least he was no longer drinking.

"You certainly have," Desmond agreed severely. "The question is, what are you going to do about it?"

"I just don't know, skipper," Ralph said helplessly, the misery evident in his face. "I thought I had this Atlantic ditching fear licked. You've flown with me for the last three years, and we've had our share of trouble in that time, but I've never lost my nerve before, have I?"

"No, you haven't. And I still don't think you have," Desmond told him, "but you're frightened of doing so, and it's having much the same result." Slowly the two men began to pace the garden, while Ralph spoke of his terrors and Desmond sought to reassure him and restore his confidence. "Every flyer has his own personal fear at the back of his mind," he told the radio officer, "but when the crunch comes, somehow they always find the strength to carry on, and I know it will be the same with you. If I didn't, I would never have taken you onto my crew."

His captain's calm words and evident trust in him went some way toward raising Ralph's morale and after another turn around the garden, he was admitting that he had allowed the problem to assume an exaggerated degree of importance in his mind and had been making a fool of himself. Anxiously he begged Desmond to let him carry on as before and not to report the matter to the airline.

"Very well," Desmond agreed. "But for God's sake, Ralph, if you find it's getting on top of you, come and talk to me about it. Don't try drinking your troubles away."

He could only pray, Desmond thought as he went up

to change for dinner, that Ralph would justify his confidence.

Entering the main dining suite, Desmond and Laura found that the majority of the guests were already present. The two of them were immediately showered with congratulations and compliments from all sides.

"We've had one bit of trouble," the senior race steward told Desmond when he was able to get him alone for a moment. "That chap d'Este's been claiming you ran him off the road; he's accused you of driving deliberately dangerously, and he's tried to file an objection to the result. Fortunately, the judges overruled him. There's the fellow over there," he pointed with his glass. "I'm surprised he's had the gall to come."

Desmond saw Luca standing beside a remarkably beautiful woman dressed in white. She seemed to have a sad, shy aura. "Is that his wife?" he inquired.

"Yes, she's the baroness, and a pretty hard time of it she's had, too, by all accounts."

Now he had managed to alienate another of his passengers, Desmond thought, just at the time when he was most in need of support.

Dinner was a prolonged affair. There were over a hundred members and their guests seated in the dining room, and the atmosphere was informal, though the scowling presence of Luca d'Este cast a slight air of awkwardness at the head table.

The Italian had invited Stewart Curtis and his wife, and, whether by design or mischance, Desmond could not tell, he found Georgina seated opposite him.

Somewhat to his surprise, she scarcely addressed a word in his direction, but from time to time she shot him a glance of such intensity that, despite himself, he felt uneasy stirrings of desire.

At last the meal and the speeches were over, and as the party moved into the adjoining room, she came up to him and touched his arm. "I must see you later," she said in a low voice. "I have something I want to give you."

"Something for me?"

"Yes, it's a small prize for being the winner today. I thought you deserved more than just a silver cup." Before he could reply, she had slipped away through the throng.

Although pressed to stay on, Desmond escaped from the after-dinner drinking as soon as he decently could. Rescuing Laura from a group of admiring men, he took her for a walk in the gardens.

The night was warm and clear, the still air scented with roses, oleander, and bougainvillea, and putting his arms round Laura, Desmond kissed her long and gently on the mouth.

"I haven't thanked you properly yet for coming in the race with me," he said.

"I thought you just did," Laura smiled happily, her head against his chest, "and anyway I loved it, even if I was scared half to death."

"You were frightened?" He stroked her hair softly. "You didn't show it."

"There were a couple of times," she confessed, tightening her arms about him. "Like when the baron hit the corner and when the Bugatti crashed, but I trusted you to bring us out alive."

They walked on in the dim light. "I must go back, I'm afraid," Laura said. "Mr. Curtis sometimes likes to give me a little work before he turns in for the night."

They kissed again, holding each other close. He was amazed at how small and light she was, and he caressed her wonderingly. Then, reluctantly letting her go, he led her back to the hotel. Laura said good night and disappeared upstairs, but several of Desmond's friends dragged him off for a nightcap, and it was some time before he was able to get away.

Thanks to his longstanding friendship with Freddy Muller, the hotel manager, Desmond had been booked into a large room with a private balcony. As he threw his dinner jacket on the bed, a faint sound from the open French windows made him look up. Georgina Curtis was framed in the doorway.

"I've brought you your prize," she said calmly. "I couldn't find you downstairs, so I came to wait for you up here."

"How on earth did you manage to get in?" Desmond asked.

Georgina laughed lightly. "I bribed one of the chambermaids. She was deliciously shocked at the idea. Aren't you going to open your present?" She held out a small, flat, silver-wrapped box.

"I can't accept a gift from you like this," Desmond protested. "It's impossible."

"Nonsense—of course you can," she told him. "I got this long before I knew who would win the race, intending to give it to whoever came first. In fact, I always thought it would be Luca. I'm so glad it's turned out to be you." And she thrust the box into his hands.

Undoing the wrapping, Desmond took off the lid and removed the layer of tissue paper inside. Georgina's prize was a gold Cartier watch on a crocodile strap.

"No," he said firmly, "I can't accept this. It's far too much." Replacing the lid he handed the box back to her.

Georgina looked crestfallen. "But you must," she said angrily. "I so much want you to have it."

"I'm sorry. It's out of the question," he told her. "And now I think you ought to go. Your husband will be wondering where you are."

"Oh, him," she said impatiently. "He's all right, he's got Laura Hartman with him."

Seeing Desmond stiffen slightly, she stared at him for a second and then with another laugh shook her head sadly. "Oh, so that's how it is, is it?" she said. "My poor man, I thought you'd realize by now—surely you know Laura's been my husband's mistress for the last three years or more?"

"I don't believe you."

Georgina said in a soft, spiteful voice, "Good, sweet, innocent little Mrs. Hartman fools everyone. Butter wouldn't melt in her mouth, but she likes nice jewelry and Schiaparelli dresses and traveling about the world. Why else do you think Stewart takes her off to South Africa and leaves me behind?"

"But three years ago she was married," Desmond said.

"Yes, and her husband was an alcoholic, and so might you have been if you had brought home a new wife and within a month of the wedding she was running around with your employer."

She had moved closer to him as she spoke, and reaching up she stroked his cheek lightly. "I know," she murmured, "it's hard; for me as well as for you, and you are not the first to be fooled like this." Desmond pushed her hand away angrily. Giving a small sigh, she put the box down on the table beside the bed. "Wear the watch," she said quietly. "If I thought you could be bought that easily, I would never have given it to you. Maybe we have more in common, you and I, than you realize." And with that she was gone, closing the door softly behind her.

III

Europe

7

By cable: PERSONAL TO CAPT. D. O'NEILL, SHEP-
HEARD'S HOTEL, CAIRO: ESSENTIAL I SEE YOU
TO DISCUSS OUR FUTURE PLANS. THIS IS IMPOR-
TANT TO BOTH OF US. WILL STAY AT THE FARM
TUESDAY NIGHT. LOVE. PAMELA.

By radio: IMPERIAL AIRWAYS OFFICE LONDON
TO CAPT. D. O'NEILL, COMMANDING G-ADHO
CATERINA IMPERIAL AIRWAYS FLIGHT 109,
CAIRO. ON ARRIVAL SOUTHAMPTON PREPARE
TO ATTEND BOARD OF INQUIRY 1700 hrs TUES-
DAY 14 MARCH INTO DEATH OF LIEUT. IAN
THORNE AT SHAMBE STATION, SUDAN ON FRI-
DAY 10 MARCH. END.

By radio: 0740 hrs MONDAY 13 MARCH 1939. IM-
PERIAL AIRWAYS CAIRO TO ALEXANDRIA AIR
TRAFFIC CONTROL. IMPERIAL AIRWAYS FLIGHT
109 G-ADHO CATERINA DEPARTED FOR ALEX-
ANDRIA - ATHENS - ROME. ETA ALEXANDRIA
0830 hrs LOCAL TIME. END.

The train journey from Venice to Rome had taken
more than seven hours, and it was not until after 2:00
A.M. that the Wienzmans arrived at Dr. Farenzi's apartment and woke him from his sleep.

Throughout the time on the train, neither Siegret nor
her father had closed their eyes for a second. They had
debated endlessly in whispers over what could possibly
have brought Gerdler to Venice. Siegret's terror had been
so great that the professor had never doubted that it was
the Nazi youth she had seen. At first the professor was

inclined to think that Hans Meyer had been arrested and forced to betray them, but in that case, they soon realized, the Nazis would have been hunting for them in Rome and not searching the streets of Venice.

"My belief is that they guessed where we would be," the professor told his daughter. "Gerdler must have been brought along because he would be able to recognize us —especially you." He patted Siegret's arm as she shivered. "Provided we were not seen boarding this train, we should be safe."

"Suppose they did see us. What will we do then?" Siegret whispered. "They may be waiting at the other end."

"Then we must take care to avoid being seen. I do not think they would dare seize us openly here in Italy, and they do not appear to be receiving help from the authorities. At worst they will follow us to Farenzi's, and we must hope he can be of some help."

They decided to leave the train separately and meet again outside the station to take a taxi across to the doctor's apartment. Siegret was so weak with fear it was almost beyond her strength to walk down the platform and through the barrier at the end. The station seemed to be full of suspicious men watching the new arrivals. She lowered her head and made for the exits.

Rome seemed very busy for so late at night. The taxi sped through the streets while Siegret and her father peered from the rear window trying to see if they were being followed. The glare of the traffic and the general activity made it hard for them to tell, and to their tired and anxious eyes, it seemed as though every car on the road was pursuing them. They passed through the gap in the Aurelian walls into the corso. Here, on a small side road, Dr. Farenzi lived in an apartment overlooking the Borghese Gardens.

It seemed an eternity before he answered his bell and hustled them inside.

"You will be safe here tonight," he assured them, fussing to make up beds and heat up drinks. "Even if you were followed as far as the building, they will have no way of discovering in which apartment you are hiding, and in the morning we will find you a safe place until we can get you off to America."

"America—" the professor echoed, then sighed deeply. "How I wish we were there."

"And so you shall be," Farenzi answered. "Mussolini and Hitler are not quite the allies many would like us to believe, and the Nazis are on their own here. In the morning we will see what must be done, but for the present you need sleep. Off to your rooms. I will lock the door, and, if anyone tries to break in, I have a gun and will not hesitate to use it."

As Siegret switched out her light, she peered out of her window into the street below. At the far end of the road under the trees was parked a black car that had not been there when they arrived.

○ ○ ○

Pat Jarrett's activities had already attracted notice. Returning from making the rounds of some outlying farms on Saturday afternoon, County Sheriff Hal Franklin had spotted tire marks in the slush at the junction of the main road and the dirt road leading up to the lake. It was unusual for anyone to come down from the cities this early in the year. Even the workers hired from nearby Keene to put the houses in order for the summer were not expected before the beginning of May.

Stopping his car and examining the marks more carefully, he saw that the vehicle had returned down the track and taken the road toward town. Most probably it was some local person who had been up to see if the lake was clear yet. Warren Lake was famous in that part of the country for the size and hunger of its trout, especially near the dam at the southern end. Hal himself spent much of his free time up there. Deciding that a check on the house could wait, he drove on.

It was not until early on Monday morning that he returned. He saw at once that the road had been used several times during his absence; there were marks of at least two different sets of tires, one of them belonging to a heavy truck, judging by the width of the tracks and the way the soft ground at the edge of the road had been gouged out.

Leaving his car halfway up the road, Hal made the rest

of the journey on foot. He was anxious that whoever was up at the lake should receive no warning.

He was surprised to see that the ice on the lake had completely vanished. He paused by the edge of the trees and swept the shore with his binoculars, but there was no sign of anything unusual. The tracks led up toward the northern end, and he peered through the binoculars at the houses there, shifting the glasses from one to another, but as far as he could see, nothing had been disturbed.

It was not until he reached the point, that he saw the truck parked off the trail beneath the trees. "Can I help you, sheriff?"

Hal spun around to face the speaker. The path was grass-covered but even so, Hal realized, the man must have come up fast and quietly.

"Sorry if I startled you, sheriff, I guess you didn't hear me coming. The name's Jarrett, and I've rented the Bosworth house for a couple of months. I see you're looking at my truck." The man gave a brief smile as he spoke, but there was no warmth in his voice.

"I was wondering what anyone was doing up here," Hal answered. "We don't normally get visitors this early in the year."

"Sure," the man nodded. "I was going to come into town tomorrow and let you know I was here."

"You on vacation?" Hal asked.

" 'Fraid not. I'm doing a meteorological survey in the area for a couple of the airlines, and I reckoned this'd be as good a base as any. I was just unpacking when you came."

It all sounded quite reasonable, Hal thought. There was nothing he could pick out as being wrong, yet he didn't like any of it. There was something in the way this man Jarrett looked and moved—something wary and alert about the eyes.

The Bosworth house was the biggest house on the lake. Why had he taken it just for himself?

Mr. Jarrett, he decided, would do well to have a discreet eye kept on him until it became clear exactly what he was up to.

○ ○ ○

Dr. Van Smit pushed aside his half-finished coffee in the breakfast room at Shepheard's. Early morning starts, necessary in air travel to avoid the turbulence that tended to increase during the late afternoon, did not usually bother him. This particular start, however, was one he had hoped to avoid. He had envisioned traveling no farther than Cairo, and after a brief but extravagant holiday, returning to South Africa, but the failure of his search of Stewart Curtis's suite had changed everything.

Without doubt, had the maid not returned, the suite would have yielded a small fortune in cash and jewelry. True, the best pieces would have been in the hotel safe, or being worn by Georgina, but there had still been a perfect opportunity to pick up some of the smaller bits, and such items were actually easier and safer to dispose of than larger and better-known stones.

Van Smit had entered the world of crime almost by chance some fifteen years earlier, when, out a job and heavily in debt as a result of his gambling, he had helped a drunk he met in a bar in Durban back to his hotel room. He had discovered the man was carrying a roll of bank notes totaling more than seventeen thousand rands.

This windfall had prompted him to experiment in robbing other wealthy travelers, until he had come to rely on the extra income. When his fortunes shrank beneath his losses at cards, he recouped them by looting the rooms of nearby hotels.

Very probably, had he not been relatively successful at his gaming during these past years, Van Smit would have been tracked down and arrested, but the comparative infrequency of his operations, as well as his skill and cunning, had so far kept him from discovery. It was even possible for him to go about under his own name, merely putting out the fiction that he was still engaged in his former occupation as a geologist.

When Van Smit had first learned of Stewart Curtis's presence in the Cape, the financier had seemed a natural target. The doctor had not in fact been particularly short of funds at that precise point, but the prospect of a visit to Cairo and its casinos had attracted him, and he had been confident of his ability to lift a large sum from the millionaire. Accordingly, he had booked on Imperial 109.

Events, however, had not gone his way. On the journey up through Africa, Curtis had been nervous and jumpy, scarcely ever leaving his private cabin even for meals, and the accident at Shambe had put the remainder of those on board in a similar mood. Once in Cairo, Van Smit had only the one opportunity to go over Curtis's rooms—owing to the constant presence of the maid, the hotel servants, or Laura Hartman—and even this had proved abortive.

Meanwhile, his nightly forays to the casinos and gambling clubs had been disastrous, so that a raid on Curtis had now become a vital necessity. At some point between Cairo and New York, he must pull off a really spectacular heist. Perhaps during the stopovers in Rome and England he might have a chance. At least, with the two d'Estes joining the flight, the number of his wealthy fellow passengers had been doubled.

Down at Kasr el Nil, the great golden disk of the sun hung on the very edge of the horizon, gilding the landscape, but its warmth had yet to stir the air, and the morning was chilly and crisp.

Caterina rode on the river once more, moored between the double-sided Braby pontoons, tail into the bank, while a stream of porters passed back and forth loading the mail bags. On the starboard wing, mechanics were making final adjustments to the inboard engine. Two other C-class boats lay moored nearby, attached to buoys in midstream.

Desmond watched from the doorway of the airline office at the head of the pier. He and the crew had been up since five-thirty to see the gold brought from the military barracks and stowed away in the holds, making sure that the weight was correctly distributed so as not to upset the aircraft's trim. Then there had followed an exhaustive inspection of every piece of equipment on board. Three or four minor faults had turned up, and even now the mechanics were righting them.

His mind kept repeating the words of Pamela's latest cable. Pulling it from his jacket, he took another look at it, puzzling again over the meaning behind the laconic phrases. "Essential to discuss our future plans." Coming so hard on her previous letter, it was difficult to know what to make of it. Most likely, he feared, Pamela was building up to one of her periodic outbursts.

He had experienced these explosions frequently and he had never ceased to dread them. Pamela would lash out indiscriminately, seeking to hurt in any way she could. Her vindictive tongue would strike without mercy, poisoning their love and tearing the relationship into shreds.

On top of Georgina Curtis's allegation concerning Laura Hartman last night, he felt emotionally drained before the day had even begun. He was disinclined to believe Georgina's story; nevertheless, her words had effectively pulled him up short and made him realize how near and how quickly he was coming to committing himself to a woman he scarcely knew.

For both their sakes, it would be better to take the affair more calmly. Laura was still in a vulnerable state after the loss of her husband, and it would be unfair to her to try and rush into a situation that might prove unworkable.

Usually, Desmond looked forward to the prospect of returning to the air after a spell on the ground. Today, the sight of the gold being loaded and the knowledge that a hostile reception awaited his arrival in England served to depress his spirits, and when Laura greeted him at the gangway, his reserve was more marked than he intended.

A look of hurt surprise passed over her face, and he felt instantly contrite. He tried clumsily to make amends, but the damage was done and his attempts only made matters worse.

"This is Mademoiselle Arlette Ducroix, Mrs. Curtis's maid," she said icily, indicating a nondescript woman of about forty in a plain gray dress who accompanied her. Her lips compressed tightly, she turned stiffly and disappeared into the aircraft, leaving him cursing under his breath, having to force himself to be polite to the other passengers.

The Kings, the Finlays, and the Johnsons were all on board, together with Van Smit, which left only the Curtises and the d'Estes. Protocol and civility demanded that

Desmond be on hand to receive them, but the thought of doing so was more than he could stand, and, handing the job over to Sandy Everett, he went back up to the flight deck.

Here the atmosphere was less strained than it had been on Saturday. Ken Frazer was whistling happily as he laid out the route maps and chinagraph marking pencils. Ralph, too, was in a noticeably happier state of mind now that he was facing up to his fears and no longer struggling to conceal them. Sliding into his seat, Desmond adjusted the safety belt.

"That's a nice watch," Frazer commented, and Desmond's eyes flicked guiltily to his wrist.

"It was a prize for winning the race—donated by Mr. and Mrs. Curtis," he explained shortly.

"A Cartier, isn't it? Mind if I have a look?" Desmond unbuckled the strap and handed the watch over to Frazer without comment. He felt angry with himself for even putting it on. Paradoxically, it had been his annoyance with Georgina for her behavior and his exasperation with the events of the last three days that had prompted him to do so. At least, he felt, he would have gained something out of the mess into which he had fallen.

Sandy stuck his head through the doorway. "All passengers aboard and settled down, skipper," he reported, "and all cargo safely stowed. Ready to take off when you are."

"Thanks, Sandy." Desmond reached forward and flicked on the main ignition switch. "Cast off the prow warps, Ralph," he called, "and let's get moving."

The time was exactly 7:35 A.M.; by 8:30 they should be in Alexandria.

Georgina had invited Jacquetta and Luca to share the after cabin, a suggestion the baron had accepted with alacrity, and the two couples were comfortably installed by the time the gangway was drawn up and the hatches closed.

Jacquetta had never been in a flying boat, and it was an exhilarating experience for her. When the noise and vibration ceased and the foaming track vanished beneath them, revealing the great city spread out below in the morning sun, she lay back in her seat with a sense of real enjoyment.

Once level flight was in progress, Andy Draper began serving coffee and hot rolls. The others chattered among themselves, but Jacquetta remained lost in her thoughts. Luca was still fawning over Georgina, yet the spectacle no longer bothered her. Ever since the ordeal in the desert, her mind had run more and more to the young sheik who had rescued her. In her fantasies she conjured up Rashid's proud, youthful face. She found she regretted not having told him her name.

Andy brought coffee to the flight deck as soon as he had attended to the passengers. Desmond had throttled back the engines and synchronized their timing. Now with the autopilot on, they were free to sit back and enjoy the view.

"How are they behaving below decks, Andy?" Ken Frazer asked jovially. He had been inspired to unusual cheerfulness by the news of the radio message about the inquiry received by his captain. "Any complaints so far?"

"Not yet, sir," Andy rejoined, "but if you like I can tell them you will be bringing us in to land at Alex." There was a snort of amusement from Kendrick at this, and even Desmond smiled. Frazer, however, was too full of himself at the thought of Desmond's impending downfall to care, and he ignored the steward's riposte.

"Baron d'Este and Mr. Curtis were asking for you," Andy went on, speaking to Desmond. "They were wondering why you weren't at the hatch when they came aboard. I told 'em you'd had an urgent radio message from the British ambassador, and that shut 'em up."

"Stewart Curtis's wife has joined him, hasn't she?" remarked Kendrick. "What's she like, Andy? Is she as bad as the old man?"

Andy shrugged. "Seems like all the others to me. Wanting this, wanting that. Why does the airplane fly so high? When do we stop for lunch?" The others on the flight deck laughed. "Tell you one who is different, though," he added, "and that's Baroness d'Este. There's a real lady, now. You can have all the rest."

"I thought Laura Hartman was your favorite, Andy," Ralph Kendrick said, with a wink at Desmond.

"Oh, well, that's different," Draper answered. "I mean, she's like one of us now—isn't she?"

○ ○ ○

In the master bedroom of Prince Suleiman's villa in Alexandria, Rashid al Senussi dressed carefully. It was fortunate that on his arrival in Cairo he had taken the trouble to have a number of suits made as well as a sufficient quantity of shirts.

He had chosen a well-cut, light gray double-breasted suit. Thanks to the reforming zeal of Mustafa Kemal, a Turkish nobleman no longer needed to wear a fez, and accordingly he chose a soft, wide-brimmed hat. His years in Rome had made him almost more at home in western dress than in his traditional robes, and it was with a sense of pride that he surveyed the finished result in the mirrors.

Soon the flying boat from Cairo would touch down on the water in the harbor, and he would go on board. When the moment was right, he would reveal his identity and watch the Italian's face dissolve in fear as he realized that he was about to be called upon to expiate his crimes.

Collecting his papers, Rashid wandered downstairs and out onto the terrace. There was something satisfying, he thought, as he strolled in the cool morning listening to the waves, in dressing with care and elegance in order to go out and kill a man.

A faint humming sound reached his ears. The airliner was approaching the coast. Rashid drew in a deep breath; it was time for Ahmed Yalchin Bey to take the stage.

○ ○ ○

At the request of Georgina Curtis and the others in the after cabin, Desmond took *Caterina* round in a slow, low level circuit of the city to give the passengers a good view of Alexandria and Lake Mareotis before beginning his run in to the harbor.

By a window in the midship cabin, Laura Hartman tried to match the enthusiasm of Harold King and his wife. Laura was feeling anything but enthusiastic. She was still trying to discover a reason for Desmond O'Neill's sudden change of attitude. In the hotel garden the previous evening, he had been loving and tender, and she had gone to sleep happier than she could remember being at any time since her marriage. His coldness this morning in the face of her affectionate greeting had hurt her desperately.

The long sweep of the Corniche facing the Mediterranean and Alexandria's famous beaches slid past beneath them as *Caterina* swung around to approach the harbor. It was possible, Laura supposed, that Desmond was feeling that they were becoming too involved too quickly, and, if so, he might well be right, but she still could not believe he would have reacted so harshly. There had to be something more.

The possibility of Georgina Curtis being involved occurred to her, but she dismissed the idea. On several occasions over the weekend, Desmond had been at pains to make it clear that he wanted nothing to do with the lady, and it was hardly likely that he would change his mind so quickly.

The flying boat came in low over the sea, dropping toward the western harbor as Desmond throttled back the engines. The white sails of the feluccas clustered around the shore were clearly visible, and several large steamers were tied up at the quays, as well as two squat warships.

Alexandria was one of the most important flying boat stations in the world, where traffic from Africa merged with that coming in from Asia, India, the Far East, and Australia to link up with European routes. This was especially true for Imperial Airways, and at any one time half a dozen of the line's aircraft might be found there, slipping crews, undergoing repairs, or simply waiting to take on more fuel, cargo, and passengers before resuming their long journeys.

For Sandy Everett, that halt at Alexandria was always one of his busiest periods. There was invariably an enormous amount of mail to be checked and transhipped to destinations in the east and more to be taken on board for carriage to Europe and North America. The bags he had sorted during the flight up to the delta had to be handed out through the mailroom hatch and the incoming ones stacked ready for him to deal with as soon as they had regained the air.

There were people to be taken care of, too. The Finlays

were disembarking to continue their journey home by sea. Perhaps fulfilling an ambition, as they claimed, but more likely, Sandy guessed, simply to put off their return to the strange and forgotten homeland where they would spend the remainder of their days.

In their place there came on board Ahmed Yalchin Bey.

Alexandria was only a refueling and loading stop for the Imperial 109. The passengers were permitted to disembark and stroll around on the piers and admire the nearby palace and the view of the city, but there was no time for them to venture farther afield. The majority of the passengers, after stretching their legs, resumed their seats and waited quietly for the flight to continue.

Jacquetta d'Este preferred to remain on the pier. It was pleasantly warm and bright, and a fresh breeze brought the scents of the sea and an interesting mixture of wood, tar, oil, and smoke from the docks. On the feluccas, the fishermen were laying out their nets to dry in the sun, picking them over carefully for holes, while a horde of small boys clambered about, swabbing the decks and furling and unfurling the sails.

From where she stood, she could see Desmond O'Neill talking with the crews from some of the other planes tied up alongside the jetties and pontoons of the airline piers. The transfer of mail to *Caterina* was still in progress, watched by a section of uniformed police. A security precaution, she supposed, to prevent packets from going astray.

She did not notice the car that approached silently from the direction of the Corniche, and it was only when she had started to walk toward the flying boat that she saw it had drawn up at the foot of the pier. The driver was talking to one of the crew members, evidently asking for directions. Possibly the man was having difficulty in making himself understood, but there was a short delay, and Jacquetta was only twenty yards away when the rear door of the car opened and an elegant young man stepped out.

She recognized him instantly, even here, in the last place on earth she had expected to find him, even in the unfamiliar European dress. As she caught sight of the lean, handsome face, her heart gave a leap. Conflicting emotions flooded through her: excitement at his presence and terror at the threat he posed.

Setting his hat firmly on his head, Rashid strode down the pier toward the gangway. The policemen moved forward to intercept him, and as they did so a fresh anxiety swept over Jacquetta. Was this why the uniformed detachment had been placed there? Had the authorities gotten wind of his plan?

Even as she watched, waiting for the moment when the police would seize him and drag him off, the officer in charge stood aside and saluted courteously, permitting him to pass up the gangway and disappear into the plane.

Jacquetta was now in a state of utter confusion. She felt mesmerized by the danger of the situation, and almost in a dream she followed Rashid's path down to the gangway.

"I'm afraid I must ask you to go aboard, baroness. We shall be leaving again very soon." Sandy Everett was smiling at her, but she scarcely realized he had spoken. Trembling with anxiety and nervous tension, she went through into *Caterina's* interior.

○ ○ ○

Thanks to a sleeping draught Dr. Farenzi had surreptitiously emptied into her nightcap, Siegret slept more soundly than she would have believed possible. Awaking, she saw at once from the sunlight on the curtains that the hour was already late, and she sprang from her bed.

The warm sparkle of the Roman sun on the rooftops and on the gardens in the park lightened her depression. The very thought that they had passed the night in safety added weight to Dr. Farenzi's assertion that the Nazis would find it no easy task to snatch them back to Germany.

Throwing a dressing gown on, she went through into the living area and found her father and the doctor having breakfast.

"Dr. Farenzi is of the opinion that we should take a ship or an airplane to the United States as soon as possible," her father said when he had kissed her. "We have been looking in the paper to see which is suitable."

"Yes," the doctor agreed, pouring her coffee and setting fruit and breakfast rolls before her. "There are no sailings until the middle of the week, but there is a flight tomorrow—British, Imperial Airways, going to England and New York. If we can get you seats, you would be in America by Friday."

"But could we leave so soon? What about the visas?" Siegret asked. "I thought we still had to wait for them."

"A good doctor, my dear, like a good cook, can always be sure of a welcome wherever he goes," Farenzi replied. "I will telegraph friends of mine in America, eminent men who will be glad to assist and to recommend your father's admittance."

"In the meantime, is it safe for us to remain here?" Siegret's father asked. "For your sake as well as our own, I think we should find a place elsewhere tonight."

"You are right," Farenzi mused.

It was agreed that while the doctor went off to the Imperial Airways office, the professor and Siegret would repack their clothes. They were to be ready to leave with him by eleven o'clock.

Rintlen and Gerdler had not been able to reach Rome before seven o'clock that morning, after traveling all night. Tired and angry from the long, frustrating day in Venice, the S.D. officer's temper had not been improved by having to share a sleeping compartment with the youth, owing to a shortage of accommodations on the train. On arrival in the capital, red-eyed and unshaven, they were driven to the German embassy.

"Well," Rintlen demanded when the secretary who received them left them alone with the head of the S.S. security section, "what have you managed to do so far?"

"We picked them out at the station, Standartenführer, although they tried to slip past us." The man launched into a lengthy description of their success in tracking the Wienzmans to the street off the Corso.

"Unfortunately, we have been unable to discover which apartment they are hiding in," he finished.

"List of occupants," Rintlen snapped curtly, and the officer hastily held out a sheet of paper.

Rintlen ran his eye down the list of names. "I see here a Dr. Augusto Farenzi living in apartment twelve. Bring me a medical listing. I want to know more about him."

The volume was produced, and he quickly turned the pages. "As I thought," he said. "Here we are: Farenzi, Augusto. Consultant physician. Student—University of Milan and"—he tapped the page triumphantly—"from 1905 until 1910, at the Department of Medicine at the University of Vienna. Where he would most certainly have met another student, there at the same time, by the name of David Wienzman."

The S.S. officer was impressed by Rintlen's resourcefulness. "Shall we go in at once and grab them?" he asked. "My men can be relied on to carry out the job."

Rintlen eyed his watch. "No," he said. "It's too early. There will be people about in the other apartments, and I want as little disturbance as possible. Tell your men to continue watching the apartment and to report anything that moves. I shall have a bath and a couple of hours' sleep. Wake me at ten o'clock, and then we will go and pay our errant professor a visit."

○ ○ ○

Entering *Caterina* through the hatchway into the promenade deck, Jacquetta found that Rashid was nowhere to be seen. The Johnsons and their daughter were standing by one of the windows watching a nearby aircraft, and Georgina Curtis's maid was occupying one of the corner seats at the rear. The steward, she realized, must have shown Rashid through into the midship cabin or the smoking saloon. With no clear idea of what she should do, Jacquetta returned to the after cabin.

Luca and Stewart Curtis were discussing the merits of empires to the obvious boredom of Georgina, who was wandering about the cabin in a desultory fashion and grumbling about the continual delay.

"I can't see why we're still waiting," she was saying as Jacquetta entered. "They finished loading the mail twenty minutes ago." Her anger, Jacquetta guessed, was because of Desmond's continued failure to put in an appearance with the passengers. The two men ignored her.

"Of course you will agree," Luca remarked, "that Italy has every right to her territories in Africa, just as Britain and France do to theirs?"

"Certainly," Curtis agreed, "but at the same time it is essential to ensure that the great powers do not come to blows over the possession of some trivial strip of land, as nearly happened at Fashoda."

Georgina shot him a venomous glance. "How a man as heavily involved in armaments as you are can say that, I can't imagine," she snapped. "Nothing would suit you better than a war."

Curtis turned to her, his face heavy with anger, but just then they heard the engines and felt the familiar trembling of the hull as the flying boat began to taxi out into the main harbor. Georgina flung herself down in her seat and gave a sigh of relief.

Jacquetta woke abruptly from the fit of abstraction into which she had fallen. She realized that she had allowed the situation to go by default. Had she sought out Rashid straightaway and confronted him, the young sheik would have had no choice but to abandon his schemes and go back on shore. In which case his chance of catching up with them before they reached America would have been slim.

Now she was left with the choice of denouncing him to the crew and seeing him arrested and perhaps condemned as a would-be murderer, or of standing by while he avenged the crimes committed against his family, killing Luca and perhaps herself as well.

The two men were still engaged in conversation, and Georgina was leafing idly through the pages of *Vogue* as *Caterina* climbed out over the Mediterranean and settled down to cruise at 4,000 feet for the hour-long flight to Crete. Jacquetta slipped quietly out of the cabin and made her way forward.

The Johnsons had been joined on the promenade deck by Dr. Van Smit and Laura Hartman; the Kings were still in their accustomed seats. Jacquetta knew before she reached the smoking saloon that she would find Rashid there alone.

He was sitting there with his back to her, a cigarette in an amber holder between his long fingers. Their eyes met instantly. He leaped to his feet in surprise.

"Who are you? And what are you doing here?"

"Please," Jacquetta begged, "don't be alarmed. I know who you are and why you are here. I won't give you away—but you must leave, get off this plane, before they realize who you are."

Rashid's eyes fastened sternly on her. "What is this? Who are you?" he demanded for the second time.

Jacquetta shrank from his gaze, and the words dried up in her mouth. Grasping her by the arm, Rashid shook her, repeating his question.

She faltered, and then unable to conceal the truth any longer, she cried, "I am Jacquetta d'Este."

There was a silence, then Rashid let out his breath in a low, slow rasp. "So you are Baron d'Este's wife." He stared at her. "What are you going to do now, baroness?" He accented the last word viciously. "Are you going to tell your husband and the rest who I am?"

Jacquetta shook her head, unable to speak.

"Why not?" he said derisively, plainly not believing her.

Jacquetta found her voice. "If I do—you'll be arrested," she said, dry-mouthed.

"And you care?"

She nodded silently.

"Why—because I saved your life? Is that it?"

"I don't know—I just care," Jacquetta told him. "I couldn't bear for you to be taken."

"And your husband? You know what lies between us, what I have sworn to avenge on him?"

Jacquetta hung her head. That question she could not answer, even to herself.

There was a noise behind her in the passageway; Dr. Van Smit was returning from the promenade deck. "Ah, baroness," he remarked, seeing them both, "have you been introduced to the newest member of our company? Ahmed Yalchin Bey—the Baroness d'Este."

Rashid bowed low.

"Thank you," she answered faintly. "We had just met. Now, if you will excuse me, I was looking for the steward." Before the others could reply, she fled from the cabin.

The peaks and pinnacles of Crete's mountain ranges were faintly visible on the horizon. The wrinkled surface of the sea was frozen motionless by the four thousand feet of air beneath them. Toylike ships could be seen crawling along the routes that led to Suez and the canal or heading northward toward the Aegean ports.

Desmond had switched to the autopilot, and he and the others watched the peaceful scene slide past. They were lulled into drowsiness by the steady drone of the engines driving them on through the clear bright air.

The memory of his behavior toward Laura filled him with guilt. He still refused to believe in Georgina Curtis's poisonous allegation; her reasons for making it were all too easy to see, yet each time he thought about it, he felt a hot surge of jealousy and anger. More than anything, he wanted to talk to Laura, to explain what had happened and apologize for the unintentional hurt he had caused her. He would have to try and see him alone in Rome that evening. Pamela, too, occupied his thoughts. Her telegram signaled the opening of a fresh struggle, just when he had thought it was all over, and he dreaded the prospect of the emotional mangling her bitter insecurity would put them both through. Worst of all was the possibility that she was having second thoughts about the divorce. The decree would not be finalized for another five weeks.

Pamela spent her life swinging from one extreme to another: hating one moment, loving the next, her fount of nervous energy forcing her to the limits of each new course she chose, sweeping aside all opposition to her decisions.

"We should be over Mirabella in a little under fifty minutes, skipper." Ralph Kendrick's voice broke in on Desmond's thoughts. "Shall I call them up and make sure they're ready for us?"

Breaking out of his reveries, Desmond examined the dial of the Cartier watch. "Yes, you'd better, Ralph," he said, yawning and stretching as he spoke. "I want to get away again to Athens as soon as we can."

Mirabella was the landing area at Crete where they would do nothing more than refill the fuel tanks. From there it was an hour or so flying time to the Greek mainland and Athens. The time was 10:40 A.M.

○ ○ ○

A somewhat hesitant and worried embassy servant woke Rintlen at quarter to eleven. "You were sleeping so deeply, Standartenführer, I did not like to disturb you," he apologized when the S.D. officer cursed him for his tardiness.

Still swearing, Rintlen rolled out of the bed and dragged himself to the bathroom. The three hours of sleep had left him feeling distinctly worse—groggy and hungover—and he regretted his weakness. Running a bath, he began to shave, calling for the latest information on the Wienzmans' movements as he did so.

"We have established that Farenzi has others in the apartment with him," the head of the S.S. section shouted to him from the bedroom. "Voices have been heard through the door. He left the building shortly before ten o'clock and drove to the Via Nazionale. Judging from his behavior, he may have been aware he was being followed, because he subsequently was seen going into the office of Imperial Airways. Our man is fairly certain that he bought tickets there."

"What flight and when? Did he find out any details?"

"No, Standartenführer, such information was impossible to obtain. You know how secretive the British are in such matters."

"Well, keep trying. Where is Farenzi now?" Rintlen rinsed the soap off his face.

"He went off in the direction of the Vatican City. There have been no reports since then," the officer told him.

"We will hit the apartment and grab the two Jews while he is absent," Rintlen decided. "That will save us having to find a way to dispose of him. Have your men ready to leave, and," he called, "bring me a glass of schnapps."

Dr. Farenzi had promised to be back by eleven. When the hour had come and gone, the fears of the two refugees grew more intense with each passing minute. Peeping from a window in the sitting room, Siegret was maintaining a watch on the street, and to her dismay, she had discovered that at least one of the cars parked below was occupied. The heads of two men were discernible in the front seat.

Her agitation increased when the quarter hour struck and still there was no sign of the doctor. She watched two men approach from the direction of the Corso and get into the same car in which the other two were sitting. She waited, praying it would drive off, but it remained an immobile, silent menace.

"Yes, it must be them," her father agreed when she called him over. "I suppose they managed to follow us last night after all." He squeezed her hand as he spoke.

"What shall we do, papa?" she asked in a trembling voice. "How shall we ever get away from here?"

"We will find a way. When Farenzi returns he will know what to do. You will see," he told her.

"I will want six men for the operation, as well as drivers for the cars," Rintlen announced. He summoned a conference to plan the assault on Farenzi's apartment. "Four will be needed to break down the door and go in with myself and Gerdler here." The youth stood listening to the proceedings with astonishment. "The other two will guard the stairs."

"What about weapons, sir? Do we have permission to shoot?" the S.S. officer asked.

"Yes, but only if you are fired upon. Remember, this operation is being carried out without the knowledge of the Italian authorities. We don't want to bring the police down on our heads."

"And if the Jews try to escape, Standartenführer?" asked another S.S. man. "Do we open fire rather than let them go?"

Rintlen hesitated. "Yes," he said at length, "but do so only if you can be sure of recovering the body. This professor and his daughter may be carrying important Party documents that cannot be allowed to fall into the wrong hands. Are there any more questions?" No one spoke. "Very well, then," he said. "As soon as the men and cars are ready, we will go."

"The Nazis must suspect you are in here," Farenzi told the Wienzmans when he finally returned sometime after eleven-thirty, "because I am fairly sure a man tried to follow me. Fortunately, I spotted him almost at once and managed to lose him in the Veneto."

"Did you get the tickets?" Siegret's father asked urgently.

"Yes," the doctor said proudly, "I have two, booked in my name." He drew a folder from an inside pocket of his jacket. "See here," he showed them, "you leave tomorrow at eight o'clock from Lake Bracciano on Imperial Flight 109, a flying boat, to England, and then on to Canada and the United States."

The tickets were thick, complicated documents, containing different sections for each stage of the journey and sets of vouchers for hotels and meals along the way. The idea that lunch had been ordered for them at a restaurant in Marseilles and rooms booked for two nights at the Ritz in London somehow went a long way toward restoring their belief in the possibility of escape.

"For your stay tonight," Farenzi continued, "I have had an excellent idea. The clerk who sold me the tickets told me that when the flight arrives this evening, all the passengers will be put up at the Grand Hotel, near the Palazzo Barberini. It is the finest hotel in Rome. So, I thought, why not ask the airline to book you there with the rest of the party?"

They looked at him uncertainly.

"Don't you see," he went on, "once you are in the hotel with the other passengers, you will immediately become part of the flight. You will have the protection of this group, and once you are among them, the Nazis will never be able to harm you. To try to do so would cause a great incident."

"The idea sounds good," Professor Wienzman agreed, "but how are we to get to the hotel? There are at least four men watching downstairs. They may well try to stop us."

Siegret gave a sudden cry. "Papa!" she cried out, "they are coming this way. The men from the car and some others, and—oh!" she let out a cry of despair, "Heinz Gerdler is with them! I can see him."

The embassy had provided six hard-bitten, well-muscled men.

"If possible," Rintlen emphasized as they collected in the street, "I want them taken alive. I gather Farenzi is back in the apartment."

"Yes, sir," replied the leader of the group who had been

keeping watch, "the Italian returned about ten minutes ago. We wondered whether to stop him, but our orders were to do nothing till you arrived."

"Quite right," Rintlen approved. "We can decide what to do about him when we have the two Jews."

"Farenzi's apartment is on the fourth floor," one of the men told him. "Two below the top."

"Good. Bring the tools for the door, and let's go," he said.

Siegret's words brought the professor and Farenzi instantly to her side at the sitting room window. Even from this height. the intentions of the half dozen men who were crossing the street were frighteningly apparent.

"They are on the stairs already!" Wienzman cried as the men disappeared from his view. "What shall we do?" He still had the doctor's pistol in his pocket, and now he drew it and looked wildly around the apartment for some means of escape.

"It's no good—we can't fight them; there are too many of them for us," Farenzi told him. "Quickly! Bring your bags and follow me. We must try to get out onto the roof before they find us here."

The suitcases had been packed and placed ready in the hall. Seizing the nearest of them, the doctor flung open the door of the apartment and led them out onto the stairs. Pausing only to snatch up the remaining bags, the other two followed him.

As Siegret began to hurry after Farenzi's vanishing figure, she could hear the sounds of many feet swiftly climbing the tile steps. Her father closed the door of the flat behind him, careful not to betray their movements by slamming it unguardedly.

Siegret ran up the stairs, past the landing of the next floor, trying to make as little noise as she could. She could hear the labored breathing of her father as he struggled to catch up to them, laden with the two heaviest suitcases. She expected to hear cries of alarm from their pursuers as soon as their escape was discovered.

At the topmost landing, Farenzi halted, his eyes darting round uncertainly. As in the rest of the building, two apartments opened off the landing, but to Siegret's dismay there appeared to be no corresponding door or hatch giving access to the roof. The doctor pressed the bell of the flat nearest the staircase while the other two gathered beside him anxiously.

There was no response, and Farenzi pressed the button urgently again. The sound of heavy blows on the door of the doctor's apartment reached them up the stairs, and there came a crash as the door was burst open, followed by shouts as the Nazis rushed into the apartment. There was still no reply to the bell Farenzi had been pressing. "Oh, hurry, please hurry, let us in," Siegret whispered in agitation.

Farenzi abandoned his efforts, and they ran to the door on the far side of the landing. Again, the ringing, and the agonizing moment as they waited, praying that this time someone would answer. Cries of anger were already coming from below. The doctor pressed his thumb on the bell and held it there.

They heard the latch being turned. The door opened a few inches, and an elderly woman peered out at them. "Who is it?" she inquired nervously. "What do you want?"

Farenzi pushed the door open and brushed past her, followed by the two Wienzmans. "Thieves and gunmen, madam," he tried to explain. "We are being pursued. You must show us the way to the roof."

At his words the old lady let out a loud wail and began attempting to push them back out onto the landing. The professor shut the door hastily, but he was too late. From outside on the stairs there came a cry as one of the Nazis, alerted by the noise, called to his fellows. There were answering shouts and a pounding of feet.

"The roof! How do we get out onto the roof?" Farenzi besought the old woman as the professor locked the door and slammed home the bolt.

The old woman cowered from them. "Through the kitchen," she quavered, pointing behind her.

All caution abandoned, they tore through the flat. Inside the kitchen, they found a back door opening onto a small flight of steps that led to the roof. Siegret had no idea of what they were going to do once they were out on the top, but she followed the doctor, pulling the suitcase after her.

The moment she stumbled onto the roof, she saw the sense in the route he had chosen. A wide, flat area lay

before them, littered with the projecting humps of stair-
wells and squat constructions that housed the building's
water tanks and other services. Makeshift clotheslines,
with clothes drying in the sun, straddled the open space.
She could see clearly where there was a way over onto
the roof of an adjoining building at the rear.

They plunged ahead, ducking under the clotheslines
and dodging in and out among the huts. They had succeeded in crossing over onto the next building, from which
a number of curious onlookers gaped at them in astonishment, before Rintlen and his gang burst through the
flat below and appeared on the roof.

Choosing a stairwell that looked as though it led down
to the street level, the doctor flung himself through it.
Both he and the professor were near the end of their
strength now, their faces streaming with sweat, their breath
labored.

Siegret pushed her father on ahead of her, worried lest
he should fall behind and be lost. He had already dropped
one of his cases. As Siegret helped her father, she heard
a sharp explosion and something struck the wall of the
stairs only a few inches from her head, sending up a
shower of dust and fragments of stone.

The shock of the bullet gave them renewed strength.
Dragging them through the door at the bottom of the
stairs, Farenzi bolted it swiftly as other shots echoed over
the rooftops. By good fortune this building was provided
with an elevator, which stood waiting before them. Piling
in, they set it rattling downward and collapsed over one
another, bent double, gasping for air.

There were few people in the street and no sign of any
Nazi agents. A taxi came toward them, and they waved
it down. "Grand Hotel," the doctor shouted to the driver.

○ ○ ○

Above the steep cliffs of the Acropolis, the marble
pediments and columns of the Parthenon, bathed in sunlight, faced out across the city. The sea formed a background of brilliant blue as Desmond circled *Caterina* low
over Athens. Banking away again, he brought her gently
down on the surface of Phalerion Bay and motored in

among the ferries, tramp steamers, and fishing vessels of the port of Piraeus.

The passengers were grateful to disembark after more than five hours aboard, with only the brief stop at Alexandria to stretch their legs. There was pleasure, too, in having a few hours to visit this most celebrated city.

Much to the annoyance of the crew, the presence of the bullion in the flying boat's holds meant they were under strict orders to remain on board or in the immediate vicinity during all daytime halts.

For Desmond, these regulations meant a further wait before he would have an opportunity to try to make peace with Laura. After they had docked, he had gone down to the lower deck to see the passengers ashore, and he attempted to say a few friendly words to her, but she walked past him with only the briefest acknowledgment.

Several chartered taxis, driven with typical Greek disregard, whisked the passengers off to Amalias Square and deposited them at the steps of the Grand Bretagne Hotel, where an elaborate lunch was waiting for them. Stewart Curtis's first action on arriving was to send Laura to rent him a sitting room upstairs and to arrange for a call to be put through to his stockbrokers in London. He badly needed to know what had happened to the price of Klerksdorp when the market opened for business after the weekend. Georgina demanded a room of her own as well, to change in and rest, and she dispatched her maid back to the aircraft to fetch several items of luggage for her.

Laura engaged a suite and a short while later reported back to Curtis that, for a variety of reasons, direct communication with London was impossible.

"Hell and damnation!" he cursed, so loudly that other people in the lounge turned and stared at him. "Can't they organize anything properly in these bloody countries? Did you tell them it was vitally urgent I get through?"

"I did everything I could," she told him, "but there's no way it can be done."

"If you were any damn use at all, you would have wired ahead and got them to arrange the call before we left Cairo. Why am I surrounded by half-witted fools?" He continued in this vein until even Georgina was moved to complain.

"Do be quiet and leave the girl alone," she said. "It's hardly her fault. You should have warned her if you wanted calls booked ahead for you. You'll have to wait till we reach Rome."

"The offices in London will be closed then," her husband snarled. "Doesn't anyone ever think except me?" Flinging down a three-day-old copy of the *Times*, he said angrily, "I shall have lunch upstairs. I'm fed up with eating with the same people day after day. Are you going to join me?"

"To eat upstairs by ourselves," Georgina looked at him in surprise, "when there is a very pleasant dining room down here? Certainly not. I shall lunch with Laura and the d'Estes."

"Very well then, please yourself," Curtis snapped.

After her recent exchange with Rashid, Jacquetta was very much on edge, reacting irritably to Luca's offhanded treatment of her and to his continued ogling of Georgina. Sitting opposite him at lunch, she tried to sort out her thoughts. She had told Rashid she could not give him or his plans away; nevertheless—she retained some vestige of loyalty toward Luca; he had, after all, been her husband for over fifteen years. She felt a desperate need for a way to make Luca aware that he was in danger without betraying the young sheik in any way or putting him at risk.

To her amazement, she heard Georgina broaching the subject. "Whatever happened to that young man you and Yousouri Pasha were telling me about?" she asked Luca. "The one who had sworn to kill you?"

"Oh, him," Luca shrugged. "Nothing at all—it was a false alarm, I suppose. The embassy was told, and the government is giving me a police guard while we are in Rome. Personally I regard it as a waste of time.

"This is a young terrorist," Luca explained to Laura, who was looking inquiringly at him, "one of a band I was obliged to put down during my time in Libya. Apparently, he wishes to avenge the death of his leaders."

"Or, to be more accurate," Jacquetta interjected, enraged by his casual distortion of the truth, "he wishes to pay you back for the callous murder of his father."

"That is a lie!" Luca retorted angrily, flushing as he spoke. "You are referring to judicial execution carried out by law."

"Is that how you describe taking old men up in airplanes and throwing them out?" Jacquetta could see the two women were wide-eyed, taking in her words.

With a great effort, Luca controlled his temper. "Such stories are nothing but lies and propaganda put about by our enemies. There is not a shred of truth behind them."

Turning to his wife, he addressed her in Italian, quivering with rage. "Never dare to repeat such things again. You are obviously incapable of grasping the concepts of political expediency and loyalty to the state. In the same way," he went on, a spiteful note creeping into his voice, "you will undoubtedly fail to understand why I found it necessary to leave instructions that your horse Balbo be sold to an Arab dealer rather than go to the unnecessary expense of having it shipped back to Italy and stabled until our return."

Staring at him in horror, Jacquetta saw that he was telling the truth. He had done exactly as he had said and must have been waiting for just such a moment to use it on her. She sprang to her feet and ran from the dining room.

Though a good ten degrees colder than Cairo, the weather in Athens was still pleasantly warm, and the tables of the cafés beneath the trees in the square were crowded with customers. Jacquetta wandered about in the sunshine, welling over with grief for the fate of Balbo and a savage hatred for Luca and his cruelty.

She sat down at a table and ordered coffee and fruit. She was eating a tangerine when a shadow fell across the table, and glancing up she saw Rashid standing beside her, very tall against the sun.

"I heard you quarrel with your husband," he said quietly. "I came to see if you were all right."

"Yes, we quarreled," Jacquetta fought to keep her voice steady, "but I didn't give you away, if that's what you're worried about."

"I never doubted it," he told her, pulling up a chair and sitting down. "Why don't you tell me what happened?"

Holding back the tears, Jacquetta recounted the substance of the quarrel and Luca's description of Balbo's fate.

Rashid listened in silence. "He was a good horse," he said when she had finished speaking, "and does not deserve to be sold off like a pack animal. I will send a message to Prince Suleiman, my uncle, asking him to buy him from whoever the dealer is and keep him for you."

"Thank you. You're very kind." she replied tonelessly, staring at the white parliament building in front of them.

"Oh—I'm sorry," she said after a rather long silence. "I didn't mean it like that—I really am grateful, but it doesn't solve the real problem, don't you see?" She seized his hand and squeezed it. "You'll never be able to get near my husband, and if you try, you'll be killed."

Rashid shook his head. "I have sworn to avenge my father, I cannot go back," he said simply.

"And what choice does that leave me with?" she cried in anguish. "I can't just stand idly by and let you kill my husband, yet if I raise a finger to save him, you'll be arrested. What am I to do? You must give up your insane venture and go home," she pleaded.

Rashid stood up; his face wore an expression of inflexible resolve. "It is time we returned to the hotel," he said. "The cars will be coming for us soon." With a slight bow, he left her.

○ ○ ○

Rintlen's seething temper finally exploded. Back in the embassy chancellery, he downed two glasses of schnapps and proceeded to castigate savagely each and every member of his unfortunate team.

Thanks entirely to their slowness in climbing the stairs and the inattention of the man left to guard the landing, he told them bitterly, the Wienzmans and their Italian companion had managed to escape. "Which makes this the third time they have been so assisted by servants of the Reich," he stormed at the apprehensive group.

The criminal stupidity of men who—in defiance of his express orders—had fired wildly during the rooftop chase, thereby drawing the attention of every person nearby, was a matter he would deal with later, just as he would deal with those who had so glibly and mistakenly assured him there was no rear escape from the buildings.

"For the moment, my only orders are to get out!" he barked. "Get out and find them. Search every hotel, every boardinghouse—search every building and house in Rome if you have to, but find them—find them at all costs!"

The men filed hurriedly from the room. Ordering Strasser, the S.S. officer, to stay behind, Rintlen poured himself another glass of schnapps and slumped back in a chair, forcing his tired brain to concentrate on what to do next. "Tell me the earliest flight by which the Wienzmans can leave, assuming they do go by Imperial Airways," he said.

Strasser consulted his notes. "The next flight, Standartenführer, is Imperial 109 for England and America, which leaves tomorrow morning at 8:30 from Lake Bracciano. We have been able to establish that this flight is now fully booked and that the remaining tickets were sold today, but no details are available as to the passenger list, except that the name Wienzman does not appear on it."

"They would have used a fake name anyway," Rintlen remarked sourly. "When's the next flight after that?"

"The day after tomorrow, Standartenführer. There are daily flights to England from here, and there are still seats available."

"But why the British airline?" the S.D. man asked, half to himself. "There are half a dozen foreign flights to London. Any one of those would have done."

Strasser cleared his throat obsequiously. "If I might make a suggestion, sir?" he said. Seeing Rintlen nod curtly, he went on. "Imperial 109 is a through flight to New York. It stops in England only to rest the crew. No other flight makes the trip this week. If the Wienzmans were intending to travel to America, that is the flight they would take."

"Of course!" Rintlen's face brightened. "You are right— that must be what they intend." He gave a grim smile of satisfaction. "Once again we have out-thought you, Herr Professor Wienzman."

"What will you do now?" Strasser asked, relieved at the reception accorded his idea.

"Try and head them off when they board, of course,"

Rintlen told him. "I have orders not to ask the Italian authorities for help, but I think we may be able to persuade the airport police that our friends' departure should be delayed. Just in case that should fail," he remarked caustically, "you had better book me on a flight, any flight that will get me into England on the same day. Rather, book two of us." He drained the remainder of his drink. "I suppose I'd better keep that little swine Gerdler with me."

○ ○ ○

Three o'clock saw *Caterina* airborne again above the Bay of Salamis where, over two thousand years earlier, the Athenian navy had destroyed the Persian fleet of Xerxes and saved Greece from conquest. In the distance, the jagged peaks of Parnassus glinted in the sun.

The passengers peered eagerly from the observation windows of the promenade deck and focused their cameras. The Ionian islands fell astern one by one—Cephalonia, Ithaca, Levkás, and the green slopes of Corfu.

Andy began to serve tea. The day had seen a distinct change in the attitudes of the passengers. Stewart Curtis, still as bad-tempered as ever, had ceased complaining, but several others on board were not nearly so pleased at having to forgo a night in Athens and press on through the afternoon and early evening, and Laura Hartman was noticeably less cheerful and easy-going.

Brindisi came in sight on the heel of Italy, another stopover on normal schedule, but today they flew steadily above the snow-laden Apennines. Another hour and Naples was behind them, Vesuvius's smoke plume lost to sight. They were drawing near to Rome just in time to see the dying rays of the sun glinting on the broad ribbon of the Tiber and catching on the great dome of Saint Peter's in a blaze of gold.

○ ○ ○

Four thousand miles to the west, Pat Jarrett made a final adjustment to the radio transmitter. Satisfied, he climbed out of the S4's cockpit onto the wing, stretching his stiff limbs gratefully. The job had taken him less

time than he had anticipated, but since dawn he had
to get at the rear of the control panel. Yesterday evening he had successfully positioned the accumulators behind the pilot's seat. A ticklish job because he had to
avoid damaging the wooden formers and stringers that
comprised the aircraft's frame.

With a last glance at his handiwork, he stepped down
been cramped in the tiny, awkward space, bent double
onto the right-hand float, his open box of tools in one
hand. The racer was firmly lashed between the walls of
the boathouse, but the float dipped sharply as his weight
came onto it, throwing him off balance. Grabbing the forward float strut with his free hand, he hauled himself
back upright, and as he did so, the tool box tilted sharply,
and several pieces fell into the water.

Jarrett swore savagely. The items lost included a set of
files essential to the proper fitting of the guns. They
would have to be replaced at once if he was to start work
in preparing the gun bays after lunch.

It was twelve-thirty. If he left straightaway, he could
drive into Keene, pick up the new files and some groceries
he needed, and maybe have a bite to eat as well.

Moreover, he thought, it might not be bad timing for
him to be seen in town. Jarrett had no doubt that the
sheriff had been satisfied by what he had seen, but any
stranger in a country district would be regarded with suspicion, and now that his presence had been discovered,
the best course was to behave as normally as possible.

Swapping his overalls for his old flying jacket, he set
off toward the main road. The day was overcast and the
weather colder than last week, but the forecast for Friday
and the weekend was good, with clear skies and temperatures around 45 degrees.

He found what he needed in a well-stocked hardware
store on Main Street, and he picked up a few items in
the grocery store. Resisting the temptation to waste time
looking around the town, he walked on up the street
until he came to a small café and bar. Peering through
the window, he saw that the tables inside were empty,
save for one nearest the counter, at which two old men
were sitting, chewing slowly on their food. Jarrett went
in and took a seat.

The two men favored him with long, hard stares. He

nodded briefly to them, and one of them mumbled a greeting of some kind. "Suzie—customer for yer out front," he called.

There was an answering cry. from the kitchen. Jarrett waited, conscious of the two men watching him. Satisfied at length, they returned to their plates. A door opened, he heard a radio playing dance music, and the girl entered.

At the sight of her, Jarrett felt a stir of excitement in his belly. She was no more than sixteen or seventeen he guessed, mature for her age and fully conscious of her power. Slouching across the room, she stood negligently in front of him, hips thrust provocatively forward. She had a sullen, sluttish expression, and her untidy brown hair was caught together loosely in back. In a few years she would have run to seed, but just now she was desirable, and she knew it.

"Want to eat?" Her voice was flat and toneless.

"A plate of whatever you are serving," Jarrett said, "and a beer."

Returning with a dish of stew, she looked him up and down curiously. "Haven't seen you in town before, mister," she said. "You just passing through, or staying for a while?"

"I'm spending a couple of weeks up at Warren Lake," he said. "Surveying a route for the airlines."

"For the airlines?" The girl's voice quickened with interest. "You a flyer then?"

Jarrett nodded. "That's right," he said. "Ever since the war. Run my own outfit doing meteorological surveys."

She fetched him the beer and poured it slowly, watching the head carefully. "I love planes," she said. "Never been in one, though. You got a plane of your own, mister?"

Jarrett was reluctant to give away any details about his activities, yet he felt a strong urge to admit to a fact that he knew would raise him in the girl's eyes. Surely there was no harm in it being revealed now that the sheriff had called. "Yes, I've got a plane," he said quietly. The effect was everything he would have wished.

"Your own plane," she breathed. "Say now, isn't that something? I never met a man with his own plane."

Jarrett was saved from having to make further comment by a call from the old men. The girl went off to fetch their apple pie. By the time she had done so, and produced cream to go with it, he had finished his stew and was downing the last of the beer.

"Nothing else?" she asked in surprise as he held out the money for the bill.

"I have to get back," he explained. "There's a lot of work to do before the sun goes in."

"Which house are you staying in—up there?" she asked, ringing the register. "Oh yeah, I know, the one on the point," she said when he told her. "Well, come in and see us again, mister." She handed him his change and gave him a knowing smile. "Who knows—maybe one of these days I'll come up there, an' you can give me a ride in your plane."

○ ○ ○

Jacquetta's outburst had caused Luca considerable embarrassment. Although he spent most of the rest of the meal denying her version of the Rashid affair, it was evident that neither of the two women were particularly convinced by his words. During the flight from Athens, his wife had gone to sit in the promenade cabin, and, since Georgina wanted to have a bed made up for her in the after cabin to rest for the afternoon and Stewart Curtis was still in an evil temper, Luca passed the trip in the smoking saloon, in conversation with Van Smit and the colonial engineer, Johnson.

Once, during the afternoon, the newcomer to the flight, Ahmed Yalchin, had joined them for a while, sitting alone in a corner, taking no part in the discussion. He seemed polite, if restrained and withdrawn; nevertheless, Luca felt as though he were being watched and was glad when the young man left them again. On landing in Rome, Luca was gratified to find an official car waiting with the news that he was wanted immediately at the Foreign Ministry, where discussions were taking place on the crisis that had arisen in Czechoslovakia: German reservists were apparently being called up, and there were reports of troop movements in Munich and Salz-

burg. Setting off at once, accompanied by two armed police guards, he left Jacquetta to make her way to the
Grand Hotel with the other passengers.

The d'Estes, in fact, owned a villa in Rome, in the fashionable area of the Largo Goldini, but this was now
rented to tenants for the period of Luca's appointment in
Washington. After the strain of the past few days, it was
a relief for Jacquetta to be able to shut herself in the
privacy of a hotel room rather than enduring the greetings and fuss of the servants. She hated the villa anyway,
with the elaborate d'Este crest over the doors and the
oppressive grandeur.

Luca would most probably not be back until late, she
guessed, and she called room service and ordered a light
supper, glad of the chance to rest. After a long, relax-
ing bath, she put on a dressing gown and brushed out
her hair. She was still no nearer finding a way out of
the dilemma before her. She was sure she ought to warn
Luca, yet each time she found herself with him, the words
froze on her lips, and instead she seemed to be led into
making increasingly bitter attacks as her husband's pom-
posity, his arrogance, and his cruelty became ever
more unbearable to her.

The other corner of the triangle, rapidly crowding out
all other considerations, was Rashid. The very idea of the
risk to him dismayed her to a point where she could
scarcely reason. As it was, the young sheik filled most of
her waking thoughts, and the mere fact of being near
him threw her into a turmoil.

There was a soft tap at the door, and two waiters entered with a trolley filled with an elaborate array of silver
tureens, dishes, and bowls. Selecting a plateful of what
she wanted and a glass of wine, she took it back into the
bedroom and, sitting on the edge of the bed, she picked at
the food mechanically.

Perhaps, she thought, she ought to talk to someone. But
there was no one in Rome she really liked or trusted. All
her acquaintances here had come to her through Luca;
her own friends were in the country, and the problem
was not something to be discussed over the telephone.

Rashid al Senussi switched out the light in his bedroom
and opened the French windows leading onto the small

balcony. He was wearing only a shirt and trousers, and the night air was chill after the warmth of Eygpt. He closed the windows carefully behind him and gauged the gap between himself and the next balcony.

The distance was no more than five feet, but six floors above the street, with the lights of Rome spread out before him in a vast panorama, it required a considerable effort of will to climb up onto the narrow balustrade, and, clinging onto the casement of the window, stretch out toward the adjoining balcony. The gap was too wide to be bridged in a single step, and Rashid was forced to throw his weight across, risking losing his footing. One hundred feet below him, the traffic swirled past like a procession of brightly lighted toys. There was a moment of heart-stopping fear, and he was across. The windows were covered by thick curtains. Drawing the service revolver from his belt, Rashid tried the door handle.

Luca d'Este left the Foreign Ministry in the Palazzo Chigi at 8:15, still accompanied by the two guards. They were broad-shouldered toughs, schooled in the brawls and street fighting of Fascism's early days, the heavy automatics in their underarm holsters bulging beneath their suits. Their presence, he was sure, was superfluous, but they added an acceptable aura of importance to his position. At the bottom of the steps, the car that had brought him stood ready.

"The Grand Hotel," he told the driver, "and wait for me there. I have to change and return to the ministry for dinner."

The sudden eruption of the Czechoslovakian crisis over the weekend had caught everyone by surprise. It was becoming obvious that the Nazis in Berlin were playing a close hand and not letting slip to the Duce any hint of their intentions. The general opinion at the palace was that Germany was planning to invade and occupy Czechoslovakia within the next two or three days. He wondered how Britain and France would react to such action, coming less than six months after the Munich agreement.

The car drew up outside the hotel, and, followed by his two guards, Luca went up to the suite, his mouth set. He still had to deal with Jacquetta.

The French windows rustled slightly and swung open. As Rashid stepped through, Jacquetta sprang up from where she was sitting and ran toward him. "How ever did you get over the balconies?" she cried in amazement. "You must be mad. You might have fallen and killed yourself."

"Not so loud," he warned her urgently. "Where is your husband?"

"He isn't here. He went straight to the Foreign Office." She noticed the revolver in his hand, and her eyes widened. "Rashid, it's impossible. He has armed guards following him everywhere. Didn't you see them at the airport? They'll kill you if they find you here. You must go."

"I cannot go back. Whatever the danger, I must keep my word."

"But not here, not in Italy. What chance have you if you're caught?" She had hardly spoken when from the far room came the sounds of the door opening and voices in the corridor.

"Quick!" With a surprising burst of strength, she pushed him back a few steps to the threshold of the windows. "Go back—please go back, for my sake if not yours," she whispered agonizingly. "If they killed you, I should die!"

Taken unawares by Jacquetta's intensity and the desperate pleading in her voice, Rashid allowed himself to be driven out onto the balcony. She had just closed the doors and was drawing the curtains when Luca appeared.

She started round guiltily, uncertain of whether he realized what she was doing. "I was just closing the curtains," she began. "I didn't expect you back for dinner."

"I'm dining at the ministry in half an hour." Luca's tone was curt. "I've only come back to change." Looking over his shoulder, he spoke to the two gunmen. "Wait in the sitting room," he told them. "I won't be more than a few minutes." Shutting the door, he turned back to Jacquetta.

"Now—I should be grateful if you would give me some kind of explanation for the disgraceful exhibition you made of yourself in Athens." His voice was icy with suppressed fury.

"I thought the disgrace was all on your side," she replied coolly. "It was the details of your behavior the other two found so shocking rather than any conduct of mine."

"How dare you question my behavior?" Luca burst out, abandoning the check he had been keeping on his temper. "I've told you time and time again—I was obeying orders, doing my duty. Would you rather I had acted like one of the rebels myself, like a traitor?"

"I would rather you were anything than a cowardly butcher who orders innocent people to be flung out of airplanes," Jacquetta retorted. "How you can live with yourself after what you've done, I don't know."

"I am an officer and a member of the government of the Duce," Luca stormed at her. "I forbid you to address me in that fashion."

"Oh, stop being so bloody pompous," she snapped angrily. "You know what I think, so why bother to argue about it."

"Yes, I do know what you think, and in the future you will keep your ridiculous ideas to yourself. Otherwise, I promise you, I shall have to take severe measures." Jacquetta made no reply. Her husband glared at her for a moment and then with a gesture of exasperation went into the bathroom.

When he emerged, twenty minutes later, dressed and ready to go out, his manner was once more controlled. Collecting his cigarette case and wallet from the dressing table, he paused in the doorway as he was about to leave.

"You had better get one thing very clear in your head," he said. "You may believe that, because you are my wife, you can criticize me, and the State I serve, with impunity. You are wrong. If it became necessary, I should not hesitate to have you placed in the care of the authorities until such time as you recovered your senses. Before that, however," he went on, "there would be other steps I would take. Your father, for instance, is widely known to hold views similar to yours. He is an old man of course, and in poor health, but a term in a desert labor camp or in a prison on one of the Lipari Islands might bring you both to heel." Seeing her expression, Luca gave a smirk of vicious satisfaction and went out, calling the guards after him.

Rather than risk detection, Rashid had climbed back to his own room and settled down to wait. Enough of the conversation in the bedroom had been audible for him to know that the Italian would be leaving again soon. He was forced to admit that Jacquetta was right about the foolhardiness of an attempt on Luca's life while he was in Italy. It would be far wiser to wait until they were in England or America. The question remained of how far Rashid could trust her not to give him away, even if inadvertently.

As soon as he heard the sounds of the baron's departure, he slipped along the corridor and tapped softly on Jacquetta's door. Letting him in, she threw herself into his arms, sobbing. Instinctively, he clasped her to him, and before they were aware of what was happening, they were locked in a passionate embrace. Rashid kissed her fiercely, her mouth meeting his with an equal hunger. He felt the softness of her body yielding urgently to him beneath the thin silk of her gown.

Pulling the tie at the waist, he slipped the gown off her shoulders, letting it fall to the floor. His fingers moved over the smoothness of her neck and caressed her breasts, fondling the hardened nipples. Jacquetta gave a small moan, and her body stiffened and trembled with longing as she pressed him to her, her nails raking his back.

With a sudden hoarse groan, Rashid swept Jacquetta off her feet and carried her naked and unresisting into the bedroom.

Ralph Kendrick had volunteered to be the one to spend the night on board to keep an eye on the gold, but there had been lengthy formalities for Desmond to go through at the lake before he could get away. The crates had to be checked and individually counted before the carabinieri and the shore staff would accept responsibility for guarding them. In part, however, Desmond well knew, the Italian authorities had instructions from the government to harass and delay all Imperial Airways flights, on the grounds that Britain was Italy's greatest rival in the Mediterranean.

It was eight o'clock by the time Desmond reached his hotel room in the center of the city, and his first action was to telephone Laura.

"I've been trying to call you myself," she said when he told her that he wanted to see her. "Can you come along to my room? There's something you ought to know about."

Laura's room was on the floor above, and he found

her waiting for him in the company of an elderly, white-haired man and a teenaged girl who looked to be his daughter. "Professor and Siegret Wienzman," Laura introduced them. The girl's eyes were reddened from crying. "They're in terrible trouble," Laura continued. "You must listen to what's happened to them."

Wearily, the old man told his story for the second time.

"They've been hiding in here ever since, not even daring to leave their rooms for meals," Laura interjected. "Siegret's room is next to mine, and I heard her crying when I was going past."

"Our greatest fear," David Wienzman continued, "is that the Nazis will prevent us from getting on your airplane tomorrow morning."

"What I don't quite understand," Desmond said in a puzzled tone, "is why the Germans should be going to such lengths to catch you if you are no more than ordinary refugees. After all, Jewish emigration is still permitted there, is it not?"

Laura gave him a sharp look. The thought had evidently not occurred to her.

Professor Wienzman sighed heavily. "Yes, you are right, captain, there is another reason why the Nazis hunt us, a reason even my daughter does not know." He patted her hand gently as he spoke. "Many years ago I learned something about a person who shall be nameless but is now in a position of great power in Germany. I did not seek the knowledge, nor would I make it public and discredit him, for I believe a patient's confidence in his doctor may not be abused. Nevertheless, the Nazis will not believe this, and they will not rest until I am in their hands."

Desmond was silent, aware of Laura's eyes on him. There was no way he could possibly refuse to help these people, yet he was conscious of being forced to take sides in a conflict he had managed to avoid for so long. "The question is," he said at length, "are the Italian police involved? If they are not, if the Nazis are operating by themselves, then there isn't too much of a problem. In that case the best way of avoiding them is probably for you both to come down to Lake Bracciano early with myself and the other crew members and go aboard a couple of hours before the passengers arrive."

"And if the Italians are watching for them, too?" asked Laura.

He could see her approval of his decision in her face. "Then the problem is more difficult. You see, the aircraft herself is under heavy guard." He told them about the gold on board. The Wienzmans' faces fell.

"But we must do something," Laura said hotly. "Surely you can think of some way of getting them on board."

"I could lend Dr. Wienzman a cap and one of my uniform jackets," Desmond answered thoughtfully. "They wouldn't fit, but they might do to get him past the port guards. Miss Wienzman isn't so easy to disguise, though."

"I know!" Laura exclaimed excitedly. "My overalls, the ones I wore in the race, I had them washed and kept them as a kind of souvenir," she explained a trifle sheepishly. "If Siegret puts them on and some kind of cap as well, to hide her hair, she could pass for a mechanic, especially in the half light."

"You're right," Desmond said. "In fact, that's a very good idea. There will be several mechanics around anyway, going over the plane."

The refugees began to brighten. "You are sure this will not bring trouble for you?" David Wienzman asked.

Desmond gave a shrug. "I'm afraid my standing with the airline is so bad at the moment I doubt if even my being arrested could make it much worse."

Laura gave him a grateful smile. "Good, then that's settled," she said. "Now I'm going to have the hotel send you two up some food. Siegret is going to spend the night here with me, sharing my bed," she added to Desmond. "I think she'll feel safer."

"In which case," Desmond suggested, "I think the professor might be wise to use the room that was mistakenly booked for Ralph Kendrick. Meanwhile though," he said to Laura, "if the Wienzmans don't mind being left for a short while, do you think you could have dinner with me? I need to talk to you."

For an instant he was afraid she would refuse. Then she nodded, "Yes, all right," she agreed. "I'll meet you downstairs in a quarter of an hour."

Dr. Van Smit approached the receptionist's desk with a feeling of annoyance. All through the evening he had been waiting for a chance to make another search of Stewart Curtis's room, but at no point had he been able to find the suite unoccupied. The maid had been in and out several times, and now it looked as though Curtis and his wife were returning for the night.

He had decided to fall back on the d'Estes. True, they were nowhere near as wealthy as the Curtises, but they still had plenty of money, and he had observed the baroness with one or two good pieces of jewelry on her. Certainly they were worth a try.

"Can you tell me if Baron d'Este is coming down to dinner?" he inquired of the clerk. "I was hoping to have the pleasure of continuing our conversation."

"I am sorry, sir," the clerk answered at once, "but you have just missed them; they left only a few minutes ago for the Foreign Ministry."

Unaware that Luca was accompanied by guards, Van Smit took the plural to refer to the baron and his wife, and, thanking the man courteously, the South African made his way back up to the sixth floor. Most of the guests were still at dinner, and the corridors were empty. Picking the lock of the sitting room without difficulty, he slipped quietly inside the suite.

The lights were on, although the room was deserted. A silk dressing gown lying in a heap on the floor caught his eye. Evidently the occupants had been in a hurry. He stirred the crumpled folds idly with the toe of his shoe, and as he did so there came a sound from beyond the half-closed bedroom door.

Instantly he froze, poised for flight, ears straining. Again the sound came, a low and drawn-out moan, and he relaxed his tense muscles, a thin smile crossing his features. Very softly he tiptoed over the carpet toward the bedroom and stooped to peer through the crack in the door.

The lights were dim, but the man and woman on the bed had thrown back the sheets so that their locked figures and slowly twining limbs were plainly visible. For several minutes Van Smit gazed at their passionate, abandoned lovemaking, feeling his own desire rising enviously as he watched Jacquetta's body moving sensuously beneath the young Arab's caresses and heard the small cries and gasps of pleasure breaking from her lips.

Tearing himself away, he crept across the suite and

went noiselessly into the corridor, his expression one of undisguised satisfaction. No longer would he have to risk the hazardous business of trying to search the Curtises' luggage.

Laura was still very much on the defensive, Desmond saw, and her response to his conversation as they sat waiting for their meal was wary and careful. Deciding that complete frankness was the best approach, he told her of his visit from Georgina, and he showed her the telegrams he had received just before leaving Cairo.

"But surely you didn't believe that Mr. Curtis and I—"

Desmond interrupted hastily. "No, of course not," he assured her, "or I wouldn't be here now. It was just that —coming on top of everything else—" He shrugged his shoulders expressively. "She must be insane, that woman," he went on, "or at the very least incredibly bitter toward you."

"I should have known something like this had happened." Laura smiled, and relief shot through him once more. "No wonder you were a bit cold this morning. You were under attack from all sides. As for Georgina Curtis," she shook her head. "I was going to resign when we got back to New York, anyway. I guess maybe I should have done it sooner."

"Well, as soon as we get back to the hotel, I'm going to give her back her damned watch and tell her exactly what I think of her," Desmond said vigorously.

"No," Laura put a hand on his arm, "don't do that, at least not until after we reach New York. Georgina can be dangerous; you mustn't underestimate her. Mr. Curtis will do anything she asks him to, and he is a powerful man, and you've got enough people against you at the moment."

Laura was studying the telegram. "How bad is this inquiry?" she asked, her face serious again. "Can't I help? I mean I was actually there, I can tell them there was nothing you could have done."

"They may ask you to appear as a witness," he told her, "even though they've already got your statement. To be honest, I've no idea how it will go. Losing a passenger is not thought highly of. I can't say I'm proud of it myself."

"They can't blame you, even so," Laura replied vehemently. "It wouldn't be fair."

Desmond smiled at her. "I'm afraid it may be more a question of settling old scores than holding a fair trial," he said ruefully. "About the only point in my favor is that they are short of crews at the moment, especially for the Atlantic division. Anyway, there's nothing to be done, so let's not discuss it anymore.

Laura was still glancing doubtfully at the second telegram—the one from Pamela.

"Listen," he told her, "my reaction to that would have been exactly the same even if I had never met you. As I told you in Cairo, Pamela and I are better apart; together we simply destroy one another."

"But this—" Laura waved the yellow slip. "She sounds as though she wants to try again."

Desmond led her through the story of his marriage, in detail, recounting the weeks of endless quarrels that had wracked them both almost before the honeymoon was over; telling her of his efforts to combat his wife's desperate insecurity, which made him the target for her savage aggression; and, finally, of the failure that had driven him further and further into the refuge of his job.

"She needs someone she can trust, someone she doesn't see as a competitor," he concluded. "We only make matters worse for each other."

"Yes, I can understand that," Laura nodded slowly. "Peter was just the same, in a way. He could never really believe he was good enough—for me, for his friends, for his job, for anything. There seemed to be no way I could reach him."

They talked for a long time, and it was near midnight when they finally left the restaurant and walked back along the Veneto toward the hotel.

"You are sure everything will go all right tomorrow morning?" Laura asked anxiously. "I mean, what happens if you and the Wienzmans are stopped?"

"I doubt if there's much danger to me." Desmond replied. "I think at the most I should be expelled from Italy. I'm much more worried about the professor and his daughter." For all his cheerfulness, he felt a growing uncertainty. Laura evidently felt the same, for she shivered and pressed her arm tightly against him as they walked on.

8

"The German army, infantry, and aircraft are beginning
the occupation of territory of the Republic at 6:00 A.M.
Their advance must nowhere be resisted."

By radio: 0830 CENTRAL EUROPEAN TIME TUES-
DAY 14 MARCH 1939. FLIGHT CONTROL BRAC-
CIANO ROME TO IMPERIAL AIRWAYS SOUTH-
AMPTON ENGLAND. IMPERIAL AIRWAY FLIGHT
109 G-ADHO CATERINA TO MARSEILLES AND
SOUTHAMPTON DELAYED ON TAKEOFF OWING
TO REFUSAL OF EMIGRATION AUTHORITIES
TO GRANT PASSENGER CLEARANCE. END.

"You must be mad, all of you!" Frazer fumed as the
car carrying *Caterina*'s crew members and the two Wienzmans sped through Rome's deserted streets.

Desmond turned on him angrily. The driver of the ancient limousine was out of earshot behind a glass partition, but even so Desmond was determined not to run
any unnecessary risks or put up with opposition from his
first officer. "I've told you already," he snapped. "If the
idea worries you, stop the car and get out. You can follow us later—that way you won't be involved—but if
you're going to stay, then shut up."

Frazer's sharp intake of breath betrayed his rage. The
others remained silent and tense. Dawn was beginning to
break behind the hills, and the gloom was taking on a
tinge of gray. It might be wiser, Desmond thought, to
take the initiative and order Frazer out of the car. But

then he would be perfectly capable of telephoning the
airline supervisor at Lake Bracciano. The supervisor would
certainly have the car intercepted and the Wienzmans returned to the hotel, for fear of causing offense to the
Italians. On balance, Frazer was probably better kept
close beside them where he could be watched.

It had already crossed Frazer's mind that here was an
excellent opportunity for ridding himself of his captain.
A few quick words to the airport police would be all
that was needed. With her captain under arrest, command
of *Caterina* would revert to him automatically, and the
airline board would have little choice but to confirm the
appointment. The only difficulty lay in making sure his
actions went undetected; otherwise, he would find himself
branded as an informer with no crew willing to serve under him.

The journey did not take long. Fifteen miles outside
the city, in the half light of early dawn, the car reached
the shores of the lake, set in the crater of a long-extinct
volcano whose walls had been ground away during eons
of erosion. The pale shapes of the flying boats were just
discernible in the thick mist rising off the water. *Caterina*
lay moored against the jetty, lights showing at her port-
holes.

Desmond felt the girl tense beside him as the car
halted at the entrance to the landing area. A policeman
swathed in a greatcoat peered in, and the driver muttered briefly to him. Winding down the window, Desmond
held out his crew identity pass, but the man was already
waving them on.

The office and maintenance hangars were open and
lighted, a few figures moving about between them. A pair
of mail vans stood by the cargo shed discharging their
loads. In the front passenger seat, Sandy directed the
driver over to the jetty where *Caterina* lay. There were
more guards here. Three men with rifles, shoulders
hunched against the cold breeze off the lake, stood at the
head of the steps, stamping their feet to keep warm.
Nearby was parked a covered military truck. It was
empty, Desmond saw, the remainder of the detachment
presumably sheltering inside the reception lounge.

He led the party up to the barrier. He had placed the
professor and Siegret carefully in the center of the group,

screened as far as possible by the rest of them. The old man looked surprisingly authentic in the peaked cap and officer's jacket. The dim light concealed the poor fit of the clothes and disguised his age. Desmond was not so sure about the girl. Instead of a cap, they had fixed her up with the flying helmet Laura had worn for the motor race in Cairo. With this and the white overalls, she looked utterly out of place to anyone familiar with airline activities, and he could only pray that the carabinieri would be more easily deceived. He had given both her and her father cases to carry in the hope of lessening the chances of their being asked to produce identity cards.

The corporal on duty barred his way in a friendly but firm manner. *"Siami i piloti,* we are the crew of the airplane," Desmond explained.

"Ah, *si, capisco,"* the man nodded, understanding. *"Il capitano?"* He glanced at the gold stripes on Desmond's sleeve.

"Si, io sono il capitano," Desmond told him. "I am the captain."

Drawing himself up, the man saluted, and as Desmond touched his cap in reply, the guard beckoned the others to follow him down the jetty and up the gangway. At the flying boat's forward entrance hatch he paused, put his head inside, and gave a call. There was a wait for a few seconds and then Ralph Kendrick appeared at the hatchway. "Yes, it's all right," he said to the guard, and the man stepped back to let them pass with no more than a cursory look at Siegret as she brushed by.

○ ○ ○

Rintlen and Gerdler arrived at the lake toward seven o'clock, a full hour before any of the passengers could be expected to put in an appearance. The failure to find the Wienzmans during the night had not worried the S.D. man unduly. After the assault on Farenzi's apartment, it was only to be anticipated that the escapees would take extreme precautions. An examination of the two rooms booked in Farenzi's name at the Grand Hotel had shown that both had been occupied until recently, and the receptionist had confirmed that neither of the supposed guests had checked out. These details had only served to confirm Rintlen's conviction that his quarry were planning to catch the England-New York flight.

The matter required precise handling. Rintlen had credentials prepared for him at the embassy, ostensibly identifying him as an officer of Germany's criminal police. A few minutes before his arrival, a telephone call had been put through to the airport emigration authority informing them that a Dr. Wienzman—wanted in the Reich on charges of performing illegal operations—was believed to be among the passengers on board Imperial 109, together with his young mistress, traveling in the guise of his daughter. Permission for this course had been wrung with much difficulty from Heydrich, and an official extradition warrant was on its way from Berlin to Rome to support the allegation.

Without the help of the Italians, Rintlen had argued, there would be little hope of apprehending the fugitives, and if the whole operation were kept deliberately low-key, then there existed a strong possibility that the Italians would simply hand the two Jews over into his keeping. A talk with the lieutenant in charge of the airport police immediately upon arrival served to confirm Rintlen's view. In a carefully casual tone, Rintlen had assured the man that the matter was no more than a routine affair with not the slightest degree of political interest involved.

"So far, only the crew of the airplane have arrived," the officer told him in English, the only language they had in common. "There is bullion, gold bullion on board today, and so we are taking special care. You can see the sentries on the jetty for yourself."

Through the office window, Rintlen saw the small knot of uniformed carabinieri at the entrance to the ramp leading down to the flying boat. This was even better than he had hoped. It was plain that the officer would risk no chance of even a remotely suspect individual approaching the aircraft.

For the next hour Rintlen and Gerdler sat watching the activities on the jetty as *Caterina*'s preflight inspection was carried out. A handcart of mail sacks was pulled up level with the freight hatch and the contents loaded aboard. It crossed Rintlen's mind that the Wienzmans might try to sneak through the security barrier dressed in some kind of airport uniform, but Gerdler remained positive that no one remotely resembling the two fugitives had gone by.

Shortly before eight o'clock, the first of the regular passengers arrived. An English couple with a little girl, the wife complaining while the husband smoked his pipe stoically. Their name would be Johnson—Rintlen ticked them off on the list he had been given. They were followed by a car containing a man and three women. Judging by the way the flying boat's purser came hurrying down the gangway to meet them, these must be the Curtises, he decided, and their secretary and their maid.

Laura Hartman was in a state of acute nervous anticipation, alert for the first sign that their plan had misfired. The sight of the armed carabinieri had terrified her until she recalled Desmond's remarks about the gold on board. She shepherded the Curtises quickly up the gangway.

From the look on Sandy Everett's face, she could tell that all had gone well. "We've got them safely hidden away upstairs," he whispered as he handed her in through the hatch. "It all went like a dream."

Inside, in the promenade lounge, Georgina Curtis found Desmond explaining to Mr. Johnson some of the construction details of a German Dornier flying boat moored nearby.

"Why captain, what a surprise," she greeted him stridently. "We see so little of you nowadays I almost thought you had left us."

"I'm afraid there's been a great deal of work to attend to in these past days, Mrs. Curtis." He answered her with all the civility he could muster, although she did not seem to notice the coldness in his voice.

"My husband and I insist you have dinner with us tonight in London," she told him.

"I'm not sure—" Desmond began.

Georgina silenced his objections immediately. "I tell you we insist," she interrupted firmly. "We won't take no for an answer or listen to any excuse."

Desmond frowned. He was in no mood to put up with more of Georgina's intrigues. "I am sorry, Mrs. Curtis," he replied in a tone of the most perfunctory regret, "but unfortunately I will not be free tonight." He was about to explain that he would be attending the inquiry instead, but then he decided that she deserved no such explanation. "I have made other arrangements," he said flatly.

Georgina went white about the mouth, her eyes widened in surprise. For a moment she appeared about to say something. He saw her bite her lower lip to keep it steady, and then she flounced off with a toss of her head.

Laura had been watching the exchange with interest, but Mr. and Mrs. King were coming aboard, followed by the d'Estes, and there was time for only a brief word and smile between Desmond and her before they had to move apart.

Stewart Curtis was unwilling to pay much attention to his wife's complaints over Desmond's behavior. He was in a highly agitated state. The BBC news broadcast from London, which he had managed to catch late last night, had reported that the current political crisis was seriously depressing stock markets around the world. Klerksdorp had already drifted substantially downward during the day's trading in London, and with the political situation worsening hourly, further falls were inevitable. If Stuttenheim, or anyone else for that matter, was to unload large lines of the mine's stock at such a time, the effect would be disastrous.

Curtis's moroseness was matched by the strained feelings between Luca and Jacquetta. The gulf caused by the quarrels of the last few days had been widened incalculably by the events of the previous evening. While Luca entertained Georgina with his forced gallantries, Jacquetta sat counting the hours and minutes before she could be alone with Rashid again.

"Those are the last of the passengers," the Italian police lieutenant informed Rintlen as Van Smit and Rashid disappeared into the flying boat. "Now we must wait to see whether these Farenzis or Wienzmans of yours attempt to board." Rintlen grunted and glanced at the time. 8:00. If the two Jews intended repeating the trick they had pulled at the station in Venice, they were cutting it very fine.

A telephone rang on a nearby desk. The lieutenant crossed the room and lifted the receiver. For a moment or two he listened. Then the two Germans heard him utter a sharp exclamation of surprise, followed by what was obviously an urgent demand for confirmation.

"I do not understand," he said, replacing the handset and confronting the others. "It is the captain of the airliner. They say he is telling the flight controllers that all his passengers are on board, and he is asking permission to begin take-off."

"It's a mistake," Rintlen retorted. "It must be. We've been watching since seven, and there are still two passengers not yet arrived. You've counted them yourself."

"I know." The lieutenant's face contorted unhappily. "That is what I said, but they tell me the crew are insisting they are ready to go."

"Damnation!" Rintlen leaped to his feet. "They've tricked us somehow. They must have managed to smuggle the two aboard disguised as crew members or workmen sometime during the night before we arrived. Quickly!" He took the startled Italian by the arm and hurried him to the door. "You search the plane!"

"I am sorry, lieutenant," Desmond O'Neill was saying a short while later. "I would like to be of assistance to you, but I am afraid what you ask if impossible. I cannot allow my ship to be searched and my passengers upset on such a slender pretext. As far as Imperial Airways is concerned, two people have failed to keep their booking and the flight must leave without them."

The police officer blinked at this refusal. "But captain, I have the permission of your airline manager," he protested.

Desmond shook his head firmly. "I am the captain and the only person whose authority matters on board *Caterina*. Until I am shown some kind of warrant informing me why these people are wanted, or proof that they may be traveling under another name, I refuse to allow a search. To do so would be to cast suspicion on myself and my crew."

Reluctant to return empty-handed to Rintlen, the Italian tried once more. "I can assure you, captain," he affirmed, "a warrant, an official request for the arrest of these persons, is even now on its way from the German embassy. It details the charges made against them and contains full descriptions and aliases."

Desmond gave him a hard look. "Are you quite sure

this is a civil matter," he asked, "or are you in reality a member of the political police?"

"I have already proved my credentials," the lieutenant snapped, stung by the question. "You will serve no useful purpose by this obstruction, and, if you persist, the consequences for you may be extremely serious."

Desmond's lips tightened angrily. "I was not aware that Italy was yet part of the Third Reich," he said crudely and was gratified to see a flush of outrage on the face of the lieutenant. "Produce your warrant if you can, but until then neither you nor your men set foot aboard my ship."

Leaving the carabinieri to guard the gangway, the lieutenant retreated to see what he could do to speed up the arrival of the warrant and other documents.

The senior management official on duty was a small, cheerful ex-naval commander named Donaldson. "I don't know what you're up to, old boy," he said to Desmond when he poked his head through the hatch a few minutes later, "but I can tell you, you can't win. If you don't let these chaps look over the place, they won't let you take off. It's as simple as that. They've got half the Italian army outside as it is, and there's a motor launch cruising off your bows into the bargain."

"How long do you think we can hold them off?" Desmond asked him. The older man pursed his lips. "The word is the police will receive authority from Rome to make a forced boarding within the next thirty minutes. There's a German fellow here representing the affair as a direct challenge to the Italian government. You can guess how sensitive the Duce will be on that point."

They were standing on the flight deck. Desmond was uncomfortably aware of Frazer watching him with a virtuous "I told you so" expression on his face. As yet no one outside the crew and Laura Hartman knew of the refugees' presence. He wondered how much longer he could maintain the charade.

"I have an idea," he said, as he escorted Donaldson down to the hatchway. "Give me ten minutes or so, and then tell the lieutenant that as a compromise I am prepared to allow him—and him alone—on board. Say I will show him all over the ship as a private visitor, but not as a police official. But make sure he realizes the offer applies to him only; I don't want any German Gestapo men coming with him."

"Sounds feasible," the manager agreed. "I'll give it a try, but I'm telling you," he warned as he ducked his head to step outside, "this is as far as I can go to help. If the lieutenant won't swallow it, you'll have to let the search go ahead."

Several of the passengers had clustered round listening to this exchange. Fending off their questions, Desmond made his way forward; at the stairway to the upper deck, Laura stopped him. "What's happening?" she asked. "Are they going to search the plane?"

"I think I may have thought of a way out," he whispered. "There will be a police officer coming around in a few minutes, so for God's sake, act naturally."

To Desmond's relief, the Italian lieutenant presented himself at the passenger gangway some quarter of an hour later. They saluted one another punctiliously.

"It is most kind of you to extend your invitation, captain," the Italian remarked in what he assumed was correct formal English.

"Not at all," Desmond assured him. "It is an honor to welcome you on board."

Eyeing each other warily, they began their conducted tour, starting with the after cabin. Stewart Curtis and the d'Estes regarded the intrusion with curiosity, especially when Desmond unlocked the door in the far bulkhead to allow the lieutenant to peer through into the freight and baggage hold beyond.

"Most interesting, captain, most interesting," he commented, betraying slight signs of embarrassment at having to carry out his task under the eyes of so distinguished a government official as the baron. "I understand there is a second hold on the upper level, also?"

"There is a small compartment beyond the flight deck," Desmond said, leading the way out through the promenade cabin. "A part of the bullion shipment is stored there." The policeman glanced surreptitiously at the passengers in the two cabins they passed through, and he took care, Desmond noticed, to look inside the cloakroom and galley as they continued forward. For all the man's apparent politeness, he was evidently determined to make a thorough inspection. In the smoking saloon he paused and rapped on the forward bulkhead. "I am told there is another compartment in the nose," he said pointedly.

"Yes, the mooring compartment," Desmond answered, praying that this was as far as the lieutenant's homework went. "It is reached from the cockpit above. We will go up there now."

At the rear of *Caterina*'s mailroom, behind a low hatch on the bulkhead, now concealed by the carefully stacked bullion crates, Siegret and her father lay amid the dark, airless confines of the narrow bedding locker. Squeezed between the high ceilings of the promenade and midship cabins and the flying boat's spine, this cramped space, nowhere more than three feet high, was the storage chamber for the mattresses, pillows, and linen used when the lower deck cabins were converted into sleeping quarters. Almost afraid to breathe, they lay beneath a layer of blankets, listening to the faint sounds of the passengers below. Sandy Everett was waiting on the flight deck, and at a slight nod from Desmond, he directed the Italian into the mailroom.

"This, as you see, lieutenant, is the second hold you were inquiring about. Normally it is used exclusively for mail." They watched their visitor poke among the mail bags. At length he straightened up and gave a look at the stacked crates at the rear.

"Ah, the gold," he exclaimed with a trace of awe in his voice. "There is really two million American dollars in these boxes?"

"Here, and in the after hold, yes, very nearly that amount," Desmond replied. "And now if you would like to see the cockpit and the mooring compartment, I'll take you forward."

Frazer was in his seat striving to maintain his expression of outraged contempt. Ralph pulled open the floor hatch, and they all waited while the lieutenant bumped and fumbled about below. When at length he emerged, his appearance was disheveled and his attitude crestfallen.

"Is there anything else you would care to see?" Desmond offered.

The Italian shook his head. "Thank you, no," he said, brushing dust off his uniform. "You have been very helpful. It seems the gentlemen from Berlin have made a mistake."

Desmond conducted the lieutenant down to the entrance hatch. The two bid each other farewell courteously. No sooner was the hatch closed than Desmond ran back up to the flight deck.

"Cast off the bow warps, Sandy. Ken, start doping up the motors. We're pulling out right away. Ralph, get flight control and tell them we've been cleared by the police and are taking off. Don't ask permission, just tell 'em we're doing it and then cut the contact."

The crew sprang to his orders. The startled passengers heard the sudden thump of the hatch doors and the burst of sound as, in rapid succession, the four engines snarled into life.

As the passengers hastily sought their seats, Rintlen was screaming at the lieutenant in the terminal building. "You must stop them, they are getting away!"

"There is nothing we can do." The officer shook his head. "Your man is not on board. I searched the aircraft from end to end."

"Fool! You half-blind, idiotic fool!" The German was beside himself with rage, and the others in the room regarded him with amazement. "They tricked you, the Wienzmans were hidden somewhere, and you missed them —why else do you think they are leaving in such a hurry?"

The lieutenant hesitated, then ordered. "Call them on the radio. Tell the captain he does not have permission to take off."

"Control is trying to get through to us, skipper," Kendrick shouted.

"Ignore them," Desmond called back. *Caterina* was already out into the open lake. "Can anyone see that blasted launch?"

"She's off the starboard bow, about half a mile downwind," Frazer told him. "She looks to be hove to."

"The plane does not reply, we cannot contact her," an anguished operator told the lieutenant.

Rintlen was plucking at his sleeve. "The launch—you

must radio the launch. Tell it to move across the plane's path and force her to stop."

On the desk the telephone rang again. "It's Rome, sir." A clerk held out the receiver. "They are saying if the airplane has not gone, you are to hold it."

If the precise words escaped Rintlen, the man's meaning was only too clear. As the lieutenant stood gaping at the news, unable to decide what to do, the S.D. officer goaded him into action. "Send a radio message to the launch out there at once," he instructed. "Tell them they are to intercept the flying boat. They still have time. See, the plane is turning into the wind, she has not yet started her take-off."

"The launch has started moving toward us, skipper; she's picking up speed. You can see the wash kicked up behind her." With his presence at the radio desk no longer necessary, Ralph Kendrick was maintaining a watch with the binoculars. Bringing *Caterina*'s nose round into the wind, Desmond eased the throttle momentarily to steady her.

"She's moving to cut across our path," Ken Frazer said in alarm. "They're going to head us off."

"Not while I'm flying this ship they're not," Desmond snapped, slamming the throttle levers open viciously. "Give me full boost." Engines roaring, the great aircraft surged forward over the surface of the lake.

"They have begun their take-off run; they are not slowing down yet," the police lieutenant commented as he and the two Germans, together with a small crowd of spectators, watched the drama on the water. Like clockwork toys, the aircraft and the launch in the distance began closing in on one another.

"He must be aiming to pass right in front of the aircraft," the lieutenant exclaimed in wonderment as he watched the launch's commander altering course slightly. "He is trying to force the pilot to turn away and abandon his take-off."

"Haven't they got guns? Why don't they shoot?" Rintlen demanded.

The lieutenant and his men were shocked. "Shoot at an unarmed passenger plane? Impossible. Even in war we could not do such a thing."

Rintlen took the rebuke in silence. It seemed certain that the suggestion was in any case unnecessary. Even from where he was standing, the launch commander's action appeared impossibly suicidal. The combined closing speed of the two vessels had to be over one hundred twenty-five knots. A devastating collision was only seconds away.

There had been no time to release the Wienzmans from their hiding place. The noise of the engines starting only feet away half-deafened them, the thunderous roar echoing through the tiny, unprotected space, drowning out all other sound, until their bodies vibrated and their ears hurt. They clung to one another in the dark. Incredible as it seemed, their plan had worked; they had slipped free from the Nazis' grasp again.

"Flaps one quarter," Desmond called out. The servomotors whined as Frazer's hand adjusted the levers. The launch was now less than two hundred feet ahead.

"Seventy knots, skipper," Frazer yelled. "Lift-off speed."

Actually, the aircraft was traveling barely fast enough to break loose from the water's grip, but they had no time. Easing the control stick back, Desmond waited for her to come away.

"She's not going to make it!" Frazer's voice rose in a cry of sheer terror. "We're going to crash!" From the windscreen they could see the appalled faces of the launch crew as her commander turned his wheel around hard in a desperate attempt to escape the bellowing leviathan racing down upon them.

Giving a savage curse, Desmond pushed the stick hard forward and as quickly dragged it fiercely back again, rocking the plane sharply in a last-ditch effort to jerk them free. For an instant he thought he had failed, and he braced himself for the crash. Then even as the launch loomed to fill the windscreen, he felt *Caterina* lift her nose.

So close overhead did they pass that at first the stunned observers on shore thought the two craft had actually collided. As *Caterina* rose off the surface, the launch disappeared in a tremendous froth of spray that reached above her stubby masthead and blotted her out completely for several seconds.

Both Bracciano and Rome air-traffic controls made repeated efforts to contact *Caterina*, but Ralph Kendrick switched off his equipment, simulating radio malfunction, and helped Sandy extract the Wienzmans from the bedding locker.

Seemingly none the worse for their ordeal, father and daughter were taken down to the lower deck cloakrooms to make themselves presentable before being introduced to the other passengers.

Mr. and Mrs. King were delighted at the adventure. "But you should have let us in on your secret," they remonstrated when Laura brought Siegret and her father in to meet them. "Why, we would have considered it our privilege to be allowed to help you all."

Luca d'Este and the Curtises remained aloof in the seclusion of the after cabin. Jacquetta herself had forsaken their company to go and sit in the smoking saloon with Rashid. Though the presence of Mrs. Johnson's husband and the enigmatic Dr. Van Smit acted as a restraint, both felt a need to be close to one another.

Van Smit himself was in a quandary. His original intention had been to demand money from the couple under threat of revealing their affair. When he had found himself sharing a taxi out to the lake with the young Arab, he had welcomed it as a perfect opportunity to open negotiations. However, something in Rashid's manner, in the way he disdainfully regarded his surroundings, had prompted Van Smit to hold his tongue. It might be wiser to approach the baroness alone, rather than risk the unpredictable reactions of her lover.

Frazer and Ralph Kendrick were plotting a route for Marseilles that would take them out of Italian territorial waters in the shortest possible time.

Desmond had withdrawn the engine boost, and the noise level in the cockpit had dropped to normal. They were flying at 7,000 feet in a clear sky, the mainland almost out of sight. "Do you think they'll send fighters after us?" Frazer asked.

Desmond shook his head. "We've got a good lead, and by the time anything could catch us, we will be in French airspace. It was close, but I think we made it back there."

Paul Rintlen had arrived at the identical conclusion. To his chagrin, the Italians were inclined to think the flying boat captain had distinguished himself by his determined exploit, and any kind of pursuit was obviously not being considered. The entire operation had turned into the kind of fiasco he had wanted to avoid. The Wienzmans, he had no doubt, would be safe in England by afternoon, leaving him with the alternative of either following them or returning to confront Heydrich—a possibility he did not relish at all.

"What shall we do now, Standartenführer?" Gerdler asked foolishly.

Goaded beyond endurance, Rintlen lashed out savagely at the youth. "We follow them, of course," he snarled.

"To England?" Gerdler cringed at the blow, his voice registering his astonishment.

"Yes, to England—where else did you think we'd go?" At least, Rintlen told himself as they sat in the car on the way back to the embassy, by continuing the pursuit to England, he was postponing the day when he would have to face Heydrich's wrath.

○ ○ ○

Georgina Curtis was bored again. "I want a drink," she told Andy Draper when he appeared in response to her summons. "A dry martini." Her husband glared at her. "Well, I'm bored," she said with a toss of her head. "What else is there to do, for heaven's sake?"

"Can't you wait a bit?" Stewart Curtis grumbled. "We'll be in Marseilles soon."

"No, I can't wait. I want a drink now," Georgina replied petulantly.

"Very good, madam," Andy answered, concealing his distaste for women who started on spirits before eleven o'clock. "Will the gentlemen be requiring anything?"

"Coffee for me," Curtis grunted, without bothering to look up.

"And I too shall have a cocktail," Luca decided and was rewarded with an approving look from Georgina.

"And hurry it up, damn you," Curtis snapped. "Last time my coffee was ice cold."

"I'll do my best, sir." Swallowing his anger, Andy returned to the galley where he found Laura mixing a glass of barley water for the Johnson child.

"I hope you don't mind," she said a little guiltily. "I thought it would be a help if you were busy."

Andy smiled. "Mrs. Hartman, it's a pleasure to fly with you," he assured her, "which is more than I can say for your boss."

"Oh, dear." Laura made a wry face. "Is he being rude again? I'm afraid he doesn't seem to be in a very good temper today."

"You never said a truer word, ma'am," Andy agreed, setting to work to mix the cocktails.

Laura watched him. "Tell me something, Andy."

"Yes, ma'am?" He looked up from the stove.

"Your trips, are they always as—" she groped for a word—"as eventful as this one? I mean things haven't stopped happening from the moment I got on the plane. First the crocodile, then the race in the desert, and now the narrow escape with those poor Jewish refugees."

"Well," Andy considered, "things do happen on these long flights. Funny," he mused. "The public, the passengers, and the rest, they don't mind at all; but the bosses hate it."

○ ○ ○

Hurrying through the imposing double doors of the German embassy in Rome, Rintlen stormed to the office he had been allocated and flung himself into a chair. The journey back to the center of Rome had coincided with the morning rush, and more than an hour had been wasted sitting in the unmoving car. He and Gerdler were booked on a K.L.M. flight to London leaving shortly after noon, but Rintlen needed to telephone ahead.

"Go and find Strasser," he said brusquely to Gerdler, "and send him to me here. Then you can pack our things."

"Yes, Standartenführer, at once." The youth turned to go.

"And find someone to send me some schnapps," Rintlen yelled after him. Christ, but he needed a drink now. The job had gone badly, and news of that was probably already on its way to Heydrich. Unless Rintlen could achieve some kind of success in England, his future was bleak indeed.

An orderly entered with a bottle of liquor and a glass, but there was no sign of the S.S. officer. Fuming at the delay, Rintlen rang the bell for the orderly again and was bawling out his demands when Strasser appeared in the doorway. Behind him stood two uniformed men. "Where the hell have you been?" Rintlen snorted. "I've been waiting twenty minutes."

Motioning to the orderly to leave, Strasser approached the desk. His subservient attitude seemed to have been shed, and now he addressed the S.D. man coldly. "I have been on the telephone to Berlin," he replied. "Before your return, the ambassador had begun to receive complaints about your actions out at Lake Bracciano. You have caused considerable embarrassment. Naturally I felt compelled to report this to the proper authorities—to Obergruppenführer Heydrich, to be exact."

For the first time in his life, Rintlen felt the fear he had so often seen in his victims. A curious numbness seemed to spread through him; his mouth became so dry he could speak only with difficulty. "Heydrich?" he croaked. "You called Heydrich?"

"Yes, I spoke to Heydrich," Strasser said with satisfaction. "He was most grateful for what I had to tell him. He also gave me orders concerning you." His voice grew abruptly harsh. "You are to be returned to Berlin forthwith under escort." He held out a hand. "You will now surrender your pistol."

There was nothing to do but obey. At a curt order, the two S.S. guards took up station on either side of the door. Pocketing the weapon, Strasser stalked out of the office without another word. Paul Rintlen reached for the schnapps with trembling hands.

○ ○ ○

Ken Frazer had taken the controls to enable Desmond to write up the flying boat's log. Normally the task was left until after they arrived at Southampton, but Desmond had little doubt that the records would be required as soon as *Caterina* landed. He wrote slowly, choosing his words with care. In the matter of the Wienzmans' escape, he had decided to adhere strictly to the truth, reporting the facts exactly as they had occurred and leaving the inquiry panel to make their own judgment.

He was still not sure whether he had taken the right

decision in not revealing Ralph Kendrick's near breakdown at Cairo. Ralph had borne up well during the last seconds of their brush with the police launch in Rome, and it seemed likely that by discussing his fears with his captain he had largely overcome them. Still, Desmond was aware that some commanders would have insisted on the man's removal.

The BBC news broadcast that had come on the air shortly after they passed over Corsica was still at the back of his mind. The threat of another war in Europe appeared to be growing with depressing speed. Soon, he would most likely be exchanging *Caterina*'s flight deck for the cramped cockpit of a carrier-borne torpedo bomber, and the world he knew now would have been swept away forever, just as the world of his boyhood had vanished in another war twenty-five years ago.

At least he had no family left to receive a black-edged telegram from the War Office, like that his parents had received on Mark's death. They had both survived only another three years themselves before the great postwar influenza epidemic claimed them.

In the right hand cockpit seat, Frazer idly observed the small movements made by the control yoke in response to the autopilot. He had no doubt that Desmond O'Neill was about to suffer severely at the hands of the airline management and that he himself was morally justified in taking the action he had. It was his duty, no less, he told himself afresh, to place the full facts before the inquiry; and a man should be proud of doing his duty. Already he was rehearsing the phrases he would use when revealing his captain's incredible behavior at Rome.

○ ○ ○

Paul Rintlen was being sent back to Germany to die. There was no room for doubt or illusion on that score. He had too good a knowledge of the mind of "Hangman Heydrich" to allow himself the luxury of thinking otherwise. Failure of any kind was punishable always; failure —coupled with the knowledge of secrets that threatened the state—could result in only one penalty. Rintlen shivered as he recalled the night of June 30, 1934, the Night of the Long Knives, when Hitler and the S.S. had settled accounts with Ernst Roehm's storm troopers, and over four hundred top figures had perished in the slaughter.

Rintlen had been a junior officer then, an Untersturmführer newly assigned to Heydrich's Sicherheitsdienst. It had been Heydrich who had masterminded the arrests and decided who should die and who should merely disappear under the shroud of a concentration camp. To demonstrate proof of his total dedication to the service of the state, Untersturmführer Rintlen had been required to participate in the executions. He was placed in command of an eight-man S.D. firing squad at the Stadelheim Prison in Munich.

They had stood in the prison's high-walled courtyard in the chill light of early dawn, as, one by one, thirty-seven frightened men had been led from the cellars by black uniformed guards who tore open their shirts and drew a charcoal circle round each one's left nipple before tying him against a wall twenty feet away.

Now, Rintlen was sitting in the rear of one of the embassy's Mercedes between Strasser and an S.S. sergeant. Gerdler slumped next to the driver. Rintlen speculated briefly on the fate of the Nazi youth; probably nothing worse than a spell in a forced labor battalion.

The car turned into the Corso Vittorio Emanuele heading for the Tiber bridges. The plane was due to take off for Berlin at midday; only a quarter of an hour before the K.L.M. flight for Paris and London on which he and Gerdler had been booked.

Strasser leaned forward and rapped the driver sharply on the shoulder. "Where do you think you're taking us? I said the airdrome, not the marine airport," Strasser snarled at him. "Turn the car around and be quick about it; we haven't much time."

Muttering apologies, the driver attempted to swing across the traffic. Within seconds, they had collided with another car. The damage was not serious, no more than a slightly scraped wing on the driver's side, but the owner of the other vehicle jumped out and proceeded to attack the occupants of the Mercedes with loud abuse.

"Tell him we will pay for the damage. Tell him to call at the embassy." Strasser wound down his window and began trying to pacify the Italian.

Almost without thinking, Rintlen saw his opportunity. Reaching quickly across the sergeant on his right, he wrenched open the door, and, before the others in the car realized what was happening, the force of his shove had sent the S.S. man and him spilling out into the road.

Rintlen was on his feet, dodging among the squeaking brakes and angry shouts and horn blasts of nearby motorists, while his captors were still staring around in bewilderment.

○ ○ ○

At quarter to twelve, *Caterina* touched down quietly on the water at Marignane, the civil airport for Marseilles. The weather was crisp and bright, and taxis were waiting to carry the passengers off to lunch at the Noallies Hotel at the top of the Canebiere, while the crew waited at the dockside berth and cursed the crated bullion.

For Siegret and her father, the air of France was intoxicating, and their happiness was communicated to the rest of the passengers, with the result that lunch was a cheerful affair in spite of the seriousness of the political crisis. Even Jacquetta momentarily forgot her dilemma, knowing that she would be able to snatch a couple of hours alone with Rashid while Luca was off on diplomatic business.

Only Stewart Curtis remained unmoved. As at Athens, his first action had been to put a call through to his brokers in London, and though he had been successful this time, the news he received had been unrelievedly bad—worse even than he expected. In the wake of the general collapse of the market, Klerksdorp had fallen sharply as news of the German invasion of Czechoslovakia had been received. More alarming still, the brokers reported that several large lines of stock were offered for sale during the past thirty-six hours. These had found buyers, but only at prices well below current market levels, and this had weakened the stock further. There could be little doubt, Curtis reckoned with an increasing sense of hopelessness, that the South African bankers had begun to unload their holdings. It was only a question of time before the news broke on the world, leaving him ruined.

He told Laura to place another call for him, this time to one of the directors of Imperial Airways, a business acquaintance of some standing.

"I'll certainly do what I can to help, Stewart," the airline director was telling him a short while later. "As a matter of fact, I've just been reading a report on your flight. The problem is, these schedules depend on three factors. The first is the weather—the Atlantic is a tricky crossing at the best of times; the second is crew availability; and the third is the convenience of the passengers. Right now I can tell you we are very short on experienced crews in the Atlantic division. What the passenger position is at the moment, I don't know."

Thanking his friend, Curtis sent Laura off to settle the phone bill with the hotel, and he went in to lunch. Laura Hartman made a call of her own to London. She spoke for almost twenty minutes from the phone booth in the foyer of the hotel, and when she came out, she paid the bill with her own money. Then she went off to talk to the Wienzmans.

By quarter to two, *Caterina* was climbing steadily to cross the mountains that lay between her and the coast of Britain, over three hours away.

Some two hundred miles to the east, a Junkers 52 of K.L.M. Airlines was approaching the Swiss-Italian border. Among the passengers, secure in the cover of his false passport proclaiming him to be a citizen of Switzerland, was Paul Rintlen. Now that the immediate danger had receded, he had begun to plan once more. If he could reach England undetected, he might still find a way of carrying out his mission and eliminating the Wienzmans. In which case, Heydrich might well be suitably impressed. If not —Rintlen tried not to think of the future if he failed. His wife and two young children were still in Germany. Even if he were to remain abroad, his family would be at the mercy of the S.D.; they called it *sippenschaft*— collective responsibility.

Pat Jarrett was still only halfway through the morning, fitting the Colts into the wing of the Supermarine. The previous evening he had worked until past midnight, only to be up again as soon as it was light.

He wiped a sleeve over his face and surveyed his progress. On the portside wing, a section of the aluminum plating had been carefully removed. The twin machine guns were snugly in their bay, held in position by diagonal steel bracing struts attached to the main spars. On the wing's leading edge, a pair of neat holes had been cut to admit the mouths of the spring-loaded blast tubes. To the right of the gun breeches lay the ammunition trays, carefully packed with enough ammunition for a full half-minute's firing. Running away behind were the leads to the fire control system, wired up to the firing button on the joy stick and the gun bay heating tube from the radiator—necessary to prevent the Colts from freezing up and jamming in the icy slipstream at several thousand feet.

On the starboard wing, the guns themselves had yet to be placed in position. Mentally he checked off the list of things still to be done: installation of the second pair of Colts and their ammunition; connecting up the fire control system—he would have to make do with the old metal ring and bead model, unchanged since his own combat days; the guns themselves would have to be test fired and adjusted; and, finally, the S4's engine would need a careful tuning.

He was well ahead of schedule. The only factor that still worried him was the weather. The sky was heavily overcast, and rain had been falling for the past hour, turning to sleet at times. Comforting himself with the knowledge that he still had three days before the bullion flight was due, he returned to his labors. With everything going so well, he might be able to afford the time to drive into Keene for lunch.

○ ○ ○

Fifty miles inland from the Mediterranean coast, the clouds began. Layers of stratocumulus stretching out on either hand to the horizon, burying the fields and villages of Languedoc beneath an impenetrable white blanket and building up ahead over the Cévennes mountains into threatening peaks.

"We should be safe at 10,000 feet," Desmond instructed. "We'll set the autopilot at that altitude for the present and keep a careful watch on the engine temperature."

"Aye, aye, skipper," Frazer lined up the indices for speed, course, and altitude on the Sperry autopilot control and clicked it into engagement. "I've turned on the carburetor heat, too," he added, flicking down the switches and watching the slight drop on the engine rev. counters as they registered the move.

Ice forming on the carburetor inlets was the Empire-class boats' only vice. In severe weather, they could be forced to 20,000 feet or more without oxygen, to the considerable discomfort of those on board, in an effort to climb above the clouds. The introduction of the exhaust heat system had gone some way toward solving the problem, but at such times all crews listened carefully to the forecasts for the weather ahead of them.

On this occasion, however, the forecasters were correct, and *Caterina* soared on untroubled in bright afternoon sunlight that reflected brilliantly off the cloud surface below. After their excellent luncheon, the passengers drowsed, occasionally scanning the papers and listening to one another's small talk. In the smoking saloon a bridge game had started, and at half-past three, Draper began serving tea and hot buttered toast.

○ ○ ○

In his office in Piccadilly, the public relations manager of Imperial Airways had just been telephoned by a big London newspaper. "We've had word that one of your airliners has rescued two Jewish refugees from under the noses of the Nazis and Italians," the reporter was saying. "An old man and his daughter. Apparently the passengers and crew smuggled them on board at Rome, and then the captain took off with the Italian secret police in hot pursuit."

"I've heard nothing of this," the manager protested. "Are you sure? What flight is it supposed to have happened on?"

"Flight 109 from Cairo to New York." The journalist consulted his notes. "We have definite confirmation at our end, anyway. The plane's due in at Southampton at four thirty, and the two escapees have agreed to give interviews. It should make a good story. Apparently the captain's quite a hero. On this trip he saved a girl's life when her companion was attacked by a crocodile, outflew a storm in the desert, won a motor race while they were in Cairo, and now he's finishing up with a Scarlet Pimpernel stunt. Chap named O'Neill—you must be pretty proud of him."

"We do have an officer by that name," the manager admitted cautiously, "and there may be an element of truth in some of your statements, but I can't confirm anything at this stage."

"Don't worry about that," his caller brushed the words aside. "We've sent someone down to meet the plane. It'll make a nice lead, what with all the news of Hitler invading Czechoslovakia. The readers will love it."

O O O

Caterina sank slowly through the clouds; the passengers stared gloomily at the swirling mist flying past the glass. Then, abruptly, the flying boat dropped clear, and the white-capped channel was visible beneath them, cold and inhospitable. A shoreline came in sight, and soon they were passing over the Isle of Wight. At Spithead and in Portsmouth harbor lay the sleek outlines and white decks of the channel fleet warships.

On schedule almost to the second, the flying boat was made fast between the pontoons of berth 108 alongside the towering superstructure of the Orient Line's *Oronsay*. Immediately the aircraft was surrounded by an eager throng of reporters and photographers.

9

From flight controller's log. Imperial Airways (Marine Division) Hythe Southampton Tuesday 14 March 1939.

1630 hrs. Durban-New York Flight 109 Caterina inbound from Marseilles on schedule, with gold bullion to U. S. value of $1,980,000 consigned to care of Federal Reserve Bank Washington. For onward carriage 15 passengers, 3 disembarking, remainder in transit for New York.
On arrival captain and crew ordered to attend inquiry into death of passenger at Shambe Station, Sudan.

The inquiry by the Imperial Airways management into Ian Thorne's death at Shambe was turning out to be everything Ken Frazer could have wished for. It was plain that the panel, composed of three of the company's senior managers (all, Frazer was glad to note, appointed before the government nationalization), was extremely annoyed at the degree of popular support being whipped up by the press for Desmond O'Neill. The panel's chairman had announced that the scope of the investigation had been widened to include the incident at Lake Bracciano and Desmond's general behavior over the whole period of the flight from Durban.

Given all this to occupy them, Frazer felt that the panel would hardly concern themselves with the possible cause of the fuel leak that had led to the landing at Shambe in the first place.

A clerk read the sections of the log dealing with the actual touchdown at Shambe. Captain Phil Harris, representing B.A.L.P.A., the Pilots' Association, was present, as well as a representative from the Foreign Office, and a naval commander sent by the Admiralty. Jack Priestly, the operations manager, was conspicuously absent. The proceedings were held in a rather shabby office, normally used for lectures and special briefings. Each time anyone moved, his seat gave off a strident squeaking that made the panel chairman—a sour, cadaverous man close to retirement age—glare irritably at the culprit.

The clerk finished reading, and immediately Phil Harris stood.

"Mr. Chairman," he began, "may I ask why this committee has not invited any of the passengers from Flight 109 to attend this inquiry?"

"I have already referred to this point, Captain Harris," the chairman answered. "The only passenger who witnessed any part of the incident was Mrs. Hartman, and we have her statement."

Harris resumed his seat, whispering a few words to Desmond as he did so. There followed a lengthy cross-examination of the entire crew. Interspersed with this were more readings from the log and quotations from airline regulations. It was evident that the panel was seeking to show that Desmond had been negligent in failing to warn the passengers of the danger from crocodiles.

"Looking back now, I suppose I should have done so," Desmond conceded, "but I can't see that it would have stopped Thorne from trying to take the launch out. He knew perfectly well he shouldn't do it. Laura—Mrs. Hartman—has already said so."

The chairman sniffed disapprovingly. "Mrs. Hartman seems to say a lot of helpful things, but then, in the opinion of many, her own part in this sorry affair is less than credible."

"I can't accept that statement." Desmond leaped to Laura's defense. "Mrs. Hartman cannot be held responsible for the behavior of an idiotic boy who insisted on showing off—any more than I can," he added bitterly.

The chairman smiled nastily. "Mrs. Hartman is not under investigation," he said. "You, on the other hand, are, and your degree of responsibility is just what we are attempting to ascertain."

Captain Harris entered the fray once more. "Are you aware, Mr. Chairman," he asked, "that Mrs. Hartman has made an additional statement before a number of witnesses, a statement that is to be published in several national newspapers, to the effect that only Captain O'Neill's prompt action prevented her from falling into the river and very possibly being seized by a crocodile herself?"

"I have told you once, we have Mrs. Hartman's statement made at the time of the incident before us," the chairman replied sharply. "Any further evidence on her part is inadmissible."

"This young lady certainly seems to be playing a most energetic role in the affair," one of the other panel members—a stout, smartly dressed man with an unhealthy, pallid face—remarked sardonically. "Is Captain O'Neill usually on such excellent terms with his passengers?"

Phil Harris interposed again, offering to produce a copy of Laura's statement to the press. This too was rejected, though with noticeable hesitation on the part of the panel's third member.

"All the fuss in the papers is putting pressure on them," Ralph Kendrick murmured to Frazer in a low voice. "I wonder how the board is taking it?"

It was just possible, Frazer realized, that if the publicity being given to the flight were sufficiently favorable, the airline board would feel unable to take disciplinary action against Desmond unless the evidence against him was so strong and the recommendation of the inquiry so severe that they couldn't be ignored.

The investigation of the events at Bracciano began quietly enough. Desmond outlined the circumstances of his introduction to the Wienzmans and his decision to help them. "I decided to smuggle them on board," he said in response to a query, "because it was clear that they would be in extreme danger if they remained in Rome. I think anyone would have."

"We are not here to listen to your speculations," the chairman told him dryly. "Kindly proceed."

The take-off drama was the crucial issue, and it was here that the panel pressed hardest. When had Desmond realized the launch was trying to stop them? At what point did the launch begin to constitute a danger to the aircraft? Why had he taken no avoiding action? Had he tried to leave against the wishes of the Italian authorities?

When it was Frazer's turn at last, he replied to the panel's questions carefully. Yes, he admitted, he had been

in the cockpit when Desmond began the take-off maneuvers. How soon had the launch begun to interfere?
Well, quite soon. Soon enough for the take-off run to be
aborted? Perhaps, Frazer hesitated, feigning conflict between his loyalty to his captain and desire to tell the truth.
Yes, perhaps in his view, the aircraft could have been
stopped. Had he suggested this to his captain? Here again
Frazer hesitated and cast an anguished sidelong glance at
Desmond. Well, as a matter of fact, yes, he had urged
that they stop the run and turn away, but the captain had
disagreed. Finally, had there, in his professional opinion as
a pilot, been a serious risk to the flying boat and its passengers? At this Frazer's acting rose to new heights. Swallowing hard, in an almost inaudible voice, he replied, yes.

Nodding in grim approval at his testimony, the panel ordered him to step down. The remainder of the inquiry was
a formality. A statement was heard from Ralph Kendrick
who stoutly defended his captain. The panel chairman
spent a few minutes summing up; then he and his two colleagues withdrew.

Desmond and the B.A.L.P.A. captain, Phil Harris, had
retired to a corner of the room and were talking together
in low voices. Frazer saw them glance in his direction,
and the knowledge that he was under discussion made him
uncomfortable. If it should come to be believed that he
had deliberately betrayed his captain, he would find himself refused a berth on any plane in the Imperial fleet,
possibly in the whole of the British Isles. None of the rest
of the crew spoke to him.

After less than a quarter of an hour, the three panel
members returned. Dusk was beginning to fall, and the
lights had been switched on, casting a harsh yellow glare
on the spartan furnishings. *Caterina*'s crew shifted uneasily in their chairs while the panel shuffled papers and
held a last minute whispered colloquy. Then the chairman
cleared his throat and waited for the noise of squeaking
wood to cease.

"This inquiry was called to investigate the death at
Shambe station, Sudan, of Lieutenant Ian Thorne and the
responsibility of Captain O'Neill for this and other incidents later in the journey, notably those at the Lake Bracciano Marine Terminal, Rome," he began. "With regard to
the former, we are of the opinion that little could have

been done to forestall the tragedy, although the panel is critical of the way in which the transport launches were left unattended and the movements of the passengers inadequately supervised." (Good, thought Frazer, they're not going to let him get away with anything.) "With regard to the extraordinary events in Rome," the chairman continued—not a sound was heard in the room as his audience concentrated on every word—"the panel is under no doubt that Captain O'Neill grossly exceeded his authority in aiding Professor Wienzman and his daughter to evade the Italian police and emigration control. The government of Signor Mussolini has made strong representations on this subject. We also find the captain responsible for unnecessarily hazarding his aircraft, the lives of his crew and passengers, and a highly valuable cargo by performing a take-off not properly cleared by Bracciano flight control."

He paused to sip from a glass of water on the table, and the crew exchanged worried glances. "Furthermore," the chairman went on, reading from his notes, "we have received several complaints concerning the highhanded way in which passengers on board Captain O'Neill's commands are sometimes treated." There was an outburst of surprised gasps from the assembled crew. "Silence please," the chairman ordered. "The management wishes to make it clear that such behavior will never be tolerated in Imperial Airways."

His mother had done her stuff after all, Frazer thought, concealing his satisfaction.

The chairman laid down his notes and surveyed the room coldly. "Normally," he intoned, "the next step would be for the panel to recommend disciplinary action. In this instance, however, we have decided to reserve our recommendations and report them, together with our findings, to the board of directors who will communicate them to those concerned in due course."

Silence greeted this last sentence as his listeners attempted to work out its significance, and the three judges filed out.

With a word of thanks to his crew and a promise to let them know the moment he heard anything, Desmond escaped into the corridor. The inquiry's result had come as no shock to him; indeed, Phil Harris had correctly forecast the reserved sentence. Even Frazer's treachery had failed to surprise him. He had sat through most of the trial in a state of curious detachment.

He set off toward the other end of the administration block. He was due to call on Jack Priestly, the flying boat operations manager immediately after the inquiry, but he wanted to sort through the mail that had accumulated for him during his absence. He often found a great bundle of letters and packets awaiting his attention, but today the haul amounted to no more than a few bills, a flying periodical, a curt note from the Admiralty requesting acknowledgment of their previous letter, and a letter from his wife's solicitors informing him that in accordance with instructions received they had arranged for a valuation to be carried out on the farm, and the results were enclosed for his consideration.

Leaving the magazine in the post rack, Desmond stuffed the letters in his pocket and went off to keep his appointment.

The flying boat operations manager had been an enemy for almost as long as Desmond had been with the airline. In some ways, Desmond considered, Jack Priestly bore an extraordinary resemblance to Stewart Curtis—large, ugly, and domineering, with a fondness for terrorizing his subordinates. Unfortunately Priestly's voice failed to match up to the rest of him; he spoke in a sharp, high-pitched key, which, when his temper grew frayed, would rise to a near hysterical scream. This afternoon it was apparent he was very angry indeed.

"Would you like to explain just what the devil you think you've been up to?" he demanded, his tone so obviously at variance with the angry nature of his words that Desmond was hard put not to laugh.

"I've already told everything to the inquiry," he answered. "You must have heard the findings by now."

"I certainly have," Priestly snapped back. "You and your escapades have caused me a great deal of trouble. The government is furious about the risk you took with the gold, and Mr. Curtis has been raising hell over your rudeness and the fact that you've been running around Cairo and Rome with his secretary."

It's just as well he doesn't know how his wife's been behaving, Desmond thought. "Mr. Curtis is lying. He has bullied my crew and the other passengers throughout the trip, and he seems to think his wealth entitles him to do as he pleases. I told him if his manners didn't improve, I'd throw him off my plane. The promise still stands."

"Well, you'd better not," the operations manager retorted, "because at Mr. Curtis's request, the board has ordered you to fly to New York tomorrow instead of the next day. You leave at 3:00 P.M."

Desmond stared at him. "What is it about this man that scares everyone so that they'll sack pilots and switch flight schedules for him?" he asked bitterly. "Ignoring, as I assume you will, any thoughts of rest for myself and the crew after eight days of flying, what about the other passengers? I mean," he went on, "why doesn't Curtis try a Pan American flight if he's in such a hurry, or even hire his own plane? He takes up a third of our list as it is."

"You know damn well the next Pan Am flight doesn't leave for two days," said Priestly, "and as it happens, the remaining passengers have been consulted and have raised no objections." Holding up a sheet of paper, he said, "The d'Estes will be staying at the Italian embassy in Washington. An earlier arrival will cause them no problem; indeed the baron would welcome it. The same applies to Mr. and Mrs. King, who are staying with friends in New York. Your protégés, the Wienzmans, have not yet booked rooms anyway. Which leaves only the Turkish fellow and Dr. Van Smit."

Desmond shrugged. "Personally, I don't mind one way or the other. The forecasters say there's a depression moving east from Labrador, but it's traveling slowly, so the weather might be clearer tomorrow than on Thursday. Is there anything else?"

"Yes, there is," Priestly answered quickly, clasping his hands together on the desk top. He looked Desmond squarely in the eye. "I've had reports of your radio officer drinking heavily. I shall not at this juncture go into your failure to report the matter; suffice it to say I intend to replace him at once."

"The hell you will!" Fury seized Desmond. Not content with destroying him, they were out to get at his crew also. "Right now you can't touch me, Priestly; you actually need me. The panel of inquiry hasn't been able to order disciplinary action because the board is too worried about the newspaper publicity, and if I refuse to captain the flight you've promised Curtis, you're in real trouble. Mine is the only available Atlantic-division crew at the moment. So Kendrick stays, and you wait till I'm gone before you start on my crew."

"How dare you?" Priestly spluttered, his voice a falsetto scream. "How dare you dictate to me?"

Standing up to leave, Desmond eyed him with contempt. "Just remember what I said," he answered, pausing in the doorway. "And one other thing since I'm here—I know very well who's been feeding you information behind my back, so when I return from New York next week you can have a new first officer waiting for me if you want me to fly again. I've had as much as I'm taking of Frazer. When he's not repeating lies and gossip to you, he's bloody useless as a pilot." Desmond walked out, slamming the door behind him.

Now he had to face Pamela. . . .

The remainder of *Caterina*'s travelers were already on their way to London. Had there been only a single day's wait before the flight resumed, rooms would have been booked in Southampton itself. However, the decision to advance the departure had been taken too late, and the passengers were on an express train on their way to the Ritz in Piccadilly in London where it had originally been assumed they would prefer to pass a two-day stopover.

Georgina Curtis and Luca d'Este were in the dining car sitting over a second cup of tea. The first green of spring was beginning to restore color to the landscape, and Georgina was enjoying the view.

"So you will understand, my dear Georgina, these stories my wife repeats could not possibly hold a word of truth."

Luca's words broke in on her thoughts, and she turned to him with a trace of irritation. The Italian was beginning to bore her. "Luca, you might as well save your breath," she said witheringly. "I don't believe you, and neither does Laura." Taking a last draw at her cigarette, she stubbed it out in the ashtray and stood up to go. "For your sake," she added as she left, "I hope that sheik never does catch up with you."

Jacquetta had known that she and Luca were due to dine with the Italian ambassador in London, and it was a simple matter for her to plead a headache after the flight and remain behind. Luca indeed had been in such an unbearable temper she doubted whether she would have gone with him even if Rashid were not in the picture. She lay on her bed while he dressed, and the moment she was sure he was safely out of the way, she slipped out and rushed to Rashid's room.

Van Smit had been waiting in the Ritz's Palm Court cocktail lounge where fashionable Londoners held rendezvous before their dinner engagements. The lounge held a commanding view of the main entrance into Piccadilly; sitting in a gilded chair beneath the palms, Van Smit watched to see who came and went.

The more he thought about it, the more convinced he was that he must make his initial approach when the baroness was alone. The Arab, her lover, was far too uncertain a factor to be included at such a delicate stage. Ideally, Van Smit would have liked to have waited until they had all reached the United States, but there was no telling how the situation might have changed by then, and he dared not wait so long.

The sight of Luca in white tie and evening tails, leaving the hotel on his own, made up Van Smit's mind.

He reached the d'Este suite just in time to see Jacquetta disappearing around the corner in the direction of Rashid's room. She vanished before he could catch up, leaving him with nothing to do but return, angry and frustrated, to the lounge. One thing was sure, he told himself. Baroness d'Este was going to pay heavily, very heavily indeed, for his trouble.

○　○　○

The consternation caused by Rintlen's escape had been considerable. Not being at first aware that his quarry was in possession of both a ticket to London and a passport as well as an ample quantity of foreign currency, and anxious to avoid any unnecessary confessions of failure to Heydrich, Strasser proceeded to call every available man to mount a search of railway stations, airports, and hotels. This operation continued until five o'clock in the

afternoon when an underling thought to suggest that Rintlen might indeed have gotten away with his air ticket
and worse still might have used it. There was nothing for
Strasser to do but contact Berlin again.

Rintlen was due to have been delivered to the S.D.
headquarters on Prinz Albrechtstrasse. Owing to the pressure of events in Czechoslovakia (Heinrich Himmler was
due in Prague on Thursday, and the first of five thousand
arrests necessary to ensure his safety were being carried
out), Heydrich was not immediately available, and it was
quarter to six before he was informed of the escape. His
fury was without precedent.

Pausing only to order Strasser's immediate arrest, he
gave instructions to his adjutant, Lindeman, to contact S.S.
sections at the German embassies in Paris and London
and have Rintlen eliminated forthwith, should he show up
in either capital. "Only our own people are to know, and
tell them to make sure there are no blunders this time
unless they want to join him."

An hour later, however, Lindeman was reporting back
that Rintlen had already passed through London airport
and was nowhere to be found. "These fools in Rome waited
till he had almost gotten there before telling us," he informed his master.

"Well, they will most certainly regret doing so," Heydrich answered. "Tell London to keep looking for him; he
shouldn't be that hard to find, and if he should murder
those two Jews openly, there will be hell to pay. What
plans have you managed to come up with for dealing with
him?"

"My staff are coordinating action to find and eliminate
him," the adjutant replied calmly, "using agents from the
embassy. I hope to have the results ready to put before
you shortly."

"Very good," Heydrich nodded approval. "Inform me
as soon as you have news." He rubbed his long hands together thoughtfully. "And now, let's see where we are with
those lists of Czech undesirables."

Rintlen had been reasonably confident of being able to
outwit an attempt by Heydrich to have him intercepted
at London's Croydon Airport. With his Swiss passport

and his good English, he felt certain of the protection of
the authorities while in a public place, and he knew that
German agents would be under strict orders to avoid any
kind of embarrassing incident.

The absence of any reception committee puzzled him.
He had expected to be followed and watched. It took him
some time to conclude that either London had not yet
been notified of his arrival, or, more probably, no one,
not even Heydrich, believed he would be so crazy as to
continue his hunt of the Wienzmans alone and unaided.
They most likely supposed he had gone underground
somewhere in Paris.

Walking through the terminal building, he noticed an
Imperial Airways sign over a ticket booth, and on an impulse he went up and inquired about the transatlantic
flight.

"Yes, there's one tomorrow at three o'clock, leaving from
Southampton," she told him. "It reaches New York at
four the next afternoon."

"No, no," Rintlen told her. "There is one the next day,
Thursday." With an effort he recalled the Wienzmans'
flight number. "Imperial 109 via Montreal."

The girl smiled. She was pretty, he noticed, with blue
eyes and curly blonde hair. "Yes," she said, "that's the
one, Imperial 109. The departure date's been put forward
twenty-four hours, though. Did you want to make a reservation, sir? I can see if there are still berths available for
you."

She looked at him expectantly, hand poised over the telephone, and Rintlen, who had not given any real thought
as to the exact means by which he was to accomplish his
objective, and thrown off stride by the discovery that he
had less than a day in which to do so, nodded.

The girl telephoned through to the head office in Piccadilly, during which time Rintlen stared around the booking
hall anxiously for any sign of German agents. Eventually
the girl laid down the receiver for a moment. "We do
have just the one berth left, sir. Do you wish me to reserve it for you?"

Rintlen had come to the conclusion that he might as
well take the flight. It would extend his opportunities for
doing away with the Wienzmans, and, in the event of fail-

ure, it would at least leave him on the other side of the world from Heydrich. He nodded again.

"Thank you, sir. Then if I could have your name, please." Rintlen pushed across his passport, and the girl repeated the name on the cover into the telephone. Hanging up she smiled at him again. "Very good, sir. I have secured you a reservation. I'm afraid I can't issue you the ticket here. You will have to collect it from the Piccadilly office before midday tomorrow."

She handed him a slip of paper with the Piccadilly address on it and the time of the flight's departure and also that of the train connection from Waterloo. Thanking her, Rintlen went off to find a taxi into London proper. It was not likely that he could do much before morning. He had yet to find where the flying boat's passengers were staying; he hadn't wanted to ask the girl at the desk for fear of causing suspicion. As it was, he felt desperately tired and in need of a drink, and he still had to find a room for the night, collect and pay for his ticket, and buy a suitcase and some fresh clothing for the journey.

The taxi was pulling out of the terminal entrance when a large black car swept into the forecourt and squealed to a halt in front of the main passenger building. Three men in raincoats and trilby hats leaped out and ran inside. To an ordinary observer, they might have seemed no more than hurrying travelers, but Rintlen recognized one of them as a man he had trained with during his first months in the S.S. The hunt was on for him in London.

○ ○ ○

There was a cold wind blowing straight down the main street of Keene. It had stopped sleeting, but the sidewalks and streets were wet with slush, and there were few people about. Pat Jarrett parked the truck opposite the café and hurried inside.

The look on Suzie's face when she saw him wiped away any doubts he had had. She was wearing the same dress as before, and its provocativeness sent a quiver of excitement through him. Hips swinging, she strolled across the room to where he sat. "Didn't expect to see you back so soon," she said casually, "specially not on a day like this."

"I like your food," he said clumsily, and the girl gave a laugh.

"Well, that's good, 'cause you get stew again." She produced a knife and fork from her apron pocket, wiped them halfheartedly, and leaned over to place them in front of him. Her skin was smooth and clear, and Jarrett had a fleeting impression of the swell of her bosom as the neck of her dress dipped open. "Want a beer as well?"

He nodded. "Like one too?" he offered.

Suzie shook her head. "Uh, uh, no thanks. Not allowed to drink with customers. I'll have coffee, though."

She brought the beer and coffee together with his plate of stew. Sitting opposite, she regarded him carefully over the rim of the cup. Embarrassed by her scrutiny, Jarrett tried to find some small talk.

"Long winter you have had up here," he began, and the girl snorted derisively.

"Sure, nine months winter and three months damn poor sleddin', that's what my step-pa says, and I guess he's not far wrong."

They both laughed. "You still got your plane, mister?" she asked. "When you going to let me see it?"

"The name's Pat—Pat Jarrett," he told her, "and you can see the plane anytime."

"An' you'll take me up in it?" She had put the cup down and was leaning forward eagerly, lips parted and eyes pleading.

"She's a single seater," Jarrett said, "but you can sit inside, even start the engine if you want."

"Can I really? You could teach me to fly, maybe?" Suzie giggled. "When can I come?"

"Like I said, anytime. Not this afternoon, though. I've work to do." He would certainly have to have the gun bays closed up before she arrived.

"Tomorrow then, after lunch? I get the afternoon and the evening off on Wednesday."

"You work here in the evenings?"

"It's the bar," she explained. "We get a few customers in at night. Can't think why." She gazed around the room, her lip curling with contempt at the flaked paint and cheap furniture. "Lousy joint. I keep telling 'em I'm going to walk out 'n leave 'em to it. Guess maybe I will one day."

"Do your people own the place?" Jarrett pushed away his plate.

The girl gave another sniff of amusement. "Not a chance," she told him. "My pa was a farmer up beyond Bellows Falls. I came down here to get away. Imagine that."

Another customer came in at that moment, and she left the table to wait on him. Jarrett finished his beer and stood up to pay the bill.

"Tomorrow, then?" she said, giving him his change.

"Yes, tomorrow after lunch," he agreed.

"I'll be ready." She shot him a sudden knowing glance as she opened the door for him. "Bye, Pat, see you soon."

Jarrett drove back to the lake, heady with excitement. It had been a long time since he had had a girl, a real young girl. Not since the war, in fact.

○ ○ ○

Stewart Curtis was not the only one among *Caterina*'s passengers who was interested in the performance of Klerksdorp shares. Laura Hartman had been studying the financial reports in the evening papers. Much as she disliked her employer, she respected his commercial judgment, and what little money she had was largely invested in the mining company's stock.

Over the past few weeks, however, she had begun to notice that Curtis's behavior was growing steadily more erratic. He was prone to bouts of deep depression, alternating with sudden, savage bits of temper. In business affairs, he seemed to have lost the dispassionate, even callous, approach that had once marked him; instead, he reacted fiercely to the slightest setback or suggestion of criticism.

He had become increasingly secretive, too, reserving far more of the details of his activities to himself than had previously been his habit. Nowadays he frequently sent her out of the room when he was making telephone calls, especially when these were to his bankers or stockbrokers. Each morning there would be three or four letters to be mailed that were handwritten and sealed by him, another departure from the normal.

Laura had been inclined to attribute these aberrations to overwork and to the strain brought about by the blatantcy of his wife's affairs. Georgina had become very nearly notorious during her stay in Cairo, and Curtis, Laura knew, felt this deeply.

Since their return from Durban, however, the financier seemed less and less interested in his wife's behavior. For long periods he ignored her altogether, and although he still displayed irritation at her flirting with Luca d'Este and her pursuit of Desmond O'Neill, he seemed often too preoccupied to notice. He no longer appeared to regard the baron as any kind of serious threat, and he even tolerated Luca's presence in the after cabin. Laura guessed that Curtis realized Luca had ceased to rate at all highly in Georgina's estimation and was now merely a source of amusement.

Georgina, Laura believed, was actually less vicious and depraved than simply bored. Born into a comfortable, protected background, her beauty and intelligence had smoothed life for her. She had met and married Stewart Curtis, who, although considerably her senior, was already an immensely successful man and a well-known figure in society. Georgina was widely admitted to have made a brilliant match, and their wedding had been one of the events of the season. Now, ten years later, life was beginning to pall for her.

Laura had grown fairly accustomed to seeing Georgina manipulating the people around her, but it had come as something of a shock to find herself caught up in one of the lady's intrigues. Her first instinct had been to hand in her notice. Only the worry and confusion over Siegret and her father had prevented her doing so at once. On the flight to Marseilles, she had begun to have doubts. Curtis was unpredictable these days, and she did not want to draw any more trouble down on Desmond's head. She still had to reach America, and the journey across the Atlantic would be vastly easier without a quarrel. It would be far wiser to wait.

She repeated those feelings to Mr. and Mrs. King over dinner that evening. Harold King had pronounced himself fed up with eating in big hotels. "I want a quiet, old-fashioned place that serves good, plain food," he said, and Laura, who knew London well, took them to a small restaurant off the Strand.

"I've thought all along you shouldn't be working for

that man," Mr. King remarked. "It's not a fit job for a young lady."

"I know, and you're so right," Laura admitted. "I should never have taken it in the first place," she sighed. "You know how it is, though. I needed the money, and there wasn't a big choice of jobs back in South Africa. I wanted to travel and meet interesting people, and I've done quite a lot of both. In many ways, I've had a marvelous time."

"Well, it's got to stop now," Mrs. King said decisively. "You can't go on having Mrs. Curtis spreading lies about you to everyone. I've a good mind to speak to her myself. I'd soon let her know what I think of such behavior. Millionaire's wife or not."

"Now, take it easy, Sarah." Harold King took a drink from a silver tankard of beer. "I'm sure Laura is capable of looking after herself; there's no cause for us to interfere."

"I still think it's disgraceful," his wife replied. She turned to Laura. "As for you, my dear, if you want any help, or a place to stay in New York, we have friends who will be glad to oblige. Isn't that so, Harold?"

"It certainly is," he agreed. "And you can be sure there'll be no trouble about finding a job. People will jump at the chance of employing someone with your experience."

"You're both very kind," Laura was touched by their genuine concern. "To be honest, I'm worried about the trouble I may have brought on Captain O'Neill. Mr. Curtis has it in for him already, I know, and he's facing enough just now, with the inquiry and the trouble in Rome."

In believing the major part of Georgina's behavior stemmed from boredom, Laura was correct. Unfortunately, Laura had underestimated the degree to which the lady's pride had been wounded and the lengths to which she was prepared to go to obtain revenge. The knowledge that Desmond had somehow seen through her attempt to discredit the American girl had aroused her anger. To lose a man to one's husband's secretary was a humiliation not to be borne.

So it was that when Laura and the Kings got back from dinner, the clerk at the reception desk informed Laura that her employer had left instructions for her to

come along to his suite the moment she returned. She
bid good night to the Kings and hurried upstairs.

Less than a quarter of an hour later, she was back in
her own room, close to tears, frantically trying over the
telephone to persuade a reluctant night staff at the head
office of Imperial Airways to divulge a number or address
where Desmond could be reached.

Desmond was in London. He was in fact sitting in the
Grill Room of the Savoy Hotel having dinner with his
wife.

The evening had started badly. Leaving Jack Priestly's
office, Desmond had put a call through to the farm only
to receive no reply. Pamela's telegram had stated specifically that she would be there on Tuesday night, but on
an off chance he tried the flat in London, where she had
moved after their separation.

"I thought we were going to meet down at the farm
this evening," he said when she answered, and he instantly
regretted his words, for Pamela took them as criticism
and came back aggressively.

"I thought you would most likely be too busy to have
time for me tonight, so I stayed up here," she answered.
"I suppose I should be flattered that you've been able
to tear yourself away from the newspaper men. You've
certainly managed to attract plenty of publicity."

"I know," Desmond agreed tiredly. "I've also had to
spend the evening being interrogated by an airline management that is trying to take my job away, so forgive me
if I sound a little short. They've also moved the schedule
up; I'm leaving for New York at three tomorrow afternoon."

"Oh really, Desmond, this is too much," Pamela's voice
snapped back over the line. "You and your damned job.
Why is it you could never find time to see me, but apparently have plenty of time to go off winning motor races
in Cairo with pretty Americans?"

"If you're going to begin slanging me, I'll hang up,"
Desmond warned her. "If you really want to see me, I
can come up to London tonight for dinner, but it will have
to be quite late, I'm afraid."

"Well, yes, perhaps that might be a solution." With her
customary abruptness, Pamela calmed down and became

briskly efficient. "Let's see now, the time is just past seven o'clock. I'll order a table for ten o'clock. You should be able to manage that easily."

"Thanks a lot," Desmond told her. "I'm glad you think so. Just tell me where it is I'm supposed to be meeting you, for God's sake."

"There's no need to get irritable," Pamela rebuked him. "The Savoy Grill. You'd better hurry if you're not going to be late. I'll meet you in the bar."

The prospect of a two-hour drive in his open MG on top of a day's flying was not an attractive one, but it was worth the effort, he knew, to clear up whatever it was Pamela had on her mind. To judge from her tone, she was not thinking of calling off the divorce; most likely it was some problem to do with selling the house. And if he stayed in London, there was a chance he might be able to see Laura the next morning. Phil Harris and his wife would always give him a bed for the night.

The second surprise of the evening had been to find that Pamela was not alone. His immediate reaction had been relief. There had been more traffic on the roads than he had bargained for, and despite his efforts, he was nearly a quarter of an hour late. Pamela, kept waiting by herself, invariably developed sufficient ill temper to poison an entire evening.

"Desmond, this is a friend of mine, Simon Collier. He's a barrister." Pamela's companion was a man of about his own age, with a thin, intelligent face and carefully brushed hair. He was immaculately dressed in a curiously old-fashioned, conservative style normally favored by men a good deal older. Barristers, that peculiarly British breed of lawyer whose work consisted almost exclusively of court appearances with little or no contact with their clients, lived a rarified and anachronistic existence in many respects.

There were two empty martini glasses on the table. Collier signaled a waiter to bring three more.

Pamela seemed unchanged—the same, elegant, chiseled face beneath the glossy blue-black hair, the same electrifying vitality, the impression she gave of restless, questing interest in the world around her, the strikingly fashionable clothes. However, there appeared to be something frenetic about the speed of her conversation, her sudden changes of subject, and her impatience with any failure to follow the mercurial workings of her mind. There were signs of strain in her expression, an almost feverish quality to her stare, which told him she was building up to an emotional crisis. He prayed fervently that they would get through the meal without a drama.

"I don't understand why they should want you to fly to America for them when they are trying to give you the sack," she remarked. "Surely the airline can't be so stupid they can't see what the public reaction would be if you were thrown out. Why you're a hero at the moment—of sorts, anyway," she added disparagingly.

"They're short of crews," Desmond told her. "Eugene's still on his way back from the Far East; Kelly Rogers is on leave. *Champion*'s captain and first officer are both down with flu. The choice was to use me or cancel and leave the field open for Pan Am. The publicity certainly helped though, I admit."

"Farouk let you buy the car, I see." Pamela extracted a cigarette from a case on the table. Collier leaned forward with his lighter. "Thanks." She inhaled deeply and blew a long stream of smoke into the room. "I'm amazed he still likes you after you refused to become his personal pilot."

Desmond shrugged. "He has hundreds of cars, one less meant nothing to him. He was pleased when it won the race, though."

The martinis arrived. Pamela took a swift gulp and began on a new topic. "I've asked Simon to be here because he's a lawyer and has been very good to me," she said. Her words were ambiguous and left Desmond and Collier regarding one another with a slight degree of embarrassment. Pamela, however, was clearly enjoying the situation. With a quick smile of satisfaction, she went on. "We —you and I that is—Desmond, still have to resolve the question of the farm. I thought it would be useful to have Simon here to clear up any legal points."

"Purely as a friend, of course," Collier put in hastily. "Pamela hasn't retained my services professionally." He cleared his throat. "But I'd be happy to give you any advice if you should want it."

"I don"t see there's really any problem," Desmond said quietly. "We bought the farm together. Now we're getting divorced, and you want your money out; it's obvious the farm has to be sold. I've seen the estate agent's valuation, and it seems fair enough. So let's go ahead and put it on the market."

"Just like that, no fuss or arguments?" Pamela said. "I thought you were desperately anxious to hold onto the place."

"I don't want to sell the farm. I would like to keep it very much if I could afford to, but since I can't, there's no point in digging my heels in against the inevitable. You can force me to sell, and anyway you have a perfect right to your money."

"Are you sure you've thought this out?" Pamela asked doubtfully. "I don't want you changing your mind tomorrow and then disappearing for a month where we can't contact you."

"Listen," Desmond told her, "I made it perfectly clear all along that I wouldn't sell until we were divorced. By the time the solicitor gets moving, the divorce will be through, so go ahead and put the farm up for sale."

"Have you considered what you will do then?" she wanted to know.

Her question irritated Desmond. "No, I haven't yet," he answered. "There's no particular urgency for me to look around for somewhere else to live. I am away most of the time."

"You don't have to tell me that," she retorted.

There was no point in replying. Fortunately, Simon Collier interrupted. "I rather think our table is ready," he announced. "Shall we go in? It's getting quite late."

The restaurant was crowded. The three followed a waiter to a table near the center of the room, and heads turned inquisitively as they passed.

"Those pictures of you in the evening papers were better than I'd expected," Pamela remarked. "You're quite a little celebrity."

The attention he was receiving was evidently annoying her, and Desmond knew from bitter experience she would spend the remainder of the meal competing with him. She began to monopolize the conversation, talking about herself and her work on the magazine, stressing the importance of her job as fashion editor. She was at pains, too, to emphasize the success Collier was enjoying at the criminal bar and the heights to which he was expected to rise.

Desmond was surprised by the detachment he felt. Though Collier was the first of his wife's new friends he had met, and it had become fairly obvious the two were having an affair, he discovered that he felt no jealousy, nor even very much interest. The barrister struck him as ineffectual. If he was able and willing to tolerate Pamela's moods, that was his business.

Desmond ordered smoked salmon to be followed by *carré d'agneau*. The salmon had barely arrived when the maitre d'hotel approached to inform them that Captain O'Neill was required on the telephone.

"I'll bet it's only the press," said Pamela. "Tell them to go away."

"Desmond?" It was with a shock that he recognized Laura's voice.

"I called Imperial," she explained, "and the girl on the switchboard gave me Captain Harris's number, and he said to try you at the Savoy. I'm sorry to interrupt your meal."

"Don't worry about it—it couldn't matter less," he assured her. "But tell me—what's happened?"

"Oh, Desmond, you won't believe this, I'm still not sure I do myself. It's the Curtises and your watch—they're accusing me of having stolen it from them and given it to you."

"They're what?" he said, stunned. "They can't be—they must be insane. Georgina gave me the watch herself."

"I know, I know, but that's not what she's saying now. Desmond, I've no idea what to do. Mr. Curtis wants the watch back first thing tomorrow."

"To hell with tomorrow. I'll come right away and ram it down his throat," Desmond told her furiously, "after which I will break his wife's neck for her."

"No, Desmond, for God's sake don't do anything," Laura begged him. "Look, could we meet for a few minutes? I need to talk."

"I'll be over in ten minutes," he told her. "Are you at the Ritz?"

"Yes. I'll wait for you downstairs."

Pamela was less than pleased when Desmond announced his intention of leaving.

"My God, you've got a nerve," she said. "This is the first time in months I've managed to make you sit down for a serious talk, and you want to run off halfway through. Why on earth can't you have a sensible job instead of this ridiculous chasing around all the time?"

"I'm sure Desmond wouldn't be leaving unless it was essential," Collier said tactfully. "Is there anything we can do to help?" he asked Desmond.

"No, thank you," Desmond shook his head. "It's something I'll have to attend to myself." The barrister was clearly relieved; the meeting had been a strain for him as well. "I'm glad we've settled about the farm," Desmond said to his wife. "I may drop by there tomorrow morning for a last look. I'm sorry to have to go now, but I'll give you a call as soon as I get back from New York next week."

Pamela seemed about to speak. Her face took on an expression of almost desperate intensity. Then her shoulders drooped and she nodded good-bye.

The Ritz was every bit as crowded as the Savoy had been. Desmond found a quiet corner in the cocktail lounge and sat Laura down beside him. She was pale and anxious, her eyes round with worry.

"You know it frightens me," she whispered, "seeing all these people here, eating and drinking and party-going as though nothing was wrong with the world, while all the time their enemies are preparing for war. Don't they know what's happening? Haven't they heard that the Nazis occupied Prague this morning? Surely people must realize that they are going to have to face the problem themselves one day soon."

"They realize it," Desmond answered quietly, thinking of the letter from the Admiralty he had found waiting for him. "We all do, and at long last we're beginning to prepare. These people," he indicated with his hand, "are simply trying to forget for a few hours."

"I suppose you're right," she agreed abstractedly. Then abruptly she broke into the account of her interview with Stewart Curtis. "He sent for me after dinner. I knew he was angry because he addressed me as Mrs. Hartman. Normally I'm Laura to them both."

She sat silent for a second or two, then she continued. "He said his wife had noticed you wearing the watch during the flight up from Marseilles. When they reached the hotel, they had checked through their baggage and found that the one she had bought from Cartier was missing!

"At this point he grew very solemn and started telling me how they had considered every possibility before coming to the inevitable conclusion, as he put it, that I must have taken it from their rooms at some time and given it to you."

"But didn't you tell him his own wife had given it to me when we were in Cairo?" Desmond demanded.

"Yes, of course I did," her voice trembled. "I told him the whole story, but he didn't believe me. He said I had taken the watch without permission and could be prosecuted for stealing."

"Well," he said angrily, "I shall make sure the truth comes out."

"Don't you see, though?" Laura said hopelessly. "We've no proof. It's your word against hers—and you know she can twist things. Anyway it doesn't matter. He said he was going to do me the kindness of assuming I had only borrowed the watch. Provided I return the watch at once, no action will be taken. I get the sack at the end of the month of course, but that's no handicap."

"I'm not standing by and seeing you accused because of Georgina Curtis's lies," Desmond said hotly. "I'll go straight to their suite and have the whole business out with them. If she thinks she can get away with a stunt like this, she's made the biggest mistake of her life."

"No, Desmond, please!" Laura clutched his arm. "Don't you see. Stewart Curtis can never admit his wife tried to—" she fumbled for the word—"buy another man. If you make an issue out of it, he will bring charges. And we haven't enough proof. I don't want to be accused of theft, which is what will happen if you try telling him the truth. Just let me take the watch back and forget about the whole business."

Desmond unbuckled the strap. The clasp had left a curious mark on the skin of his wrist, shaped like the letter

D. He gave a rueful smile. "What's so annoying about the whole thing is that I was seduced into accepting it," he confessed. "I should have thrown it back at her in the first place."

He passed it to Laura, and she shut it hastily away inside her evening bag. "Tomorrow morning, however," he said, "after you've seen him, I will still have a few words with him myself. Don't worry." He held up his hand as Laura began to protest afresh. "Once the watch is in his possession again, he will have no grounds for accusing you. All he can do is accuse me directly, and the threat doesn't frighten me. I very much doubt if he would ever actually dare to bring charges. The publicity would make him look ridiculous."

"But Desmond, you can't be sure. Why take the risk?" Laura begged. "The Curtises aren't worth it. Let them go, out of our lives. I was stupid ever to have let myself become mixed up with them."

Desmond shook his head. "No," he said firmly. "The Curtises get away with too many things and have bullied enough people. I mean to see they're stood up to for once. Besides," he added, "Curtis is not in a very strong position where I'm concerned: he needs me to fly him across the Atlantic."

"Well, if you're sure," Laura said doubtfully. "But I do wish you'd let it alone."

Desmond smiled at her. "You'll see. I'll even make them offer you your job back," he said. "And afterward, how would you like to leave London early and have lunch in the country? I want to drive down and have a last look at the farm before we fly off."

This time there was no hesitation in her voice. "I'd love to come," she said, smiling back, "so whatever you do, don't get me my job again, or I won't be able to."

"Good, then that's settled. I'll pick you up at ten, after I've dealt with the Curtises."

Leaving the lounge, they made their way out into the foyer. "Desmond, I am sorry," she said, putting a hand on his sleeve as he was about to go. "I've been so wrapped up in my own problems I forgot to ask you how it went at the inquiry."

"The outcome was pretty much as I expected," he

said. "Except for the publicity in the papers and the fact that they need a crew to fly tomorrow, I think it might have been a good deal worse."

Laura looked relieved. "I am glad," she said. "I was a bit worried the publicity might only make things more difficult for you."

Desmond laughed. "I guess it was you who spread the story. I suppose I should be angry, but to tell the truth, I'm very grateful. But for you, I might now be without a command."

Bidding good night to her in the foyer, Desmond went out into Piccadilly, declining the doorman's offer of a taxi. He had left his MG on Jermyn Street. The clouds had disappeared, and the night was clear and cold. With luck, he thought, tomorrow would be a fine day. As he walked, he passed a newspaper placard. BRITISH PILOT IN DARING RESCUE the black letters proclaimed, and underneath in smaller print, *German Troops Parade in Prague.*

Jacquetta d'Este propped herself up on her elbows in Rashid's bed and kissed him on the shoulder. "I must go back soon," she said. "Luca will be returning."

Rashid was lying on his back, one arm around her waist, stroking her gently. Reaching out with his other hand, he felt for his watch on the night table. "Eleven o'clock," he said, glancing at the dial. "When do you expect him back?"

"He said not before midnight. The Slovak business should keep them late at the embassy, but he might be tired and leave early."

"Wait a little longer." He pulled her body across him to rest on his chest, her silky hair brushing his face.

"No, I must go," she protested halfheartedly. But he drew her head down and kissed her lingeringly on the mouth.

"There is time," he murmured, "again, before you go." And his hands began moving over her body. "Again—once more," he repeated.

Under his touch, her belly and thighs responded, growing heavy with desire. "Rashid, no, no," she cried softly, but her pleadings were already giving way to quick moans of pleasure. Passion swept over her in a wave, and she abandoned herself to it, hugging him fiercely to her as he rolled her over beneath him.

Later, when they were lying in each other's arms, she lifted her head from his shoulder and said, "Rashid, I must talk to you for a minute."

"About your husband?" he replied, his fingers toying idly with her hair.

"Yes, about Luca."

"What is there to say? You know what I have to do."

"Yes—but," Jacquetta insisted, "you must see that our being together makes a difference. I mean," she continued, speaking plainly, "I can't be the lover of my husband's murderer."

"And how can I forsake my word to avenge the killer of my father and my sister?" he asked.

"Luca did not do the actual killing, though. He was with the governor's office. Why don't you take your revenge on the unit involved?"

Rashid let his hand drop from her hair. "We did," he answered in a flat, hard voice. "My men and I, we laid an ambush on the edge of the sands last year. We killed many of the men and all the officers."

"Then surely you have had your revenge a dozen times over," Jacquetta urged. "At worst Luca was only one link in the chain. If you have to kill those responsible, try the generals, or the Duce himself. They're the guilty ones."

"And my sister, what of her?" he asked bitterly. "She was only fifteen when the soldiers carried her away to the governor's palace; she killed herself because of the things they did to her."

Jacquetta's eyes filled with tears. "Rashid, look at me," she said. "Rashid, do I matter? Am I important to you?"

His hand stroked her cheek and wiped a teardrop from the corner of her eye. "You are more than any other person to me," he told her gravely, "and will always be so."

Jacquetta held his hand tightly. "Then listen," she said. "The Fascists have murdered your father and your sister and enslaved your country. Are you going to let them destroy us as well? Because that is what will happen if you kill Luca. Is he worth that? Will his death help your people, or will it only mean more misery and pointless waste of life? You alive and leading your men are a far greater threat to the tyrants in Rome than the killing of Luca. He's not worth sacrificing yourself for; better to avenge your family by freeing their land."

Rashid sighed deeply. "There may be some truth in what you tell me." At length he said, "I must think." He lay there staring up at the ceiling. "As you say, I must consider not only myself, but my people as well."

"Oh, my love," Jacquetta felt a surge of hope. "I know I'm right." She sat up and kissed him tenderly. "I must go, or I'll be missed. I'll come and see you in the morning after breakfast."

○ ○ ○

In his apartment at the Abdin Palace in Cairo, Yousouri Pasha lay back against the embroidered cushions of a divan and sucked a sweet. Though forty-eight hours had passed without incident since his conversation with Prince Suleiman on the subject of Rashid and Baron d'Este, he nevertheless felt a faint unease. Intensive investigation by his spies had not yet come up with any clue as to the young Senussi shiek's whereabouts, and Yousouri was an instinctively fastidious person who preferred to gather up the loose ends of his plots.

A second interview with the prince had failed to elicit any further information and had ended with the old man querulously threatening to go to the king to demand a stop to "this insolent detective work," as he had so contemptuously phrased it.

If Rashid was no longer in the country, where had he gone? There were only two logical possibilities—Libya or Italy. Italy would seem an almost suicidal choice, yet Yousouri was reasonably sure Rashid had not passed westward over the border between Egypt and Libya.

If Rashid had returned to Italy, perhaps abandoning his pursuit of d'Este to wreck his vengeance on some other important figure, the consequences—if he was found to have entered the country from Egypt—would be extremely serious.

A direct warning to the Italians could do no harm and might even prove useful in the light of current—and covert—approaches being made by the palace with a view to providing a counter to British influence.

Clapping his hands, Yousouri ordered a secretary to be summoned. A friendly note to the Italian ambassador would be sufficient. No direct or definite knowledge need be claimed, simply a passing on of chance-heard rumor that might be of benefit to an ally. The court, he thought, would be pleased at this delicate solution.

○ ○ ○

The security roundup in the Czech capital and elsewhere in the newly occupied territories was proceeding sufficiently smoothly for Heydrich to take time off to attend a gala dinner at the Italian embassy in Berlin, and it was here his adjutant, Lindeman, came to report on the progress of the Rintlen affair.

The embassy, in the most elegant and exclusive part of the city, had been bought from a banker in 1934 and restored by the previous ambassador, Vittorio Cerutti. Inside, the illusion was created of being in Venice, in one of the fabulous sunlit palaces of the doges. Flowers were everywhere among the vast expanse of marble, light glittered from the countless facets of Venetian chandeliers reflected back in tall mirrors, and priceless paintings by old Italian masters adorned the walls.

Dinner was over, and the guests had spilled out of the dining room. Footmen in blue silk tail coats and white wigs moved among the guests, bearing trays of coffee and liqueurs. Lindeman went from room to room in search of his chief. The cream of Berlin society, both diplomatic and social, was present, as well as nearly all the most high-ranking Party politicians.

Lindeman finally ran Heydrich down in a small salon. He was in conversation with the president of the Reichsbank, Dr. Schacht, an anxious, colorless man who seized the adjutant's arrival as a pretext for slipping away. "The good doctor," Heydrich remarked sarcastically, regarding the banker's retreating figure, "has been most unwise. He has recently presented the Führer with evidence that Ribbentrop, Goering, and several other high officials had been illegally purchasing foreign currency. Now he wonders why he has enemies."

Together they wandered back in the direction of the hall. Lindeman noted with amusement the alarm caused by the presence of the black-uniformed security chief. Heydrich inspired greater fear in Germany than any other single man. The mere sight of the unsmiling features of "Himmler's Black Ghost," as he was widely named, was sufficient to halt conversations and drive away the more nervous guests.

They passed Magda Goebbels—she was sitting, sour and angry, with Count Ciano. "Her husband's lechery has become a scandal," Heydrich observed in an undertone. "I am told this evening he was dancing with a pretty Jewish girl from one of the embassies. 'You should go to the Anthropological Institute for a consultation,' he said to her. 'I think it is absurd that you should be Jewish. Your skull has the perfect Aryan formation.'"

Lindeman smiled. Heydrich's contempt for the Party's leaders was well known. Their self-indulgence served only to highlight his own ruthless efficiency.

"Goebbels," Heydrich continued when they were in the car and on their way back to Prinz Albrechtstrasse— "Goebbels" he mouthed the propaganda minister's name with distaste—"saw fit to complain to me about British press reports concerning the Wienzmans' escape from Rome. Fortunately I silenced him by saying the matter was proceeding under the Führer's personal supervision. Which, in a sense, it is. However you'd better see to it that Rintlen is gotten out of the way quickly. What news of our plans?"

"Our people in London are still looking for him," Lindeman answered. "They are checking hotels and boarding houses. Unfortunately, there are a great many such places."

"Curse you, I don't need you to tell me that," Heydrich's voice lashed back. "What I want is Rintlen found —and in the shortest possible time."

"It will be done—Obergruppenführer, have no doubt," Lindeman assured him hastily. "There is one point that has arisen however," he cleared his throat nervously.

"Well?" Heydrich demanded coldly.

"It seems, Obergruppenführer," Lindeman went on, "Rintlen has booked a seat on the flight taking the Wienzmans to America. It is possible he may still be intending action of some kind against them."

"You mean he plans to kill them?" Heydrich exclaimed in disbelief. "After the publicity given to their escape? He must be insane!"

"I agree," Lindeman replied unhappily, "but that, it seems, may be the case."

The car swayed as it rounded a corner. Heydrich gripped the armrest to steady himself. "Mark this, Lindeman," he said in a low, savage voice, "if Rintlen succeeds and brings down any more unfavorable publicity on the Reich, it will go ill with you and everyone concerned with this operation. He is to be found and dealt with at once. This whole damned business has been mishandled from the start. Wienzman alive and in our hands would have been of some value. His death serves no useful purpose whatsoever, except to rid the world of another Jew."

"Rintlen will be found and eliminated, Obergruppenführer," Lindeman promised. "I expect confirmation hourly."

"It had better come soon," Heydrich told him, "and let his punishment serve as a warning to the rest of you of the penalty for failure."

○ ○ ○

In his battle for survival, Rintlen was using all the skills picked up during scores of similar operations in which he had been the hunter, tracking down enemies and suspects of the Third Reich. All the techniques and stratagems he had learned to anticipate and watch for were ironically now enabling him to stay ahead of his pursuers.

He knew better than to use a hotel or lodging house. Any place that could be checked was a potential trap. True, London had far too many addresses to be covered by Heydrich's agents working alone, but there was no telling whether or not the British police might have been persuaded to assist, just as he himself had used the Italians in Rome.

After collecting his ticket, he spent the evening in a West End cinema near Leicester Square. Emerging toward ten o'clock, he ate a meal alone in a nearby Italian restaurant, and after a much-needed drink, he set out to organize his accommodations for the night. It did not take him long; by the entrance to Piccadilly Circus he found what he was seeking. From out of the shadows a woman stepped forward.

"You on your own, mister?" The invitation was casual, but unmistakable.

"Do you have a room?" he asked.

The woman nodded. "Five minutes in a cab."

"For the whole night, until morning."

She shrugged. "Sure, if that's what you want. Cost you, though."

People were passing by, and he moved out of the way. The woman looked at him intently. "Twenty pounds," she said, "for the whole night, anything you like." Rintlen hesitated, mentally converting pounds into Reichmarks. "It's a nice room," she assured him. "Quiet, an' there's a bath. It's not far. Anything you like," she repeated.

Rintlen inclined his head curtly. "Very well," he agreed. "Twenty pounds for the night." It was a small price to pay, he reflected, for immunity from Heydrich's killers, and his new companion was attractive enough that the experience promised to be interesting.

Only a few hundred yards away, in the Ritz Hotel, Siegret kissed her father good night and went back to her own room. The events of the past four days had left the professor utterly exhausted, and the strain of conducting interviews with the hordes of reporters who had met them at the dockside had almost been too much for him. An evening in bed and a good night's sleep would see him greatly recovered, she did not doubt, and tomorrow they would start the final leg of their journey.

Siegret was determined not to give herself any false hope again. Though she felt immeasurably happier and more secure in England, she refused to count herself safe until she actually set foot upon the soil of the United States. In England, as in Austria and Italy and France, she had seen the preparations for approaching war: the recruiting posters on the billboards; the air raid warning notices; the newspaper pictures of battle fleets and troop reviews. The news from Czechoslovakia had frightened her further; yet another country had fallen beneath the domination of the Nazis. How long would it be before the whole of Europe followed, and perhaps England, too?

○ ○ ○

The completion of the second gun bay kept Jarrett up late, but he was feeling thoroughly pleased with the day's work. Not only had he installed all four machine guns together with their ammunition trays and replaced the wing panels, but another hour or two would see the Supermarine operational. He estimated he was running more than a day in advance of his allotted schedule, a most satisfactory state of affairs.

Back in the house, he went down to the cellar and returned with another cloth-wrapped bundle. Opening this up on the kitchen table, he drew out a carefully oiled Thompson submachine gun. Once the flying boat was forced to land on the lake, a weapon of some kind would be necessary. The Thompson was easily obtainable, it had a solid, dependable feel, and it was sufficiently formidable to deter all but the most suicidal from attempting resistance. Satisfied with his purchase, he took it upstairs and stowed it in the cupboard in his bedroom with the rest of his flying gear.

Tomorrow, he told himself, his pulse quickening, he would take the afternoon off and with luck, the evening as well, to enjoy himself with Suzie. He would taxi the airplane out onto the water for her and even let her sit inside.

○ ○ ○

Ralph Kendrick's scream woke him from sleep. For a moment he lay exhausted and trembling in the darkness, uncertain of where he was. Then there was a click as his wife, Anne, switched on the lamp and light flooded the room.

"You've been having that nightmare again," she said, peering anxiously at him.

"Yes. I know. I'm sorry I woke you." He felt drained, almost unable to speak as the fear ebbed slowly from him. The bedclothes were drenched with sweat.

"Was it the same one?" she asked.

Ralph nodded wearily, "Yes, the same as before, the fire and the plane going down into the sea."

Morning had come at last, but it had brought no comfort to the three fliers. Beneath them stretched only the bitter North Atlantic, an endless vista of white-capped gray waves that were frequently obscured by drifting banks of mist. According to Ralph's calculations, the coast of Newfoundland was less than two hundred miles away, but the performance of the compass had deteriorated even further during the night, and they could only guess at their true position. It was easily possible that they were hundreds of miles to the north of their intended course, and the weather they were experiencing made this seem all too likely.

The icing on the wings and fuselage had grown more serious, too, affecting the aircraft's handling, and the temperature inside the cabin had dropped noticeably. "What's our altitude now?" Bell demanded.

Carl Huessen scanned the altimeter. "Eight hundred feet," he answered. "Do you think we ought to take her a bit higher?"

"I've been trying, but it's all I can do to hold her at this level," Bell told him. *Sudden rain squalls were forcing the plane down. In the rear of the cramped cabin, Ralph worked with numbed fingers, vainly seeking a way to make radio contact.*

"What's that ahead?" Carl *pointed to a grayish-white cloud looming ominously in their path.*

"It's snow," Bell answered.

All three men's eyes remained locked on the flickering altimeter needle as the Junker plunged into the cloud and their view was blotted out by the swirling whiteness. The needle oscillated, swinging down to zero and then up again, and at any moment they expected to feel waves thrashing against the fuselage.

On and on they flew amid what proved to be a blizzard of arctic intensity. Occasionally they would strike a clear path, and their hearts would lift, but inevitably the snow would close in around them once more.

It was Carl who first drew attention to the red warning light on the engine temperature gauge. "I know," Bell said tersely. "She's way over the limit, but there's *nothing I can do. It's taking every scrap of power we can get just to keep us out of the water. I daren't ease up."* Ralph peered over his shoulder at the altimeter again; four hundred feet was now the upper limit of the needle's travel, and for much of the time it was registering less than half that figure.

Through the snow and cloud vapor, the angry surface of the ocean was visible, the crests of the waves being torn into ragged streaks of foam by the wind. Ralph thought of the small escape dinghy they carried in the rear of the plane. How long could they survive in such a sea?

"We must gain height. We're being forced into the water," Bell shouted to him. "Throw out everything you can to save weight; spare nothing, not even the radio; it's no use anyway."

Hastily Ralph unlatched the door in the rear of the cabin and pushed it open. A freezing wind lashed the interior with stinging snow. Half-blinded and numb with cold, he worked frantically, dragging the heavy radio set across the floor and tipping it out. It was followed by tool boxes, spare parts, and their supplies of food and extra clothing. The two large oil drums they carried for emergencies in case of a leak were jettisoned, as was all the meteorological equipment, ironically the reason behind the whole flight. Ralph even unscrewed his seat and chart table. When everything movable had been stripped out, he tugged the door shut again and returned to the others.

"What about the dinghy?" he asked. They were now between eight and nine hundred feet, but the warning light remained on. "Yes, get rid of that, too," Bell told him.

Carl Huessen protested, "No, the dinghy is our only hope if we do crash in the sea. It weighs nothing. Leave it on." They were still arguing when the engine gave a sudden cough and started to run with an unnaturally loud roaring.

"Christ, what's the matter?" Bell exclaimed, throttling back.

The nose dipped with the loss of power, and as it did so, a long plume of black smoke spurted from the nacelle. Another series of sharp coughs sounded from the engine, followed by a terrible clattering vibration. "We're

going to ditch!" he cried as the plane went into a dive.
He pulled desperately back on the control column.

Suddenly the entire nose of the Junker was enveloped
in flames that were streaming back over the windscreen,
the roar and crackle of the blaze engulfing the front of
the cabin. Ralph could hear the screams of the two
pilots above the howl of the slipstream as the aircraft
plunged.

They struck the water with a jarring, bouncing crash
that seemed to go on and on, shaking and hammering as
though the aircraft were being torn to pieces. Water and
spray poured in through the broken windscreen and a
dozen other places, and steam mingled with the smoke and
fumes from the fire. Stunned and dizzy, Ralph picked
himself up from the floor where he had been thrown by
the impact. Engine noise had ceased, and the slap of
waves against the fuselage, and the whistle of the wind
were audible, but they seemed unnaturally quiet after
the shattering ordeal of the crash.

Still amazed to find himself uninjured, he dragged the
dinghy out from the recess in the tail and prepared to
launch it. The door had jammed shut and required all
his strength to force it open. At once a rush of water
swept in, submerging the floor knee-deep. Through the
hatch he glimpsed the terrifyingly heavy seas, spray breaking over the fuselage.

Carl came stumbling up from the nose, half carrying
Bell with him. The German was badly burned about the
face, neck, and hands, and his flying jacket was smolder-
ing in patches. The skipper, too, had burns, though less
serious. He appeared to be unconscious, and there was
blood in his mouth. "The stick crushed his chest," Carl
said, speaking through blistered lips. "I had to cut him
free. Help me get him into the boat."

The airplane was sinking fast. Hampered by the seas
bursting through the opening, they scrambled aboard the
dinghy, dragging Bell's limp form after them, and pushed
off from the wreck. Minutes later, they watched the
Junker's tail lift high into the air and then slide slowly
beneath the waves, leaving them alone in the rubber
boat.

Fortunately the memory of those terrible days in the
boat had been blurred by the delirium he had endured

toward the end. Bell had died the first morning without regaining consciousness. Carl Huessen, in intense pain from his burns, had followed him two days later, after suffering with great courage the agony caused by the salt spray on his skin. Only the thick, fur-lined clothes he had been wearing had kept Ralph alive until a sharp-eyed lookout on a freighter had spotted the dinghy and its lone survivor. It had taken two months in a hospital for his injuries to heal.

Ralph pushed back the bedclothes and swung his legs to the floor.

"What are you doing?" Anne asked.

He parted the curtains and stood staring out into the night. "Looking to see what the weather will be like for tomorrow," he said.

The sky over Southampton and the estuary was clear—not a wisp of cloud to be seen. Sighing, he drew the curtains closed again and climbed back into bed.

"Don't go tomorrow," Anne pleaded. "Stay behind, say you're sick. You'll only make it worse for yourself."

"I have to go," he told her. "And I'll be fine once I've made the flight again. Now go back to sleep." His words seemed to reassure her, for she switched out the light and settled down among the pillows, but Ralph lay awake for a long time, his mind filled with foreboding.

IV

Transatlantic

10

By radio: 0800 hrs GMT. WEDNESDAY 15 MARCH. IMPERIAL AIRWAYS SOUTHAMPTON ENGLAND TO BRANCH OFFICE LA GUARDIA MARINE TERMINAL NEW YORK. IMPERIAL AIRWAYS FLIGHT 109 G-ADHO CATERINA TO BOTWOOD - MONTREAL - NEW YORK DEPARTS SOUTHAMPTON 1500 hrs GMT TODAY. ETA NEW YORK 1600 hrs EST THURSDAY 16 MARCH. END.

By radio: (Trans. from Italian Diplomatic Code) URGENT AND SECRET. TO MINISTER BARON LUCA D'ESTE ITALIAN EMBASSY LONDON. FROM FOREIGN MINISTRY ROME. INFORMATION RECENTLY RECEIVED RASHID AL SENUSSI NOW IN EUROPE, POSSIBLY ATTEMPTING TO REACH ENGLAND. URGENTLY RECOMMEND EXTREME CAUTION. END.

UNITED PRESS INTERNATIONAL—
WALL STREET MARKET REPORT
OPENING TRADING—MINING: FURTHER FALLS.
KLERKSDORP GOLD—$1.35: DOWN 4½.

As he drove to the Ritz, Desmond was aware of a tension growing within him at the thought of the upcoming flight. The most difficult and dangerous journey in the world—he had said as much to Georgina Curtis in Cairo, and he had been speaking the truth; 1,800 miles of ocean, through the worst weather conditions anywhere on earth. The smallest error or breakdown in equipment, unimportant on an ordinary trip, could result in catastrophe. *Caterina* was immensely reliable, and he himself had made the crossing in perfect safety half a dozen times, but even so, it was only twelve years since Charles Lindbergh's epoch-making flight.

Laura was waiting in the foyer, well prepared for the car journey in a warm, fur-trimmed coat. "I've some bad news for you, I'm afraid," she said, jumping up as he came through the door from the street.

"What's that?" he asked with a grin. From the smile on her face he could see nothing serious had gone wrong.

"It's Stewart Curtis. He's not there," she told him. "He went off first thing. Where, I've no idea, but I guess it's something important. Normally he doesn't start work so early. I won't say I'm not relieved," she admitted, buttoning up her coat, "but maybe it is as well if you don't see him."

"I'll see him all right," Desmond replied. "I've no intention of letting either him or his wife get away with treating you in the way they have. If I can't talk to him now, I'll catch him at Southampton before we take off."

The MG was parked outside the Saint James entrance. Laura gave a cry of delight when she saw the porter loading her suitcase. "Desmond," she turned to him, "I can only come with you today on one condition."

"Which is what?" he asked with a laugh.

Laura held out her hand. "The keys," she demanded. "I let you drive me in the race to Fayum; now you're going to sit beside me while I drive you down to Hampshire."

Desmond looked at her suspiciously. "Are you sure you can handle her?" he asked. "I mean a sports car isn't the easiest machine in the world to drive."

"Can I handle her?" Laura responded with outrage. "Just you get in the left-hand seat, Desmond O'Neill, and I'll show you what real motoring is like!"

Moments later they were roaring down Piccadilly, and she was cutting through traffic, with verve and dexterity.

"At least I've done one thing you'll approve of," she cried as they flashed past the fountains in Trafalgar Square. "I sent a telegram to my stockbroker in New York asking him to sell all my Klerksdorp shares and put my savings into something else. I've so few it's no more than a gesture, but it's given me a lot of satisfaction."

They drove happily on in the crisp spring morning, and

neither gave much more attention to her words. However, Laura had underestimated the effects of her action.

Stewart Curtis had left the Ritz early to keep an appointment with his stockbrokers. Until recently, he had maintained a London office to manage his British and European business, but since his interests had become almost exclusively concentrated in Africa and the United States, he now divided the majority of his time between these two continents.

Klerksdorp, however, was quoted on both the London and Wall Street exchanges, and the considerable shares held by British investors, combined with London's close links with South Africa, had prompted him to retain advisors here as well as in New York.

Curtis's relationship with his brokers was ambivalent. Raikes, Saumarez, and Company was an established, immensely prestigious firm with a well-deserved reputation for scrupulous honesty. His acceptance by them as a client shortly after his marriage to Georgina—and partly as a result of her social connections—had seemed to him to put the seal upon his acceptance in the British world of finance. His satisfaction, however, was mixed with annoyance at the condescending, frequently arrogant tone that many of the partners adopted in dealing with him. Curtis, they made it plain, might be a very rich man; he might even be a business genius; but he was also a parvenu, and the city had seen them before. Until now, the brokers' behavior, though irritating, had not upset him greatly since he had been able to dominate any situation with little difficulty. Today things were different.

Jervase Raike's office, looking out over Threadneedle Street to the Bank of England opposite and the Stock Exchange building itself, spoke of generations of wealth and social position, and the senior partner himself mirrored the qualities of the room. Tall, silver-haired, and soldierly, dressed in morning tails, gray waistcoat, and striped trousers, he regarded Curtis across the wide Georgian desk.

"The fact is, Curtis," he was saying in cold tones, "there is very little we can do unless you are prepared to contribute something for us to work with. When someone starts selling stock in a market as weak as this one, it is bound to affect the price. If you won't release more details about Klerksdorp's progress, my only suggestion is to begin buying on your own behalf and try to drive the price up."

"I've already said once that I'm doing so at this very minute on Wall Street," Curtis snapped. "You can't expect me to support the price single-handed in every country."

Raikes consulted a note on his desk. "Then I'm afraid it doesn't seem to be reflected in the share price," he remarked dryly. "What do you think, Giles? Wall Street is more your pigeon."

Giles Raikes was a slimmer, darker version of his uncle, and some twenty years his junior. He was not lacking, Curtis knew, in either initiative or intelligence, and his urbane manner hid shrewd business insight.

"I don't know quite on what scale your purchases in America have been, Mr. Curtis," he said quietly, "nor exactly at what point they were made. Since the time in New York at this moment is approximately five in the morning, I assume your statement is not to be taken literally. The price of Klerksdorp, however, has moved down steadily over the past ten days, just as it has in London. Kimber, Crossfield, and Smith, the company's brokers on Wall Street, report a similar pattern to the one we find. Sizable lines of stock are being offered for sale at regular intervals, and bargains being struck at ten to fifteen percent beneath the current bidding. Incidentally," he added, "their report yesterday made no mention of recent buying of any significance."

Curtis frowned. The inference was perfectly clear. The man was calling him a liar. Accustomed to behaving as though he were a financial wizard whose statements were not to be disputed, he was finding the Raikeses' attitude an unpleasant surprise. They had always been content to sit passively while he dictated his instructions, even if their manner in doing so had been one of fastidious distaste. This new toughness was wholly unexpected.

Jervase Raikes was speaking again. "Can you shed any light on who is behind this persistent selling?" he asked. "Certainly some of it appears to be originating in South Africa, and since you yourself have so recently returned—"

Curtis shook his head. "I've not the slightest idea," he

retorted angrily. "Which is why I'm here asking you."

The two brokers exchanged glances. This time it was Giles who spoke. "Of course, during the past twelve months," he said casually, "our firm has put more than one million pounds worth of Klerksdorp stock through the London market, on your personal behalf—"

Curtis interrupted him. "You know damn well those sales were made as part of a worldwide rationalization of my business interests," he said hotly. "And the money was used to finance further exploration at the mine. Are you suggesting I've been selling my own stock short?"

"No, of course not, Curtis. Everyone knows how ridiculous such an idea would be," the senior partner responded smoothly. "Nevertheless, I'm sure you can see that in the face of all this confusion some form of positive action on your part is highly desirable, if not vital."

"Damn it, I've told you once. I can't support the price here and in New York," Curtis swore angrily. "Why don't you put some more of your clients' money in? A bit of outside buying is all it needs."

Jervase Raikes gave him a long, hard look. "I am afraid we should find that impossible at this juncture," he said succinctly. "In fact, we are having to do the very opposite."

Curtis stared at him in amazement. "You mean you're advising your clients to sell? My God—I won't stand for that! You're brokers to the company, it's unethical. I'll go to the courts."

Giles stood up and gazed out of the window, watching the figures streaming in and out of the Stock Exchange. Turning back to the room, he cut through Curtis's frothing complaints. "What my uncle means," he said crisply, "is that we no longer consider Klerksdorp an acceptable risk, and nothing you've said to us today has done anything to change our minds. You don't seem to realize that the market is in a dangerously weak state, and your company is now on a knife edge. Unless you can come up with some way to stop the slide in your share price, the quotation may have to be suspended. As it is, rumors are beginning to go around. The slightest thing could cause a run on the stock, which might bring bankruptcy."

It was only too easy to read their minds. Uncle and nephew both believed he had sold stock earlier in the year because he had known then the company was insolvent. Ironically, the money he had raised had been loaned to Klerksdorp—in a desperate attempt to stave off disaster for a few more months—in the hope new ore loads could be discovered in the meantime.

There was no point in trying to argue the matter further; the meeting was clearly at an end. He had failed to allay their suspicions, and their intentions were obvious. They would continue the process they had already initiated—clearing the Klerksdorp shares from their clients' portfolios and feeding the stock onto the market. The effects would gather momentum, and within forty-eight hours, the steady selling of the past fortnight would have become a wave, touching off a chain reaction across the Atlantic.

Unless he could reach New York before the news broke, and complete the option sale, he was ruined.

$$\circ \quad \circ \quad \circ$$

Paul Rintlen was shaving in the prostitute's room in Covent Garden. The mirror above the basin was placed so low he was forced to stoop at an uncomfortable angle in order to see his reflection. To add to his difficulties, he was using a miniature razor that belonged to the woman.

He swore as he scraped awkwardly around his chin, and a trickle of blood appeared among the lather. He had cut himself for the second time.

He was rinsing his face in the basin when the door opened. "I bought everything you wanted," she said. "Socks, underwear, three white shirts and collars, pajamas, and a dressing gown." Reaching into her coat pocket she pulled out a handful of bills and loose change. "I kept the receipts like you said, only I'll need a bit more for the suitcase if it's got to be a good one."

Rintlen's suit had been hung tidily on the back of a chair. Taking out his wallet, he extracted another note. "I want a bath," he told her, handing it over, "and breakfast as soon as you get back." The woman nodded. "I'll run it now; it takes awhile."

She showed no curiosity about the purchases she had been sent to make. In the daylight, without the heavy make-up, she appeared younger and more attractive. The evening before, she had displayed considerable expertise at her profession, and Rintlen had been able to respond with an enthusiasm that had surprised him, considering his exhaustion. Her room, though cheap, was clean and pleasant, its colors and furnishings unexpectedly imaginative.

A little later, soaping himself in the bath, he directed his mind to the task ahead. He was inclined to think it would be safe for him to take the train down to Southampton with the other passengers. There was no reason to suppose Heydrich's men had guessed that he was still intending to fulfill his mission, and even if they had, there would be little they could do in public to prevent him. The flight to New York took more than twenty-four hours and involved two stops in Canada on the way. At some point on the journey there would be the opportunity to finish with Wienzman and his daughter.

Back in the bedroom he found the woman packing his new belongings neatly inside a smart brown suitcase. "I'll start your breakfast," she said. There was an oddly innocent air about her that brought a reassuringly commonplace touch to their relationship. Under normal conditions, Rintlen would probably have felt contempt, even revulsion, by now. As it was, however, hunted and an outcast himself, with the life he was accustomed to slipping from his grasp, he felt a bond of sympathy. It occurred to him that he did not even know her name.

"Not yet," he said firmly. Taking another five-pound note from his wallet, he laid it on the mantelpiece. His train, after all, did not leave until one o'clock.

○ ○ ○

The journey through Surrey and Hampshire on such a glorious day had thoroughly restored the spirits of Desmond and Laura. Laura was delighted at the chance to show off her skill at the wheel. The MG was a joy to drive, and she sped along the twisting roads, the wind blowing through her hair and bringing color to her cheeks.

Past the ancient town of Winchester, Desmond directed her off the main road, and through the narrow lanes in the valley of the Itchen River. They passed small villages set among water meadows and rolling fields whose earth lay freshly turned after the spring plowing. Then turning down a track that wound for a quarter of a mile between high-banked hedges, they came upon the farm in a fold among the downland, gazing back up the valley.

On the way down, Desmond had described the house and its surroundings, but even so she was struck by its beauty.

"Do you like it?" Desmond asked, smiling.

"Do I like it? It's the loveliest house I've ever seen! I can't believe you really live here." The driveway opened out into a wide square of gravel, bordered by a lawn.

"I'm afraid the place hasn't been very well looked after these last few months," he apologized, glancing at the weeds pushing up through the stones and the unkempt grass.

Scrambling out, Laura filled her lungs with deep breaths of the invigorating air. In the distance she could see the river sparkling in the sun and the rust red roofs of a village amid the green and brown patchwork of the fields. She turned to him, her face flushed with happiness. "No wonder you wanted to live here."

Desmond laughed. "I'm glad you approve," he said, searching in his pocket for the key. "Come on and I'll show you around inside." He opened the heavy oak door, and they went in.

"It's a pity Pamela had all the furniture put into storage," he said as he led her through the hallway to another door. "This is the sitting room. It was in a terrible state when we first arrived. The last owner was a farmer who used to store hay in the ground-floor rooms. The beams had all been covered with plaster, which we had to strip off by hand."

"It's incredible," Laura said. The light here was bright, giving the room a rich, warm glow.

He led her through the rooms, downstairs and up, and then he took her out into the paved courtyard between the rear of the house and the old stables and barn.

"In the summer, we used to bring out a table and have dinner here on fine nights," he told her, recalling the early days of his marriage. Laura was interested in the well in the middle of the yard, with its stone surround and wooden canopy, and Desmond obligingly hauled up a bucketful of clear water for her to taste.

"It's delicious," she gasped, "but so cold." They both laughed; their eyes met, and, moving together, they kissed happily.

They were still embracing when a hard voice broke suddenly upon their private world. "Well, this is a charming spectacle, I must say."

Springing guiltily apart, they looked around to see the figure of Pamela standing by the kitchen door.

"I came down in the hope of having a talk with my husband, and what do I discover?" she said, coming across the yard, "but him and his girlfriend making love in the stables." Her face was very pale, accentuating the crimson of her mouth, her dark eyes glittering dangerously. "This, I suppose, is the celebrated Mrs. Hartman." She gave Laura a venomous glance.

Desmond pulled himself together with an effort. "Laura, I am sorry," he apologized. "This is my wife. I wasn't expecting you," he said to Pamela. "Why didn't you tell me you were coming down?"

"I only decided this morning. It never occurred to me you'd bring your airline pick-ups here."

"Pamela, that's enough," Desmond warned her sharply.

Laura had recovered her composure. "I'd better leave you two alone," she said to Desmond. "I'll wait for you by the car."

"Running out on us already?" Pamela sneered, stepping forward to bar the girl's way. "Afraid you might have to listen to a few homely truths?"

To Pamela's surprise, Laura faced up to her. "Did you really come here because you wanted to speak with your husband, Mrs. O'Neill?" she asked witheringly. "Or do you simply want to pick a fight with me? Because I've been pushed around for the most of this past week, and I'd just love a chance to hit back." The two women faced each other angrily. Then Pamela abruptly dropped her gaze and with a contemptuous sniff stood aside, allowing Laura to pass.

Desmond waited until the sound of Laura's footsteps had died away inside the house. "Well?" he said shortly. "Here we are alone. Now why did you want to see me?"

"Why the hell shouldn't I want to see you? You're still my husband, aren't you?" Pamela stormed at him. "Or does it mean nothing to you that we are about to be divorced after only four years of marriage? Do you imagine it's very pleasant for me to come down to try for a last attempt to reason things out with you, only to find you in the arms of another woman?"

"Almost as pleasant as for me to find you with Simon Collier last night," he answered. In truth, he couldn't have cared less, but her talk of wanting to reason things out had worried him.

Fortunately, she was in too much of a rage to pass up a chance for an argument. "Simon—he's just a friend." She dismissed the barrister with a toss of her head. "And even if he weren't, I certainly would not go bringing him down here. This was our home, or had you forgotten?"

"Of course I hadn't, and I'm not likely to, either," he retorted. "In any case you seem to forget it's you who has been so keen to sell the place."

"I know—which is why I'm here." Pamela had been facing him, hands thrust into the pockets of her coat. Now she began pacing up and down. "I want to be quite certain you're aware of what you're doing."

"Of course I know what I'm doing," Desmond said irritably. "I've been perfectly sure all along. We made a mistake, you and I, in believing we could ever live together. The only sensible thing to do is to cut ourselves loose."

"And suppose I said I was willing to have one last try. What then?" she demanded, checking her stride and looking at him intently.

Desmond shrugged his shoulders wearily. "We've been through this before. You have no more wish to stay married than I have; you'll be much better off with some other man. Someone like Simon Collier, who doesn't disappear for weeks at a time."

"Leave Simon out of it," Pamela snapped. "The truth is you can't wait to be free so you can marry your new girlfriend: Nice fools you'd both look if I called off the divorce."

Desmond had had enough. "Pamela," he said to his wife quietly, "if you really want to believe I would jump straight from one marriage into another, I can't help you, and I'm certainly not staying here to argue over it. You must do what seems best for you, but as far as I am concerned, we're finished. I'm not standing for any more emotional indulgences; these scenes are pointless, they do neither of us any good, and we end up hurting each other more. Now that we have agreed to sell the farm, I don't want to see you again."

He had spoken more brutally than he had intended, and he felt a momentary pang. Pamela stared at him in astonishment, her mouth working soundlessly. The shock of rejection seemed to have left her momentarily speechless. "You bastard!" she said at last, between tightly clenched teeth, her voice shaking with hatred. "You unutterable bastard! I swear I'll make you regret you ever said that, if it's the last thing I ever do. I'll never give you a divorce, do you hear? Never. I'll make you beg me first."

Overwhelmed by emotion, she screamed savage denunciations at him in a blind, unreasoning rage. There was no point in staying to listen, Desmond knew, or in attempting to calm her; his very presence was the cause of her bitterness.

"Do you think she meant what she said?" Laura asked as they drove back down the valley. Desmond had taken the wheel this time, and he was giving her the gist of his confrontation with Pamela.

"I don't know," he said, shaking his head. "Maybe not. I doubt if she really knew what she was saying most of the time. When one of these nervous crises breaks on her, she simply strikes without thinking. I'm only sorry you had to be there when it happened."

"Oh, that doesn't matter." Laura smiled. "I've had much worse things thrown at me. I feel sorry for her."

"Well, it had to be faced sooner or later," Desmond said. "I always knew I'd probably have to have it out with her once more before we finally cut ourselves free. Poor Pamela doesn't know any other way." He drove on thoughtfully. In the sky, a formation of planes etched white vapor trails with unerring precision. Fighters, he guessed. Hurricanes or Spitfires from the nearby base at Tangmere. How long would it be before they were patrolling in earnest?

○ ○ ○

Toward half past eleven, Jacquetta d'Este returned to her room at the Ritz from a walk in the park with Rashid. There was no doubt that he had very nearly been persuaded to switch the target of his revenge from Luca to some other more prominent figure. Not that this was without its dangers. Jacquetta shuddered at the idea of the risks he might run. At the back of their minds, though so far unvoiced, was the hope they might one day be able to return together to Egypt and live there under the protection of Prince Suleiman and the king. Such a course would be impossible if Rashid were in serious trouble with the Italian government.

Against all this was the disturbing news that the Italians suspected Rashid's presence in London. The telegram to the embassy from Cairo had been relayed to Luca at breakfast. Luca had hurried off to the embassy to consult with the authorities, while Jacquetta, with equal anxiety, had hastened down the corridor to tell Rashid.

It was only when Rashid had calmed her down and made her repeat everything her husband had said that she realized she had been exaggerating the dangers. The Italians, it was clear, had only learned of Rashid's disappearance from Cairo. The rest was pure conjecture. Besides, Jacquetta knew, her husband pictured Rashid as a vengeful figure in Arab robes, mounted on a horse. A far cry from the elegant Turkish nobleman traveling aboard Imperial 109.

A soft tap at the door interrupted her thoughts. Rushing to open it, she was surprised to find Dr. Van Smit standing outside. "Are you certain I am the one you want to see?" she asked when she had let him in. "My husband will be back before we go to the station, but I am not sure at exactly what time."

"Thank you, baroness, but it is you to whom I wish to speak," Van Smit answered in his clipped accent. "I have a matter of great delicacy to discuss."

"A matter of great delicacy?" Jacquetta repeated in amazement. "Whatever can you mean?" Even as she spoke, a terrible suspicion shot through her. The South African was eyeing her intently. Here in England his deep tan was even more noticeable, making him seem grotesquely out of place in the luxurious comfort of the room.

"I am sure you are already aware of my meaning, baroness?" Van Smit answered, observing the sudden loss of color from her face, "but since you ask, I will make my meaning clear. The night before last, while we were in Rome, I had occasion to come to your suite during the evening. I wished to see if your husband would be interested in a game of cards.

"The door to your suite was not quite fastened," he continued, "nor was the door to your bedroom——"

"Very well, you need not go on. We both know what you saw," Jacquetta interrupted sharply. "What is it you want of me?"

The doctor's thin lips twitched briefly. He was clearly enjoying the situation. "I should have thought that was obvious," he replied. "I want money, and a great deal of it. We will start with twenty-five thousand dollars, payable as soon as you reach America."

"Twenty-five thousand dollars!" Jacquetta echoed in astonishment. "You can't possibly be serious. How do you imagine I can obtain such a sum? It is out of the question. We are not rich."

"Not in comparison with Mr. Curtis, I agree," Van Smit said calmly, "but you most certainly have money. Also jewelry," he added. "Like the nice diamond brooch you're wearing now." Jacquetta's hand went instinctively to the hooped clasp pinned to the shoulder of her dress. The piece was one of her favorites, left to her by her mother, and the thought of losing it to this loathsome man enraged her.

"Get out!" she cried furiously. "Get out, and go to my husband with your tales. Do you think I care? It was finished between us long ago. And when you do, I shall go to the police. In both England and America, the penalty for what you are doing is severe. Then we shall see who is the loser after all."

Van Smit was surprised by her spirited attack. "You'd better think again," he said menacingly. "Imagine the reaction of your family and friends if they were to hear about your affair. How would you feel then?"

Jacquetta, however, was not to be beaten so easily. "It is you who should think again, doctor," she said with contempt. "Among my friends are men of honor who will know what to do to prevent my disgrace."

"Don't threaten me, baroness," Van Smit spat back. "I

took the precaution before coming to see you of leaving a letter with lawyers explaining everything, to be sent to your husband in the event of my death or disappearance. So tell that to your lover, baroness. You can also tell him from me that he may be able to fool everyone else on this flight, but I've met his kind before. He's a desert Arab from out of the deep sands; you can see it in his eyes and face." Seeing Jacquetta's look of alarm, he chuckled briefly. "Yes, I thought maybe there would be people interested in knowing we have an imposter among us. So find the money between you—twenty-five thousand dollars. I'll give you forty-eight hours from the moment we land in New York."

Jacquetta could only stare at him, paralyzed by the thought of what would follow were Luca to learn of Rashid's identity.

"Good day, baroness." Satisfied with the outcome of the interview, Van Smit took his leave of her. "Remember," he said with one hand on the door, "twenty-five thousand dollars by Saturday afternoon—or your husband will learn everything."

○ ○ ○

At Warren Lake, dawn was breaking on another day of mist and a dull, overcast sky. Pat Jarrett edged the Supermarine out from the boathouse. According to the most recent weather forecasts, the cold front was moving eastward; by tomorrow the skies would probably be clear, and the fine weather was expected to last through the weekend.

Jarrett listened with a glow of satisfaction to the familiar roar of the 700 horsepower beneath the long cowling. A quick check of his instruments, and he was racing across the lake into the wind. At 3000 revs he lifted off and hurtled over the tree-covered slopes of the opposite shore. The little racer was handling as sweetly as he could wish, the extra weight of the guns making only a fractional difference in her performance. He shot up over the dam wall, pressed hard down on the starboard rudder bar to bring her around in another tight turn, and dived low over the lake's surface.

Leveling off, he flicked on the firing button and sighted

in on his target. A quarter of a mile from the house, close to the water's edge, lay the decaying remains of a small cabin cruiser. Rocketing in at fifty feet, Jarrett opened fire at a range of four hundred yards, holding the burst for three seconds. Even above the slipstream, he could hear the blast as the whole aircraft trembled with the recoil.

Jarrett had a fleeting glimpse of timber and paneling bursting apart before he dragged the stick back, pulling the aircraft up to scrape clear of the trees. A fierce joy swept through him, and he found his whole body quivering with excitement as all his old war memories came surging back. When he reached the scene minutes later, he stared amazed at the effect of his handiwork. There could certainly be no doubt as to either the alignment of his sights or the efficiency of his guns. The cabin cruiser was scarcely recognizable.

Back in the boathouse, he cleaned and reoiled the guns and fed in fresh ammunition, lapping the long belts carefully into the feed chutes. Resisting the temptation to go up for a second practice shoot, he replaced the doped-on fabric patches over the muzzles of the blast tubes as a protection against dirt and spray and returned to the house for breakfast. By conducting his firing test this early, and with the added advantage of the low cloud to muffle the noise within the valley, it was unlikely in the extreme, he thought, that the gunfire would have attracted attention.

O O O

At quarter to one, *Caterina*'s passengers boarded the Southampton express at London's Waterloo Station. They had been conducted from the Ritz Hotel under the watchful eyes of two Imperial Airways staff who were delegated to make sure no one went astray and thus delayed the flight. Installing their charges in the Pullman compartments with the reminder that luncheon would be served in the first-class dining car as soon as the train started, they went to check the luggage aboard and to await the arrival of the new passenger—Mr. Ernst Perler, of Bern, Switzerland.

Rintlen himself was already in the station. For the past

half hour, he had been watching the approaches to the platform from the corner of a nearby buffet. He had observed nothing to alarm him, but he was still apprehensive. The station was very crowded; numerous men in uniform were passing through, no doubt part of Britain's recently introduced armed forces call-up, making it difficult for him to detect anyone suspicious lurking in the vicinity. Several times he thought he spotted one or more of Heydrich's men, but on each occasion they had been ordinary travelers, merely waiting for family or friends. Perhaps he had managed to slip his pursuers successfully.

Slinging his raincoat over his arm, he approached the ticket barrier. The two airline staff members waiting there led him at once to join the remainder of the flying boat's passengers. There was just time for a seat to be found for him in a compartment with Rashid, Dr. Van Smit, and Georgina Curtis's maid, Arlette. With a shriek of its whistle and a blast of white smoke, the train began to move.

Jacquetta was sitting two doors along in the window seat of a compartment occupied by her husband and the Curtises. The men were discussing the latest developments in the Czechoslovakian crisis and their significance for Europe and the world at large. Jacquetta listened with half an ear while keeping up a chatter with Georgina about the clothes Georgina had bought on her shopping spree in London. Jacquetta was trying to think of a way to break Dr. Van Smit's hold on her. She had been unable to find a moment to speak to Rashid and tell him what had occurred. Luca had returned to the hotel moments after the doctor's departure from their room. Fortunately, he had ascribed his wife's nervousness and distress to the effects of the telegram he had received at breakfast.

To no small degree, her worries were caused by fear of Rashid's reaction. He would be outraged, she knew, and he might easily take violent steps against Van Smit, the results of which might be calamitous. If the South African was to vanish or be found dead, having indeed left a letter with lawyers to be sent to Luca, she and Rashid would most certainly be indicted for murder.

As the train steamed out of Winchester, Rintlen ate a light lunch, then left the dining car early. He was fortified by a bottle of wine he shared with the doctor, who had proved an interesting companion, full of gossip and considerable information on the flight ahead.

He wandered back down the train to find the lavatory. The first two he came to displayed engaged signs in the slot above the door handles. Continuing down the corridor, he passed through the second-class section, where there seemed to be fewer passengers. He had reached the end of the next-to-the-last carriage when, looking back, he saw two men coming toward him.

Without the need for a second glance, he recognized them. Tall, athletic-looking men, both in their late twenties or early thirties, fair-haired and smartly but unobtrusively dressed, they could have passed unnoticed as Englishmen in any group, which was how they must have escaped his attention. However, Rintlen had no doubt that they were an execution team sent by Heydrich to kill him.

Immediately to Rintlen's right was the door to another lavatory. He seized hold of the handle, praying that it would not be occupied. The door opened, and he slipped inside, turning the lock behind him.

Expecting at any moment to hear the rattle of the handle as the door was tried, he waited, ear pressed to the woodwork, straining to catch the sounds in the corridor above the noise of the wheels on the track. He hoped desperately that the two men had not seen him duck inside. If they had. . . . He looked around the small, cramped cubicle. There was no way out; above the window his eyes fell on a red emergency chain. If worse came to worst, he would have to pull that and trust to the resulting confusion to save him.

He was still listening when, without warning, the door was smashed violently inward, tearing the lock from the frame, striking him a savage blow on the side of the face, and hurling him onto the floor against the toilet bowl. In the same moment the two men burst through and flung themselves on him. Dazed by the suddenness of the attack, Rintlen lashed out fiercely, kicking and punching blindly. Blows rained down on his head and body, his arms were pinned, and he was hauled struggling to his feet.

Pushing the door shut again, his captors faced him grimly. Producing a small caliber automatic from an inside holster, the leader of the two pointed it at Rintlen's chest. "Foolish to try to escape from us, Standarten-führer," he said, breathing heavily. "You only make things worse for yourself." He had gingery fair hair, gray eyes, and freckled skin.

Rintlen's head was still singing from the effects of the beating he had received, and his body ached. "What are you going to do with me?" he gasped, knowing it was pointless to dispute his identity. The man behind him twisted his arms viciously, and Rintlen let out a cry of pain.

The other agent smiled thinly. "In approximately six minutes," he said, looking at his wristwatch, "this train enters a long tunnel. When that happens, we take you into the passage, open the door"—he jerked his head—"a little push, and out you go. We are traveling at one hundred and twenty kilometers per hour. The authorities will have some difficulty in identifying your remains. In the meantime," he went on, "we will wait quietly here together."

Jacquetta d'Este had at last managed to snatch a few moments alone with Rashid in the corridor. Luca and Curtis were lingering in the dining car over coffee and brandy, and Georgina had returned to her seat in the Pullman coach.

It was only with the greatest of difficulty that Jacquetta was able to prevent Rashid from seeking out and confronting Van Smit immediately.

"It is useless to try and buy off such a man," he told her. "He will demand more and more until you are bled dry, and in the end he will still go to your husband."

"Not so loud," she begged him, terrified. "I know—but what else is there to be done?"

"What should have been done long before now," Rashid whispered fiercely. "Your husband must die—and this Van Smit must die with him."

"Please, Rashid, for God's sake," Jacquetta pleaded with him frantically, "couldn't we just go away together, you and I, back to Egypt—and forget about them both? Then none of this would matter."

"No, it is impossible," Rashid shook his head decisively. "I should never have allowed myself to forget my duty."

She tried to reason with him, but he remained adamant. "Afterward, yes, perhaps we can go away," he said to her. "But first, I must do what I set out to do."

Before Jacquetta could reply, the sound of voices down the corridor warned them that Luca and Stewart Curtis were returning. Shooting a last anguished look at her lover, she fled in the direction of her compartment.

In the lavatory at the rear of the train, the leader of Rintlen's two captors looked at his watch again. "About two more minutes," he said. "We'd better bring him out into the passageway." Changing the gun over into his left hand, he opened the door a fraction and checked to see that all was clear. Backing out, he motioned to his companion to push Rintlen after him.

In the corridor they took up positions on either side of the exit, holding the S.D. officer firmly between them. The leader squinted through the window at the ground speeding past them. "Here it comes," he said. "Get ready with the handle."

Releasing one hand from Rintlen's arm, the other man reached down and fumbled with the latch of the door. As he did so, the train plunged into the mouth of the tunnel with a sudden deafening shriek. Taken unawares, the man allowed the door to be jerked from his grasp, and, caught in the slipstream, it flew open and slammed back against the side of the carriage.

Seeing the agent suspended between himself and the roaring black void, Rintlen seized the only chance he was likely to get. Lunging forward with all his weight, he drove his shoulder and hip into the man's left side. His assailants were totally unprepared, both of them had been bracing themselves to prevent Rintlen from trying to break backward, away from the yawning exit. Caught off balance, the man was pitched headlong through the doorway. He clawed desperately at Rintlen's arm, trying to maintain his grip, but the momentum of his fall and the pull of the slipstream were too much for him. His fingers tore loose, and he was whirled away into the darkness of the tunnel, his scream cutting off abruptly as his body thudded sickeningly against the rear carriage.

The force of Rintlen's lunge had sent both him and the remaining agent crashing to the floor in a furious struggle for the gun. Though Rintlen had the advantage of surprise, the other man was stronger. The agent fought back savagely, twisting the weapon free from Rintlen's grip and using his superior strength to heave his opponent half out of the open door.

Choking and half-blinded in the smoke and soot-laden blast of air, with his head and shoulders hanging out the door as the train thundered through the tunnel, Rintlen tightened his grip frantically on the other's gun hand, attempting to pull himself back inside. Panic rose within him as he fancied himself slipping, and he thrashed convulsively, striking out with his feet. All of a sudden there was a sharp report; he felt a stinging, burning sensation in the fingers of one hand, then the body on top of him relaxed and went limp.

Rintlen's one thought was still only to save himself from falling under the wheels. Grasping the edge of the door frame, he jerked himself back into the carriage and squirmed out from under his attacker. The agent was either dead or seriously wounded, and Rintlen did not stop to find out which. Snatching up the pistol, he seized the man's legs and tipped him out through the exit, dragging the door shut behind him just as the express flashed out into the sunlight.

Twenty minutes later, shortly before the train pulled into Southampton, Rintlen emerged from the lavatory. He had successfully removed the traces of dirt and damage suffered in the struggle, with the exception of a bruise on one cheek and a powder burn on the fingers of his right hand, neither of which would attract particular attention. Though the fight had left him weak and shaky, he was elated. No one else on the train seemed to have heard the gunshot above the noise in the tunnel, and there was a good chance that the bodies of the two men would not be discovered for some time. Even when they were, there was nothing to link him with their deaths. The German embassy would certainly maintain silence in the affair. And he himself was now armed once again.

○ ○ ○

Pat Jarrett had switched on the big shortwave wireless receiver set, and he was listening in, over his breakfast, to the early morning radio traffic between Botwood in Newfoundland and New York's La Guardia Airport. He heard the Botwood operator acknowledging the prior receipt of the overnight message from England concerning the rescheduling of Imperial 109.

A momentary anxiety passed over him at the realization that he had only thirty hours to go before the plane was due, and for an instant he considered calling off his afternoon date with Suzie. On reflection, however, he told himself there was ample time. He anticipated little trouble over the final engine tuning, and he actually had few worries of not being ready in time.

He looked out across the lake. A fresh breeze had sprung up, ruffling the surface of the water. Overhead, the leaden cloud base was starting to thin, and patches of blue sky and sunlight were showing through; fine weather was on its way. He would be sorry to leave the lake; he had enjoyed working in this lonely place with its clear waters and hills of dark trees and clean air. The life had suited him. Perhaps when it was all over, he would find another place like this.

○ ○ ○

A pleasant lunch in a small restaurant outside Southampton had done much to dispel the gloom Desmond felt after his meeting with Pamela. Laura had contrived to turn the conversation to more cheerful topics: his boyhood in the Wicklow Mountains south of Dublin, his early days with Imperial Airways. "Those were marvelous times," he said nostalgically as they drove on toward the marine terminal. "Each journey was a tremendous challenge. New routes were being pioneered everywhere; people were performing unheard of feats—night flights, flying over deserts and mountain ranges, crossing the Atlantic."

Parking inside the dock, they made their way down to *Caterina*'s berth. "There's a fine sight," Desmond exclaimed. "The *Queen Mary* leaving harbor."

Laura watched as the blue liner slid slowly out toward the open sea to a chorus of whistle blasts and sirens from the other ships. "Come on," he said, taking her arm, "and I'll show you around the flight deck before the others arrive."

In the main passenger terminal of the port, Junior Emigration Officer Ian Smallpage impatiently awaited the arrival of the contingent that was traveling on Imperial 109. He was a gangling young man whose thick glasses and generally studious air had earned him the nickname of "Professor" among his colleagues. Conscientious and meticulous at his work, off duty he was quiet and unadventurous, living with his parents in Southampton's northern suburbs, and spending most of his evenings studying for promotion to a higher grade. Today, however, was especially important for him. He was about to get engaged.

Ian Smallpage and Helen Rowe had been going out together since Ian's sixteenth birthday, and it had never occurred to either of them that they would not one day marry each other. All the same, he was in a hurry to be away. His shift was due to finish at three o'clock, and he was meeting Helen outside the terminal. He would take her for a cream tea in the center of town, he would tell her the promotion he had been waiting for had finally been confirmed for the end of the month, and he would ask her to marry him.

The passengers appeared through the doors of the departure lounge at last and advanced toward Ian in a struggling bunch. He began flicking through the proffered passports, canceling the entry stamps of the foreigners among them, and, out of long habit, automatically checking the photographs and descriptions for errors. Emigration procedure was largely a formality, he knew, but an ingrained sense of duty forced him to go through it without skipping.

Suddenly he paused, frowning; something in one of the passports had struck a jarring note. "Mr. Perler?" he looked up inquiringly.

"Yes?" The man before him was of medium height, slimly built, dark, with a narrow face. He wore a brown, double-breasted suit of continental cut, somewhat crumpled. "Is there anything wrong?" His English was good, with a slight German accent, reasonable enough in a Swiss. His left cheek bore the mark of a recent bruise.

Ian wavered. Over the past three years, he had acquired a certain instinct for sniffing out frauds and for-

geries. A retouched photograph, blurred lettering, a smear
of faint chemical stains on a page; he had learned to spot
small signs that betrayed an imposter. This time there
was nothing obvious, there was merely a feeling that
warned him something was not quite right. "You are
traveling through to New York?" he asked as he turned
the pages again, seeking a clue that would shake the passport's authenticity, but if anything it was too perfect.

"Yes, from Rome via Paris and London," the man answered.

Other passengers were lining up at the desk now, beginning to look impatient. Ian handed the passport back
and moved on to the next. After all, he consoled himself,
what did it matter? The man was leaving the country
anyway.

Although *Caterina* had had a thorough one-hundred-hour
service at Cairo, the engineers had been over her again
in preparation for the Atlantic crossing. There was still
much preliminary work for Desmond and the crew. The
flying boat would take off, lightly loaded with fuel, and
two hours later they would rendezvous with a tanker aircraft over Foynes on the mouth of the river Shannon in
Ireland. After a midair refueling, they would head on out
over the North Atlantic. It would take approximately
twelve hours to cover the 1,800 miles to Botwood, Newfoundland, though it might be longer if strong head winds
were encountered. For part of the trip, the cabins would
be converted into bedrooms equipped with comfortable
bunks to enable those who wished to do so to rest.

Landing at Botwood, the local time would be only 3:00
or 4:00 A.M., owing to the 3½-hour difference between
London and Newfoundland, and the next morning would
see them in Montreal in time for a leisurely lunch before
the final two-hour stage over the Adirondack and Cat-
skill Mountains to New York, touching down on the East
River at 4:00 P.M. on Thursday.

Ralph Kendrick was already on board checking his wireless equipment and radio direction-finding sets. The rest
of the crew turned up shortly afterward, including Ken
Frazer, who had spent the previous evening and morning
pleading with Jack Priestly for a transfer to another flight,

and whose colleagues were now punishing him for his betrayal of their captain. They refused to speak to him except on technical matters.

Laura was interested to look around the flight deck, but she saw that the men were busy; moreover, there was an awkwardness in the atmosphere, caused by the first officer's presence. Retreating tactfully into the mailroom, she passed the time until the other passengers arrived helping Sandy Everett sort the mail.

The three officers completed their checks, then retired to the airline meteorological office for a comprehensive briefing on the conditions likely to be encountered on the crossing.

"The only weather system you really have to worry about," the senior meteorological officer told them as they examined a wall chart of the North Atlantic, "is here." He indicated an area in the extreme northeast of Canada. "There is a deep depression moving eastward out of Labrador toward Greenland. We've been watching it for a couple of days now, and by all accounts it's pretty bad; storm-force winds, snow blizzards, severe electrical interference—the lot. Fortunately, however, it is merging on a track that will take it well to the north of your course, so you shouldn't experience any difficulties, apart from slightly increased head winds.

"Otherwise, the reports we've been getting in from Canada and from shipping indicate that you will have very little to worry about," he went on. "The skies should remain fairly clear until you are about five hundred miles or so out into the Atlantic. From there on, it will probably begin to cloud over, and you'll meet fairly continuous cover—up to about eight or ten thousand feet, I'd say, with winds mainly easterly, force four to five at maximum. Temperatures about average for the period."

"What about isolated thunderstorms or rain squalls?" Desmond inquired.

"No reports of any," the met. officer answered. "As I said, provided that the storm over Labrador holds its present course and speed, the bad weather will all pass to the north of you."

Cheered by this optimistic view, the three men returned to *Caterina* in time to greet the returning passengers.

The approach of the passengers was signaled by the appearance of a number of photographers and journalists intent on obtaining a follow-up to the previous night's story. They were accompanied by an irate Jack Priestly who was equally determined to ensure that Desmond, at least, received no further publicity. "No interviews! You're to give absolutely no interviews to anyone. I forbid it categorically," he said hurrying up the gangway to where Desmond stood greeting the arrivals.

"I've not the slightest intention of doing so," the Irishman told him coldly, shaking hands with the Kings as they climbed aboard. Priestly looked relieved, but his anger returned when Laura stepped out of the plane and, standing on the side of the pontoon, conducted a lengthy conversation with the reporters, in the course of which she was deliberately loud in Desmond's praises.

Jack Priestly was infuriated, but there was nothing he could do, and Desmond slipped back inside the hatch.

He had quite a different matter on his mind. He made his way to the after cabin. Entering without knocking, Desmond found Stewart Curtis slumped in a chair with a copy of the *Wall Street Journal*.

"What the devil do you want?" Curtis scowled at the interruption.

"I've got something to say to you about the allegations you made last night concerning Mrs. Hartman and the Cartier watch," Desmond said with icy calm.

"Well, I've no wish to hear it," Curtis retorted. "As far as I am concerned, the matter is closed." He resumed his study of the paper.

"You'll listen," Desmond told him, "because unless you do, you're not going to reach America tomorrow."

Curtis glanced up sharply. "What exactly do you mean by that?"

"It's quite simple," Desmond answered. "The watch was given to me by your wife last Sunday as a prize for winning the motor race. I didn't want to accept, but she pressed it on me; I've no wish to have it back. What I *will* have, though, is a signed admission from you that the watch was a gift freely given by Mrs. Curtis and equally freely returned by me, and, furthermore, that Laura Hartman played no part in the affair."

Stewart Curtis flushed angrily. "If you think I'm going

to sit here and listen to you insult my wife and myself,"
he growled, "you're mad. I shall see what your superiors
have to say about this. You wouldn't dare to refuse to take
the flight out."

"I don't have to refuse outright," Desmond replied coolly. "It's too simple. We haven't finished the preflight checks
yet. I only have to say I'm dissatisfied with the functioning of one of the instruments for a complete test to be
ordered. By the time that's been completed, or by the
time you've made your complaint, it would be too late
in the day when we reached Ireland for there to be light
enough for refueling. They'll have no alternative but to
postpone the flight twenty-four hours."

"I'll see you're fired for this," Curtis began, getting to his
feet. Just then the door behind them opened, and Georgina entered.

"I just want to get my camera," she said. Seeing Desmond, she stopped abruptly, alarm registering in her expression.

Her reaction was not lost on Curtis. "Welcome, my
dear," he went on, tight-lipped. "Perhaps you can clear up
this argument. Captain O'Neill here," he nodded contemptuously in Desmond's direction, "has the effrontery to con-
tend that you actually gave him the watch as a present
when we were in Cairo."

Georgina shot Desmond a single, searching glance.
Meeting his steadfast, hostile gaze, she looked away.
"Yes, it's true," she answered.

"It's what?" her husband shouted. "You mean you lied
to me last night?"

"That's right." Georgina leaned over the back of the
chair to get her camera, affording Desmond a display of
her silk-stockinged legs. "Yes, I lied." She straightened
up, her voice hard and bitter. "People lie all the time. I
did it last night. I know," she continued to Desmond as he
started to speak, "it was inexcusable, and I'm sorry."

"Laura's the one who deserves an apology," he told her
curtly.

Georgina's eyes flashed. "Damn Laura! And damn you!"
she snapped and made for the door again.

"Georgina, where are you going?" Curtis cried.

"Oh, go to hell, both of you!" she yelled and ran out,
slamming the door.

The two men stared at one another. Without a word, the financier crossed to a table against the bulkhead, and pulling a sheet of paper from his briefcase, he began writing.

To Ian Smallpage's annoyance, the feeling of disquiet aroused by the passenger from Switzerland persisted. As he handed in his record sheets, he mentioned the matter to his supervisor. "There was nothing definite—more of a hunch, I suppose, than anything else. He just didn't seem quite right for what he claimed to be."

The supervisor had respect for Ian's judgment. "A refugee of some kind," he hazarded.

"No, sir," Ian was definite. "It was too good a job for that, and the man was too sure of himself to be a refugee. If it was a fake, it was a professional one."

The supervisor thought for a moment. "It's not worth taking action over," he said at length. "As you say, the man was only passing through, and he'll have to face a much tougher screening when he arrives in New York. Make a note of the incident on your report, and we'll pass it on to Police Special Branch later."

Relieved to have the responsibility removed from his shoulders, Ian hurried away to do as he was told. He left the terminal building just in time to see *Caterina* lift off from Southampton water in the direction of Ireland.

○ ○ ○

The body of the agent Paul Rintlen had shot had fallen just at the mouth of the tunnel and was spotted from the cab of another train passing through shortly after three o'clock. It was nearly four o'clock before the body was finally located by a maintenance unit sent to investigate. A police search was then made of the tunnel's entire length, and the corpse of the second agent was discovered. A murder inquiry was instituted, and Chief Inspector Joe Moyers of the Hampshire constabulary was placed in control.

By the time Moyers reached the scene, the bodies had been removed from the tunnel and were lying beside the track on the grass bank of the cutting. "We had to shift them as soon as possible, I'm afraid, sir," he was told by the detective sergeant who had been in charge of the situation. "It's a busy line, and we couldn't keep it blocked. I had a complete search made on both sides of the track, and we brought out everything we found."

"I may as well have a look at them," Moyers answered. He was a slow-speaking West country man, looking more like a farmer than a policeman, with his broad, weather-beaten face and ill-fitting suit, who possessed, nevertheless, a formidable reputation. "Then you can send them off for a post-mortem."

Climbing over the wire fence at the top of the cutting, they scrambled heavily down the steep bank to where the bodies lay covered by sheets. Other police were still engaged in scouring the track beyond the tunnel mouth, and a little distance away, three railway signalmen stood ready to give warning of approaching trains.

"This was the one we found first, sir." The sergeant lifted back the canvas sheet. "As you can see, he's been shot once in the chest. Otherwise he's not in too bad condition, a bit battered, but that's all. The other one's in a right mess. He must have fallen under the wheels."

"Any sign of the weapon?" Moyers asked.

"No, sir," the detective told him. "But see this." Stooping down, he turned back the left side of the dead man's jacket. "He's wearing a shoulder holster. We've searched the whole tunnel and both sides of the track for five hundred yards beyond, but so far we've found no trace of a pistol to fit it. The railway police are checking the coaches of every train that passed through during the previous six hours, so it may turn up in one of them."

"What about identification?" Moyers asked, pulling the sheet back over the body.

"Both German nationals, living and working in this country as far as we can tell. Names of Keller and Scherf."

"You'd better contact the German consulate in London and ask for any information they have on these two." Moyers stepped down onto the track. "Is it all right to go into the tunnel?" he called to the signalmen.

"Aye, there's nothing due for another ten minutes," one of them shouted back. "We'll hold everything until you come out again." Lifting the portable field telephone beside him, he began cranking the handle vigorously.

There was little enough to be seen in the tunnel. The

search the men had conducted had been exhaustive. Only a few dark splashes of blood on the ties and gravel two-thirds of the way along marked the spot where the second man had been found. After examining them by the light of torches, Moyers returned to the entrance once more and began trying to piece together the sequence of events.

"The bodies were both found on the left-hand side of the track leading away from the tunnel entrance," he said, "which means, therefore, they either fell or were pushed from a train proceeding in the direction of Southampton. They were first spotted at around ten after three. Have we established whether anyone else thinks they might have seen them before then?"

"No, sir," the detective shook his head. "So far we've only been able to trace the drivers of the preceding train. The one o'clock express from London. They are fairly sure the body wasn't by the tunnel mouth when they came through. They think they would have noticed it. I must say I'm inclined to believe them," he added grimly. "I think I'd have noticed it myself."

"In which case," Moyers continued slowly, "it would not be unreasonable to assume that both men might have been on that train." He paused for a moment, then went on. "Two German nationals on the Southampton express? What does that suggest to you, sergeant?"

"They were on their way to catch a boat, I should think, sir," the policeman answered brightly.

"Yes, or an airplane," Moyers agreed. "So perhaps whoever was responsible for their deaths was doing the same. We'll start by obtaining lists of all passengers going through Southampton today."

Climbing back up to the top of the cutting, he had another thought. "What kind of man goes around carrying a pistol in a shoulder holster?" he remarked. "We'll get onto Special Branch as soon as we get back, sergeant. Maybe they'll have some ideas about this business."

○ ○ ○

"Tanker coming up astern now, skipper," Ralph Kendrick called out from the radio desk. "The captain is starting to make his approach."

"Very good," Desmond acknowledged. "Tell him I

will maintain my present height, course, and speed." Three thousand feet above the lush Irish countryside, *Caterina* and her crew were about to engage in one of the most complicated of all aerial maneuvers. In a few moments, a tanker aircraft—a converted R.A.F. twin-engined Harrow bomber—would endeavor to pass a hose across to the flying boat and transfer some eight hundred to one thousand gallons of aviation fuel into her tanks. It called for strong nerves on the part of all concerned—as well as supreme flying ability and fine judgment.

Desmond and Ralph were alone in the cockpit. Ken Frazer was in the rear hold on the lower deck, in the extreme tail of the aircraft, crouched beside an open hatch in the floor, through which the refuel hose would be passed. Sandy Everett had unclipped the door of the mailroom freight hatch and was maintaining a running commentary as the heavily laden tanker closed in.

"Looks like she's just about right," Sandy shouted, straining to make himself heard above the noise of the engines. He was shivering in the freezing draft of the slipstream, clinging to the side of the door to prevent himself from being sucked out. "She's about fifty feet above us, and a length behind on the starboard quarter, and she's coming up slowly."

Turning his head a fraction, Desmond could just catch a glimpse out of the side windows of the bomber's black nose creeping into view. Behind him there was a crackle from the radio. "Tanker's ready to start the pickup, skipper," Ralph told him.

"Right. Stand by everybody," Desmond ordered, gripping the control yoke firmly. Though a few patches of cloud had appeared in the sky as the afternoon had worn on, the air was still calm and free from any trace of turbulence. Pressing the intercom button, Desmond called through to Frazer in the tail. "You can begin letting out the line now, Ken."

"Aye, aye, skipper," Frazer's voice came back, distorted by the earphones.

There was a short pause, then the radio crackled again. "The tanker's spotted our line; it's trailing out nicely," Kendrick told him. "They're preparing to lower their grapnel." Seconds later, there came a confirming shout from Sandy.

While the passengers watched excitedly through the starboard windows, Ken Frazer peered out behind him at the two thousand feet of weighted line he had paid out on the power winch. The line was streaming back, nearly horizontal, in the flying boat's wake. As he watched, a second line appeared in his field of vision, dropping down from above like a black thread. Attached to its end was a small grapnel, the steel barbs glinting in the sun as it twisted and jerked.

Frazer observed its progress carefully, reporting over the intercom to the flight deck. For the tanker crew this was the trickiest part of the operation—maneuvering close in to the huge flying boat, in danger of being buffeted by its slipstream, while attempting with their grapnel to hook and fish up the line being trailed from *Caterina*'s stem. It was extraordinarily difficult to judge the distance separating the two cables and to anticipate their behavior in the aircraft's wake.

"They've got her, skipper!" Frazer had seen the tanker's grapnel snag against his own line. Slowly and painstakingly the men in the bomber reeled it in. Frazer released the brake on his winch, ready to pay out more cable if necessary.

Then the intercom came alive again with Desmond's voice. "The tanker has attached the hose to the cable, Ken. You can start winching her back in."

Throwing the switch on the machine behind him, Frazer set the drum in motion again, watching carefully to be sure the line was running in smoothly.

Over the intercom Desmond relayed observations from Sandy in the mailroom and messages passed on by Ralph Kendrick from the tanker's commander.

The winch wound away steadily, hauling in on the cable; a thicker line appeared, the tanker's hose curving down in a wide arc from the second aircraft. Fifty feet above him, the other crew were paying out their winch. The hose swam nearer; a heavy metal nozzle at its end became visible. Then it was bumping and grating at the entrance to the hatch. Reaching down, Frazer gave it a tug to help it through and into the mouth of the auxiliary fuel inlet, hearing the union click home solidly as he did so. "Fuel hose engaged," he called over the intercom.

There was a brief acknowledgment from Desmond, a

short pause, and then the hose began to pulsate. There was a sound of fuel gushing into the tank, and a stench of petrol filled the hold.

This was a tense period in the maneuver. Desmond had to take on nearly 900 gallons, and the tanker's pumps were capable of transferring at a rate of 120 gallons a minute. For the next seven or eight minutes, therefore, he must maintain *Caterina* in exactly her present position in relation to the other aircraft. Any sudden deviation, any widening of the gap separating them, and the hose would be ripped away.

The problem was made more difficult by the extra weight being pumped aboard, nearly two and a quarter tons in all, altering the trim of both craft. Five minutes into the transfer, they hit a small patch of turbulence, but Desmond was alert for the faintest sign of trouble, and he eased *Caterina* through, catching her smartly before her nose could drop.

"Cease pumping," he ordered as the gauge needles reached their limits. "You can release the hose now, Frazer," he told his first officer as soon as the tanker had acknowledged his signal. "Secure the hatch and return to the flight deck."

"You should have told him to jump out after it," Kendrick muttered from the radio desk. "No one would miss the bastard." From the rear, there came a thump and a bang as Sandy slammed the mailroom door shut.

"OK, everyone," Desmond called, "stand down and resume normal flying routine. Give me a course for Newfoundland, will you, Ralph?" he said to the radio operator, and, bringing *Caterina* around toward the red disk of the slowly sinking sun, he headed out over the ocean.

11

By radio: 1900 hrs GMT WEDNESDAY 15 MARCH. IMPERIAL AIRWAYS SOUTHAMPTON ENGLAND TO IMPERIAL AIRWAYS FLIGHT 109 G-ADHO CATERINA TO BOTWOOD, NEWFOUNDLAND - MONTREAL - NEW YORK. CANADIAN WEATHER BUREAU REPORTS MAJOR DEPRESSION MOVING EAST INTO CENTRAL NORTH ATLANTIC FROM LABRADOR. SEVERE STORM CONDITIONS NOW PREVAILING OVER DAVIS STRAIT AND SOUTHERN GREENLAND. WINDS FORCE NINE RISING TEN. SEVERE ICING AND SNOW. CLOUD BASE 3000 FEET. RECOMMEND ALTERATION TO PROPOSED COURSE TO ALLOW DEVIATION SOUTHWARD. ADVISE INTENTIONS. END.

With a sense of mounting anger, Desmond studied the contents of the radio message Kendrick had brought him. The weather picture had changed radically since the last forecast from Canada had been received. The depression first noticed two days ago over the Beaufort Sea had moved across Franklin District, north of Hudson Bay and over Baffin Island, to link up with a second pressure trough near the coast of Greenland, deepening as it went until it had developed into a storm front of major proportions.

Of this Desmond had been aware when they took off from London, but it had seemed that the track of the storm would take it well to the north of *Caterina*'s proposed route, leaving them with little to fear beyond some slight turbulence and poor visibility should they be brushed by the system's fringe. Now it appeared that the entire front had altered direction and was veering southward.

Unless the speed of the storm increased markedly during the intervening period, they should be able to dog-leg around the threatened area, making a wide detour out toward the south into mid-Atlantic. Even so, there was a strong suspicion in Desmond's mind that Jack Priestly had deliberately held over this late report until the flying boat was well out to sea. Had he relayed it when they were still within sight of the Irish coast, it was conceivable that Desmond might have decided to abort the flight altogether.

It was probably also true, he guessed, that Perritt himself was under strong pressure from the government in London, to whom the urgency of the gold delivery appeared to be all important. Desmond was tempted to send a sharply worded riposte to those responsible, pointing out that by their actions they were endangering the entire plane and the cargo, as well as the people on board.

It would be an empty gesture, nothing more. Now all he could do was to crack on with all possible speed and hope to avoid the worst of the weather. He ordered Ralph Kendrick to prepare the necessary alterations to the flight plan.

In *Caterina*'s galley, Andy Draper prepared for the evening. Although of the flying boat's crew only Desmond and Ralph had actually made the crossing before, Andy knew the importance of forecasting the passenger's morale correctly. At the moment, they were relaxed and cheerful. There was still an element of adventure and romance about the flight.

For the past hour and a half, as *Caterina* headed out across the hazy purple surface of the great ocean, Andy had been busy mixing round after round of drinks as his charges celebrated this start of their journey. The present clear weather conditions had enabled Desmond to play host at the cocktail party in the promenade lounge, organized by Sandy on company instructions. Even the Curtises had consented to put in an appearance, and, after some initial strain, the atmosphere had become unexpectedly good-natured.

Despite this, Andy could see, there would come a point when the enjoyment would begin to wear thin. They had still another twelve or thirteen hours before they reached the Newfoundland coast, and, thanks to the flying boat's constant westward progress, the evening would seem long. It was Andy's job to anticipate the moment when boredom would start to set in and to be ready with a thoroughly excellent dinner. The meal, he was determined, would be memorable. The time by the wall clock was 7:15 P.M., and already he had some of the cold hors d'oeuvres prepared, and the chicken was cooking. It would be another hour before the passengers were ready to eat; with luck, he could prolong the meal until ten, by which time they would be ready to start thinking of their beds.

The galley door clicked open, and Sandy's head appeared. "Pass me out another bottle of champagne, will you, Andy?" he said. "Mrs. Curtis and the baroness are fairly mopping the stuff up. I think you'd better get around with your shaker again soon, too. Some of the others look as though they'll want another cocktail."

"I'll be out in a moment," Andy told him, opening the refrigerator and removing a champagne bottle. "Just as soon as I finish setting out this salmon. I don't mind 'em drinking a lot before dinner; it'll mean they'll sleep better afterward. Less trouble for you an' me if there's bad weather."

"Do you think we'll have some?" Sandy asked as he uncorked the champagne.

The steward pursed his lips. "You saw the forecast. Storms are normal on these trips. Don't worry about that lot, though," he nodded in the direction of the promenade lounge. "They'll be all right once they're tucked up in bed."

The cork came out with a loud pop, and Sandy caught the spurting wine neatly in a glass. "The skipper was telling me you want to turn the Curtises out of the after cabin for the night," he said. "Isn't that going to make them furious?"

"Their hard luck," Andy replied with indifference. "We can make up all the beds in the first three cabins and leave the after cabin for those who don't want to sleep. It's better for everyone that way."

"I suppose you're right," Sandy agreed. "It's the farthest from the wash rooms, too. We can put the Curtises and the d'Estes in the smoking saloon together. They'll be out of the way of the others then. How do you think we should divide up the rest?"

"The Kings and the professor and his daughter in the midship cabin," Andy began.

"Won't Laura want to be in with the Kings, though?" the purser objected. It was a measure of the American girl's popularity with the crew that among themselves they referred to her by her Christian name.

"No. I've already spoken to her," Andy replied. "She says the Wienzmans will be happier in the smaller room with the Kings. They've gotten to know each other now."

"And the remaining five in the promenade lounge." Sandy nodded thoughtfully. "I agree it's a good plan—if the Curtises will buy it. Someone's bound not to want to turn in with everybody else." Closing the galley door again, he returned to the party with the champagne.

Behind him the steward chuckled. Up in the bedding loft there was one particularly uncomfortable mattress normally kept only as a spare; Andy had earmarked it specially for Stewart Curtis.

Given the existing tensions, it was not surprising that the party before dinner was such a success. Desmond certainly had had his doubts as to the wisdom of holding the affair, but company policy had ordained that the passengers be entertained in this fashion, weather permitting, and he had faced up to it as best he could. It proved to be far less of a strain than he had expected.

The two Wienzmans were bubbling with good humor and gratitude. "We owe everything to you, Captain O'Neill," David Wienzman assured him repeatedly. "Our lives, our freedom, all the kindness we have been shown since leaving Rome."

"Mrs. Hartman and the rest of the passengers and crew helped every bit as much as I did," he said with some embarrassment.

"But I understand there has been trouble for you on our account?" the professor continued, a worried expression on his face.

Desmond hastened to reassure him. "I think the airline was a little surprised, but nothing more really. To be honest, I believe the board was quite pleased with the publicity."

The professor looked relieved. "That's good. I am glad. We are both glad—my daughter and I."

At the mention of her name, Siegret smiled. She still seemed wary and uncertain, Desmond thought, but the fear had begun to fade from her eyes. She had put on a new dress for the flight, and he complimented her on it.

"Yes, we bought it this morning to celebrate our escape. It makes her look pretty, don't you think?" her father said proudly while his daughter blushed.

She did indeed look very pretty, Desmond thought. Sandy Everett was standing nearby, unable to keep his eyes off her.

"This morning, too, I obtained this," Wienzman continued happily. From an inside pocket he produced a heavily embossed and sealed document, held together by a tasseled cord. "American visas for Siegret and myself. The officials at the consulate were very kind. I had worried we might have to wait many days for it."

"Do you ever hope to be able to return to Austria?" It was Harold King who spoke. "I mean, do you believe the persecution of your people will cease?"

David Wienzman shook his head sadly. "I hope so, I hope so. Vienna is my home. I cannot believe this evil will last. There are still many good people in Austria. Men like Herr Meyer, who helped us to get away and in Italy, too, my old friend Farenzi. I pray no harm will come to them. At least now, though, Siegret and I will be able to live in peace again."

Paul Rintlen had been following the exchange closely, pretending all the while to listen to a conversation between Mrs. King, Laura, and Luca d'Este in which d'Este was explaining how he would have won the race to Fayum had he not been forced off the road. Rintlen had been deliberately avoiding the two Austrians. Though neither they nor anyone else on board had ever seen him before, and he had no reason to believe his cover story would be suspected, he intended taking no unnecessary risks. The Wienzmans were still plainly on their guard, the girl very much so, and with his German accent and obviously Continental origins, he was afraid of causing them to take fright unwittingly.

Even so, he could not help but be drawn by the mention of Meyer's name. He had been right all along in hold-

ing the police chief responsible for the escape. If he did
succeed in bringing the mission to a successful conclusion, there was going to be a score to settle there. He
strained to catch more of the old professor's words, and
he heard him describing how the research notes and case
histories had been smuggled past the border guards. There
flashed into his mind the words of Heydrich when the arrest of the Wienzmans had first been ordered: "Bring away
unread all personal documents you find."

At the time those words had seemed unimportant; now
they assumed special significance. Suppose the professor
was in possession of some vital secret? It would have to be
political, of course. Secret information on a person of
high standing in the Reich. That was exactly the kind
of scandal the S.D. chief was always most eager for. If,
as well as eliminating the Jews, he could recover those
notes, he would indeed have no fears about returning to
Berlin.

While Rintlen was speculating in this fashion, Desmond
was observing the behavior of the Curtises. He had not
expected either of them to put in an appearance, and he
was struck with their cordiality. Georgina had been avoiding meeting his eyes, and there was a forced quality to the
gaiety with which she was chatting to Jacquetta d'Este
and the quiet young Turk from Alexandria. She was also
getting through the champagne, he noticed.

Like his wife, Curtis seemed to be making an effort
to be pleasant and was behaving as though the angry
scene between Desmond and himself had not occurred.
Perhaps the financier's anxieties were diminishing now
that they were actually on their way to New York, or
perhaps the exposure of his wife's lies had brought about
the change. Whichever it was, Desmond wondered whether it would withstand the pressure of being made to give
up his private cabin tonight. For the sake of preserving
peace, it might be diplomatic to wait before springing
the news on him.

The guests seemed to be enjoying themselves, and it
looked as though he might safely return to the flight
deck. He checked the time—7:15. *Caterina* was two hours
and three hundred miles out into the Atlantic, with another twelve hours and seventeen hundred miles to go

before the lights of the landing area at Botwood became visible.

"There's a report due in from the ocean weather ship about now," he said to Laura.

"Are you expecting to run into bad weather, captain?" Van Smit inquired as he turned to go.

"Not at all," Desmond answered. There was no point in causing alarm among the passengers, and it was by no means certain that the storm ahead would cross their path. "But it's important for us to have as much information as possible on the strength and direction of the winds we're encountering because they can greatly affect our speed. Strong head winds can delay us seriously, and on an east-west flight, they are not uncommon."

Stewart Curtis, who had been staring out of the window pointedly ignoring the conversation, broke in. "Delayed," he snapped. "Delayed by how much?"

"I only said delays were possible," Desmond replied. "Any time lost on the actual crossing can nearly always be made up on the following day. Whatever happens, we should still arrive in New York tomorrow afternoon."

Leaving the financier mollified, he excused himself. It was time to check on *Caterina*'s progress and see how Ralph Kendrick was standing up to the demands being placed on him.

Ralph had been kept too busy to give much thought to the fears that had troubled him earlier in the week. Although both Desmond and Frazer held master's certificates in navigation, it was on Ralph's shoulders that the bulk of the work lay. Spread out in front of him on the table was a chart for the North Atlantic, the immense void of ocean, fringed along either side by the shores of two continents. Projecting from the right-hand edge, a red line struck out to follow the start of the great circle route between Ireland and Newfoundland. Scattered on the table were other instruments and paraphernalia employed in plotting the flying boat's course. A Byrd bubble sextant, drift-bearing plates, a stopwatch, parallel rulers, dividers, books of astronomical tables, and scraps of paper covered with intricate calculations.

As they were at the moment three hundred miles from the coast of Ireland, Ralph was still relying primarily on the Marconi radio direction finder to enable him to establish their position, using dead reckoning and astronomical observation as a safety check and as a means of discovering such details as rate of wind drift. Further on, however, when the range became too great for accurate radio fixes, or if weather conditions should interfere, he must be ready to fall back on the older methods.

Taking a straightedge and a crayon, he bent over the chart and, with infinite precision, fractionally extended the red line of *Caterina*'s track to meet the tiny penciled cross representing her latest position. Navigation was demanding work; all the same, Ralph found it immensely satisfying. To guide an airplane across two thousand miles of featureless ocean, much of the time in darkness or poor visibility and in the face of constantly varying winds, would be no mean achievement and one he could be proud of. Moreover, by occupying his mind in this way, he hoped to crowd out the nagging images from his dreams.

He took *Caterina*'s preflight plan as well as a sheet of transparent film onto which he had traced a summary of the details passed on by the Jacques Cartier weather ship out in the ocean ahead and the Canadian weather bureau. Comparing the three, it was possible to see that the storm center from Labrador was moving southeast more swiftly than they had originally anticipated, and at its current progress, it would intercept the flying boat's projected course in approximately six hundred miles. The detour they had originally proposed would clearly have to be extended southward to enable the aircraft to skirt around the now widened danger zone. Ralph began to calculate the course alteration.

"Hell!" Frazer exclaimed in disgust when he was shown the proposed change. "That'll add at least another two hours to our time; we're bending far enough out of our way as it is."

"I know," Ralph agreed, "and I've cut us in as far as I dare, but the whole front is moving across our path. We'll have a rough passage even so."

"I don't see what you're getting in such a panic about," Ken remarked maliciously. "It's only a thunderstorm, and we've flown through plenty of those before."

"They weren't over the North Atlantic though, and they

didn't consist of sixty knot winds driving snow from the Arctic," Ralph replied. "There's cloud up to 20,000 feet, severe icing, and storm force winds covering a 200,000 square-mile area between the Hudson Strait and the coast of Greenland, and the whole lot is moving out toward mid-ocean right into our path. If we make this course alteration, we can still skate around the worst of it."

"You mean you want us to steer an additional three hundred and fifty miles off our course because you're afraid to fly through a storm." The jeer was unmistakable, but Ralph ignored it.

"It's the skipper's decision," he said tersely, "and you know bloody well what he'll order, so what's the point in arguing?"

"Lucky for you. No other captain would carry a radio officer who had lost his nerve," Ken sneered. "Must make it a lot easier for you."

Ralph's jaw tightened. "You treacherous little bastard," he grated. "Wait till I get you on the ground. Then we'll see who's scared."

Frazer sniffed contemptuously. "Better see if you've got the guts to make it first, hadn't you? Only two hours out of Ireland, and you're cracking up already."

Shaking with rage, Ralph tried to resume his work on the charts, but the lines and figures swam across the page, and his mind refused to hold the calculations. Staring at the storm track he had sketched on the map, he knew Frazer was right. He was afraid, deeply and terribly afraid. Afraid of the empty waste of the endless ocean beneath them, and of the cold, hungry waves waiting for him.

Desmond noticed the change in the radio officer's manner immediately when he returned, and though he made no comment, he could not help but worry. He backed up Ralph's judgment on the need for a change of course, and, after a brief glance at the charts, he ordered Frazer to make the necessary alterations to deepen the flying boat's sweep around to the south.

Even this detour would not enable them to escape all the effects of the storm. Desmond ran his eyes over the instrument panel. *Caterina* was flying at 3,000 feet and the airspeed indicator was reading 160 miles per hour, though Ralph's calculations indicated that head winds were reducing this to 140. The sky was starting to cloud over with patches of drifting cumulus, merging into a solid line on the horizon. The air temperature was forty-two degrees, no danger of icing yet.

Switching off the autopilot, Desmond flew manually for a while, testing the flying boat's response to the controls. The heavy load of fuel was unevenly distributed at present, making her handle a trifle sluggishly, but by the time the storm reached them, much of the excess would have been consumed. With luck, the passengers would be comfortably in bed by then.

Ahead of them, the sun was sliding slowly into the sea, casting a yellow glare on the white-capped waves of the heavy swell and on the great rack of clouds building up in the west, straining them with a lurid, unhealthy glow.

o o o

Laura Hartman had observed the steady fall in Klerksdorp share prices over the past fortnight, but she had ascribed its cause to no more than market nervousness in the wake of the unstable political climate. She would have been surprised to learn that the company's difficulties were serious and even more surprised had she known that the telegram she had sent to the firm of Wall Street brokers was the subject of intense debate among the partners.

These were the senior members of the firm of Kimber, Crossfield, Smith, and Company, to which Jervase Raikes had referred only that morning. The general attitude of those present was much the same as that of their English counterparts. Like the Raikeses, they had seen large blocks of stock being offered for sale at below the ruling prices, with no clues as to who the sellers might be or the reason behind the disposals.

Stewart Curtis, it was true, had sent a telegram that morning to the head of the firm, but the message had contained little beyond a string of meaningless and unsubstantiated assertions about the vast, though admittedly so far unproven, reserves of ore within the mine and the intrinsic asset backing to the shares that these implied.

The firm's senior vice-president was summing up his argument. "Mrs. Hartman is Curtis's personal secretary, so she probably knows as much as anyone of what's happening." He ticked the points off on his fingers as he spoke. "We also know she's been with him in South Africa and is traveling back with him at this moment; in fact, she's the only person who has been in touch with him during the whole of the last fortnight. She is due here in New York tomorrow afternoon, yet all of a sudden she seems to think it necessary to cable across the Atlantic, only a day before she arrives. Finally, her instructions are quite specific. She asks for no advice, she makes no suggestions: "Sell all stock held by me in Klerksdorp immediately, at best possible price."

"Maybe she's only panicking because of the slide she's seen in the price?" someone suggested.

"The price has slipped back before, and she hasn't run to the nearest phone," the vice-president countered. "I say the stock is in danger of collapsing, and Mrs. Hartman knows it. She's getting out, and so should we. What do you say, Harvey?"

All eyes in the room swung to the man behind the desk. For more than a quarter of a century, Harvey Tilset Kimber had run the firm with rigid adherence to the principles of the proud, conservative New England background from which he sprang. Now, at seventy, his grasp of affairs was as firm as ever, and the gaze from beneath the thick white eyebrows still keen and penetrating. "If anyone has panicked, it is Curtis," he remarked in dry tones. "Racing about the world in this fashion and trying to hoodwink us with fairy stories. Something is badly wrong, and he's running scared. Never liked the man," he said with contempt. "Never trusted him, either, no more than does Raikes in London. If he's going down, none of our clients are going to be caught in the crash. I want the firm's books cleared of Klerksdorp stock by four o'clock this afternoon." There was a short pause, then the old man permitted himself an instant's cold humor. "And that includes Mrs. Hartman, gentlemen. We'll put her first in line; she deserves a decent price for her pains."

As the men in the room filed out to put his orders into effect, Kimber was struck by another thought. Motioning the vice-president to stay for a moment, he said, "I want you to get a cable off to the people in South Africa. Let them know what we intend doing. Maybe they'll start letting us in on what's wrong with Curtis and Klerksdorp."

O   O   O

At Southampton Police Headquarters, Joe Moyers was making progress with his investigation. An examination of the one o'clock express from London had revealed blood splashes on the wheel bogies of the rear carriage and also a bullet embedded in the paneling inside the corridor, eighteen inches up from the floor and close to one of the doors.

In addition, although the German consulate had been unhelpful and seemingly embarrassed when contacted about the incident, a call to the Metropolitan Police Special Branch concerned with political offenses had yielded the information that the man, Keller, who had been found at the tunnel mouth with the bullet wound in his chest, was a known agent. "More of a secret police thing really," the officer on duty told Moyers. "We think they used him to keep their countrymen over here in line. He was supposed to be under surveillance; he must have slipped away somehow and joined the train. We've no idea why, but we're doing what we can to find out."

"They're sending men down," Moyers informed Dewhurst, the detective sergeant working with him on the case, as Dewhurst entered the office. "Did you get those passenger lists I asked for?"

"Here they are, sir." Dewhurst handed a sheaf of papers across the desk. "Being able to establish definitely which train the victims were on has been a big help. It let us rule out the *Queen Mary,* for a start. A big Italian liner left for Geneva at four o'clock, and the P & O's *Oriana* departed around the same time. There was also a Swedish ship headed for Copenhagen and Stockholm. The passenger lists are all there in front of you."

"Is this the lot?" Moyers asked, sifting through the lists.

"I'm afraid not, sir," the sergeant told him. "Several cargo vessels and coasters left during the period in question—and I'm still trying to get details on those. And of course there were the ferries; they don't keep lists. Also there were two airplanes: Imperial 109, to Canada and

New York; and a Pan American flight on its way to Lisbon."

Moyers examined one of the lists thoughtfully. "Which of all these people would have been most likely to travel down on the one o'clock?" he asked.

"We have some idea, sir," the detective sergeant answered, "but not a list. Any of the passengers on the channel ferries might have been aboard—it's a very good connection. Some of those for the *Oriana* and the Italian liner might have done so too, but the majority would probably have taken an earlier train. One thing we do know for certain, though. Imperial Airways reserved a coach for the passengers boarding their transatlantic flight. But they're only thirteen out of nearly six hundred."

"Well, we'd better start getting down to it," Moyers said heavily. "I'm issuing a local appeal for anyone who was on the train and heard or saw anything suspicious to contact us. In the meantime we'll start checking through these lists for German citizens and just hope the Special Branch can come up with something in the way of motive. They should be here by nine."

Settling in at their desks, the two men began working steadily down the columns of names.

○ ○ ○

The same winds that were driving the storm out into the northern Atlantic had cleared the skies over New England, and the warm afternoon sun was melting the remaining snow on the hills around Warren Lake. Suzie had not been in the café when Jarrett arrived to keep their appointment. Instead, a sour-faced, slatternly old woman was serving behind the bar, and she scowled when he asked after the girl. "She's gone. Sent 'er packing myself. Dirty-mouthed little hussy. 'I'll teach you to speak proper to me,' I says. 'You can take your money due an' git out,' an' she did. Left this mornin'.'"

Jarrett finished his meal in moody silence and returned to the truck. He was just starting up when the door on the passenger side was jerked open, and he saw Suzie standing there in a dirty black coat, clutching a battered suitcase. "Thought you had run out on me," he grinned as he helped her up beside him. "The woman back there said you had left for good."

"The old rat," Suzie said vindictively. "She wanted me to stay in this afternoon an' clean out her filthy kitchen. I told her she could clean her own damn floor, so she threw me out." She sighed. "I was goin' to leave soon anyway. Figured maybe you'd give me a run over to Bellows Falls after we've been out to the lake."

"Sure, glad to. You going back to your stepfather's place?" Jarrett pushed the truck into gear and began driving up the street.

"Maybe. I'll see." Suzie shrugged. "He doesn't like me stayin' around for long. Might find a job near there, though," she said listlessly.

As they drove up to the lake, she told him about herself. Her father had spent a lifetime clearing his small farm in the woods of Vermont. He had married late, and Suzie had been only ten years old when he had died one winter, prematurely worn out by the struggle for survival. Less than a year later, her mother had married again, a hard man with an evil temper, who allowed the land to fall into decay while he spent the time drinking and hunting with his cronies. Suzie had never liked her stepfather, and he had resented the little girl and begrudged the money spent on her keep. At fifteen, she had left home when he started forcing his way into her room at night.

Now, three years later, her mother was dead, too, and the farm would soon be sold to pay off her stepfather's debts. There was nothing to go back to. She told the tale philosophically, but Jarrett could sense her bitterness. Life had never held out a great deal for her, but what little there was had been taken away.

Up at the lake, her spirits brightened. The Supermarine was a brilliant success. Jarrett sat her in the cockpit and explained the controls while she fiddled with the steering yoke and worked the rudder bar with her feet. Then, sitting her on the jetty, he put the silver plane through its paces in the air, flying a series of aerobatics over the water for her, ending with a shallow loop out in mid-lake and a low, level swoop across the head of the jetty that had her flattening herself against the planking.

"Some more—do some more," she pleaded when he taxied in. "I never had my own stunt show before."

"Later," he promised. "If you're good and behave yourself." The warmth of her approval sent a glow of pleasure through him.

The girl giggled. "Do you really promise, if I'm very good?" she said in a deliberately provocative voice. Reaching out, he pulled her to him, and for an instant he felt her mouth hard against his own and the firmness of her body beneath his hands. Giggling again, she slipped free and giving a shriek of laughter fled up the path toward the house.

He caught up with her as she burst into the kitchen, and they tussled briefly before he pinned her against the wall, forcing his lips on hers once more and working his hands hungrily over her body.

○ ○ ○

Dinner on board *Caterina* was not the success Andy had hoped it would be, yet it would have been hard to fault a single detail. Much of the passengers' earlier gaiety had vanished, and even the excellence of Andy's cooking was not sufficient to restore their good humor. They were beginning to experience the full import of the voyage they had undertaken.

While the flying boat droned on across the seemingly endless ocean, they stared out at the never-changing sea three thousand feet beneath them, gripped by a consciousness of their own frailty. England had been left behind, America lay yet further ahead. Two-thirds of the journey was still before them: 1,400 miles without a sight of land. All sense of time and movement had vanished, leaving them suspended in a tiny bubble of warmth and light above a darkening, lifeless world.

Jacquetta had dined in the after cabin with her husband and the Curtises in an atmosphere of unrelieved gloom despite Luca's attempts to maintain a flow of conversation. The champagne had left Georgina in a mood of sour depression, which alone had been sufficient to put a blight on the meal, and Curtis sat morose and withdrawn, scarcely bothering to reply when addressed.

Jacquetta longed for the meal to be over. Rashid, she knew, was having dinner in the same cabin as Van Smit, and she was in a fever of anxiety lest the facade of indifference between them should break down. Added to this was the fear that seized her each time the young sheik entered a room in which her husband was present. Like Rashid, Luca was now armed. On receipt of the telegram from Rome, he had acquired a pistol from the embassy, thus turning the situation into a powder keg that a single out-of-place gesture could explode.

Andy entered with a tray and began clearing away the remains of the dessert. "I suppose you're wanting us to hurry up and make way for the rest of them?" Georgina observed with distaste.

Andy smiled back politely. He was perfectly aware that the Curtises had been deliberately prolonging their meal in order to delay the moment when they would have to vacate their cabin. "There's no need for you to worry just yet, ma'am," he said condescendingly. "We've made up the beds for you in the smoking saloon, and we'll be starting on the midship cabin shortly, but we'll probably leave the promenade lounge as it is for a while until more people are wanting to go to bed. Of course," he added casually as he backed toward the door with the loaded tray, "the purser and I will be having to pass through here a lot to get the passengers' cases out from the rear hold for them to use tonight. You might be more comfortable in your own sleeping cabin up for'ard."

"Blasted insolence," Stewart Curtis complained as soon as Andy was gone. "He's going out of his way to make life as difficult for us as possible."

"It is all the doing of the captain," said Luca, for whom Desmond had been an established enemy ever since Cairo. "He has taken a dislike to the four of us, and he permits his crew to treat us rudely."

"Not without reason where some of us are concerned," Georgina remarked dryly, reaching out to press the bell push on the wall of the cabin as she spoke, and Jacquetta hid a smile at the flush that rose to her husband's cheeks at the rebuke. "Personally," Georgina continued, "I'm feeling quite tired already, and so too I should imagine is Jacquetta. When the steward sends my maid, I will tell her to start getting our night cases out and laying out our things. Ah, there you are, Arlette," she said as the French woman appeared silently in the doorway. *"Bien, écoutez. Madame la baronne et moi . . ."*

Georgina and Jacquetta were not the only ones on board who wanted to turn in early. The sight of the comfortable twin-tier beds, complete with fresh linen, each cunningly designed to have its own window, reading lamp, and individual curtains, was sufficient to start most of the passengers making preparations to retire.

Rintlen observed the changeover with interest. As soon as the Curtises and d'Estes had been dispatched forward out of the way, Andy Draper fastened back the door from the after cabin into the tail of the aircraft and began bringing out the rest of the passengers' baggage. In mid-Atlantic, the safety of the bullion was less of a worry, and a number of the passengers were allowed into the cavernous hold to assist in identifying their luggage.

It might be, Rintlen reasoned, as he waited to use the washroom, that whatever documents or papers the professor had escaped with he would be careful to keep in his possession. On the other hand, a surreptitious watch on the couple had revealed that at least one case of theirs remained untouched in the hold. Rintlen was determined to attempt a search of this once the rest of the airplane was asleep.

Preoccupied with the business of getting ready for bed and distracted by the novelty of the new arrangements, few of those on the lower deck were especially aware of the growing turbulence through which the flying boat had begun to pass.

The crew, however, were finding themselves under increasing strain. *Caterina* was flying between dense cloud banks, and Desmond struggled to hold her steady in the face of the eddying winds whose strong crosscurrents were causing her to pitch and yaw uncomfortably. Ominously, the outside air temperature had dropped to thirty-four degrees. Since leaving Ireland, Desmond had had the carburetor heat full on, but all three of them knew it was only a matter of time before they were driven to descend to a lower altitude to avoid the danger of icing.

At the portside navigation window, Ralph Kendrick leveled his sextant and peered through the eyepiece at the reflected image of a star, fleetingly visible through a gap in the clouds. For the past half hour he had been trying to obtain a fix on Rigel; now, in desperation, he had switched to Aldebaran in the constellation of Taurus. Adjusting the arm of the instrument, he managed to read off the angle before the pinprick of light in his mirror faded out again.

Resuming his position at the table, he forced himself to concentrate while he plotted the fix against his own dead reckoning. *Caterina* was already brushing against the storm's leading edge. The front itself, four hundred miles or more in breadth, was still an hour away. Behind it, blizzards of hurricane intensity raged over the ocean. His fingers shook as he drew the converging paths of the aircraft and the storm. Their margin of safety was frighteningly narrow.

○ ○ ○

The team of investigators from the Special Branch arrived at ten o'clock, headed by a sharply dressed superintendent some years Moyer's junior, who gave his name as Maclain and announced that he had been placed in charge of the case. "Of course," he added patronizingly, "we shall be glad to accept any help you local chaps can give us." Moyers eyed the man's elegant city suit doubtfully; policemen, he felt, should look like policemen—not like stockbrokers.

"So far, sir, the only facts we've discovered that might have a bearing," Moyers said when the superintendent returned from a protracted inspection of the bodies and an examination of the dead men's clothes and other possessions, "is that this flight Imperial 109 is carrying the two refugees who escaped from Rome. Their name has been in all the papers. The plane is also carrying a large sum in gold bullion." He spoke with a slight edge to his voice. Owing to poor communication, this last information had only a short while ago been passed on to him.

"I'm sure that will be most helpful," the superintendent replied loftily, "though I rather doubt if one old man and a girl would have accounted for two trained agents. And, whatever else we may be dealing with there, it is certainly not a case of simple theft. Don't worry, though, we'll keep you informed of anything we come up with."

Concealing their anger, Moyers and the sergeant returned to the tedious job of reconstructing a list of the train's passengers. Their revenge came toward eleven o'clock, when one of the superintendent's men came into the office.

"It seems you may have been right after all about that Imperial Airways flight, chief inspector," he said with a trace of embarrassment. "The fact is, the Yard has called through with a report sent in by one of the emigration people down at the terminal. One of the passengers on board may have had a suspect passport. A man by the name of Perler, Ernst Perler."

"Then why on earth did they let him on?" Moyers asked. "It was a bullion flight. Wasn't that reason enough to pull in whoever it was?"

"Apparently no one had told them about the gold," the officer replied. "There was too much secrecy. The point is, it looks as though there may be a connection between these Austrian refugees, the dead agents, and whoever this man Perler is. We need to get hold of the emigration fellow who spotted him."

Ian Smallpage arrived at Southampton Police Headquarters in a state of near shock. He had been at Helen's parents' home, happily celebrating the formal announcement of his engagement by allowing himself to become as near drunk as he ever had in his life. Then the bell of a police car had sounded in the street, there had been a loud knocking at the door, and the party had been brought to a rude halt by the entry of several policemen who demanded he return immediately with them to the station.

Pandemonium followed. Helen burst into tears, and both sets of parents angrily wanted to know what offense Ian was being accused of. The men in the patrol car could only reply that they had been ordered to bring him in at the request of the Special Branch.

The rapidly sobering Smallpage had been accompanied to the station by his new and tearful fiancée as well as by both sets of parents. Their arrival en masse created instant chaos at the reception desk, which lasted until Moyers appeared. Explaining that Ian was only required to help identify a traveler, Moyers calmed the situation and led the young man away for questioning.

Fortunately, Smallpage was gifted with a retentive memory and he was able to supply an accurate description of

the man calling himself Ernst Perler, along with the information that his flight to London had originated from
Rome.

"Sounds as though he's the chap we want, all right,"
Superintendent Maclain agreed when he had heard the
story. "What exactly is behind it all I don't know, but it
seems clear this man Perler followed the Wienzmans from
Rome—and is himself an agent. Why he should have
killed his two colleagues is puzzling, but one thing is sure
—we'd better get a message out to that plane fast."
Moyers's gaze flicked to the clock. The time was 11:15.
The flying boat had been airborne for eight hours and
would be over a thousand miles out into the Atlantic.

The night staff of Imperial Airways were contacted immediately by telephone, and the situation was explained
to them. "At least the crew are armed—thanks to the
bullion they're carrying," Maclain murmured as they
waited for news.

A little after midnight, a worried Jack Priestly came on
the line, having been summoned from his bed by the
emergency. "I have to tell you," he said, "we can't raise
the plane, and neither can the Canadians. We've completely lost contact with her. She's flying through an area of
bad storm that must be blocking our transmissions."

"Either that," someone in the room remarked when Moyers repeated the message, "or else she's gone down."

○ ○ ○

"You're going to hold up a plane? I don't believe you,
you're crazy!" Jarrett and Suzie had been lying in one another's arms exchanging lovers' confidences, when his sudden confession jerked her bolt upright. "I don't believe
you," she repeated, frowning at him. "You're just teasing
me."

Jarrett smiled up at her. She had allowed the bed clothes
to slip away, and he ran his hand up from her hip over
her rib cage to her firm, high breast. "It's true," he said
gently. "Tomorrow afternoon at three o'clock I am going
to hold up a plane and take off it two million dollars in
gold."

The girl pressed his hand tightly against her breasts as
though afraid of losing him, her eyes serious and troubled

as she sensed the purpose behind his words. "Tell me," she commanded. "Tell me it all." And lying there beneath her gaze, Jarrett revealed every detail of his plan.

If anyone had ever asked him why he had chosen to unburden himself in this way to a young girl he had met for only the third time, he would probably have been unable to reply. He had spoken almost without conscious thought; it had never crossed his mind that he might be putting himself in danger. He had simply taken it for granted that the girl would understand.

"And when we've got the money," he concluded, "we'll go away together—you and me—and start a decent life somewhere." They stared at one another gravely. Jarrett saw conviction and hope gradually replacing the incredulity in her feelings, and he knew his instinct had not played him false.

He waited for her questions, ready to dispel any uncertainties, but there was only one thing she wanted to know.

"Where would we go to?" she asked, wrinkling her brow.

"We can go anywhere you like. We could go to Europe maybe, see England or France."

"France!" Suzie's face lit up, and her eyes sparkled. "France, could we really go there—to Paris, even? You were there, before, in the war. Tell me about it." And she snuggled up against him, drawing the bedclothes around them.

○ ○ ○

In mid-Atlantic, weather conditions had worsened considerably during the hour before midnight. The first sign of the deterioration had been the rapid build-up of dense banks of low-lying clouds. *Caterina*'s crew found themselves flying blind, hemmed in by opaque drifts of vapor. At first Desmond had attempted to climb above the cloud layers. The temperature was still dropping ominously, and in these wet-fog conditions, the ice danger was very real. Gunning the motors, he had taken the flying boat up to 12,000 feet, and for a short while they had found relatively clear air.

Then, in the light from the distorted ball of the moon that showed the patchy cover above, they had seen an enormous bank of black clouds looming ahead of them, as solid as a mountain range, the menacing thunderheads rearing up to twenty thousand feet or more. The moment they entered these, they encountered severe rain squalls and strong gusts. The temperature soon dropped well below zero, and the wings became covered with a crust of frozen sleet. There was nothing to do but descend.

They plunged down through a blackness so intense that the wing tips and even the outer engines were at times obscured. The turbulence increased, rocking the plane. Desmond was unable to distinguish either sea or sky. Only by keeping a close watch on the artificial horizon and the turn-and-bank indicators could he tell what was happening to the flying boat. The effect on the augean canals in a man's ears of the centrifugal force developed by a turn caused such a complete loss of equilibrium that a pilot who had no frame of reference was inclined to believe his aircraft was level even when it was actually at a steep angle. If he went into a spiral or a spin, he would have no way of telling how to pull out.

Lightning flickered off to starboard, revealing boiling, storm-rent cloud banks churning beneath the force of giant vortexes, through which the pilots strained for a glimpse of the ocean. The altimeter showed less than twelve hundred feet between them and the surface, and in such conditions Desmond dared not continue the descent much longer unless the visibility improved.

The lightning flashed again, this time almost dead ahead. A seering double pulse, so near that Desmond's retinas were dazzled for several seconds, and *Caterina* bucked wildly. The rain squalls turned to sleet mixed with snow, blasting at them from out of the darkness with malevolent fury. The outside temperature was still only twenty-three degrees, and Desmond could see the ice patches on the leading surface of the wing and on the cowling of the inboard engine, gleaming dully in the light from the cockpit.

More lightning crackles and Desmond was sure *Caterina* had been struck. Caught in the grip of a monstrous down draft, the plane dropped horrifyingly. The altimeter needle wound back through five hundred-foot revolutions in as many seconds. Engines racing, the propellors clutched at the falling air as Desmond dragged the stick back and opened the throttles to pull her out of the dive. The port wing dipped sharply, threatening to put them into a spin, and he stamped down on the rudder bar to level her up again, feeling the aircraft shaking beneath the strain as he did so.

Then, almost miraculously, they broke through the bottom of the cloud layer, and the storm-whitened surface of the sea was faintly visible below. "Jesus! What on earth's that?" Frazer exclaimed in awe, peering down through the sleet at the waves only four hundred feet below them.

A scant quarter of a mile ahead, a huge whitish mass was distinguishable against the darker background of the ocean, nearing rapidly. Reaching down on the left-hand side of the instrument panel, Desmond flicked on a pair of switches, and twin searchlights stabbed the night. Their 10,000 candle-power brilliance was pitifully inadequate to pierce the near solid sheets of rain and sleet, but their beams enabled the stunned fliers to pick out the glinting, perpendicular cliffs and sweeping, humpbacked crest of the giant iceberg in their path.

"We're going to hit it!" Frazer cried, and for an instant Desmond was of the same opinion as the mountain of gray-streaked ice seemed to fill the windscreen.

Jerking the stick back, he felt the flying boat lift, and they soared overhead, scraping above the drifting menace by feet, or so it seemed.

"Jesus!" Frazer repeated. In the glow of the cabin light, his face was green with fear. "I didn't think bergs that big came this far south."

"Ever heard of the *Titanic?*" Desmond replied shortly, with little breath to spare from the effort demanded to control the plane. A shiver ran through him as he spoke, at the memory of the White Star liner and her fifteen hundred passengers lost in this very area twenty-seven years before.

On the lower deck, a number of the passengers were managing to sleep through the storm. Those who could not lay, largely unworried by the noise and erratic motion, in the warmth and comfort of their beds, fortunately unaware of the gravity of their situation.

Paul Rintlen was wide awake. The promenade lounge had been made up with five beds, occupied by Laura Hartman, Charlotte Curtis's maid Arlette, Rashid al Senussi, Van Smit, and Rintlen himself. In the rear of the plane, screened off by a thick curtain, the after cabin remained

lighted for the use of those who might find themselves
unable to sleep and unwilling to stay in their beds. At
present it was unoccupied.

The S.D. officer intended to make his way through into
the lighted cabin and into the hold beyond. With reasonable luck, he should be able to carry out a thorough
search of the Wienzmans' luggage.

○ ○ ○

In England, attempts to contact the flying boat were
still being made. Reports from weather ships and other
vessels near the area hit by the storm drew a bleak picture
of the conditions a thousand miles out in the Atlantic.
The storm had moved directly across the path *Caterina*
had intended to follow, and even allowing for the detour
she was to have made in her efforts to avoid it, there could
be little doubt that the aircraft must be in serious difficulty.

At the police station, Moyers and the other officers
waited for news. The air was thick with cigarette smoke,
the tables littered with heaped ashtrays and half-finished
cups of coffee. Conversation was desultory, but, exhausted
as they were, no one was willing to leave before hearing
some positive indication of the flying boat's fate. From
time to time, one of the telephones on Moyers's desk
would ring, but always the message was the same: still
no news.

By 2:00 A.M. when under normal circumstances *Caterina* would have been nearing the Newfoundland coast,
the government in London was informed. Instructions were
then beamed to two Royal Naval Aurora-class light cruis-
ers, which were riding out the storm in heavy seas some
four hundred miles south of *Caterina*'s projected track, to
close the distance and try to raise her on their wireless.
In addition, ships of the United States Coast Guard were
asked to keep a watch for the missing plane.

But still there was no reply from Imperial 109.

○ ○ ○

The strength of the storm was increasing. Desmond had
begun to fear their course was taking them into its very

heart. They were still flying at less than a thousand feet, amidst sleet and snow squalls of unremitting ferocity, and they were being shaken by violent quartering winds that threatened to dash *Caterina* into the sea below at any moment. The temperature outside had fallen further to twenty degrees, and the weight of the ice buildup on the wings and fuselage was beginning to create a noticeable drag. Much of this was because of the thick banks of freezing fog they were encountering.

Most of all, Desmond was worried by their inability to fix their positon. Ralph's last accurate plotting had been made more than three hours ago and had indicated that they were drifting south much faster than they had expected. Desmond had tried to compensate for this tendency in the subsequent period, but the result was that they were left with only a poor idea of their actual course, calculated by dead reckoning without checking it by another means.

They were still trying to make radio contact, either with Newfoundland or with some passing ship, but static from the electrical discharges in the storm made it impossible to tell if their transmissions were being answered; it also ruled out any hope of their being able to use the radio direction-finding equipment.

Until he could be more sure of their position, Desmond was unwilling to risk heading any further south and trying to run before the storm or skate through its fringes. They had been flying now for almost ten hours, during which time they had maintained an average speed of 160 mph. Actually, their true ground speed had been considerably less, thanks to the effect of the wind, leaving them still seven or eight hundred miles short of their destination.

Caterina had taken off with an adequate margin of fuel to allow for extra consumption owing to head winds, but from early on in the voyage, they had been forced to add two or three hundred miles to the total length of the trip. This figure was being increased by the impetus of the winds that carried them constantly southward, and it was possible that they might reach a point where the flying boat no longer carried sufficient fuel to permit another, still wider, sweep out into the middle reaches of the ocean.

Another fog bank loomed before them. It was virtually

impossible to tell where the sea ended and the cloud vapor began. Already ice crystals might be forming in the slender intakes of the carburetors; Desmond had been listening for the dreaded shutter and misfire that would indicate a blocked fuel jet. Once that occurred out here in midocean, the end would be very near.

The fog belt was narrow, but no sooner did they merge on the other side than they struck a squall so violent and twisting it made the plane tremble along her entire length, the wings bending and flexing in an alarming fashion, while hail rattled against the glass and drummed noisily on the metal plating.

An ice floe was slipping past below, the jagged blocks smaller than the giant berg they had seen earlier, but more numerous, an indication of the bitterly cold temperature of the seas. Then another patch of wet mist enveloped them, blotting out the way ahead for several minutes, and the moisture-laden air condensed on the aircraft's exposed metal skin.

Desmond came to a decision: to remain as they were for very much longer was impossible. The danger of icing had grown acute; moreover, the flying boat was taking a terrible hammering. The passengers, too, Sandy had warned him, were beginning to grow frightened, and though their comfort was not a major consideration when weighing the safety of the plane, it was nevertheless a factor to be taken into account.

"I'm taking another shot at climbing out of the fog," he announced. "If we stay on the deck much longer, we'll soon be carrying so much ice we'll fall out of the sky." He half turned his head to call out to the radio operator. "Ralph! I want you to have that sextant of yours ready; stand by to try to make a star fix the moment there is any kind of break in the cover. I must have an idea of our position." The engine tone deepened as the plane used increased power to lift her through the cloud layers. Desmond watched the rev. counters carefully. "Did you hear me, Ralph?" he called out.

"Aye, aye, skipper, I heard you," the radio officer's voice came back faintly.

Ever since the weather had closed in on them, Ralph had been sitting at his desk working at the radio sets with an inner conviction of hopelessness. *Caterina* carried a

Marconi telegraphy transmitter working on the short and medium wave bands as well as a medium wave telephony transmitter and a loop aerial direction finder. In addition, transmitter, receiver, and direction finder were duplicated by Hermes aircraft trans-receiver auxiliary apparatus, designed to provide a fallback should the main system fail. The appalling atmospherics were drowning out all sound in a wash of static, rendering this array of complex equipment useless.

As their course had taken them deeper into the depression, Ralph's fears had deepened, too, rising in him like a slow, cold tide, numbing his limbs and dulling his mind. He felt as if he were being sucked into a morass of despair that was enveloping him in its freezing embrace, slowly stifling the life out of him. Paralyzed, he stared at the useless flickering dials of the wireless. For him, for all of them on board, death was only a short while away. He was almost resigned to it.

Desmond's words reached him as though from a vast distance, like a voice echoing in his sleep. He managed to force a reply. He reached toward the sextant lying on top of the pile of charts. His movements appeared to him to be slow and distorted, as though he were walking in his sleep. He was dimly aware of Frazer watching him, the first officer's expression a mixture of vindicated revenge and dismay. What did it matter? Kendrick thought. There was so little time left.

The flying boat droned on through the darkness, only the slowly winding arm of the altimeter telling the men in the cabin that they were ascending. All sense of speed and altitude, even of motion itself, save for the unwavering vibration of the engines, had vanished. They felt the concussion of thunder near at hand occasionally, but no lightning penetrated the obscurity. Between six and eight thousand feet, the turbulence increased sharply, but gradually the bumping died away.

They were climbing at six hundred feet per minute, the air around them growing colder with every second, multiplying the ice threat to the carburetors and adding to the burden the flying boat was hoisting aloft. Even in the heated cockpit, the temperature had fallen noticeably, setting the two pilots shivering in their seats. Sandy Everett came in with a pair of sheepskin jackets and joined them in scanning the windows for a sign that the clouds were thinning out. Outside, the temperature had fallen to below zero, and the altimeter indicated a height of more than 13,000 feet. Desmond was forced to open the engine throttles to their maximum extent to maintain their climbing altitude—14,000 feet—15,000. The engines were laboring, and now a new hazard was added. The engine temperature gauges were moving toward the red danger zone; there was a serious risk of fire or of seizure within the engine blocks themselves, as well as the continued fear of ice buildup in the air inlets. Desmond held his course.

Frazer's nerve was the first to give way. "It's no good!" he burst out. "We're taking on too much ice; she's overheating; there could easily be another ten thousand feet of cloud above us."

Desmond made no answer. He could sense that the nerves of the others were also stretched to the breaking point, but he was determined to press on. Rather than turn back, he would jettison some of the cargo—better to lose that than the lives of everyone on board. The altimeter needle had slowed; they were scarcely rising at all now: 16,000 feet, 16,300. The needle steadied, quivering. The engines were straining to their limit. The temperature gauges were firmly into the red, their speed was falling off, and at any second the flying boat would stall. The controls were growing sluggish already.

"We're going to stall! You must ease off—she can't make it!" Frazer cried out again.

"Shut up and give me full boost," Desmond snarled at him, holding the stick tightly back.

The first officer gaped at him. "You're mad! She won't take it, I tell you! Do you want to kill us all? If she goes into a spin, we'll never pull her out in these conditions."

"Give me full boost, I said," Desmond repeated savagely. Seeing Frazer making no move to obey, he leaned across and yanked the switches open himself. The engines roared out as the superchargers cut in, and the altimeter needle began to climb again.

They saw a streak of light ahead and, for a single instant, the moon shone through a rent in the black pall above them. "Ralph!" he called out. "Get ready—here it comes!"

Ralph Kendrick was unable to move. Now that the moment had come for him to perform his duty, he seemed bereft of will, rigid and transfixed. He knew their only hope depended on his making a star fix. He was aware of how vital it was and how little time there was left. He wanted to act, but his limbs refused to obey his brain. He heard Desmond's cry and saw the sextant on the table before him, but his fingers refused to move across the intervening inches.

Again he heard Desmond's voice. "Ralph, get to the window!"

Desmond's order was followed by Frazer's panic-stricken cry. "Can't you see he's too bloody scared?"

Scared! Were they going to die because he was scared? Desmond and Sandy, Andy Draper, Frazer even, the passengers below—the Wienzmans, with their escape so near? Was he about to let all of them down? Anne, too. She had begged him not to go on this flight—was he going to fail her now? Very slowly—so slowly it seemed to him he could measure the time in minutes—the finger of his right hand flexed, moved, and gripped the sextant. Deep inside him a small residue of will was fighting the fear that was trying to choke him.

Ralph pressed down on the table and—using every ounce of effort he had—heaved himself to his feet. As he did so, the spell broke; the spark of resistance within him was fanned into a blaze. High above them the winds had torn the cloud veil open, and in the gap, three stars glittered, the brightest of them very clear and brilliant, with a faint bluish tinge.

"Ralph, can you see anything?" Desmond was calling.

A wave of exultation passed over Kendrick. He had experienced the awful, appalling, naked terror of the certainty of death, and he knew he would never be afraid of it again.

Lifting the sextant he caught the image of the bright star in its mirror. "Just hold on a moment, skipper," he called out. "I've got a sighting on Vega for you."

Minutes later, Ralph had taken three separate fixes on the star, calculated their position, and worked out the fuel range. Though they were some one hundred fifty miles farther south than they should have been, there were still sufficient reserves in the tanks for them to try to

Imperial 109

break away from the storm track. Withdrawing the boost, Desmond banked away to port, relieving the straining engines as the aircraft descended.

That his decision had been a wise one was shown less than half an hour later when they found themselves cruising easily above the cloud layers at 8,000 feet in bright moonlight, still experiencing head winds, but out of the worst effects of the storm, the danger of icing receding.

There was a mood of elation and satisfaction in the cockpit, but Frazer sat sullen and dispirited, jealous of the radio officer's resilience as compared with his own weakness. Desmond handed the controls to Frazer.

"Any luck with the radio?" he inquired of Ralph as he squeezed past the wireless desk.

Kendrick shook his head. " 'Fraid not, skipper. There must still be too much electrical interference below. It should be clearer in another hour or so. I'll keep trying."

"Fine, let me know if there's anything important." And stretching out on the bunk in the mailroom, Desmond fell asleep instantly.

The resumption of normal flight was a considerable relief to everyone. Reassured by the steady drone of the engines in the calm air and by the moonlight gleaming silver on the backs of the clouds below, the passengers drifted comfortably off to sleep again.

One exception was David Wienzman. He had slept well during the early part of the night, waking only as the airplane began its climb up through the cloud banks. For a while he lay talking quietly with his daughter in the berth above and the Kings on the opposite side of the room, but gradually his companions had fallen silent, as sleep overcame them. Unable to follow their example, Wienzman sat up and reached for his dressing gown. If he could not sleep, he might as well read. His case notes were still in his bag in the hold.

He got out of his bed and crept from the cabin. The overhead bulbs had been turned low, and there was barely enough light for him to see where he was going. The long promenade lounge was full of sleeping forms, none of them stirring. The professor found the after cabin empty, and the strong light made him blink. Opening the door in the far bulkhead, he went through into the hold beyond.

The light was on in there, too, somewhat to his surprise, and the figure of a man was bending over one of the suitcases. Thinking it must be the steward or purser, the professor started to explain what he had come for. Then he saw his suitcase open on the floor. The man who was straightening up and turning toward him was the Swiss, Ernst Perler, and in his hand he held a gun.

"Come in, Professor Wienzman," he said softly in German, "and shut the door. You have led me a long chase from Vienna."

It seemed to Desmond he had barely fallen asleep when Sandy was shaking him awake. "Skipper, we've managed to get through on the wireless to Saint John. They've an urgent message for you. They've been trying to contact us for the last four hours."

Cursing, Desmond sleepily followed Sandy into the cockpit, pulling on his jacket as he went.

"It sounds serious." Ralph handed him a copy of the message.

Desmond studied the form, then read the official phrases aloud. " 'Ernst Perler, traveling on a Swiss passport believed to be a forgery, boarded at Southampton. Urgently wanted for questioning in connection with killing of two men. Almost certainly armed and dangerous. To be approached with extreme caution.'

"Who the hell do they think we are," he exclaimed in exasperation, "the U.S. Marines?"

"What do you guess we ought to do?" Kendrick asked.

Desmond stared at the paper again. "I suppose the best course is for two of us to go down now and grab him while there's a chance he's still asleep. We can lock him in with the gold behind the grill in the mailroom."

"Couldn't we leave him and let the Mounties handle it when we reach Botwood?" Sandy suggested.

Desmond dismissed the idea. "No,'" he said firmly. "The authorities wouldn't have been so anxious to get through to us if they didn't think this man was a threat. If he has a gun and realizes that we're on to him, or that the police are waiting, God knows what might happen.

It'll be safer if we act at once." He turned to Ken Frazer. "How's she handling?" he asked.

"Fine," the first officer told him without looking up. "Steady as a rock."

"How do you want to play it, skipper?" Ralph looked up at him. "Sandy here says Perler's berthed down at the after end of the promenade lounge."

"Starboard side, far end, lower berth," the purser interjected. "With Dr. Van Smit above and the Turkish chap opposite."

"Anyone else in there?" Desmond opened the locker by his seat and took out the two pistols.

"Laura—Mrs. Hartman—and Mrs. Curtis's maid," Sandy told him.

"We'll still have to risk it; there will never be a time when he'll be totally alone." Desmond handed one of the revolvers to Ralph. "I'll go down, and you follow, and we'll take him between us. You're quite sure which is his bed?" he said to the young purser.

"Positively, skipper," Sandy affirmed. "I checked all the cabins just before the message came over the radio, and he was there. He seemed to be asleep, too."

"Right, then." Desmond spun the chambers of his revolver, checking the action. "Get Saint John again on the wireless, Ralph, and tell them what we intend doing; then we'll go down."

Horror and amazement dawned slowly on David Wienzman. "You are a German?" he blurted incredulously.

"Standartenführer Rintlen of the Sicherheitsdienst," the man smiled tightly. "Did you really think you could ever escape from us, professor?"

"But please, what is it you want of me? Why can you not leave us alone?" Wienzman begged. "We have done no harm, my daughter and I."

"Yes, you have done immeasurable harm as you are well aware," Rintlen snapped. "Why else did you flee from the Reich and try so hard to evade our attempts to recapture you in Italy?"

"We were frightened. My daughter was frightened— that lout Gerdler was with you—"

Rintlen waved him to silence. "Enough of this, there is

no time for talking. You have papers, important papers with you. I want them, at once."

"My notes you mean? They are in the suitcase, labeled as school books. If they are all you want, take them. I would have given them to you gladly. Believe me, it was never my intention to publish the names of my patients. Take them by all means and let me go."

The S.D. officer gave a chuckle. "Let you go," he mimicked. "Oh, no, professor, it is not as simple as that. We have come too far to let you go. You are a threat to me personally, as well as an enemy of the Reich."

"But you cannot touch me here, in the plane!" The professor's voice rose in anguish as the words sank home. "They could find out. There would be an investigation, you would be arrested!"

Rintlen laughed again. "They will find nothing, my dear professor, for the simple reason that there will be nothing to find, only the evidence of a most unfortunate accident." Stepping around the baggage, he moved to the massive door of the freight hatch in the side of the hold. "You are about to take a walk, professor, a very long walk—straight down."

Reaching up, he snapped back the first of the four heavy latches securing the hatch. "Come over this way," he ordered, motioning with his gun. As if in a dream, the professor obeyed, mesmerized by the gun and the harsh stare of the S.D. man. He took a couple of faltering steps and then stopped.

"Come on—more." Rintlen had unclipped two more latches and was stooping to reach the bottom one, still keeping the pistol trained on Wienzman's chest. "And don't worry," he said cruelly, "your daughter will soon be joining you. I will attend to her when we reach America." Grunting, he snapped open the last of the latches.

David Wienzman was a man of peace, a man who believed that war and violence could be avoided if people would only come together and talk reasonably to each other. He had never raised his hand against anyone or threatened to do so. But now, as he heard the gloating promise to destroy his daughter, as he watched the man who had persecuted and pursued them for so many days, fury and hatred welled up within him.

The German had begun to wrench open the handle of

the door lock. Close by Wienzman's side, on top of a leather cabin trunk, stood a lizard-skin hatbox belonging to Charlotte Curtis. With a surge of courage, the professor seized it and flung it at the Nazi's head.

Rintlen's fingers tightened instinctively on the trigger. In the confined space of the hold, the crash of the shot was deafening. Flinging himself down, Wienzman felt the bullet part the air—scant inches from his head. At the same instant there came a terrible cry from Rintlen, and a violent blast of air swept through the hold.

Jerking his head up an appalling vision met the professor's eyes. The great metal door of the freight hatch had swung open. Dangling from it, clawing on the handle, was the figure of the Nazi agent, his head hanging back, his mouth open in a scream that was torn soundlessly away by the slipstream.

Even as Wienzman stared, transfixed, he saw the man's fingers slip and break loose.

He was still staring at the empty hatchway when Desmond and Ralph Kendrick burst into the hold.

"The old man must be tougher than I thought," Ralph Kendrick remarked when he and Desmond were back in their seats on the flight deck. "It took a lot of guts to do what he did."

David Wienzman certainly was tough, Desmond thought. When he and Ralph had secured the freight hatch and helped him through into the after cabin, dismissing the other passengers who had crowded in, the professor had been able to give a lucid account of what had happened in the hold, as well as to comfort his daughter's renewed anxieties.

Taking a statement from him, Desmond had dispatched it by radio to the authorities, and on receiving a lengthy reply, he had been able to dispel the refugees' fears of further pursuit. "London is pretty certain this was one man acting on his own without orders, and it seems likely that the agents from his own country had actually been trying to prevent him from getting near you," Desmond told them. "So you should be safe from now on."

Explanations to the excited passengers—and the stream of messages that continued to pour in from the Canadian wireless stations—took longer, and it was five o'clock before he was able to take the controls once more.

The clouds had vanished, and some predawn light was beginning to creep into the sky ahead of them. Below, a swell was still running in the sea, but the angry whitecaps had vanished. From time to time they flew over thick belts of sea fog hanging low above the water, sure proof that they were in the area of the Grand Banks fishing grounds, where the cold Labrador current coming down from the Arctic met a branch of the warmer Gulf Stream.

Ken Frazer was scanning the way ahead through binoculars. Adjusting the focus, he let out a sharp cry of excitement. "There it is! Five degrees to starboard," he sang out jubilantly. "Land! We've made it across!"

12

By radio: 1400 hrs EST. THURSDAY 16 MARCH 1939.
AIR TRAFFIC CONTROL MONTREAL CANADA TO
LA GUARDIA MARINE TERMINAL NEW YORK.
TRANSATLANTIC MAIL PLANE IMPERIAL AIR-
WAYS FLIGHT 109 G-ADHO CATERINA LEFT
HERE. ETA NEW YORK 1600 hrs EST. END.

The afternoon sun was shining brilliantly on the waters
of Lake Champlain as *Caterina* climbed away from the
Saint Lawrence and flew over the Canadian border into
Vermont. They were flying at 7,000 feet following the
line of the lake, between the long ridges of high ground
on either side. The air was clear, with only a few patches
of drifting white cumulus clouds, and free of turbulence.

Desmond yawned; with the aircraft on autopilot there
was little for him and Frazer to do but check the instruments occasionally and watch the snow-streaked terrain
unfolding beneath them.

Fighting his tiredness, Desmond turned his attention to
the log and began filling in the remaining details of the
flight from Europe. They had landed at Botwood amid
the bleak, stony Newfoundland landscape at 6:15 A.M.
just before the sun rose, thankful to be able to stretch
their limbs. Much of the time on the ground had been
taken up with inspecting the hull of the flying boat, which
fortunately had suffered no damage in the storm, and
there were reports to be made to the police on the events
of the night and the death of the Nazi agent. Apparently
an inquest was necessary, though there was doubt as to
whether this would be held in England or Canada. At least
there had been no newspaper men at Botwood.

At Montreal, where they landed at midday, their reception was tumultuous. They were besieged by journalists and photographers. Everything about *Caterina* was news. Her glamorous passengers, her journey through the storm, the attack on Professor Wienzman. Even poor Ian Thorne's death on the river at Shambe was dragged up again.

Desmond had been one of the newsmen's prime targets, and he had been thankful when the airline management had come to his rescue. With the weather reports fair, everyone was anxious to be away, and by two o'clock the passengers were back on board, and *Caterina* was nosing out into the river while a crowd of waving spectators lined the river bank to watch her take off.

Glancing out of the window, Desmond saw they had reached the middle of the lake and were passing above Burlington, Vermont. The time was 2:30. In another ninety minutes they would be arriving at La Guardia.

○　○　○

Seventy-five miles to the Southeast, Pat Jarrett and Suzie were making their final preparations. They had been up since dawn, monitoring the radio traffic between Botwood, Montreal, and New York. From these and from news broadcasts had gathered something of the dramatic adventures of the night crossing and of the intense worldwide interest that had been generated in the Imperial 109.

The publicity the flight was receiving had caused Jarrett some moments of anxiety, and he had even considered abandoning the attack. A thorough reexamination of his plans however, had convinced him that the new developments would have a minimal effect as far as he was concerned. The flying boat might be located sooner than he had anticipated, but, even allowing for this, he and Suzie would still have plenty of time to cover their tracks.

So they had maneuvered the seaplane out from the boathouse and moored her fast to the jetty, where Jarrett had made a final inspection of the Napier engine. Then the two of them had rolled the drums of aviation fuel down to the end of the jetty and replenished the tanks in her twin floats.

"That will give me enough for two hundred miles, provided I'm careful," he told Suzie as he screwed back the caps.

"Why do you need so much?" she asked. "I thought the plane was coming close by."

"She is—reasonably close," he replied. "I'll make the interception about forty miles from here, between Hudson Falls and Saratoga Springs, but I want to have plenty of fuel on hand in case I don't spot her right away. It shouldn't be too difficult. I know her height and course and the speed she's making. All the same I want to have the extra fuel just in case I have to go looking."

"How long will you be gone for?" They began rolling the empty drums back up the jetty to the rear of the boathouse.

"Not more than three-quarters of an hour if it all pans out," he answered. "But don't get worried if I happen to take longer."

Returning to the house, Jarrett went through the painstaking ritual of preparing himself for action. He washed and shaved again, put on fresh underclothes and shirt, and donned his old Army Air Corps uniform. Then the girl helped him into the fur-lined boots and heavy leather greatcoat he had last worn in combat over the Western Front twenty-one years ago. Even with these and his leather gloves and leather flying helmet, he knew he would be freezing cold 7,000 feet up, flying in the open cockpit at 240 miles an hour.

Taking out the Thompson submachine gun, he showed Suzie how to work the action and change the magazine. "Are you sure you know what to do?" he asked.

The girl gripped the weapon tightly. "As soon as the flying boat lands, I go down to the jetty and cover the crew with the gun while they tie up." She slapped the butt of the Thompson as she spoke.

"That's right," Jarrett nodded approvingly. "The jetty is very low, and the airliner will be able to get her starboard wing and props over the top and nose right in alongside, with the pier fitting easily between her hull and the starboard wing float, like a pontoon mooring. So make sure you keep well out of the way until the captain has switched off the engines. Then what do you do?"

"Then you'll tell them over the radio to get out, and I'll line them up and keep covering them while you come in on the water in your plane and tie up on the other side between them and the shore." Suzie repeated the briefing she had been given.

"Yes. There should be plenty of room. The flying boat can't come all the way up because the boathouse is in the way," Jarrett affirmed. "As soon as I'm out of the cockpit, I'll take over, and we'll set them to work unloading the gold."

"Couldn't we leave the gold on the plane and just fly off with it?" Suzie suggested. "We could go anywhere then."

"No. It's the plane they'll be searching for," Jarrett told her. "Until they find her, they won't have a clue to what's happened, and you and I will be safe. Their best guess will probably be that she's gone down somewhere in the Adirondacks, I reckon. No, we'll stick to our plans." Going out through the kitchen, he stopped to switch on the main wireless set.

"Can you hear the flying boat?" Suzie asked, watching him tune the dial.

"Nothing but ordinary traffic between the ground stations," he answered, laying down the headphones and switching off. "The captain made his last report soon after he crossed the Canadian border. It's unlikely he'll come on the air again until he's drawing near New York."

For the hundredth time that day, he looked at his watch. "It's nearly 2:30, time I was getting down to the plane." Taking his arm, Suzie walked with him to the pier and stood holding his navigating pad while he put on his helmet and glasses.

"This is it," he said. "If you want to back out, now's the time to say so."

By way of answer, Suzie put her arms around him and kissed him. "I'll be ready," she promised. "Don't worry about me."

Once in the cockpit he made a quick check of the fittings; all seemed well. He switched on the master ignition, feeling his excitement surge as the dials and gauges flickered into life. Meticulously, he scanned each one. All were functioning as they should. He pressed the black start button.

Without a moment's hesitation, the engine roared, puffs of blue-gray smoke spouting from the exhaust cowls. He let the engine run for a few seconds, working the throttle as it warmed up. As it settled down to run smoothly, he lifted his hand to the girl, signaling her to unleash the stern lines. The little plane began to taxi across the water.

Pulling down his goggles, he steered out into the middle of the lake. The wind was light, hardly more than three or four knots from the south. With a final wave to Suzie, he let the silver racer have her head.

A fierce wave of elation swept through him. Now he was about to show the world what he could do. This was his moment—the years of frustration and poverty, rejection and indifference, were to be repaid. He was back where he belonged, in the seat of a high-performance fighter, fueled and armed. His mouth set, he set a course to intercept Imperial 109.

○ ○ ○

While *Caterina* was cruising peacefully over the New England countryside, and in New York City's financial district, people were settling down to the afternoon's work, Harvey Tilset Kimber left his office in the Bankers Trust Company building opposite the New York Stock Exchange and instructed his chauffeur to drive him to the Saint Regis Hotel.

Smaller and more exclusive than the nearby Waldorf-Astoria, the Saint Regis appealed to Harvey's discriminating taste, and he was accustomed to dining frequently at its celebrated La Boîte restaurant. It also made an admirably discreet place for the meeting about to occur with those parties who held a financial interest in the affairs of Stewart Curtis and Klerksdorp.

In the elegant double drawing room overlooking Fifth Avenue, Harvey found half a dozen men waiting for him. They stood as he entered, and one of them came forward to meet him. "Harvey, it was good of you to come."

Edgar Mathers was a big, genial man who, like Harvey, lived in a brownstone mansion on Murray Hill and was a member of the influential and prestigious University Club.

"Gentlemen," Mathers announced, "I'm sure I don't need to introduce Harvey Kimber, president of Kimber, Crossfield, Smith, brokers to Klerksdrop Gold."

One by one the men shook hands. Harvey knew them all by sight and reputation if not by actual acquaintance. Like Edgar Mathers, they were bankers and investment barons. They took their seats. "We are meeting here this afternoon to discuss—" Mathers began.

He was interrupted by a small, dried-up husk of a man in a tight black suit and a wing collar; this was Statten, president of First Financial Trust Company. "No need for all that," Statten snapped petulantly. "There's only one thing we want to know. Is Klerksdorp sound?" His colleagues echoed his remarks, and everyone in the room looked expectantly at the stockbroker.

Sitting upright, Harvey marshaled his thoughts before replying. "No, Klerksdorp is not sound," he said clearly. "I received confirmation from Stuttenheim in South Africa only a short time ago. The Securities Exchange Commission is being informed, and the share quotation will be suspended in a few minutes." Obviously the verdict was not unexpected. "A survey of the mine carried out over the past fortnight," he continued, "has shown the reserves were grossly overstated. It is doubtful whether it would be viable at all, and certainly not on the scale on which it is being operated at the moment."

"And the options on the surrounding mineral rights and real estate?" Mathers inquired, a worried frown on his face.

"Worthless," Harvey told him, seeing no point in mincing his words.

This time the murmurs were louder, and it was Statten who summed up the general feeling once more. "That crook, Curtis," he spat the words out vindictively, "has taken four million dollars from us as a down payment on those options, and three hours from now he'll be in the city demanding the balance of sixteen million. He won't see any of that, but I want to get back what we've already paid him."

"I agree, of course," Mathers said, "but Curtis is a slippery bastard. The contract for the sale was with him personally; it wasn't linked specifically to the fortunes of Klerksdorp. The mine isn't even mentioned in the word-

ing. A court might say we still had to pay up even
though the mine had failed."

"I won't hand over another cent, whatever the courts
say," Statten retorted vigorously. "Everyone knows these
options were only of value because of Klerksdorp's gold
strike."

"Curtis will argue that mining is always a gamble and
we knew what we were doing," interjected another.

"It might be cheaper in the long run to buy him off,"
suggested Mathers.

"Never. I won't hear of it," Statten snapped back
shrilly.

"There may be another way," Harvey interposed quietly,
and the conversation ceased. "This whole affair probably
originated from an introduction I gave Curtis to Edgar
Mathers," he nodded in the direction of his friend, "some
years ago. I have felt all along that I have a duty to do
what I can to help you. Whether we can recover the money already paid is hard to say; knowing Curtis, I would
doubt it.

"As far as preventing him from trying to enforce the
contract, I think there is hope. Our South African friends
have informed me that charges of fraud will be brought
against Curtis in the Union. On my suggestion, they are
contacting the Department of Justice even as we sit here,
with a view to having an extradition order made against
him. I am glad to say there is every possibility that Stewart Curtis will be arrested the moment he steps off the
airplane at La Guardia."

○ ○ ○

With the flying boat's arrival in American airspace, Stewart Curtis's confidence returned and with it the arrogance
and contempt for his inferiors that had been so marked
earlier on in the trip. Not many men, he told himself,
would have been able to keep up the facade of Klerksdorp's
prosperity sufficiently well to persuade a syndicate of
bankers to part with twenty million dollars simply for the
right to mine nearby.

Already he had been highly abusive toward Andy Draper
about the discomfort of the bed he had been given. "Your

captain may be able to protect you while you're on this plane," he had stormed at the steward, "but I can promise you that when we reach New York I shall make personal representations to the airline management. After all," he remarked with crude self-satisfaction, "if I can have one of their flights rescheduled, I should be able to have a miserable steward sacked."

Draper thus dispensed with, Curtis turned his attention to Laura. Summoning her to the after cabin, now returned to his private use, he subjected her to a long harangue, accusing her of treachery and theft, while Luca d'Este looked on, smiling at her discomfiture. The baron had not forgiven Laura for taking his wife's part against him during their lunch at Athens.

"But Mr. Curtis, I thought Captain O'Neill had explained things," Laura tried to protest.

"Captain O'Neill has explained nothing," Curtis cut her short. "He came to me with a pack of lies that he demanded I accept or he would delay the flight. Well, he can't hold that threat against me now, and I have no hesitation in repudiating my agreement. You're sacked as from last Sunday when you committed the theft, and as soon as we reach New York, I intend to have you both arrested."

"I think you are quite right, Curtis," Luca egged him on. "One has, after all, a moral duty in these matters."

Laura reacted fiercely. "Don't waste your time trying to frighten me with talk about police," she said contemptuously. "We both know perfectly well all you're saying is lies, and the admission you signed proves it. Don't think you can sack me, either, because as far as I'm concerned, I've already resigned. I've had enough of your boasting and bullying. You two make a fine pair." She included Luca in a scornful glance. "An intentional swindler who ought to be in jail himself—and a common murderer."

She gave them no chance to respond. "You're both very fine at ill-treating servants and people who have to depend on you," she continued hotly, "but it's easy to see the moment you come up against someone your own size, you're shown up for the cowards you are. From now on I don't have to worry about being polite to either of you, so mind how you speak to me because I'm likely to let fly in a way you won't be forgetting in a hurry."

She made for the door before they could begin to reply. As she did so, however, it opened suddenly, and Georgina entered.

"Oh, hello, Laura," she said pleasantly. Then, peering more closely at the girl's face, she said, "You look rather upset. Are you all right?"

"If I am upset, Mrs. Curtis," Laura replied freezingly, "it is only because the people in this cabin seem to think they can treat people as though they own them, and as I've just told your husband, I am one person he doesn't own anymore." Without waiting for an answer, she strode past Georgina.

Georgina turned on Luca and her husband. "What the hell have you two been saying to her?" she demanded. "Have you been going on about the watch again?"

"There's no need for you to concern yourself." Curtis attempted to dismiss the matter. "I simply told the girl that she was being sacked for theft and that I was putting the matter in the hands of the police."

"My God, you've got nerve!" his wife exploded. "Don't you realize that after what you've been saying about her, she could well sue for slander? I told you I took the watch. Laura never had anything to do with it. You'll have to apologize to her at once."

"Don't start telling me what to do," Curtis rebuked her angrily. "None of this would have happened in the first place if you hadn't made such a fool of yourself over that bloody pilot. I can't possibly keep the girl on now."

At this point, Luca d'Este made the mistake of interrupting on Curtis's behalf. "Your husband is right you know, Georgina. One must be able to have absolute confidence in one's employees."

His words drew the full weight of Georgina's wrath. "Be quiet, you sycophantic little man—it has nothing to do with you. Why don't you get out of here, anyway," she snapped savagely. "I'm fed up with you always hanging around."

Luca could only stammer with embarrassment. Rising hastily to his feet, he scuttled out of the cabin, muttering apologies.

"Ridiculous little toad," Georgina snorted contemptuously as the door closed behind him. "I can't think why you have him in here."

"You found the baron amusing enough in Cairo while
I was away," her husband observed acidly. "Until Captain
O'Neill came on the scene and you decided he was a more
attractive prospect."

"For Christ's sake, stop going on about him, will you?"
Georgina answered, growing suddenly weary. "The affair
is ended, let's leave it at that."

Luca's first thought was that he badly needed a cigarette, and he made his way to the smoking saloon. In the
midship cabin he found Laura Hartman obviously engaged in recounting to the Kings what had just happened.
All three glared at him as he walked past, and he hurried
on through into the passageway beyond.

In the smoking saloon, Jacquetta and Rashid found themselves alone together for the first time since boarding the
train for Southampton on Wednesday afternoon. Until a
few moments before, the presence of Harold King had
forced them to maintain their apparent indifference
to each other. Then, to their relief, he had been summoned aft by his wife.

Jacquetta ran into the young sheik's arms, and they embraced, tense and afraid at the thought of being discovered, yet unwilling to let each other go. "Rashid," she
whispered, "what are we to do? In a little while we land
in New York, and in two days Dr. Van Smit will go to
Luca."

"If he does that, the Italians will demand that I be returned to them in Rome," he answered, "to stand trial for
rebellion." He spoke matter-of-factly.

"The Americans wouldn't do that. It would mean sending you to your death." She tightened her arms about him
in terror.

"Perhaps—who can tell?" Rashid shrugged. "I do not
intend to take the risk." He did not elaborate.

"Rashid, please," she begged him. "For my sake, forget
both of them and let us go back to Egypt. You can do
more good there."

"Listen," he said grimly, "there is no other way. Would
you really have me break my word, forget my father and
my sister? My oath means more to me than the fear of
what might follow."

Sobbing, Jacquetta buried her face in his chest, hugging him fiercely to her, as though trying to force the resolve from him with her own strength. They were still holding one another when Luca entered the saloon.

Jacquetta had been right in thinking her husband was aware of the strained atmosphere that existed between himself and the young Turkish nobleman who had joined *Caterina* at Alexandria. Several times on the flight, Luca had spotted the man watching him with a peculiarly disquieting intensity. It had never crossed Luca's mind for a moment, though, that his wife was carrying on an affair right under his very nose—still less that his rival was in reality the Senussi sheik whose retribution he so feared.

Luca, outraged by what he saw, immediately seized his wife by the arm and jerked her roughly across the room, throwing her against the chairs by the door. As she stumbled and fell, she let out a cry of pain.

This was all Rashid needed. Springing forward, he struck the Italian a terrific blow on the side of the head, sending him crashing against the bulkhead. Luca slid to the floor, and Jacquetta, seeing him lying at the Arab's feet, let out a frantic cry. "No, Rashid!" she screamed, thinking in the confusion that the Arab was about to carry out his threat to kill Luca. "Don't harm him."

At her words, both men froze. The Italian had been picking himself up, but now he stiffened and stared up at the man standing over him, his face white with fear. "Rashid—" he croaked, dry-mouthed. "Rashid al Senussi?" he repeated slowly, as if unable to believe what he heard.

"Yes, that is my name," Rashid nodded tersely. "I am the man whose father and whose sister you murdered and whose people you enslaved," he said. "I have trekked half across the world to find you and avenge your crimes."

Luca continued to stare open-mouthed at the figure above him. Then, as though coming out of a trance, he fumbled beneath his jacket for his pistol. Seeing Rashid going for his own gun, Jacquetta gave a desperate cry and flung herself between them.

○ ○ ○

Pat Jarrett had a more difficult task than he had anticipated in locating *Caterina*. He began to fear that he had made a miscalculation. Desperately he searched among the clouds for the glint of sunlight on metal. Though he was carrying fuel enough to enable him to loiter, his greatest worry was that the airliner might have increased her speed and placed herself well to the south, thereby forcing him into a long, stern chase and perhaps carrying him too near the populated areas where the attack might be witnessed from the ground.

Increasing altitude to 8,000 feet, he began following the line of the Hudson River toward Albany, and almost at once he spotted his quarry a thousand feet or so below him, cruising majestically out from the cover of a white drift of cumulus. She was about half a mile ahead, he estimated, some ten miles beyond her expected position. Probably she had met with following winds on her flight down the valley.

A sharp current of excitement fired through him at the sight of the sleek, white target flying below. He was tempted to roar down on her in a power dive, attacking from the classic "upsun" position, but, checking himself, he resolved to stick to his plan.

He put the Supermarine into a shallow swoop, and, leveling off about a hundred feet beneath the flying boat, he increased power to bring himself up until he was only a length behind. This was another classic attack position, against the undefended belly. Tucked up forward on the flight deck, the crew would be totally unaware of his presence. He was close enough to make out every detail of the white hull; he could even distinguish the scratches on the step of the flying boat's planing bottom.

Jarrett felt dwarfed in the tiny racer beside the lumbering giant that cruised on, blissfully ignorant of her danger, and for the first time he was struck by a sense of the enormity of what he was about to do. Taking a deep breath, he gripped the stick tightly in his gloved hands. With a flick of his right thumb, he switched on the firing button.

Giving a light touch to the starboard rudder and slightly increasing the speed, he eased the racer out from behind the flying boat and brought her up until the two were almost level. Very deliberately, he sighted on the extreme tip of the starboard wing. He did not want to cause any real damage with his first burst, merely to prove to the crew that he had guns and was prepared to use them. With a second intake of breath, he pressed the firing button.

He held it down for about a half second, no more, and deliberately aimed to miss the important wing flap. The Supermarine shuddered with the recoil, and a brief scatter of red dots appeared in the sighting ring. Instantly, it seemed the flying boat's wing tip shredded like cardboard under buckshot, pieces of debris splintering off in a burst of metallic fragments as some thirty of the heavy caliber bullets smashed through it.

Now he was committed. Jarrett hesitated no longer. In front of him, he saw the stricken plane buck wildly and then dip as the pilot banked away frantically. Matching their maneuver, he tucked the racer tight in beside them and switched down the transmit button of his radio, preset to the flying boat's normal communication frequency. *"Caterina,* Imperial Airways *Caterina.* Do not use your radio. I repeat, do not use your radio," he intoned, praying that the transmission was getting through and that the airliner's captain would obey. "I say again, do not use your radio." His own equipment was specifically low powered to reduce the chances of ground stations overhearing. "Steer course 273 degrees. Repeat 273 degrees. Maintain current height and speed. Do not use your radio."

For what seemed to the anxious flyer like several minutes but in reality was a period of only some thirty seconds, the airliner continued in her banking descent, sliding earthward against a tilted horizon. At last, to Jarrett's exultant relief, he saw the flying boat's wings level up.

The captain was obeying. The bullion flight Imperial 109 was now under his command. In the open seat of the tiny Supermarine, Pat Jarrett shouted aloud in triumph.

○ ○ ○

"Passengers are all OK, skipper," Ken Frazer reported. "We've got them packed into the galley passageway. They're frightened and nervous but so far under control."

"Good. They'll be safest there with the mailroom above and the extra walls of the galley and washrooms to protect them," Desmond said, "just in case that bastard decides to start firing at us again. You'd better get up to the mailroom windows and keep an eye on him for me."

"What do you think he intends doing?" Ralph Kendrick asked. He was at the radio ready to receive further instructions from their assailant. Already they had been told to drop to one thousand feet and had been given two course alterations.

"My guess is that he and his friends are going to make us land somewhere," Desmond answered, "where they can remove the gold." He glanced out the window at the heavily wooded country they were flying over. "This is a pretty remote area by the look of it. Ideal for the job."

"And what about us and the passengers?" asked Kendrick. Desmond shook his head. "I've no idea what they'll do once they get us ashore," he said, "but I know one thing. I'd rather face it out on the ground than start taking chances up here with that fighter. He made a hell of a mess of our starboard wing. Whatever he's using carries a hefty punch, and he's a good shot."

"It's definitely a Supermarine type," Ken shouted back from the mailroom. "I can't tell what model, though. I think I can see the two gun ports in his nearside wing."

The Supermarine had been the prototype for the new Spitfire, Desmond recalled, which flew at more than three hundred fifty miles per hour. He doubted whether the plane would be able to manage more than three hundred with the extra drag of the floats. All the same, it would still have speed enough to overhaul and destroy the slow, unarmed *Caterina*.

He felt a deep hatred for the helmeted figure in the other cockpit, a sense of personal outrage that anyone should dare shoot at *Caterina*. If only they had some means of firing back, of defending themselves.

"He's calling again, skipper," Ralph said suddenly. "He says you should be able to see a small lake about two miles ahead and ten degrees to starboard."

"I have it," Desmond answered. "Is that the place he wants us to come down?"

"Yes. You're to land from the southern end, without circling around. He says the water is clear and deep."

"It's going to be a bloody steep descent," Desmond growled back, "if I'm not allowed to circle. Those hills are closer than I like. Tell Frazer to get below and send the passengers back to their seats for the touchdown."

○ ○ ○

Suzie had never seen a big airliner before. Indeed, the Supermarine was the only plane she had ever been close to. Consequently, she was unprepared for the sheer size of the great flying boat appearing suddenly over the rim of the hills to the south.

Her amazement was coupled with fear and a degree of awe at the enormous bulk that came swooping steeply down, the noise of its descent echoing off the hillside. The flying boat alighted on the water with a burst of spray so high and wide that Suzie thought it had crashed and was about to sink. Then she saw the airliner breasting smoothly over the lake's surface and, taking a firm grip on the submachine gun, she prepared to receive the plane.

○ ○ ○

"Christ! The man's bloody crazy!" Desmond swore as Ralph relayed the latest of the fighter's commands. "How the hell does he think I can maneuver an eighteen-ton aircraft onto a tiny little jetty like that without the help of a boat? Call him up and tell him it can't be done without damaging the airplane."

"He's just coming down onto the water behind us now," Frazer called out. "He must have been waiting for our wash to die away."

There was silence for a moment or two, then Ralph turned back to his captain with a helpless gesture. "He says to do what he orders or he'll start shooting again."

"Hell!" Desmond swore again. "If he makes me damage *Caterina*, I'll take him apart with my bare hands if I have to." Gritting his teeth, he began to line the flying boat up for the attempt. "Cut the power to the outer engines, will you, Ken?" he said. "We'll go in as slowly as we can."

On the lower deck, the passengers huddled in the narrow passage between the smoking saloon and the midship cabin, where Sandy Everett and Draper had made them return the moment the flying boat had touched down. No one had argued with the order, though they knew the thin partition walls would give them little extra protection against machine gun bullets. At least there was an illusion of safety—and an added sense of security in being close together.

The initial panic had been swiftly checked by the steward and the purser, aided by Frazer. Now they all stood pressed against one another, sometimes whispering nervously, but for the most part in frightened silence. They strained to catch every sound around them—the water slapping against the hull, the slow beat of the two inboard engines as Desmond steered cautiously in toward the pier, and the occasional muted exchange of voices from the flight deck above. To each sound, their imaginations ascribed innumerable and ominous meanings, fear of the unknown magnifying their anxiety.

Laura stood squeezed between Georgina Curtis and Siegret Wienzman, trying vainly to still her quivering limbs. Siegret's father held her tightly, but Laura could see the young girl's shoulders shaking. Turning to look the other way, Laura found herself face to face with Georgina. Pale and plainly terrified as she was, the older woman forced a brief smile; reaching out, she gripped Laura's hand, and the two stood holding on to each other for comfort.

At the end of the passage, Rashid held his arms protectively around Jacquetta, his quarrel with the baron abandoned as he concentrated on the fresh threat to their lives. In the pandemonium that had followed the attack, he and Luca had barely had time to struggle to their feet before Sandy Everett had come running in, shouting at them all to take cover in the corridor.

Rashid felt trapped and helpless inside the plane, unable to see his opponents and forced to rely on the judgment of the men in the cockpit. If only they could get out onto the shore, perhaps they could begin fighting back.

"Two of us here, the baron and myself, have guns," he whispered over Jacquetta's head at Sandy, who stood at the entrance to the saloon peering around the corner through the windows, trying to make out where they were. "Tell the captain he can count on my help."

"We have some pistols on the flight deck ourselves," the purser whispered back, "but the captain's afraid of what will happen if anyone starts shooting. We're a sitting duck for the machine guns."

"What can you see?" Rashid asked him.

Sandy put his head around the corner again. "We're coming in at a small pier," he said, turning back again. "There's at least one person on it carrying what looks like a Tommy gun."

Rashid's heart sank. Their enemies outgunned them overwhelmingly. Even at close range, their revolvers would be useless against the concentrated fire of a single such weapon. With one sustained burst, the rawest shot could cut down every person on board; and with the heavy armament of the fighter at their backs . . . Rashid could visualize the bullet-riddled aircraft, shattered and in flames, drifting out to sink in mid-lake, her interior a bloody shambles of dead and injured.

"You'd better get down into the mooring compartment and open the hatch," Desmond told Ken as *Caterina* closed in on the jetty. "I'll need you to tell me how to steer." The first officer hesitated, visibly dismayed by the prospect. "Come on, hurry up," Desmond said tersely.

"Can I have a pistol with me?" Frazer asked, getting slowly out from his seat.

"If it will make you feel braver," Desmond answered, "but hurry it up. We're practically on the jetty now."

Sticking the weapon in the waistband of his trousers, Frazer lifted the trap in the cockpit floor and lowered himself through. Moments later, they heard the sound of the hatch opening below.

○ ○ ○

Suzie backed slowly off from the foot of the pier as the airliner crept across the last few feet of water. The noise drowned out the sound of the Supermarine approaching from the side, and she could feel the vibration through the planking under her feet. The size of the flying boat was overwhelming, making her feel small and scared. She clutched the Tommy gun tightly, wishing Jarrett would hurry down to help her. Glancing nervously behind, she

saw he had reached the jetty and was preparing to switch
off and tie up.

The sudden opening of *Caterina's* hatch caught her by
surprise. Seeing a man's figure emerging, she jerked the
muzzle of the gun up toward him. The events that followed came so swiftly it was impossible to be definite as
to their correct sequence. Whether Frazer saw the submachine gun swinging up and panicked, or whether he saw
that the girl was alone and decided on a mad attempt at
heroics will never be known. All that is certain is that
he drew his pistol and fired.

His aim from the unsteady platform was poor, and the
round struck the water on the far side of the jetty without
passing closer than two feet to the girl. For Suzie, however, it was sufficient to know that she was being shot at.
Tightening her finger on the trigger, she sent a long, ragged burst of fire toward him.

Her reaction was instinctive and unaimed, and the thun-
dering blast from the heavy weapon almost deafened her.
A cone of bullets screamed over the man's head and
smashed into the side of *Caterina's* cockpit. The thin
duralumin plating was little hindrance to the big slugs
at such a range, and they tore through into the flight deck.
By some miracle, they all missed Desmond, although the
windscreen by his left shoulder disintegrated in a shower
of glass, and one bullet ripped into the padding of his
seat back. Ralph Kendrick was less lucky. Both radio sets
in front of him took several hits, and a jagged lump of
metal ricocheted off one of the casings and slammed into
his chest.

Desmond jerked open the throttles on the inboard engines and pushed down hard on the rudder bar, slewing
the flying boat across to port in a desperate attempt to
scrape clear of the jetty. He heard Ralph's cry, but there
was no time to consider what had happened. Their only
chance lay in getting into mid-lake again where the aircraft could maneuver.

Another volley of shots echoed out, and again he felt the
shock of bullets striking the aircraft, lower down on the
fuselage this time. He punched the starter buttons of the
two outer engines. *Caterina* was coming around but not
nearly fast enough; they were going to hit the wooden
piling at the end of the jetty. He could see the pilot of the

Supermarine trying to swing the nose of his plane around
so that his guns would be in position; any moment
now he would be pouring fire into the helpless airliner.

○   ○   ○

With the prow of the flying boat bearing down on her;
with the sudden roar of the two propellors starting up
again; and with Frazer in the nose hatch still firing aimed
shots at her, Suzie lost her head completely. Holding down
the Thompson's trigger, she blazed away the entire contents
of the fifty-round magazine. The fierce recoil of the submachine gun made it impossible for her to aim with any
pretense at accuracy, but *Caterina* was a big target. Suzie saw the man with the pistol tossed suddenly backward
beneath the impact of the heavy shells. Then he tumbled
out of the hatch into the water beneath the aircraft, but
in her terror she could only keep firing. Round after
round pumped into the white hull, punching through the
metal skin.

Too late, she realized the danger she was in. Before she
had time to turn and run, the airliner's raked prow
crashed into the jetty. The worn old timbering stood no
chance. *Caterina*'s nose lifted for an instant and then
burst through the obstruction, disintegrating some thirty
feet of the jetty into a mass of debris surging in the
foaming wake thrown up by her passage. The harsh stutter
of the gun was choked off abruptly as, caught in the
devastating collision, Suzie vanished into the boiling mael-
strom.

Desmond felt the jarring shock of the crash, but he had
no time to worry about the probable damage it had
caused. All four engines were biting at the air, and the
plane was beginning to pick up speed. The starboard
wing came around, and there was another heavy shock as
the wing float rammed into the stump of the jetty. The
Supermarine fighter was turning too, but *Caterina*'s
wing swept on past and, as her tail followed, the tiny plane
began to buck and wallow in her wash. Desmond saw
sparkles from her gun ports, but the fire went wide, and
the next instant the airliner's tremendous slipstream was
driving the fighter shoreward, spinning her nose around
again so that her armament no longer pointed at them.

Desmond could only pray that the damage had left *Caterina* still flyable. The starboard wing float was trailing uselessly, threatening to dip the wing onto the surface at any moment, but the controls seemed unaffected. Running the engine up onto maximum boost and setting half flaps, he streaked across the width of the lake, desperate to get away before the pilot in the fighter could regain control of his craft and come after them. There was barely sufficient distance for a takeoff, but Desmond had no time to alter course. He waited until the last moment before pulling back the stick hard, and, almost unbelievably, he felt *Caterina* lift off, scrape above the trees, and skim over the crest of the surrounding hillside.

"Ralph, how badly are you hit?" They were streaking southward, Desmond hugging close to the ground, navigating by instinct. He had forced the throttle levers as far open against the stops as they would go, holding the engine straining at maximum power, heedless of the rapidly rising needles of the temperature gauges. Amazing as it seemed, *Caterina* appeared to have suffered no major damage to either airframe or engines. If they could hold this speed for another twenty minutes, they would reach New York and safety.

To his relief, he heard the radio officer answering, "I'm all right I think, skipper. I seem to have stopped one in the ribs, but it doesn't feel serious. I'm trying to call up some help on the radio; the main set's had it, but the auxiliary sounds as though it may be repairable."

Sandy came leaping up the stairs, followed by Laura and Professor Wienzman who was carrying the emergency first aid kit. "We've lost one passenger," Sandy reported quickly while the old man set to work at once on Ralph's injury, assisted by Laura. "Van Smit was killed outright by a bullet in the head. Andy's been hit in the leg, but it's not bad according to the professor, and Baroness d'Este has a grazed shoulder. Everyone else is fine except for a few bruises. We've taken a lot of holes, but so far we seem to be in one piece—apart from the starboard float—and the hull seems to have survived the smash through the pier."

"Frazer's gone," Desmond told him in reply. "I saw him fall into the lake just before we hit the jetty. Otherwise we seem to have gotten away more lightly than I'd have thought possible. I want you to go to the rear, Sandy," he went on, "and keep a look out in case that fighter tries to have another pass at us. Open the freight hatch and keep in contact over the refueling intercom. It still seems to be working."

"Desmond, are you OK?" Laura leaned over and asked him as the purser hurried away. Her face was scratched. She had rolled up her sleeves, and there was blood on her hands from where she had been helping the professor.

"I'm fine," he smiled briefly. "How about you?"

"Nothing worse than a bump on the head," she told him. "Do you think that other plane will come after us?"

"He's crazy if he does, but I'm afraid it's possible," Desmond answered grimly. "He'll have found it pretty difficult to get into position for a takeoff run, thanks to the swell we kicked up as we left. I reckon that's given us several minutes start, which—with luck—will mean that by the time he catches up, we'll be too close to New York for him to hurt us."

○ ○ ○

Conditions at the lake were in fact worse than Desmond guessed. The slipstream of the flying boat had driven the Supermarine hard aground on the muddy shore. Leaping out onto the bank, Jarrett ran down the jetty until he came to the tangle of broken timbers at the end. Fully one third of the pier had been torn away by the airliner's hull, and only a few bits of shattered planking remained in the swirling water to show where it had been.

Of Suzie there was no sign. The girl had disappeared completely. Her body had evidently been sucked under by the flying boat's wake and, like that of the crewman who had started the shooting, swept out into the middle of the lake. There was not a trace of either of them. A deep anger welled up within Jarrett as he gazed at the desolate aftermath of the battle. There had been no need for any of it. The man who had died had killed himself and Suzie and probably many others as well, all to no purpose.

Rage, frustration, and grief left him empty, save for a desire for revenge—revenge on the flying boat and its crew, who had been responsible. Running back up the jetty, he pushed the silver fighter off from the mud and clambered aboard again.

○ ○ ○

Two Marine Corps TBD-1 Devastator torpedo bombers had just taken off from the airbase at Floyd Bennett Field and were heading out toward the gunnery practice range off the New Jersey coast. They were flying at an altitude of 10,000 feet. The Devastators, the standard U.S. Naval and Marine bombers, were all-metal, low-winged monoplanes, with 800-horsepower engines that had a top speed of 206 miles per hour. Normally carrying a crew of three—pilot, bombardier, and radio officer/rear gunner —seated one behind the other, they were on this occasion flying without their bombardier, who had no part to play in gunnery practice.

In the cockpit of the lead aircraft, Lieutenant Phil DeMartino heard the voice of twenty-one-year-old Sergeant Al Murray crackle unexpectedly over the intercom. "Skipper, the base has just been on the air," he called excitedly. "We're to break off and head over to Manhattan. It seems some looney in a homemade fighter is taking shots at an airliner, and we've been ordered to see him off."

"They want us to do what?" Phil replied. "Are you serious?"

"Never more so," the young sergeant's voice came back. "They say we are the nearest planes in the sky carrying ammunition, and we're to get on over." He sounded cheerful. Phil could picture him in his rear-facing cockpit, grinning as he cocked his gun, happy at the prospect of actually being able to shoot at a real target.

The Devastator's armament consisted of one fixed forward-firing .30-caliber machine gun mounted on the right hand side of Phil's windscreen and a similar weapon fixed on a scarf mount, giving limited traverse in Al's position, firing rearward. Hardly an excess of armament, Phil thought as he reached up to cock the gun beside him. Glancing out at the aircraft flying at his starboard wing, he saw that his fellow pilot Bob Wood had just done the same and was giving him a thumbs up sign.

"OK," he called back to Al, "Manhattan it is." And

banking hard around to port, he set a course toward the north.

Jacquetta d'Este and Andy Draper had each been made comfortable on beds in the midship cabin. Their injuries had been expertly attended to by Dr. Wienzman, aided by Laura and Georgina.

With the arrival of the Devastators to protect them, the passengers had been allowed back to their seats. The professor and Laura had returned to the flight deck to take a second look at Ralph Kendrick's wound, which, though not serious, was causing him pain. Jacquetta's injury had been less severe; the bullet had scored the side of her left shoulder, stinging and breaking the skin, but fortunately inflicting no further damage. She was sitting up in bed talking to Rashid.

"What can we do?" she was saying despondently. "There is so little time left. What is going to happen when Luca tells the authorities about you?" The aircraft was wheeling over Long Island. Through the window Jacquetta could see the panorama of lower Manhattan spread out beneath them, the gleaming towers stretching up through the haze; the busy harbor—a maze of interlocking waterways and islands held together by the slender spans of bridges in a complex and delicate tracery. Ordinarily she would have been excited and fascinated by this view of the richest and most powerful city on earth, but as it was she could think only of the imminent arrest and deportation it signaled for her lover.

As if on cue, Luca appeared in the doorway. Now that the emergency was over, he had recovered his customary suavity, and with a smugly complacent smile, he answered his wife's question. "I can tell you exactly what will happen, my dear," he said. "The Americans will have no choice but to deport a man who has not only entered the country on a false passport but has threatened the life of an accredited diplomat. In which case, acting on behalf of our government, I shall request that he be returned to Italy at once to stand trial. The verdict will not, I think," he concluded, "be hard to predict."

"You may not find me so easy to dispose of, baron," Rashid retorted, stepping toward the Italian. "And I shall have my revenge. Of that you may be sure."

Luca continued to smile. "I anticipated your attitude," he remarked coldly. Bringing his hand out from behind his back, he leveled his pistol at the young sheik. "So I intend taking no chances. You will now please hand me your gun. If you refuse," he added as Rashid glared at him defiantly, "I can assure you I shall have not the slightest compunction in shooting you where you stand."

○ ○ ○

As he spoke, Pat Jarrett opened fire on the flying boat again.

Despite the superior speed of the Supermarine, Jarrett had underestimated the lead the flying boat had acquired. By the time he was in a position to make his second attack, *Caterina* was already passing over the Queensboro Bridge and Welfare Island at a little over a thousand feet, and Desmond O'Neill was preparing to the final approach to La Guardia six miles ahead around the bend of the East River.

Jarrett saw the two Devastators flying in close formation on either side, but by now he no longer cared who his opponents were or how great their numbers. The sight of the city spread out below served in a curious way to heighten his desperate need for revenge. It was as though the whole of New York had been selected as a gigantic backdrop against which the final act in the drama was to be played out.

Coming in from the west at 8,000 feet, he was perfectly placed to swoop down out of the sun at the three unsuspecting aircraft. This time there was no reason to hold his fire or stick to prearranged plans; putting the seaplane into a steep power dive, he screamed down on the slow-moving airliner.

All thoughts of his own survival vanished. His brain singing with the force of the acceleration, he held the dive until the flying boat's hull swam up to fill his sights, the black bead in the center of the ring set squarely in the middle of her back between the wing roots. At a range of four hundred yards, he pressed the firing button and sent a stream of tracer bullets into the helpless plane.

He felt the heavy vibration running through the fighter as the four Colts pumped their shells across the intervening space. The huge slugs tore into the white fuselage in a pulverizing blast that ripped through the mailroom and into the passenger deck. Lifting the Supermarine's nose, Jarrett watched the line of holes punched by the seven-hundred grain bullets march across the hull to the inner-most starboard engine. A thick, oily trail of black smoke began to pour from the nacelle.

The crews of the Devastators had failed to spot the deadly silver racer streaking down on them. Not until they heard the rattle of Jarrett's guns and saw the airliner shudder beneath the terrible impact of his fire did they realize what was happening. As *Caterina* fell away, trailing smoke, they saw the fighter flash by close overhead, and the two pilots slammed their throttles open, flinging the Devastators into an urgent climb in pursuit.

Wrenching the stick back hard, Jarrett pulled the Super-marine up sharply and as his speed began to fall away, he flicked over to starboard and rolled out above them. Both rear gunners had swung their weapons up and were engaging him, but the pitiful fire from the single-barreled light-caliber guns went easily wide. Pushing the fighter into another dive, he cut down through the sky on top of them. Before the Marines realized the danger they were in, he opened fire on Bob Wood's aircraft.

Jarrett raked the bomber with a full five-second burst. During that fraction of time, the Colts poured over one hundred seventy bullets into the plane, with a total strik-ing impact of over one ton. The Devastator did not stand a chance. With a bright orange flare from the exploding petrol tanks, it blew up, disintegrating instantaneously in a cloud of fragments that showered down onto the river.

Stricken with horror, Phil DeMartino hurled his machine into a tight turn, frantic to get clear before the fighter could lock onto his tail, but the Devastator was no match for the Supermarine. There were a series of stunning concussions at the rear of the fuselage, and over his ear-phones he heard a scream of agony from Al in the rear cockpit. The elevator controls went heavy, and the plane began to spin earthward.

Caterina was still airborne. Her inherent ruggedness and strength had enabled her to withstand Jarrett's initial and shorter burst, and by a fortunate chance, the stacked gold and mail sacks had absorbed a considerable portion of the ammunition. But she had suffered serious harm. One engine was burning and running raggedly. The hail of bullets had also sliced through the cables linking the wing flaps, rendering the aircraft's rate of descent almost impossible to control.

On the lower deck, Andy Draper and Luca d'Este had died in the same instant, their bodies riddled by the Colt's fire. Only the shielding of the gold crates above them had saved Jacquetta and Rashid from a similar fate.

Desmond was struggling desperately to control the airliner. His one thought was to get down to the river before the fighter came back for a second pass. The Triborough Bridge loomed ahead of him; beyond that, Hell Gate Bridge. He was feathering the outer port engine to try and keep it going, but the flames were spreading down the wing along the fuel lines. He needed another two or three minutes until they reached clear water on which to land.

Laura screamed suddenly from the radio desk where she had been helping the professor bind Ralph's chest. "He's coming at us again!" Through the window of the navigation hatch, she had caught sight of Jarrett plunging down on them.

At the same time, Ralph shouted, "Break to port, skipper! Break to port!"

With no time to think of what the airliner could stand, Desmond drove the rudder into the floor and forced the stick hard over, peeling *Caterina* away, low across northern Manhattan, praying that the sudden maneuver would throw the seaplane off. Before they could claw out of range, they felt the violent shock of machine-gun bullets impacting on the starboard wing and the tail as the fighter swept past.

Above the noise of smashing metal, Desmond heard both starboard engines break into a shuddering rattle of coughing and felt the immediate loss of power. The rudder assembly went slack beneath his feet as the concentrated fire ripped apart the flying boat's tail.

With almost total engine failure, badly on fire, and losing height rapidly, *Caterina* was limping out of control over the roofs of Spanish Harlem. Desmond knew instinctively that the Supermarine was looping round again to administer the coup de grâce. Within seconds, the airliner would be a blazing wreck plummeting down on one of the most densely populated pieces of land in the world.

Miraculously, no further passengers had been injured during the last attack, for the stream of bullets had missed the main fuselage, spending their force on the control surfaces and power plants. In the bloody shambles of the midship cabin, Jacquetta clung screaming to Rashid as the sea of brown roofs below rose to meet them.

As Jarrett powered his machine around over the Bronx to make his final pass, to his amazement he saw the remaining Devastator coming straight toward him, fire spitting from its single machine gun. Badly damaged as his aircraft was, his rear gunner dead in his seat, Phil De-Martino knew that he had to stop the fighter from shooting the airliner down over Manhattan. Pointing the Devastator at the Supermarine's nose, he kept his finger on the firing button.

Flames flickered along the seaplane's gun ports, and Jarrett felt the bullets striking home around him, but he held his course without flinching. Too late, he saw the pilot of the other plane try to pull up in a last effort to escape above him. At a combined closing speed of four hundred fifty miles an hour, the two aircraft smashed into one another and exploded in a terrific ball of flame that seemed to hang suspended in the air before toppling into the docks of the Harlem River.

Caterina was now skimming the tenement rooftops. There was no hope, Desmond knew, of their making the far side of Manhattan. Only the fact that the buildings here were significantly lower than those to the south had delayed the crash even this long. However, one faint chance remained.

Seeing the green expanse of Central Park, Desmond yelled at the others behind him to brace themselves. With feet to spare, *Caterina* flew over the buildings on Cathedral Parkway and the ancient blockhouses around Harlem Meer. The green of the meadow beyond flashed by, barely missing their keel, and there ahead of them lay the clear, hundred-acre expanse of the receiving reservoir.

Caterina was on her last gasp. With three propellers twirling uselessly and flames streaming back to envelop the whole of the port wing, she plunged into the water with a terrific violence that bounced her twice shatteringly clear of the surface, throwing bursts of spray two hundred feet into the air. Surging through the waves created by her landing, she sped helplessly toward the southern bank, hitting it with another crunching impact that carried her halfway up the grass. There, battered, bullet-riddled, but miraculously intact, she rested.

Although dazed and stunned by the successive impacts of the crash and their minds numbed, the passengers' instinct for survival drove them to their feet and sent them reeling through the smoke-filled cabins toward the hatches.

The shock of the landing had flung all on board about like toys, and the floors were slippery with blood from the dead and injured. As well as killing Andy and Luca d'Este, the Supermarine's final pass had seriously wounded Stewart Curtis. Mrs. King had received a broken shoulder, but with characteristic determination had refused offers of assistance and together with her husband had taken charge of the badly shocked Siegret Wienzman. All three succeeded in making their way forward to the promenade cabin hatchway, which Sandy Everett had just managed to force open.

The drenching spray thrown up by the plane's crash-landing on the surface of the reservoir had doused the flames pouring from the wings, and it was this fact more than anything else that saved the lives of *Caterina*'s travelers. Rashid seized Jacquetta and hastened out with her after the Kings. Closely followed by Arlette Ducroix, they stumbled out onto the grass before a swiftly gathering crowd of amazed spectators who hurried forward to help them.

In the after cabin, Georgina Curtis had escaped the burst of fire that had struck her husband, but the concussion of the crash flung her against the rear bulkhead knocking her unconscious for several seconds. Coming to in the smoke-choked cabin, she saw Stewart lying on his side, and a single glance at the ominously spreading dark stains across his suit was enough to tell her of the seriousness of his injuries.

Terror gripped her at the thought of being trapped in the blazing aircraft, and she attempted to drag him through toward the hatch. He groaned, and a froth of red bubbles appeared at his mouth. His weight was too much for her, but her frantic cries brought Sandy to her aid.

Some little while later, Desmond watched as the last of the ambulances moved slowly off through the crowd. The entire northern end of the park seemed to be filled with a horde of onlookers who had come to gaze at the huge smoke-streaked hull of the flying boat, lying half out of the water. Near at hand were four fire trucks, summoned to the crash, their crews waiting idly by as Caterina's remaining fuel was drained from her tanks. About them were grouped an ever-increasing swarm of police cars and official vehicles, as well as scores of journalists and newsmen who had flocked to the scene.

It seemed likely that Stewart Curtis would succumb to his wounds. Should he survive it would be to face a series of charges for fraud.

Looking up at his former command, Desmond shook his head in wonder. It was almost impossible to believe that any aircraft could withstand so much punishment. All at once he gave a chuckle.

"What on earth are you laughing at?" Laura was standing beside him.

Desmond slipped his arm through hers as he answered, "I was just wondering," he said, still smiling, "how we're ever going to get her out of here."

ABOUT THE AUTHOR

A descendant of Sir Arthur Conan Doyle (and a great-great-great-nephew of Richard Doyle the *Punch* illustrator), RICHARD DOYLE was born in the Channel Islands in 1948 and spent the first twenty years of his life in Ethiopia, the Middle East and North Africa. After leaving school at the age of fifteen, he educated himself for the next two years before going to Oxford University where he took a degree in law. Between 1970 and 1974 he worked on the stock exchange doing investment analysis before deciding to try to earn his living as a writer. His interests include literature, history, philosophy, comparative religion, mathematics and traveling. A nomadic existence has led Doyle, for the moment, to Rockport, Massachusetts, where he is working on his third novel.

Turn the page for an exciting
Special Preview of another book.

A Special Preview of
the tension-filled new novel of
the world on the brink of global war

THE DRAGON

By the author of
THIRTY-FOUR EAST

Alfred Coppel

"As tingling as anything since *Seven Days in
May*."

—*The New York Times*

1

The wind that blew across the Talimupendi Plain came from the Altai Mountains and it had the frightening cold of those ancient lonely peaks in it. The sky was a threatening gray darkness; there would be snow by nightfall. But Choy Balsan was not concerned about that. He was certain that both he and his captive would be dead before the last light of this bitter day faded.

Colonel Balsan was a thick, stocky man, with the broad, brown face of the Mongol. There were ice crystals on his sparse beard and drooping mustache and on the shaggy fur of his hat and parka. His felt vest and half boots were stiff with the cold, and his face ached at each cut of the cruel wind.

The captive, a petty officer of the Chinese People's Liberation Army, had stopped struggling and now produced only an occasional moan. Balsan carried him trussed like a deer across the bow of his fur saddle, and the man involuntarily twitched with each step the shaggy pony took across the rocky plateau.

Balsan drew from his parka the map showing the minefields. He hoped it was reasonably accurate. It was a miracle that the KGB had been able to produce a usable map at all. He was traversing a part of the most heavily guarded military reservations in northern China. At the moment, there was nothing to be seen but the empty expanse of the frigid Talimupendi: a high plateau of rocky desert, lichen-covered outcrops, and dry salt pans. It was a Martian vista that seemed both vast and unpopulated, but that was an illusion. The true nature of the region could be seen in the occasional tangle of rusting barbed wire, the places (obvious to Balsan's eyes) where the earth had been disturbed to place a mine, a heat or pressure sensor, or even a television spy.

He did his best, with the help of the map and the information he had coldly tortured from his prisoner, to avoid these secret traps. But he knew with absolute certainty that he was pursued, that soon there would be aircraft and mounted soldiers, and that he would be cornered and killed or captured. He did not plan to let the Chinese take him alive. He knew their methods of interrogation too well for that, and there would be special treatments devised for an officer of the Glavnoye Razvedyvatelnoye Upravleniye, the Intelligence Directorate of the General Staff of the Soviet Army.

The Chinese soldier stirred, and Balsan pressed a fist against the small of his back and spoke in Mandarin. "Be still, Comrade. Your pain will not last much longer."

Balsan was sorry that the single survivor of the three-man patrol he had ambushed had turned out to be only a noncommissioned officer. It would have been too much to expect that he might have snared one of the scientists or engineers the GRU believed were working down in the marshy sink of the Turfan Depression, but a commissioned officer, at least, would have been more useful. Still, it was remarkable that he had been able to penetrate this desolate fortress, make his observations, and—thus far—survive. The man he carried across his pony's withers like a hunter's kill was a bonus. His captive had already talked, under persuasion, about the security patrols. Under more severe inducements he might yield a few words about the installation he and ten thousand other soldiers were guarding in the Turfan.

Balsan turned in the saddle to look to the northeast. The dull light made distances deceptive, but the wind had swept away the bitter dust and he could see the dark loom of the snow-laden hills beyond the Turfan. Of the Depression itself, he could see nothing now. It dropped from the high plateau like a vast oblong bowl. Fifty meters below the surrounding land, the sluggish Algoy River fed a network of marshy streams in the sink, the ground soft in what passed for summer in these latitudes, and frozen into a salty, alkaline waste in winter. A hellish place to have built a scientific installation. The labor involved, Balsan thought, must have been immense. But the very harshness of the terrain was a defense of sorts against discovery, and the Siberian storms that swept down from the northeast made satellite observations extremely difficult.

There had been speculation in Moscow that the Americans, with their more advanced space-spy technology, were watching the developments in the Turfan. But if they were, they were not sharing their information with the Russians. . .

It was beginning to grow dark when he reached his campsite among the rock outcrops. He dismounted, removed the saddle-bags, and let the reins drag so that the horse would stand. There was much to do, but he took the time to put a few handfuls of grain into a depression scooped in the cold earth for the pony to eat. Then he unpacked the tapes and the radiosonde, and inserted the cassette into the transmitting case.

This done, he paused to listen to the sounds the wind brought him. The helicopter was still five to six kilometers distant, he judged. But it had been joined by others.

He took a gas cylinder from his saddlebag and

checked the pressure on the gauge. The tank was full. He broke the seal and adjusted the valve and nozzle. He unfolded the balloon from the kit taken from the bag. The material was somehting the Americans had developed. It was called Mylar, and it was so thin and transparent he could scarcely believe that it would not tear in his hands. It seemed almost weightless. Next he assembled the twenty-meter trailing line and the radiosonde harness. He assembled the transmitting module and connected it to the trailing line.

He paused again to face the wind. It blew steadily from the northeast, as the meteorologist in Moscow had assured him that it would.

The helicopters were getting nearer. He caught sight of the first, approaching slowly out of the north. He suppressed a wry smile. Even at a distance, he recognized the Russian Yak, old now, but quite serviceable. He had flown such a machine himself many times. Since it was a troop carrier, there would be at least a section of fifteen soldiers aboard. Three helicopters—forty-five men. The odds were unfortunate.

He crawled into the felt yurt and emerged with a length of plastic tubing affixed to a stock, reel, and sending unit. A second trip produced three RPG wire-guided rockets. The odds would improve soon, he thought. He assembled the weapon, placed it aside with its two reloads, and began inflating the Mylar balloon from the gas cylinder. . .

He watched the Mylar balloon rising in wind-shivered bubbles as the gas filled it. He secured the holding line to a jutting spur of rock and went back into the yurt. When he emerged again he had four magazines of nine-millimeter bullets for the machine pistol. He placed these with the rockets. The helicopters were very near; he could see them circling to the south. The pilots must be using infrared sighting gear, he thought, to see so well in this half-light.

North of his position, an armored personnel carrier crested a rise in the ground six hundred meters away. Each time the engine accelerated, he could see blue fire through the inefficient flame-arrestors on the exhaust. The engine sounded as though it was laboring and detonating. The refineries the Americans had helped the Chinese build to exploit the great new oil finds in the south were still incapable of producing military-grade diesel fuel.

But the lumbering machine came on, and Balsan reached for the rocket launcher.

The helicopters were landing somewhere behind the rise against which he had erected his yurt.

The balloon, half filled now, was rising from the ground like a quivering, translucent ghost. Much of the gasbag still trailed on the ground, but he knew that he must not fill it more lest increased internal pressure at high altitude burst the Mylar before its work was done. . .

The balloon was clear of the ground and tugging at the holding line. Even half filled, the Mylar globe towered eight meters above him, slanting to the southwest, bobbing and shuddering to be free with each gust of the wind.

It was nearly dark now. Balsan considered the fate that had caused him to be found one half hour too early to allow him any hope of escape.

He set the pressure switch on the radiosonde so that the device would begin to transmit at two thousand meters. He would have preferred to wait until it had reached at least ten thousand. That way he would be sure that the listening stations in the Kazakh Soviet Socialist Republic would get the first transmission. But with his pursuers so near, he dared not delay.

In the gloom it was difficult to judge ranges accurately, but he estimated the armored vehicle was now within range of the RPGs. A file of soldiers had deployed around it and advanced at a walking pace.

Balsan looked carefully at the balloon and slashed the line. For a dozen meters the balloon dragged the sending unit along the ground, tumbling and crashing into the rock outcrops. He held his breath and hoped that the device was strong enough to take the abuse. Between one puff of wind and another the balloon rose enough to clear the ground, but it seemed to gain height with agonizing slowness.

He heard a shout behind him and the sudden clatter of a helicopter taking off. One of his pursuers, more quick-witted than the rest, had realized what it was that was rising into the darkening sky.

Balsan glanced at the approaching armored vehicle and then at the balloon, which now scudded southwestward, driven, but held down, by the wind, the black shape of a helicopter moving to overtake it. He did not hesitate. He loaded an RPG into the shoulder launcher and fired at the helicopter. The rocket, trailing glowing exhaust gases and a thread of wire, arced upward. He tried to hold the sight on the target, but the wind affected his aim and the rocket missed. He saw it explode with a flash of yellow and white far to the southwest.

He reloaded and fired again, knowing that the helicopter could easily destroy the Mylar balloon. Another miss, and another useless explosion down-range.

He glanced for only a moment at the approaching armor. If he used the last RPG on the helicopter, there would be nothing to use against the steel-skinned vehicle coming toward him.

He turned away and fired again at the helicopter, now at extreme range. He held the sight on the point of fire made by the Yak's exhaust pipes as the rocket, spilling wire, flew into the night.

The helicopter seemed to dissolve in a bubble of fire. It fell, raining fragments. The balloon was out of sight.

Balsan dropped the empty launcher and picked

up his machine pistol. He removed the silencer and began to shoot at the advancing Chinese soldiers. He heard a shout, a scream of pain, and a rattle of return fire. The armored vehicle rumbled closer.

He discarded an empty magazine, reloaded, and turned to fire at the soldiers approaching from the opposite direction. Frightened by the noise, the pony rose to his feet and bolted. He had not gone a dozen meters before he was cut down by a fusillade of automatic fire from the approaching Chinese. . .

2

_____

The rain, battering the tall, draped windows, made a rattling sound. Harry Grant, with an airman's instinctive sensitivity to the weather, noted that the wind was from the northwest and would drive the storm past Washington by morning. There would be sunshine, of a sort, for the President's departure.

He lay naked in the bed, his hands behind his head, staring at the dark ceiling. A thin shaft of light from the Georgetown street penetrated the narrow gap bewteen the drapes, and a branch, swayed by the wind, interrupted the beam of light with each movement, sending a black needle across the illumination.

He was a thin man. His bare chest was badly scarred by burns that had seared his flesh. His injuries had come from an F-4 crash into a flaming, oily sea. He called them his legacy from Ho Chi Minh.

The woman beside Grant slept quietly, with deep regular breathing. He wondered again how she, so spring-tight and aggressive in her waking moments, could sleep so peacefully. Perhaps, he thought sardonically, it was the peace of convinced righteousness. No one in Washington was more certain than Jane McNary that she stood on the side of the angels.

Grant stole a glance at his wrist watch on the nightstand. The luminous hands of the complicated steel chronograph (a belligerent gift from Jane—she had presented it with a speech about "steel from the Iron Colonel") showed twenty minutes after five. By seven he was due at Andrews to inspect Air Force One and talk to Ortiz and the flight crew about accommodations for the President's guests. And by afternoon, the aerial caravan of President, politicians ("statesmen" would be a kinder word), and news people would be over the Atlantic on the way to England. With the President's Senior Air Force Aide, General Tillotson, nursing an ulcer at the Bethesda hospital, the travel arrangements had fallen to Colonel Grant. Serving as an aide to the President was not an appointment to Grant's liking, but Cleveland Scott Lambert, President of the United States, need not inquire about the personal preferences of officers on the Colonels List of the Air Force.

Jane stirred and put a hand on Grant's chest. He suppressed an instinctive urge to pull away. Even after so many years, he was still conscious of the ugliness of his own mutilated flesh. The treatment he had received from the North Vietnamese medics had been primitive and, understandably, not gentle.

The woman beside him was slender, almost to emaciation, not at all like Bethany. Not in any way. His wife (he still thought of Bethany as his wife) had been soft to the touch, voluptuous. And she had lived with a cloying dependence that had held him in a kind of bondage until the unexpected day she told him that she no longer wished to live as a service wife. She had the honesty to add that she had found a man more suited to her tastes. There had been a hard core under the smooth skin and the sweet manner.

With McNary the metal was on the surface. She was thin, intense, consumed with self-righteousness and pugnacity. She had served her time in what she still called "the Women's Movement"—like that, with an upper-case emphasis. She had served her time in other movements, too, though she imagined, naïvely or wishfully, that few, including Grant, knew about her youthful fling with Marxism.

Tyler Davis, one of the sentinels of the National Security Council charged with reviewing the personal lives of the men who stood near the President, had presented McNary's dossier to Grant long ago, insisting that he read it through. The implication was quite plain. It was unsuitable for one of the President's White House staff to be conducting a liaison (Davis had actually called it that) with an unfriendly member of the press corps whose political past was suspect.

To his credit, the President had never broached the subject to Grant. Nor had he ever suggested what would have been worse—that Grant use his friendship with the radical Ms. McNary to soften her attacks on the administration.

Davis had taken the trouble to catalogue all of McNary's affairs, and they were many. She slept with writers, politicians, bureaucrats, and, on occasion, with men she picked up in the street. It was Davis's considered opinion—and the opinion, Grant assumed, of the National Security Agency computer —that Jane McNary, syndicated columnist, politically unreliable, was a flaming nymphomaniac.

The investigation had outraged Grant and he had told Tyler so. Tyler had responded with an appeal to a nonexistent friendship, asking how one so dedicatedly apolitical as Colonel Harry Simpson Grant could indulge himself emotionally with a militant fire stick like McNary.

What Tyler did not know, and what McNary understood with great clarity, was that Grant was not emotionally involved, that he had not been involved emotionally with any human being since his return from three years as a prisoner of the North Vietnamese. He had seen life reduced to bare minimums. He had lived in circumstances where emotional ties to other human beings could be manipulated by torturers and used to obliterate personality, human dignity, and honor. And Grant was a man who lived by such unfashionable notions as honor and dignity.

He disagreed with most of what McNary believed. He disliked her politics, her cynicism, her stridency. But he respected her quickness and intelligence, could not fault her sincerity and the strength of her convictions. And he was a man. McNary, as dozens, and possibly hundreds, of men in Washington had cause to know, was a rare experience in bed.

She opened her eyes now and said, "He never tires, he never sleeps. The Iron Colonel."

Grant suppressed a rueful smile. She had used him hard and often, and, despite the fact that he was in good shape, he was nearing fifty and felt it. He said, "It's near time for me to leave."

"Screw and run, you sexist." Her eyes seemed to glow in the darkness; her fine-boned face was like a carved mask.

"I am due at Andrews soon."

McNary sat up in the bed. Her breasts were hard and flat, but feminine for all that, with small dark nipples. She said, "Do I get to ride with the first team or am I stuck with the workers?"

At the suggestion of her Washington editors, she had been included in the press contingent traveling to the Sissinghurst conference with the Presidential party. Paul Lyman, the White House Press Secretary, had done his best to have her stricken from the list, quoting from her last phillipic against the administration's "reactionary stand" on nuclear disarmament, which was the purpose of the meeting in Britain between NATO and Warsaw Pact countries. But the President was certain that he could charm even the militant Ms. McNary, given time and the gracious surrounding of Sissinghurst Castle's rose gardens. Grant was less sure of this than his President, but Grant was a soldier and such decisions were not within his purview—for which he was grateful.

"You ride the Number-One Bird," he said. "The President's orders."

"I suppose I'm expected to be impressed . . ."

Grant, buttoning his shirt, said nothing. He had been expecting her to ask about the messages that had been flying between Washington and Moscow. Somehow no secret was ever secure in Washington. There always seemed to be some bureaucrat or politician who was willing to curry favor with the press by leaking classified information. The long-past, almost-forgotten case of the Pentagon Papers had set a style that still persisted.

McNary said, "I've heard that Kirov is suffering a case of Peking jitters."

Who could have put her onto that, Grant wondered. Not Margaret Kendrick or her people. Since her appointment as Secretary of State, Mrs. Kendrick had rigidly tightened State Department security. Senator Prior? The old man was bitter against the administration and had old scores to settle with the President. But Grant was reasonably certain that the Senate Foreign Relations Committee had not yet been told about First Secretary Kirov's appeal to the President.

"The Iron Colonel's lips are sealed," McNary said caustically. "That's why Lambert the Dinosaur lets him come play at my house."

Grant controlled the familiar surge of irritation at her manner. This was the McNary touch. She never stopped trying to use the people she knew, even those with whom she shared her bed.

"I'm not one of your White House sources," he said.

"I don't have any White House sources, Colonel. I don't need them."

"Good, then," he said, and took his raincoat from a chair.

"But there have been messages from Moscow," McNary said. "You can tell me that."

"Good night, Jane. Or good morning," he said.

"I'll get the story, Harry."

"There is no story."

"Fuck you, Colonel. Button up. It's raining outside..."

He reached Andrews early, at 0630 hours. The rain had diminished to a drizzle and there were breaks in the clouds to the northwest. A pale star showed through a gap in the overcast.

Colonel Carlos Ortiz, the President's pilot, had Air Force One on the ramp before the VIP terminal. One was a giant C-9, converted to the President's needs. The follow-up aircraft, a wide-bodied Lockheed, stood behind One, dwarfed by the white-and-silver monster. The flight attendants were mustered; the airplanes were stocked with food, drink, and fuel. Now, typically, there was nothing for the crews to do but wait.

Ortiz, a dapper American of Mexican descent, greeted Grant warmly. The two pilots had served together in Vietnam and had high regard for one another. With Ortiz at his side, Grant inspected the aircraft. Carlos Ortiz knew his job too well to need close supervision, so the inspection was a formality.

Back in the Operations Room, the two men drank coffee and watched the weather sequences as they appeared on the Weather Service computer. Grant was preparing to return to his quarters at Fort Myer to shave and change uniform when Ortiz said, "We had a strange one this morning, Harry. A call came from State asking that we dispatch the standby Presidential 767 to Hurn. That's near Bourne-mouth—miles from Sissinghurst. You hear anything about this?"

"Nothing. You say the request came from State?"

Ortiz sipped at the tasteless brew in the Styro-foam cup and nodded. "From State with a capital S. The Secretary made the request. Herself. In person. I sent George Barrow out with a stand-by crew on the 767. They cleared Washington Flight Control at 0540."

Ortiz waited for him to comment, but Grant remained thoughtfully silent. It was strange indeed that an old aircraft be added without prior planning to the President's flight, that it should be dispatched to a minor British airport this way, and stranger still that the request should have been made by Secretary of State Kendrick in person and at such an early hour.

Presently, Grant asked, "Any special instructions to Major Barrow and his crew?"

Ortiz nodded, his dark eyes alert and curious. "He is to land at Hurn and stand by there until he receives further orders. Oh, yes. The aircraft is to be parked away from the main operations area and there will be RAF security troops on hand to guard it. What do you make of that?"

Grant felt a premonitory tightness in his belly. It was a feeling familiar from his days of combat. The before-a-mission sense of alertness. . .

He was opposite Anacostia when the light began to flash on his car telephone. It was Silas Davenport from the Military and Naval Aides' Office.

"Where are you now, Colonel?"

Grant instantly detected a note of excitement in the naval officer's voice, though it was standard procedure to be extremely guarded in radiotelephone communications. "Anacostia," he said. "I'm on my way to Fort Myer."

"You'll have to cancel that, Colonel. You are to come right in."

Grant had worked for the President long enough to expect the unexpected. But Cleveland Lambert was not one of those politicians who made a practice of starting the working day before eight in the morning. Something was up. . .

As Grant walked swiftly in the direction of the Oval Office, he was aware of tension in the air of the Executive Mansion. Entering the office of the President's secretary, he caught sight of General Clinton Devore, the Chairman of the Joint Chiefs of Staff, and Admiral Jay Muller, the Chief of Naval Operations, hurrying out to a waiting staff car. Devore, a sleekly handsome Air Force officer, newly appointed chairman, looked angry. Muller, a less temperamental sort, accustomed to serving the Navy in the Washington jungles, looked concerned. The two men were the most dynamic officers of the Joint Chiefs, and neither was given to dramatics.

Ivy O'Donnell, the sixtyish spinster who commanded the President's corps of secretaries, looked up as Grant came into the room.

"You're late, Colonel," she said severely. "You'll have to wait."

Grant, accustomed to Miss O'Donnell's brusqueness, acknowledged his cold reception with a nod and, prepared for a long wait, took a seat next to a warrant officer, one of the specially selected custodians of the nuclear codes who waited always within voice call of the President, the grim black briefcase chained to his wrist.

The door of the Oval Office opened, and Grant received the first of the many mild shocks that were to continue throughout this day. The two men who hurried by without a glance were Mikhail Baturin, the Soviet Ambassador to the U.S., and Reuben Ritter Richards, the Secretary of Defense. Grant could imagine no stranger companions. Richards was a draftee from the inner bastions of Wall Street, a man so given to lecturing the nation on the threat of Communism that he was known to the liberal Washington press corps as "Three R Richards," for Rapid Rearmed Reaction. He had also been dubbed "the Last of the Cold Warriors." Richards accepted both tags without protest. To find him in close company with Baturin, the latest silky-smooth Soviet salesman for détente (a word Richards was said to have difficulty even pronouncing), was surprising. To find them leaving the President's office together at eight-fifteen in the morning was far more so.

Grant thought again about Jane McNary's probing for information about hot-line traffic. Apparently even the talkative Senator Sutton was in for surprises today. Grant's warning mechanisms, the instincts that had kept him alive in th sky over Indochina and sane in the camps of the North Vietnamese, were fully alert.

The intercom on Ivy O'Donnell's desk pinged, and he heard Cleveland Lambert's resonant murmur. Miss O'Donnell fixed Grant with a steely eye and said. "The President will see you now, Colonel."

As he walked to the door of the Oval Office, he almost collided with Christopher Rosen, the President's Special Adviser for Scientific Affairs, who was exiting in haste and with considerable agitation.

The laser antimissile device becomes the focus of an international power struggle involving the U.S. President's trip to Moscow, the ailing Russian Premier, and Chinese agents.

(The complete Bantam Book will be available July 1, on sale wherever paperbacks are sold.)

RELAX!
SIT DOWN
and Catch Up On Your Reading!

☐	11877	**HOLOCAUST** by Gerald Green	$2.25
☐	11260	**THE CHANCELLOR MANUSCRIPT** by Robert Ludlum	$2.25
☐	10077	**TRINITY** by Leon Uris	$2.75
☐	2300	**THE MONEYCHANGERS** by Arthur Hailey	$1.95
☐	11266	**THE MEDITERRANEAN CAPER** by Clive Cussler	$1.95
☐	2500	**THE EAGLE HAS LANDED** by Jack Higgins	$1.95
☐	2600	**RAGTIME** by E. L. Doctorow	$2.25
☐	10888	**RAISE THE TITANIC!** by Clive Cussler	$2.25
☐	11966	**THE ODESSA FILE** by Frederick Forsyth	$2.25
☐	11770	**ONCE IS NOT ENOUGH** by Jacqueline Susann	$2.25
☐	11708	**JAWS 2** by Hank Searls	$2.25
☐	8844	**TINKER, TAILOR, SOLDIER, SPY** by John Le Carre	$1.95
☐	11929	**THE DOGS OF WAR** by Frederick Forsyth	$2.25
☐	10526	**INDIA ALLEN** by Elizabeth B. Coker	$1.95
☐	10357	**THE HARRAD EXPERIMENT** by Robert Rimmer	$1.95
☐	10422	**THE DEEP** by Peter Benchley	$2.25
☐	10500	**DOLORES** by Jacqueline Susann	$1.95
☐	11601	**THE LOVE MACHINE** by Jacqueline Susann	$2.25
☐	10600	**BURR** by Gore Vidal	$2.25
☐	10857	**THE DAY OF THE JACKAL** by Frederick Forsyth	$1.95
☐	11952	**DRAGONARD** by Rupert Gilchrist	$1.95
☐	2491	**ASPEN** by Burt Hirschfeld	$1.95
☐	11330	**THE BEGGARS ARE COMING** by Mary Loos	$1.95

Buy them at your local bookstore or use this handy coupon for ordering:

We Deliver!
And So Do These Bestsellers.

DON'T MISS
THESE CURRENT
Bantam Bestsellers

Bantam Book Catalog

Here's your up-to-the-minute listing of every book currently available from Bantam.

This easy-to-use catalog is divided into categories and contains over 1400 titles by your favorite authors.

So don't delay—take advantage of this special opportunity to increase your reading pleasure.

Just send us your name and address and 25¢ (to help defray postage and handling costs).

BANTAM BOOKS, INC.
Dept. FC, 414 East Golf Road, Des Plaines, Ill. 60016

Mr./Mrs./Miss_____
(please print)

Address_____

City_____State_____Zip_____

Do you know someone who enjoys books? Just give us their names and addresses and we'll send them a catalog too!

Mr./Mrs./Miss_____

Address_____

City_____State_____Zip_____

Mr./Mrs./Miss_____

Address_____

City_____State_____Zip_____

FC—6/77